KINGDOM KEEPERS

THE INSIDER

BOOK SEVEN

RIDLEY PEARSON

KINGDOM KEEPERS

THE INSIDER

> BOOK SEVEN

𝒟ISNEY • HYPERION BOOKS

New York

SUSTAINABLE FORESTRY INITIATIVE   Certified Sourcing   www.sfiprogram.org   SFI-00993

THIS LABEL APPLIES TO TEXT STOCK

This, the final installment of the Kingdom Keepers, is dedicated to all the hardworking Disney Cast Members and Imagineers who provide the rest of us with boundless entertainment in the parks, on the ships, and on our television and movie screens. I also offer a metaphoric tip of my hat to those who are right now dreaming of things yet to come. We can't wait!

No dedication would be complete without thanking you, the reader, the Insider, who has come along with me on this ride. What a thrill it has been and continues to be. It ain't over yet. . . .

Ridley
11/12/13
St. Louis, Missouri

*Have nothing to do with the fruitless deeds
of darkness, but rather expose them.*
—*Ephesians 5:11*

About This Book

Somewhere around the time *Kingdom Keepers IV: Power Play* was published, I was thrilled to discover that the books in the series were being read multiple times—not just twice, but six, nine, even eleven times!

As a writer, I'm an outliner—I want to know where my story (and the series) is going before I get behind the wheel. Now I don't always strictly follow this outline; but if I don't, I modify it as I go to allow me to reach a satisfactory ending.

In writing the final book—*Kingdom Keepers VII*—I faced a difficult decision. Write the novel as outlined, or—and here was the tricky part—seek input from my readers about *how the series should end*. Eventually, I became obsessed with the idea that Kingdom Keepers like me should be able to direct the conclusion of the series.

After months of conference calls, e-mails, and planning, Disney-Hyperion hired an e-book publisher, Coliloquy, to create a free app and Web site called Kingdom Keepers Insider. The idea was that I would post an outline for a new chapter each week, and Kingdom Keepers Insiders would vote on direction, setting, and character. I would then customize that week's chapter, post it, and start the process all over again. I also asked Insiders to write in response to specific challenges. If we felt the writing was strong enough, I would edit the excerpt and place it in the novel. My readers would literally help me write the book.

It worked!

The first day we opened the Kingdom Keepers Insider app/Web site, we had 1,000 people register—three times what I expected for the entire run. That week we had more than 700 fiction entries. By day three, we had crossed 5,000 registered users. Ten days in, we passed 16,000. On one Friday night in May, we received more than 1,700 fiction entries responding to my request for help with a certain passage. That is, college, high school, and middle school students were staying home to *write* on a Friday night!

Soon, we'd reached 50,000 registered users and over 150,000 regular visitors. We had people from all over the world and all 50 states voting on the direction of my outline and submitting writing pieces.

The result is *Kingdom Keepers VII: The Insider*. In these pages you will occasionally notice the ЖК logo. This denotes the start of an Insider's contribution. The contributed passage is followed (and closed) with a number. At the bottom of the page you'll see the Insider's User_Name. Because the Insider environment is anonymous, we didn't know who these wonderful writers were. Only as the project neared its end did Disney contact the "winners." Some of these writers and their parents agreed to use their real names, and these are listed at the back of the book.

Together, we crowd-sourced the writing of a novel! It was an exciting, always entertaining, never-a-dull-moment experience that we may repeat on a future project. Thanks to each and every Insider. There were so many incredible writing pieces submitted. The choice was never easy. Everyone who contributed helped "raise the bar" and improve the contributions week to week. It was as if we were engaged in a six-month writing seminar. I hope the Insiders learned as much as I did. Learning as a writer never stops!

Thank you to my readers, and especially the Insiders, for thrilling to the stories as much as I do, for telling your friends and families about the books, and keeping the Keepers alive! I've said it before, but I'll say it again: I have the best (writers!) readers an author could ask for.

Yours, *always*,

Ridley Pearson

Hailey, Idaho
Christmas 2013

1

SHE HAS BEEN CALLED MANY THINGS: the Black Mamba, Calypso, Tia Dalma. And worse. Much worse.

The scratching of rat claws on stone at her bare feet is accompanied by the disturbing squeals of the rodents as they stream past. Consumed by the darkness of the tunnel, she shuffles forward, her toes stabbing into the void like a cockroach's antennae.

Her stubby fingers feed twine from the ball she carries. Slowly she plays out the lifeline, measuring the ball's diminishing diameter with a slight pressure of her left thumb. It is the third such ball she has knotted, one to the other, in as many days. She has no idea how long it may take for her captors to realize she has escaped; some spells outlast time itself, others prove themselves fleeting.

The string now stretches more than fifteen hundred feet behind her—nearly a third of a mile—as it winds through the unmarked turns and dead ends of the Devil's Labyrinth, the name she has given this seemingly endless underground maze. Carved from caves by an ancient civilization, the interconnecting subterranean passageways might have once connected temples or burial monuments, might have provided safe harbor from hurricanes or served as death traps for exiled citizens, prisoners, or the sick and elderly. Her torch burned out twenty minutes and two tunnels ago. She has considered going back, chasing the twine to the daylight, but what would be the point? Though she cannot see in the dark, Tia Dalma is not without her ways. She has her voodoo, her visions, is able to direct wormholes through reality to sense Danger, Desire, and Death—the three Ds.

She does so now, but detects only the worry and scurry of the rats and a looming menace that hangs like a stink. Bad things have happened here. Evil stains these walls. Where some would feel fear so intense as to set teeth to gnashing, this woman warms at the very thought.

Getting close now.

A slight breeze, fainter than the breath of a bumblebee bat, flutters the two mole whiskers on the underside of her chin, tickles her tattooed eyelids with delicious warmth, fills her dilated nostrils with the fetid odor of moldering organic matter. Proof of life. Somewhere, perhaps far from her current position, perhaps as near as the other side of a two-ton slab of rock, something lives. Or it once did. Candidates include blind wolves, dead snakes, dragons, or bubbling gases from the corpses of sacrificed animals stacked like cordwood two thousand years earlier. Tia Dalma picks up on it with the instincts of a bloodhound. Won't let it go. Sniffs the air loudly as she pursues the frail thread of decomposition.

The twine uncoils as the ball spins on her fingers. Even a maze as complicated and devious as this must contain compromises, secret passageways connecting one to the other, hidden exits, covert companionways. This whiff of decay is her first encouragement. But it proves fleeting, no more than a temptation to hurry her forward to the fraying end of her rope, where she stops, eager to press forward even without the connection back.

Not daring to release the twine, she stretches her body, pushing her fingertips as far as she can reach, tickling the dark with pointed purple nails like a relay runner reaching for the baton. It is a risky business, this, for she could inadvertently release the stretched string and send it recoiling from her, elusively difficult to locate. Divorced from the certainty of survival, a person could go mad in such darkness.

But Tia Dalma is no person. If she were, she would prove herself less susceptible than most: she's mad already.

Once again the fetid, rank odor of rot overcomes her. It comes from stone rubble to her left caused by a cave-in. She approaches and begins to dig, driven by a gnawing suspicion that whatever corpse is causing this foul report, it is meaningful to her, pertains to her. This thought causes a spike of energy, determination and—dare she admit it?—apprehension.

The digging is surprisingly easy. She pulls a stone loose only to cause a small rockslide. The grave comes open for her. A few more rocks is all and—

She gasps as her fingers touch not rock but scales—large scales, the size of dinner plates, but with the rough texture of giant fingernails. *Dragon scales,* she realizes. She howls into the dark like a lone wolf. Maleficent transfigures herself into a dragon—*or did*, Tia Dalma realizes. No longer. In her mind's eye she can see the willful boy who trapped and killed one of the greatest practitioners of black magic ever to live.

The boy who did this!

A second haunting cry reels though the catacombs. It's a high-pitched complaint tinged with pain and anger, grief, and agonizing uncertainty. There should be others even if the one is lost. The Evil Queen. The Beast. Tia Dalma has made it her charge to collect these principals and rebuild. No battle is without losses; no army survives with all its generals. Hope is ephemeral, defying her wish to hold on to it. Who needs hope when there is hate to take its place? Who needs even hate when there is an attack planned for later this same night many, many miles to the north? An attack set to bring the Kingdom to its knees?

With one hand she searches the rubble and makes contact with neither wood nor rock. She pulls hard, extricating what turns out to be a length of bone, her treasure found. Still, she has not let go of the twine. She twists it in her fingers as she reverses direction, begins collecting the twine around itself, the ball in her hand growing thicker as it directs her back along a route well traveled.

2

$\mathcal{T}$HROUGH THE WINDOWS, an image. At first, the Security guard—appropriately named Bert; he looks like a Bert, and was even named for the character in *Mary Poppins*—can hardly believe it. Here? At this hour? Waving to him like they're old friends?

Bert glances at a photograph hanging on the interior wall of the Frank G. Wells building at the Disney Studios. In the photo is the the same man, much younger, standing with Becky Cline and Mickey Mouse at the grand opening of the Disney Archives. They call him a Disney Legend. In the court-yard terrace outside, this man's palm prints and name adorn a ceramic-tile plaque on a pillar supporting the trellis. A child prodigy, he worked with Walt Disney himself, helped design Disneyland and later, Walt Disney World, overseeing the cre-ation of attractions. He was a founding member of what would come to be called "the Imagineers"—those Cast Members whose job it is to have vision.

He is old now, his hair white as cotton, but his ruddy face is youthful and full of surprise. Bert feels better just seeing him out there. Wayne Kresky has the power of personality, of confidence and willful joy. It almost looks like he's glowing.

Wayne motions for Bert to unlock the door. Later, this will strike Bert as odd; surely Wayne possesses every key, every code needed to access any building anywhere in the Disney kingdom—so why signal for Bert's help?

But Bert does not hesitate. Who is he to deny Wayne

5

Kresky anything? It might as well be a royal prince making the request. As Bert moves toward the door, he is once again struck by Wayne's charisma. Against the backdrop of night, the man appears cloaked in incandescence—almost shimmering.

Bert bumps the door's push bar and heaves it open with his hip.

"Good evening, sir."

"I have business to attend to. . . . Do you mind?"

The two sentences seem—somehow—prerecorded, like two different pieces of dialogue edited together. But Bert is overcome by the man's presence. Wayne Kresky, here! Bert doesn't stop to question anything about the situation. Hindsight will help others fill in the blanks. For now, the Security man is awestruck. Albert Pujols or Kobe Bryant would have less of an impact upon him than Wayne Kresky.

"Of course!"

"The Archives."

"I was just looking at the picture of you and—"

Wayne's face is devoid of emotion as he pulls the door farther open and blocks it with his foot. It's an aggressive act: so unexpected, it stops Bert cold, in midsentence.

"Welcome to Walt Disney World!" Wayne says in a theatrical voice different from any inflection he's used thus far.

Bert thinks, *But this is Burbank. South of here is Anaheim, home to Disneyland. Disney World? Why did he say that? Can the old dog no longer hunt?*

Just above the courtyard, a string of specks appears in the night sky. If this wasn't Southern California, Bert might think they were snowflakes. Fireflies, perhaps. Hummingbirds. The specks grow in size and proximity quickly—they are flying, flying fast, straight toward an openmouthed Bert, whose expression changes now from wonder to dread. Not snowflakes. Not hummingbirds. If he didn't work for Disney, he would have thought, *not possible!*

The first three or four come into focus: brooms, brooms with buckets—the nemeses of Mickey in his role as the Sorcerer's Apprentice. Flying brooms. No, not flying—the brooms are carried by ghosts, the ghosts followed by demons and monsters, hollow-eyed, horrid creatures from unseen graveyards, decayed and fetid, so grotesque that Bert averts his eyes, recoiling as they swoop under the courtyard's trellis and flow inside the building driven by a ferocious wind.

"No!" Bert hollers. "Please! No!"

But who's to hear? A demon hovers over him, gray and toothless with the shriveled, sunken cheeks of a two-thousand-year-old mummy and eyes like wrinkled dates. The demon points the bony nub of one long, skeletal finger at Bert as he floats lower . . . lower. . . .

Bert shrinks into a tight ball, moaning in terror. The finger pokes him.

And then . . . blackness.

3

WHY DOES SENIOR PROM have to be held at Disney World? In every other way, the evening is perfect: the hotel ballroom is decked out with life-size photographs of high school seniors set to graduate in three weeks, colorful crepe paper streamers, and a mirror ball suspended over the crowded dance floor; blue and gold lasers blast from each corner of the cavernous room; the two DJs are laying down jams that produce massive cheers as the thumping rhythms play nonstop. It's dreamy, even for a boy.

Finn Whitman is dancing with Amanda Lockhart. Truth be told, he doesn't hear the music. He's pretty much in an alternate universe—a realm in which Amanda is the sun. She throws off heat and brilliance that make his cheeks redden. Four whole hours of this—whoever came up with the idea of prom night should be immortalized, Finn thinks. They deserve a national monument in Washington, D.C., a library on the banks of the Mississippi, and a statue in Central Park.

Amanda's arms are clasped around his neck; his hands hold her waist. They aren't all glued together the way some of the other kids are. There's a sliver of distance between them that feels magnetic; Finn has to hold himself back from pressing closer.

"This is nice," Amanda says. The queen of understatement.

"Not really," Finn says. He feels her body tense in apprehension. A cloud of confusion suddenly hangs between them. Amanda seems ready to push away. He speaks in a whisper.

"It goes so far beyond 'nice,' so far beyond amazing and perfect and brilliant and glorious and supercalifragilisticexpialidocious, that you ought to have to sit in the corner for making it sound so underwhelming."

Amanda's arms slip down from around his neck to his back and she compresses the space between them. For an instant, they hug. It's quick, but powerful.

"Thank you."

Her breath, so close to his ear, sends chills down his spine.

"My only complaint, and it's a small one: it had to be Disney World."

"Can you believe it?" She laughs. "More work than treasure."

He nearly corrects her. The expression is "more work than pleasure" or "more work than leisure." But he lets it go. Learning to care about someone means trying not to correct or criticize.

By *work*, Amanda is referring to Finn's own version of an alternate universe, a universe in which she and her sister, Jess (who isn't her biological sister) have become full-fledged citizens. Amanda and Jess now travel in the same orbit as Finn and his four closest friends, who have all earned full college scholarships by serving as models for Disney hologram hosts in the theme parks.

The internal Disney technical term for the role Finn and his four friends play in the parks is Disney Host Interactive or Daylight Hologram Image: DHI. What started essentially as a modeling job has grown into something more complex; the kids—they were so young when they all started, Finn thinks—learned that they'd actually been recruited to form a five-person strike force, the Kingdom Keepers. That's the nickname the Internet community has assigned Finn and the other DHIs.

Their real job was to enter the parks at night and battle a dark force attempting to corrupt the park experience. Disney villains who wanted to take over the parks—dubbed Overtakers—were wreaking havoc. The DHIs were meant to put an end to all that.

It turned out that the OTs' ambitions went far beyond stealing cars from Buzz Lightyear's Space Ranger Spin; they meant to destroy the magic of the parks, the magic of Disney. They were instigating a revolution, and the DHIs turned out to be the only force standing in their way.

For the past several years, Finn and his co-DHIs, Philby, Charlene, Maybeck, and Willa, have been more Navy SEAL than hologram host. And even though Amanda and Jess are not official DHIs, Philby and the Keepers have secretly installed the girls' data onto the DHI computer servers, enabling them as holograms. All of the Keepers have, on numerous occasions, risked their lives to keep the magic alive. If they'd known from the start what they were getting into, maybe they wouldn't have volunteered. But the expansion of their responsibilities just kind of crept up on them. On one level, Finn thinks, their mentor and leader, an original Disney Imagineer, tricked them into accepting their roles: they were told that if they bailed, Disney would never be the same. Thanks for the warning, Finn thinks grimly.

It has been three years since Finn lost his friend Dillard Cole in the Mexican jungle. Dillard died because of the Overtakers. Since that dark day, the Kingdom Keepers have enjoyed three years of relative quiet. Yet not a single night has passed that Finn hasn't dreamed of that awful moment. Finn can't help but feel that he was responsible for Dillard's death. But according to their fellow DHIs, that is far from the truth.

After he returned from Mexico, Finn's parents made him go to counseling. That came to an abrupt halt when Finn showed up one day as a DHI and shocked the psychologist by walking through the office door without opening it. It was the psychologist who needed therapy after that.

Next, they put Finn on "medication." That ill-conceived solution lasted all of one week. He slept better and didn't dream about Dillard, but he didn't feel like himself. Finn and his parents decided it wasn't worth it. Weirdly, the ordeal drew him closer to his parents, especially his mom. For a long time he'd felt alone as a Kingdom Keeper. His mom eventually rallied behind him, but then became a victim of the Overtakers herself. Not a good situation. Throughout an entire fifteen-day voyage on a Disney cruise ship, Finn worried he might never get his real mother back. Now their family was reunited, feeling somehow stronger than before. And Finn's mom knew what it was like to live with the fear of the Overtakers.

"Can you believe how long we've known each other?" Finn asks, and then feels stupid. "Sorry! That came out awkward."

"No it didn't."

"I just meant—"

"I know what you meant—what you mean. I know you, remember? You mean that we've been friends—just friends— for a long time now. That both of us . . . that sometimes it doesn't feel exactly like friends." Amanda giggles softly. Nervously.

For Finn, the sound of her laughter is sweeter than any of the songs the DJ has played.

"So I'm just going to say it," Amanda continues.

"Why don't you?"

Another giggle. He wills the song to keep playing. He wants this dance to go on for the rest of the night.

"We're more than just friends," she says.

"We are." Can she hear his heart beating?

"But we've kept it like this because to lose this isn't worth what we might gain by it not being like this. Does that make any sense?"

"It does." Did it just get hotter in here? Is anyone else sweating the way he is? "But things change."

"They do," she says.

She can't look at him. Is that good or bad? he wonders. "And as much as we'd like for things to stay the same, that isn't how it works."

"No," she says.

He's not sure how to take that. Does she mean that's not how it works? Did he overstep? He says, "It could ruin things, right?"

"Totally."

"And that would be horrible. The worst thing ever."

"The apocalypse."

They laugh. The couple next to them shoots them a look that says, *Shut up!*

"Vampires," he says. He kisses her neck, pretending to bite her.

"Werewol—" His kiss catches her off guard. She stops talking so quickly that it sounds as if she inhaled an insect. "Do that again," she whispers. "Please."

"I was just kidding around."

"Oh . . ."

The moment passes. Finn could slap himself. *She asked you to bite her neck again, you jerk!* So he aims for the same spot.

"No!" She stops him. "Never mind."

They dance through a chorus and another verse. "See?" Finn says, "I'd be horrible at this."

"I had to stop you because I didn't want to faint on the dance floor."

It takes him a few seconds to process this. He relaxes. She isn't angry. She isn't going to walk off the dance floor and leave him standing alone.

"Maybe just friends is a good thing," he says.

"Definitely."

He leans back so that he can see her eyes. Colored lights spin across her face. She seems to be glowing from within. Finn knows it's just an effect of the lighting, but he convinces himself it's more than that. They've stopped dancing despite the continuing music. She didn't mean it. He didn't mean it. This is it: the moment. He never quite pictured it like this. But here it is. Their heads move slowly closer. Her lips part ever so slightly. He can't believe it's finally going to happen—again, now—a lifetime after their first kiss.

"Finn!"

Finn and Amanda jump away from each other. Whatever they just had shatters into pieces on the floor and melts away. Finn can't breathe—but he could put a fist through Philby's face.

What is he doing here? Philby doesn't even go to their school. And he isn't dressed up for a prom; he's dressed the way he always is, like . . . well, like Philby: preppie, with the Scottish air that comes from his red hair and freckles. But Philby has clearly finally hit his long-delayed growth spurt— he looks like he's grown about six inches since the end of the DHIs' Disney cruise. In fact, all the Keepers look different now, Finn realizes. It's like they're not themselves anymore.

Except Amanda. She's the same person, but somehow better than back then. Amazing Amanda.

"What the—?" Finn is trying to process the interruption.

Philby keeps his voice low so that the nearby dancers cannot hear him over the throbbing music. But Finn hears, Amanda hears. "Your phone," Philby hisses in a patronizing tone.

"I'm dancing here," Finn says, gesturing toward Amanda, whom Philby has yet to acknowledge.

"Hey, Mandy," Philby says. "Sorry." Polite, gentlemanly. Then back to Finn, and now he's condescending again. "Your phone is off."

"It's on Do Not Disturb. As in: Do Not Disturb!"

"Something's going down. They need us." Philby looks at his friends intently. "They need us to take a 'nap.'"

For the last three years since the cruise, things have been quiet. The Keepers have officially done little more than some image maintenance and new voice recordings for their in-park holographic guides. Unofficially, they have gone on occasional DHI "surprise inspections" of the Walt Disney World parks— late night walkabouts to make sure the peace is being kept. Now this.

One everyday skill that all the Keepers have developed as a result of their DHI service is the ability to fall asleep easily. All the Keepers, and Amanda and Jess too, can lie down and drift off in a matter of minutes. Once asleep, they can be "crossed over" and make the jump to their DHI hologram form—a bio-electronic mechanism that hasn't ever been fully explained to any of them. Nor is it fully understood by anyone but the old man who serves as their mentor, Wayne Kresky.

"Where?" Finn asks.

"Everyone else is in the back of Maybeck's van, waiting."

Finn looks Philby up and down, taking the measure of his seriousness, and decides this is not a practical joke.

With one word, Amanda lets Finn know that she both understands the situation and feels hurt nonetheless—a one-two punch that leaves his stomach in a knot. "Go," she says.

4

OUTSIDE THE TUNNELS, Tia Dalma takes her rest in the shade of a tree beneath the blue moonlight. It is sweltering, the air thick as mud. Jungle birds caw and complain. Creeping critters crush and disturb the oversize foliage, their intrusion very much felt though they go unseen.

Tia Dalma raises her hand like a priestess. The buzzing jungle goes instantly quiet. As still as a pond on a windless morning.

A rhythmic thumping intrudes, like a hammer striking metal. It amplifies the pain in her head, encouraging anger to rise from her belly like lava. A mechanical, entirely human sound, it has no place in the thick of the Mexican jungle. She wills it away, but to no effect. The unwanted clanging is as steady as a heartbeat.

The remains of the walls and temples are revealed in the moonlight as rubble, oversize cubes of weathered limestone tossed about as if a child has wrecked his castle of wooden blocks. They form a festive weed-and-vine-covered courtyard, with a sacrificial table at its center. Two pyramids have been lopped off at the top, like bridal cakes decapitated. A third remains intact, the stones stacked in diminishing tiers like massive stairs rising to the heavens. The rock is crusted with colorful lichen, reminding Tia Dalma of spilled blood, with white splashes of bird droppings and vivid green weeds, air plants, and orchids forgoing dirt and living off the wet of the air itself. The pyramid has stood scabbed in silence for thousands of years, has no doubt witnessed atrocities, marriages, deaths and births, cyclones, deluge, and drought. But this constant, dull pounding from the distance arrives as an abomination.

Already agitated by her general lack of progress in the catacombs, Tia Dalma can take it no longer. A woman who gets what she wants and suffers no fools, she plots her course, electing to climb the stepped central stripe that symmetrically divides the pyramid. No stranger to religious ceremony, she is mindful of this elaborately carved aisle's possible significance, imagining—even sensing—a procession of high priests ascending it in colorful robes as thousands of jungle-dwelling peasants gather to witness the spectacle. She can see herself among them—a high priestess, in gold and jewels, clad in a breastplate of hammered silver and a necklace of mummified animal heads, carrying a black ironwood staff topped with the hollow-eyed stare of a human skull. She carries herself accordingly as she climbs: square-shouldered, straight-backed. Her mystic powers transcend the present; instead of the intrusive pounding, she hears thousands of voices chanting a guttural language she cannot understand. It drives her and the priests ever higher. No commoner is allowed the privilege of seeing the world from the top of the temple's peak, of looking into the future, of viewing the past, of talking directly to the gods.

Wooden drums take up the beat of the chant as the priests climb higher. The high priest arrives at the summit, stops, and turns dramatically to look down on his flock. His face is painted like a monster's. Bare-chested men in the crushing crowd begin leaping and cheering; women faint. Children cry.

Tia Dalma finds herself standing upon the flat-topped pyramid, her right arm extended as if holding a staff, looking down at the tangle of jungle that has consumed everything in its path but the most inhospitable rock.

From behind her comes the rhythmic punch of metal on metal, the sound like the ticking of a giant clock. She spins to address the intruder, but is faced with the treetops of jungle as far as she can see. If there are roads, they do not reveal themselves; nor do structures or villages. Tiny specks—flying birds—interrupt the sky, some in groups, some solo. Only through focused concentration is Tia Dalma able to detect a smudge of gray at treetop level—a faint stain of discoloration in the verdant green, like a watermark on a kitchen window.

The longer she stares, the more evident the tiny cloud becomes. There must be lights beneath it. This place is the source of the mechanical heartbeat. This surgical hole in the jungle's perfection. Humans. Environmental cancer.

She thinks to stop this sound, to inflict her powers of witchcraft upon anyone vulgar enough to imagine they can disturb a holy shrine such as the one upon which she stands. The hubris! How reprehensible are those who disturb and disrupt without awareness of those around them.

But the longer she stands atop the temple, her foul mood festering like an open sore, the more she feels a slight vibration rising through her bare feet, into her ankle bones, and up her shins. She kneels and places her open palms on the warm rock. Yes, the ground is shaking.

She zeroes in on the underbrush below and to the right, the earthen roof of the catacombs through which she has just wandered. The tunnels are part of the limestone cave systems that can be found in abundance throughout Central America. Here, the priests dictated a human fashioning, carving and connecting, blocking and redirecting, turning what nature offered into a labyrinthine puzzle that only they could navigate. If a commoner entered, he or she never came back. The priests' abilities anointed them as superior and god-chosen. Untouchable.

But if Tia Dalma's knees feel the tremor, so too do the limestone walls and ceilings of the catacombs.

Only now, as her unflinching eyes tear up, does she realize she has gone about this all wrong. Worse, she has condemned the people—the humans—responsible for the vexing sound. Instead of condemnation, she should have tried understanding. Instead of repulsion, she should have embraced, even praised their technology!

She sees so clearly where she has gone wrong. If the Beast remains alive in the suffocating chambers beneath her, there may yet be a way to free him.

5

THE WORKER'S SUN-BAKED SKIN is the color of tobacco, his unfocused eyes bloodshot. He stands, facing the jungle lit primarily by moonlight. Behind him, several electric lights reveal a tangled mass of machinery that connects to an assemblage of aluminum and steel rising like a church steeple. From here tolls the impertinent pounding of metal on metal that drew Tia Dalma. If the temple from which she has just walked represents a sacred place where humanity can connect to the gods, this place is quite the opposite.

In her hand, Tia Dalma holds a doll crudely fashioned from leaves and twigs, bound together with tendrils of green vine. It follows a human form: legs, arms, the stub of a neck upon which is lanced a *chicozapote* fruit to symbolize the head. Reminiscent of a child's plaything, it is anything but. It serves no little girl's purpose. It is not a soldier in a boy's imaginary army. This doll serves a far more devious purpose. Her purpose.

Following her silent summons, the worker is drawn to the jungle's edge.

Tia Dalma adjusts the doll's left arm—and grins perversely as the worker's left arm moves accordingly. Right arm. Echo. Swivel of the head left to right—perfection!

"The process must be compromised," she says, speaking the man's native Spanish so fluently, and with such a fine accent, that she might be this man's mother. In his mind, the voice sounds like a fusion of his mother's bidding and commandments from God. There is no denying it, no refuting its authority. To disobey would be tantamount to committing a sin.

"You will do what must be done, or suffer the consequences," Tia Dalma whispers. With that, she stabs a twig into the doll's belly. The man buckles over, groaning in agony. "Yes," she says. "You must obey the Black Mamba."

Tia Dalma works the doll. It is routine for her; she could do it in her sleep. Only the pesky Kingdom Keepers—five teenagers empowered by hologram technology who serve the good of Disney—are not fully susceptible to her black magic. The effects of her powers on the young people sent to defeat her are wholly unpredictable. Otherwise, she might have prevailed already, she and the other dark masters, the ones who have come together to overtake the parks—the entire Disney kingdom—for the good of bad, the dark of night, the sake of corruption and control. And don't forget the three Ds: Danger, Desire, and Death.

The worker responds to Tia Dalma's manipulations like a child's remote-controlled robot, pivoting and walking stiff-legged in time with the relentless, rhythmic clanging toward the machinery, the dials and tanks, pumps and pipes that sit like an open sore amid a swill of mud. The muck oozes around the man's bare feet as he reaches the metal tangle. He is not without consciousness: to a point, he can think for himself. Tia Dalma has taken control of him physically and impaired him mentally; they work as smoothly as dancing partners, like a well-oiled machine.

The man marches directly to a control panel of digital readouts so bright that Tia Dalma can make out their neon greens, ambers, and reds from where she lurks in the shadows of the jungle. He acts without haste as she raises the doll's right arm, giving his brain a cue to work the controls.

Immediately, the wheezing of pressurized pipes rises like a chorus. Steam valves cough; the generator revs to keep up with the demand for electricity. Three of the green displays turn amber; two of the amber, red. A wiry man with slicked-back hair and a tattoo of a snake that winds from his wrist to his neck approaches her worker. The supervisor wears a DayGlo orange hard hat, distinguishing himself from the yellow hard hats of his team. He barks angrily at the worker.

Three more amber displays become red. The supervisor rants, gesticulating at the panel, and moves in to correct the changes his worker has made.

Tia Dalma lifts the doll's arms, pushes the hands together, and lowers them fast, like a sledgehammer driving down a tent spike. The supervisor collapses to his knees. Her worker smashes the man's back a second time; now he's down on all fours, shouting. Four other workers emerge from a small trailer.

All the green is gone from the panel, replaced by amber, red . . . and flashing red. The sounds intensify. Tia Dalma doesn't understand the process—she is no mechanical engineer—but by the look of it, steam and chemicals are being injected into the ground, flushing or pressurizing the cavity far below and causing it to disgorge its valuable natural gas. Some form of extraction that goes well beyond her limited knowledge. Whatever the case, the worker's efforts are charging the well with added pressure; she needs no gauge or display to tell her that. The earth beneath her feet is trembling now, more strongly than she felt from the top of the temple.

The four men rush toward her worker, hollering. The ground shakes so violently that one of the men loses his balance and falls, comically. It feels to Tia Dalma like the earth itself is sliding. Shifting.

She works the doll's feet and arms in a flurry of inhuman gestures that knock the other three men aside. They go down like bowling pins, and then jump to their feet as the supervisor recovers and stands.

Her priorities set, Tia Dalma turns her worker, holding him upright as the three men attack him from behind. She hears the cracking of her worker's bones, but keeps the doll steady; it will not yield. The worker swings at the supervisor. The wiry man soars through the air, crashing hard into a rusted pickup truck.

The sight stops the other three men. In an instant, they understand that they are dealing with something cursed, something from another realm. They back up as Tia Dalma turns her worker and marches him forward. Two of the three men hesitate. The other runs, screaming.

Her worker's legs are broken in several places, the bones showing through the skin—and yet he walks on, undeterred.

The vibration in the earth gives way to shaking, and the shaking to quaking. Tia Dalma steadies herself, reaching out for a palm tree. Behind her, other trees begin to fall, their roots torn from the loosening soil.

From a bird's-eye view, a ring of destruction emanates outward from the drilling rig, with ever-expanding concentric circles formed by rippling shock waves. The jungle growth inside this ring falls silently, as though a wind has toppled everything taller than a few inches. Birds, snakes, and other creatures scatter. On and on the ring spreads, like ripples in a pond in the wake of a stone's splash.

As the leading edge of the ring reaches the temple compound, dust rises. The earth collapses, folding inward, swallowing the surface whole.

Against the backdrop of a low rumble, so terrifying that

the very birds take flight, can be heard the cackle of a witch doctor's cruel laugh.

There, in the midst of the mud and grime, as the drill tower teeters and collapses, Tia Dalma has her dull-eyed, broken-boned worker dancing an Irish jig in celebration.

6

Tia Dalma observes her work by night, an artist in the privacy of her studio.

She studies the destruction she has caused. The gray stones of the temple lie on the ground, wearing a crust of dirt and debris. The grass and plants that once surrounded the temple look as if they belong on an ancient gravestone.[1] The temple, at one time tall, and proud as the forces of nature it was modeled after, now is little more than a child's broken tower of building blocks. Water trickles through the blocks and pieces of the once majestic pyramid, the very stream that defeated the Beast, Chernabog, years before. A miasma of evil fills the dusty air. This was a place of sacred ritual, untouched by the commoners, now desecrated by outsiders—worse, foreigners—who have no right to be here. The tears in the earth scream like wounds, spitting hate. Who knows what ancient powers have been released?[2]

A snorting, heavy-breathing sound summons Tia Dalma closer—the sound made by a ferocious bull trapped in a branding chute. Despite all the magnificent horrors her eyes have seen, many of her own making, she approaches with trepidation and unusual reserve. But this is hardly a usual situation. Only as she nears the grating noise does it dawn on her that these catacombs have been dormant for thousands of years;

---

[1] WillaTree_Circles
[2] Freedom_Kingdom

24

that high priests perhaps more powerful than she (a terrifying thought in itself) utilized them as a place of banishment for thieves, those unwanted outcasts deemed a danger to the greater community.

Danger. Desire. Death. Evil spirits would have been expelled to this labyrinth, led into its tangled tunnels with no hope of finding their way out.

Until now.

In all her impatience, Tia Dalma thinks, she may have liberated these festering forces. She may have inadvertently torn the lid off Pandora's box. Tia Dalma is not one to experience chills of fear rippling up her spine, and yet the sensation invades her now, as unwanted and unfamiliar as disease. The very location of the labyrinth, below the earth, its proximity to the realm of fire and darkness that has fed her all these years, allows a faint possibility to enter her mind: she could be standing atop an access to the Underworld. A portal to the kingdom of Hades himself—one so powerful, so ultimate, that she would be made to look the infant by comparison.

She wants no contact with Hades. Briefly, she considers running. Tia Dalma—flee like a frightened child? Unthinkable! Inexcusable! And yet . . . the urge is there, ever present and gnawing her brain raw.

She lays one bare foot in front of the other. She has carved her own way through this murky world, no doubt troubling the likes of Hades—assuming powers she might have been better off leaving to others, misusing those powers, abusing, torturing. He might smile at what she has done. Pain could raise a chuckle. But in the past she has forgiven, nurtured, nursed, and assisted those in need: violations, all. She has allowed herself to act—dare she even think it?—human. If caught, she will be punished. Pulled deeper into the realm through the cavernous cracks in the earth that spread before her.

She must hurry! A power such as this knows no compassion, has no sense of time. Should he find his way out, she—and perhaps those she seeks to liberate—will be fugitives from his all-encompassing wrath for time immemorial. Never safe, always on the run.

The solution is plain to see: she must free her associates and search for a way to cause an even bigger earthquake, something to fold the dirt and stone back in on itself, closing off the very chambers she has now exposed.

But for now, her skin crawling, she marches steadily forward, only yards from the nearest exposed tunnel. She must peer inside—which goes against every fiber of her being.

She must free the Beast.

I T'S NOT JUST THE OTHER KEEPERS—Philby, Maybeck, Willa—who are in the back of Maybeck's van. Brad is there too. Brad, the Imagineer technician responsible for all the studio green-screen work involved in digitizing the Keepers' actions and speech to create their holograms. Brad, who worked with them during the upgrade to DHI version 2.0, stabilizing their holograms. He's maybe thirty now, but still has a youthful face, dark hair, and thick eyebrows. He works calmly but intensely, making sure that each Keeper is comfortable lying down on a few yoga mats.

Finn is shoulder-to-shoulder with the fiercely intelligent and sometimes brooding Willa. At their heads, Maybeck lies sideways across the van. Next to him, and immediately behind the front two seats, is Philby, also sideways on the floor.

Brad climbs into the driver's seat and turns the ignition. "For the past three years," he says, "it's been mostly exercises. Right?"

His words trigger memories and images for Finn, most of them good. He pushes past the pain of losing Dillard to the harrowing events of the cruise, and past those to the long year spent battling Maleficent in all four of the Disney World parks. As a team, they've come through a great deal together and grown closer as a result. They battled back the dolls of It's a Small World and endured the rage of Judge Frollo; they've had crushes and learned to distinguish them from real feelings;

27

they've experienced loss, rage, determination, and frustration as they've battled the Overtakers.

The reality-TV crew that broadcast their actions without their knowledge during the second half of the cruise has come and gone. For a time, their show drew the highest ratings of any program on the Disney Channel. The only good that came of it—if you can call it good—is that television executives in L.A. noticed Charlene's all-American good looks and gymnastic athleticism and gave her a shot at the big time. She's had several guest appearances on *Good Luck Charlie*, and there's talk she may be offered a starring role in a new Disney Channel show. The thought that Charlene could be the next Hannah Montana is a little off-putting to all the Keepers, especially Maybeck, who texts with her constantly and hasn't been himself since her departure. They've all missed her, but for Maybeck it has been agony.

"This is not an exercise," Brad continues. "There's been a breach in security at the Studio Archives."

"But wait," Willa says, "aren't they in—"

"Burbank. You'll be crossed over onto the Disney Legend outdoor terrace between the Team Disney and Frank G. Wells buildings. Finn has the Return."

Finn taps his pocket, ensuring that the small fob-size remote device Brad is referring to is where it belongs. Items in pockets cross over; handheld objects are less predictable: sometimes they make it, sometimes not. It's crucial that the Return crosses over successfully; it's what enables the Keepers to trigger their emergence from their hologram state. Although the Imagineers could return the DHIs manually, the Keepers have learned through hard experience that initiating their exit themselves is critical to their survival.

It is not an exact science. Research into the DHI

phenomena of crossing over into hologram form is ongoing, and conducted by the very people who created the DHI program in the first place.

The best explanation the Imagineers have so far offered the Keepers is that crossing over involves each Keeper's consciousness making a jump "into" his or her hologram at the moment of drifting off to sleep. In that fragile moment between wakefulness and slumber, a kind of portal opens to supercomputers operated by the Disney Imagineers running artificial intelligence software. The Imagineers believe that each DHI operates in a dream state controlled by the sleeping Keeper. This hypothesis is at least partly confirmed by the all-too-real fact that while crossed over, a Keeper can get stuck—in what they call the Sleeping Beauty Syndrome, or SBS. If a DHI is not returned, the sleeping host is trapped in what appears to be a coma while the spark of waking consciousness is unable to make the jump back to the sleeping body.

"You're being dropped into a hot zone," Brad cautions. "Fair warning: this isn't like crossing over at the Hub in the Magic Kingdom and going off searching for OTs. Tonight, you'll be dropped into the middle of an active operation. The security breach is a well-organized raid. It's imperative that it be thwarted. We are Code Jiminy."

A collective gasp. On a scale from one to five, Jiminy is code for the second-highest threat level, surpassed only by Tink. Its invocation authorizes the Keepers to use any means necessary to accomplish the specified goal, including "loss of property"—an Imagineer euphemism for the destruction of Disney characters. Tink allows further for the destruction of physical property, attractions, and systems within the park, as well as for the use of "enhancers"—meaning, dark magic and specialized implements of destruction.

This new military-style regimen is a direct result of the ordeal in Mexico that cost Dillard his life. Since the Imagineers adopted it, the Keepers have never been authorized to go beyond Code Alice, the second of the five levels. By establishing the higher risk level, Brad is warning them that they're being dumped into a dogfight.

"Mission objective?" Philby asks. The Professor wants to get the facts straight.

"Protect assets; restore video surveillance; determine the target or objective of the raid."

"Layout?" Philby, again.

"You will cross over onto the terrace. There's a Starbucks in the corner of the lobby of the target building. The doors are straight ahead. Inside the lobby, the Archives' entrance is forty feet ahead and on your left."

"'Restore video,'" Finn says, quoting Brad. "So, will we go dark once inside?" The holograms need to be projected. If a Keeper goes into "DHI shadow," their hologram disappears, and the Keeper becomes invisible to others, which can be a blessing or a curse.

"We can't confirm. Currently, we have eyes on a few spots in there, so I suppose it's more a case of you encountering extended DHI shadow."

"Until and unless we fix the cameras that aren't projecting," Philby says.

"Correct."

"So, basically," Maybeck says, "we won't know what's going on until the Overtakers are throwing everything they have at us."

"Basically," Brad says.

The van rolls. The Keepers rock from side to side on the yoga mats.

Finn says, "Everyone okay with this? It's voluntary, you know."

No one speaks up.

"All right, then," Brad says. "Good luck."

8

FINN AWAKENS TO THE HUM of traffic. Overhead, flashing jet lights punctuate a colorless night sky void of stars. He's lying on a stone terrace. A hand holding a wand looms over him. He rolls out of the way before a curse is landed, only then identifying the hand and wand as part of a bronze statue—a ten-foot-high replica of the Disney Legend award, the emblem of imagination: Mickey's gloved hand hoisting his powerful wand skyward.

The image sticks in Finn's mind; he thinks it's no coincidence that the DHI server has crossed them over to this particular spot.

Maybeck and Philby appear at nearly the same instant. They both react defensively to the ominous wand hovering over them, scurrying out of the way, only to realize that it's immobile. Nearly in unison, all three glance in the direction of the Frank G. Wells Building; ghostly wraiths swirl in and out like angry bees around a hive. Possessed demons march like zombies toward the door. It's like nothing any of the boys has seen before, and the sight temporarily paralyzes them. Finn finds himself checking his pocket for the Return.

"What are they?" Maybeck asks.

Professor Philby answers. "Wraiths and demons. Possibly from the Haunted Mansion. More likely *Princess and the Frog*. Dr. Facilier and his 'friends on the other side.' Makes one think of New Orleans, and therefore Tia Dalma. Chernabog summoned harpies and all sorts of ghouls. What's important to us is that wraiths are immortals and remain so as long as they can find humans to feed upon. That would be us—or so they will think, since I doubt they're versed in hologram technology. They're agile—can jump over fifteen feet. Apparently this variety can fly as well. They feed through their palms. Drain your soul by placing their hand to your heart. As much as I'd like to think they can't drain a DHI's heart, it's the life energy they crave, and we are, after all—"

"Energy," Finn says.

"Light energy. Yes." Philby considers their situation. "Since we're highly concentrated arrays of photons, I'm pretty sure they can suck us dry if they want to."

"And if they do, we'll be where, exactly?" Maybeck asks.

"SBS, I suppose," Philby says, sounding more like a scientist than a possible victim: Sleeping Beauty Syndrome.

Finn shudders instinctively. "Fascinating."

Maybeck snorts.

"A demon, on the other hand," Philby continues, "to be distinguished from *daemon*—is a spiritual, paranormal entity. It takes human form and can be conjured and/or controlled. Demons first appeared—"

"Save it," Maybeck snaps, pointing to the base of the statue.

A girl's translucent shape appears and then vanishes. Then reappears, flickers, and solidifies. Willa's DHI looks at the boys—and then at the swirling wraiths at the far end of the terrace.

"That's interesting," she whispers. A moment later she takes in the Legend statue without reaction; she might as well have crossed over beneath an oak tree.

"Let's go," Finn says.

The Keepers pair up without discussion. Philby and Willa

crouch and move to the right of the terrace; Maybeck and Finn crouch and scurry to the left.

"You ever see something like that before?" Maybeck whispers.

Finn doesn't answer. A memory of Splash Mountain is playing in a loop in his head: he's wet from the waist down, hearing a sound as creepy and unexplained as these ghostly shadows swirling in and around the office building door.

The wraiths have shriveled human skulls, and black smoky capes trail behind them. Witchlike, they appear more female—and uglier—up close.

"Can you say 'Dementors'?" Maybeck cracks. "If they try to suck your face off, my suggestion is to bolt."

Maybeck and his wisecracks. Finn shakes his head wryly, lost in the memory of another encounter: the frightening sounds behind him and Philby that turned out to be a *T. rex* breaking loose from a painted scene on the wall in Big Thunder Mountain Railroad. The dinosaur chased the boys down the train tracks, its jaws snapping like a hungry alligator's. They outwitted it, but only because it was so big and clumsy. These wraiths and demons do not look big and clumsy.

"You're not helping," Finn says.

"Chill," Maybeck snaps.

"I will once we're returned."

"So serious. We're 2.0, dude. What are they going to do to us?"

Finn can't argue about the benefits of the software upgrade. Among other problems, version 1.6 had stability issues: personal fear could trigger a decay of the hologram and therefore physical vulnerability, and physical objects that were not part of their DHIs when they crossed over could present difficulties. It could be—unpredictably—impossible to move or pick up certain things in certain circumstances. The 2.0 upgrade—carefully protected and secured by the Imagineers—has removed those bugs and more: they've gained high-definition projection and audio; their sensory stimuli have been enhanced. All in all, there's no comparison.

"And then there's your Superman thing," Maybeck says, reminding Finn of the perplexing but welcome strength he inherited after a brush with electricity in the bowels of the Disney *Dream* cruise ship. Struggling with Tia Dalma, he'd collided with a power source. Finn still doesn't know if it was the electricity, some miscalculated spell that backfired on the Creole witch doctor, or a combination of the two, but he came away from the encounter with surprising strength, the kind of strength associated with guys who are six feet six and two hundred forty pounds. More than that, even. Much more.

"Do you actually think Chern—?" Finn starts.

Maybeck cuts him off. "I don't know."

The Keepers have been together so long that they can complete each other's sentences, share each other's thoughts. But despite all their experience, neither of them knows how to battle wraiths and demons.

"I just hope it's not like bear cubs," Maybeck says.

"Chernabog's dead or, at the very least, still trapped in the labyrinth," Finn says. "Philby's right: if these belong to anyone, it's Tia Dalma."

"I know that, and you know that. But do they?"

The boys move closer, within a few yards of the door.

"No blue lines," Maybeck says. DHIs rendered in version 1.6 had thin glowing blue borders around the projected images, signaling that they were holograms, not real. The absence of blue edges suggests that the wraiths and demons are not holograms either. Projected in 2.0, the boys lack the blue outlines as well, which should convince their opponents they too are real.

Philby and Willa have worked their way on their bellies through the grass to the edge of the patio walkway bordering the building. Philby points up. Finn nods.

"Does he think we don't see them?" Finn says softly to Maybeck.

"No idea what he's doing."

Finn nods more enthusiastically. Philby shakes his head and points sharply again, gesturing to a spot above the door. The wraiths are swirling like black smoke into a vent.

"You okay?" Maybeck asks.

"Not really," Finn admits, unconcerned about being teased—even by Maybeck. The Keepers have long since crossed such boundaries. There's no need to exaggerate with each other, no need to lie. Finn can say what he feels and thinks, more so even than he can at home. It's the safest group of friends he's ever had.

"I hear you," Maybeck says. This is as close as Maybeck will get to an admission of fear; at such moments, he is still something less than one-hundred-percent candid, as if that makes him older or cooler than the others. They've learned to accept this. Maybeck is never the first to adapt.

"The lights!" Finn says. "Philby's pointing to the lights."

"There are no lights."

"That's the point."

The only light emanating from the Frank G. Wells Building is the sterile bluish-white brilliance of the emergency fixtures, the same kind of lighting the Keepers have encountered in attractions throughout Disney World when they are inside the parks after hours.

Behind the glare cast by the emergency lights, the edifice

looms, a gray obelisk against an eerily glowing sky lit by the light pollution from urban sprawl. The cardboardlike silhouette of mountains serves as a backdrop.

"Power's out." Maybeck speaks reverently, a hush whispered in a cathedral.

"Yup," says Finn.

By lifting his arms with his hands gripping an invisible lever, Philby signals back that he and Willa will attempt to reinstate the electricity. The two turn and slither off through the grass like gators, moving away from the entrance. Typical Philby, Finn thinks; he's probably memorized the studio map and all the buildings' blueprints, including mechanical specifications.

Maybeck attempts to sing. "'Just the two of us . . .'" A music machine, Maybeck has managed to mine the database of his aunt's oldies collection and come up with a Bill Withers hit from forever ago. Finn only recognizes the lyric because his parents play the same music in their car nonstop and sing along like college freshmen.

"Not now," Finn says. "There's work to do."

"*Work* is a term for those who don't enjoy their particular enterprise. You and I, on the other hand, relish the chance to put the Overtakers back where they belong. This isn't work, Finn. This is what we do. And we do it well."

"We've never battled wraiths."

"It's the brooms I'm worried about. And that green goo in their buckets."

The *Fantasia* brooms have been known to carry a toxic acid in their work buckets that is capable of melting glass—and more frighteningly, metal, wood, flesh, and bone. The only broom Finn can make out through the floor-to-ceiling windows appears to be standing guard at an internal door. The body of a Security guard lying on the floor against a wall—hopefully unconscious, not dead—remains a top priority for Finn.

He hatches a plan. Maybeck is strength and quickness deployed with the creative accuracy of a painter's mind. Finn is strategy, cunning, and calculation. They make a good pair.

"You see Starbucks?" Finn asks.

"Hardly a good time for a latte."

"That's you. In behind the bar, you'll find a fire extinguisher—"

"Says who?"

"—that you'll use to hit the flying uglies. There's toxic powder in those canisters, Maybeck. It'll blind them at the very least."

"You can be very mean."

"As you crash and blast your way through them, I'll make for the door and check the guy on the floor over there. That'll draw the bucket brigade, so don't dawdle. I'm going to need reinforcements."

"Crafty. Even devious. I approve."

"You first," Finn says.

* * *

At the westernmost side of the building, across from the electrical substation, Philby and Willa's DHIs rise to their feet. Philby takes Willa's hand and heads about eight feet to the left of a door. The two disappear through the solid wall.

* * *

Maybeck's DHI walks through the plate glass window as if it isn't there; technically, he's the one who isn't there. He enters the Starbucks and walks through, not around, the counter. A fire extinguisher is strapped to the wall next to a first aid kit. Maybeck doesn't waste any time wondering how Finn knew the extinguisher would be there or doubting his faith in Finn's knowledge. Maybeck is not the type to get all sentimental about how they have each other's backs, how they complement each other's deficits, how they work so well as a team. He's not a sports guy; he doesn't have "team" in him. He's an artist, and he considers himself something of a loner (though that has changed since his feelings for Charlene have grown); he feels like a discard, because he's been raised by his aunt Jelly and not by his biological parents. He has issues.

Maybeck focuses. The 2.0 software makes touching, smelling, hearing—all five senses—seem perfectly normal and real. He unclamps the fire extinguisher, turns, pulls the safety pin, and squeezes the handle.

He spots an attacking airborne wraith in a reflection on the plastic face of a coffee timer. Yellow dust hits the wraith in its horrid, withered face. A sound like a baby pig being sat upon ricochets off the walls, rattles the coffee mugs, and shakes the teacups. Maybeck identifies terror bubbling up in his DHI, a sensation he does not expect and could never have anticipated. It's uncomfortable and irritating.

The wraith crashes into a wall, sending a stack of mugs to the floor. It writhes on a shelf, clearly injured by the impact. Regaining its strength, the wraith turns its hooded, hollow-eyed leathery head and stares darkly at Maybeck. A bony hand shoots out from beneath its smoky cape. Palm to chest, the hand attaches to Maybeck's sternum like a suction cup.

Maybeck looks down in surprise: the gray hand should have passed *through* his DHI, but as Philby warned, something is wrong. The hand attaches to his chest, palm forward. Colored pixels collect at his chest in a brilliant flare, first red, then blue, yellow, white, and suddenly a blinding burst brighter than sunshine. The particles migrate from Maybeck's side and extremities like electronic blood draining away. His DHI turns gray at the edges. His arms and legs grow weaker; it's harder to think. He's losing consciousness. This creature is sucking the light out of him. The melody of "Killing Me Softly" floats through his head.

It's a light show. Maybeck can't take his eyes off the sparking, shooting rays leaping from his chest. It's a supernova, beautiful in a way. He understands the creature is killing him, but he's so transfixed, he's helpless to do much about it. This, he realizes, is the secret of the wraiths' power—they mesmerize.

The realization briefly breaks the spell. Maybeck struggles to lift one pale, dimming arm. It takes all his concentration. His hand and skin are dull gray, the tips of his fingers dissolving as the last of the photons flow up his forearm to collect at his shoulder. With his other hand, he manages to take hold of the espresso machine's steam tube and bends it to aim at the creature. The thing sees him—its skull shifts slightly in the machine's direction—but the wraith has conjoined with Maybeck using its right arm, and it lacks the flexibility to reach far enough.

Wraith and Keeper look at each other. The creature smiles.

All of Maybeck's color is now drained, gathered in a ball in his chest like a backed-up sink. Maybeck turns the plastic knob, opening the valve.

Boiling hot steam rushes from the nozzle with a delicious hiss and blasts the wraith directly in its hollow eye sockets. The leathery skin bubbles and sizzles. Tethered as it is to Maybeck, there's no way for the wraith to avoid the scalding blast.

Seconds before passing out, Maybeck feels the cold inside

him replaced by a welcome warmth. The ball in his chest disperses as luminous color rushes back into his extremities.

The wraith finally releases Maybeck in order to shield its face from the steam. The struggle has taken only perhaps twenty seconds—twenty seconds that feel like many long minutes.

Maybeck swings the fire extinguisher overhead and crushes the wraith's skull. Bone cracks and shatters. There's a puff of gray ash, and the creature is gone.

Staggering, finding his strength and balance, Maybeck turns to face the onslaught of wraiths flying toward him. But he's got game now. He understands the objective. He swings the fire extinguisher canister like a baseball bat back and forth, connecting with the skull of each wraith as it nosedives to attack. The creatures burst into gray ash on contact.

He dispatches four, then spins around to check behind him and sees the impossible: the wisps of ash are drawing together on the floor like magnetic particles; re-forming, the ash begins to take shape—the edge of a cape; the top of a skull. Wraiths are immortal, Maybeck thinks. Maybeck can't guess how long it will take for the wraiths to restore themselves, and he's not sticking around to find out. He charges through to the lobby, where he sees Finn leaning over the fallen Security guard.

Overhead, a wraith. It slows and hovers above Finn. His full attention is on the guard.

"Look out!" Maybeck shouts.

* * *

After passing through the wall, Philby and Willa find themselves in a stairwell.

"Perfect," Philby says.

"You amaze me!" Willa says, a little too adoringly, and

stutters. "Your . . . accuracy. Your . . . aim. Right where we want to be."

She hopes he can't see her blushing face, but the emergency lights in the stairwell are superbright and not hiding much.

Ignoring her discomfort, Philby takes off down the stairs. "It's likely they—" He cuts himself off as, rounding a landing, he finds himself fifteen feet from a broom. The broom is having trouble with its small legs on the stairs. One hand holds the rail; the broom clearly needs the support for balance.

Willa can see the green goo in the broom's bucket—it's the same stuff Maybeck and Charlene encountered in Disney Hollywood Studios three years earlier, an acid that would quickly dissolve human flesh and bone. Willa accepts that she's not the most physically coordinated Keeper. But she has better balance than most and can hold her own on a climbing wall. Her fellow Keepers think of her as brainy and quiet. Philby knows her better than any of the others, but even he probably considers her more bookworm than athlete.

It's not what others think of you, Willa reminds herself; it's the truth you know about yourself. Since the devastating confrontation in the Mexican jungle at the end of the Panama passage, the Keepers have adopted the motto No Limits. Willa doesn't remember who came up with it, and she doesn't care. She only knows that it resonates inside her, reminding her that she is limitless in her abilities, effort, and success. The Keepers battle for good; only good can come of it. Only one person can stop her from accomplishing her objectives: herself.

She mounts the railing sidesaddle, balances, and lets go with her hands, racing down before Philby can stop her. The broom is slow to turn; Willa catches the upper part of one of its arms and slides off the railing, spinning the broom around in a full circle. Her momentum dislodges the broom's grip. It staggers, its bucket swinging nearly horizontal. Willa grabs hold of the opposite handrail and whips the broom behind her, propelling it off the stairs and onto the lower landing. The bucket spills its contents across the cinder block wall and door, instantly burning a small hole through the door and scarring the concrete wall.

Philby practically flies past Willa and leaps from the fourth step. He lands directly on the yellow wood of the broom handle, splintering it in two. Its hands spasm, twitch, and stop moving.

"Kindling," Philby says. "Nice move."

"Thank you."

He sizes her up, head to toe, seeing something in her he hasn't glimpsed in a long time. "Really *nice* move."

"Again: thank you." She feels like an idiot.

With Philby in the lead, they step over the broken broom. Together, he and Willa pass through the acid-burned hole in the wall and approach an unmarked steel door halfway down the long corridor—and step right through.

"Yes!" Willa cheers, sounding a little too much like Charlene for her liking.

They face an array of gray electronic panels, conduits, and boxes. A metal lever with a red rubber end cap is in the off position. Philby grabs it and forces it up.

"And then there was light," he says.

* * *

As Finn looks up, the wraith floating above him dives, aiming at him, one palm outstretched as if to push him.

"Don't let it touch you!" Maybeck shouts.

Finn tears a metal sign off the wall, swings it, and bats the wraith across the room. Seeing Maybeck's stunned expression, Finn realizes that the sign probably weighs more than he does. His unusual strength has kicked in.

The lights come on.

The wraiths shriek and twist and roll in the air. They waste no time fleeing, swirling out the door and into the night, where they disappear. File folders and papers, notebooks and binders cascade to the floor in their wake.

The demons—there are fewer of them, more slow-moving and plodding—remain, not to mention the broom that stands sentry, blocking the door to the Archives.

"These guys aren't terribly smart," Finn says, leading Maybeck's DHI through a section of glass wall. He slams the door on the broom and locks it before the thing has time to turn around.

"He's just going to burn his way through," Maybeck says.

"Let's hope it takes him a moment."

Sure enough, the doorknob starts to rattle.

"I told you," Finn says, "not smart."

The two boys find themselves in the Archives' small library with several tables in the center of the room surrounded by chairs and walls of shelves packed tightly with books. There's an administrator's desk at the far end, and an open doorway to its right shimmers with fluorescent-tube lighting. From this room comes the sound of items falling to the floor.

Finn and Maybeck hurry farther inside—and stop short.

Wayne Kresky, the Keepers' mentor and team organizer, Finn's personal hero, stares back at them unflinchingly.

"Continue the search," Wayne says, directing two brooms beside him. The creatures have paused, startled by the intrusion.

"Stop them!" Finn pleads. "Order them to stop!"

44

"Careful, Witless," Maybeck says, reaching for Finn and pulling him back a few steps. "The animals bite."

"Continue the search!" Wayne repeats.

The brooms go back to clearing the shelves.

"Order—them—to—stop!" Finn can't believe he's seeing this: Wayne, a traitor! "There's a man out there who needs medical attention."

Maybeck quips, "The man out there needs something more like an exorcism."

"Buckets up!" Wayne orders.

The brooms abandon their search and take hold of their buckets, ready to splash.

"Back off, or it burns," Wayne says to Finn and Maybeck. "All of it."

Maybeck tugs Finn's shoulder a second time, but Finn slaps his hand away and steps toward the white-haired old man. He takes in the ruddy face, his strong nose and bushy eyebrows. He thinks of all the lessons Wayne has taught him: leadership, confidence, teamwork.

"Why?" Finn asks. It's not an easy question to ask; Wayne has reasons for everything. But this? Betrayal?

Wayne repositions himself, turning slightly. He's wearing khaki pants and a black Windbreaker with a chest patch emblem and a stripe down the sleeves. His leg bumps a cardboard file box. He looks down. Back up at Finn. Back at the box.

"When you wish upon a star . . ." he says, smiling. "Been looking for this box."

Handwritten in black marker across the side of the box is one word: *Fantasia.*

Wayne knocks the lid off, squats, and withdraws a manila folder. Slipping it under his arm, he calls out, "Back off, or it all burns!"

"Why?" Finn repeats, not moving.

"Buckets!" Wayne shouts.

The brooms hurl the contents of their buckets against the moveable shelving. Instead of acid instantly eating a hole through the walls and the floor, the shelves catch fire.

The boys jump back.

Maybeck sprints for the brooms before they can complete a second dousing. Finn rushes past Wayne to the fire alarm box on a distant wall, elbows the box's glass face to pieces, and pushes the silver button inside.

The ceiling erupts with a gray gas.

* * *

As Philby and Willa slip back outside, they encounter two adults: a man who could be a farmer and a woman dressed for a charity luncheon. Judging by the jet-black eyes sunk deep in their sockets, they aren't . . . *human.*

"Hello?" Willa says tentatively, beginning to shake with fear.

"Demons," Philby whispers. "Don't look into their eyes, no matter what you do."

"What were you going to tell us about demons?" she asks.

"Nothing you want to hear."

"Try me."

Philby and Willa take two steps back. The demons match them step for step, their footfalls scraping on the concrete.

"The souls inside these two aren't under their control. They're recently dead, back on Earth's surface for a particular mission."

"Earth's surface . . ." Willa mutters.

"Right at the moment, these two want to use us. Enter

us. Possess us. If they do, we end up down under with them, or . . ."

"'Or'? I don't like 'or'!"

The Keepers step back again. The demons step forward. Again, their shoes make a scratching sound with each step.

"No, you won't," says Professor Philby. "You'll like it even less when you hear the full story. Believe me."

"So we're out of here," Willa says.

"One problem: they are fast. Believe it or not, they're part angel."

"Not." Willa understands the source of that strange sound: the demons are leaving slight trails of sand behind them.

"Demons can be good. The ancient Greeks used the same word for angels. These, maybe not so much. Chances are, they can fly," Philby says.

"We can't outrun them?" Willa sounds terrified. "Do we even have to? We're DHIs."

"Doesn't seem like a good time to test their powers. We might outsmart them. Maybe not. But we won't outrun them."

"How do you outsmart a demon?"

"Depends on the variety," Philby says, taking another careful step backward.

"I hope you're kidding."

"I wish I were."

"'Variety,'" Willa says dubiously.

"They could be Biblical. Or Greek. Or Hindu. Or . . . a lot of other cultures. The point is, they're under divine control."

"Divine? As in . . . ?" Willa takes a big step back, drawing even with Philby. "Can they hear us?"

"They can't think for themselves. That's our advantage. We have to make them try to use their brains, because they can't—it'll confuse them. Maybe we buy some time to run for it."

"Riddle them?"

"That's it!" Philby says enthusiastically. "That's what I'm talking about! Riddles. Puzzles. Yes! Exactly!"

"Tie them up in thought while we escape."

"You're good at this," he says.

"Why do you always sound so surprised? You know how many times you've said that to me? Is it really so shocking that—"

"Riddles. Yes! Great idea, Willa. Got any riddles for a brain-dead, remote-controlled, soulless demon?"

Willa raises her voice and speaks to the two monsters ambling toward them. "Answer me something: I never was, but am always to be. No one has ever seen me, nor will they. Yet I am the hope of all who live. What am I?"

The demons glance at each other as they continue to march forward. The male answers, "Him," and strains his head to look up.

"No! Wrong." Willa repeats the riddle. Under her breath she tells Philby, "Get ready . . ."

The second challenge does the trick. The demons stop to ponder.

"Now!"

Philby and Willa run. The former studio back lot is laid out like a small town or community college, with city blocks of buildings separated by lanes. Philby leads Willa down Donald Avenue, between a building marked PLUMBING to their left and one marked TEAM to their right. He heads for a barnlike structure marked THE MILL.

At the door, Philby stops, out of breath. He and Willa glance back and see the demon duo coming at them, flying like puppets. They're not like Superman or Iron Man—there's nothing glamorous or cool about their form of levitation. They look like floating corpses, with their arms held stiffly at their sides as if they were still lying in their coffins. The sight turns Philby's stomach. These monstrosities can't possibly represent anything good. They are black holes in the world of good. They don't belong here.

"What was the answer?" Philby asks Willa in a whisper.

"Tomorrow."

"Intriguing!"

Willa pushes through the metal barn doors just as the demons arrive, flying insanely fast despite their awkward posture. The demons crash into the door with a screeching thud; Philby makes sure it's locked, but an ominous scratching sound echoes through the space, followed by the unmistakable noise of metal tearing.

"They're ripping through the door with their bare hands," Willa says.

At that moment, a bony finger punches through the metal, nearly poking Willa in the eye. She screams and falls back.

"Told you we didn't want to conduct tests," Professor Philby says.

Willa's fall knocks some lumber loose into a tangle on the floor. Willa glances around. "If we were looking for tools—"

The hand tears through the metal skin of the door and scrabbles down, trying to unlock the doorknob.

"—we've come to the right place."

A carved wooden sign on the wall reads: THE MILL. There are workbenches and suspended light fixtures, and every available square inch is dedicated to storage or tools. Willa realizes that they are in a workshop for fabricating objects from all kinds of materials—wood, metal, glass, plastic, everything.

Philby slips one of a dozen wood chisels from its leather sheath. He stabs it into the hand. There's no reaction, no apparent pain. He stabs it again. And again. Some brown powder leaks out, like flakes of rust.

"That's disgusting," Willa says.

The hand tries to work the doorknob, but it's broken; nothing is working properly. Fingers flutter every which way in a comical dance.

A different hand—the female's—punches through the concrete wall and turns the knob. Philby attempts to stab it, but the hand moves too quickly: an instant later, the door is unlocked and open. The demons lurch inside.

"How do we kill them?" Willa shouts.

"That could be a problem," Philby says, "since they're already dead."

The two Keepers run to the far end of the room, where a group of handmade bows strung with nylon hang from a hook. On the worktable is a quiver of arrows. But the arrowheads are plastic and therefore useless.

Philby launches a hammer end over end—and misses the demons by a good five feet.

"That was effective," Willa says drily, taking hold of a bow and stringing an arrow.

"Are you any good with—?"

But Willa answers Philby's question before he can finish asking it, driving an arrow into the chest of the male demon. He doesn't flinch.

"With demons . . . you have to remove the curse," Philby says. "We aren't strong enough! "

The male demon takes the near side of the workbenches; the female, the far side. They lumber steadily forward.

"Look at me," the male says. His voice is distant, like the echo of claws scratching stone a very long time ago.

Willa shuts her eyes and unleashes a second arrow. Its plastic arrowhead nicks the male demon's cheek, but he doesn't seem to notice. Rust-brown sand leaks out like tears.

"We're dead," Philby says. His voice is desperate; he wants her to correct him.

Willa reloads another arrow.

The female demon springs from the floor, soars over the workbench, and lands on Willa, taking her down. Willa kicks out, throwing the demon off her.

"Cold!" Willa says. "She's ice-cold!"

The demon reaches for Willa's eyes, trying to open them. "Look at me!"

Squinting his eyes shut, Philby dives, knocks the female demon off Willa, and wrestles blindly to pin her. The demon is ten times more powerful than he is.

He dares to blink: the male demon is nearly upon him.

The barn doors at the far end slide open.

All four look at the door at once.

A young woman's figure in silhouette fills the door.

"Charlie!" Willa shouts.

It's Charlene Turner—the fifth member of the Kingdom Keepers. She has sandy blond hair, a gymnast's body, and an angry look on her face.

Charlene calls out. "Off of them!"

Philby manages to push the female demon away, sending her reeling so that she catches the male demon at the knees. Willa and Philby scramble to stand up.

Charlene collapses an easel and breaks off one of its aluminum legs. "Hey!"

The female demon pivots. Charlene launches the metal

leg like a spear. Lands it in the female's eye socket. The demon goes down like a popped blowup toy.

"Eyes!" she calls out.

"Eyes!" Philby says. "Of course! I should have—"

Understanding now, Willa picks up the bow, takes careful aim, and looses an arrow. The arrow hits it mark. Plastic tip or not, it penetrates the demon's soft eyeball. The male demon falls, raising a cloud of sawdust.

"I've missed you all so much," Charlene says.

"Glad you didn't miss *him*," Philby says.

* * *

Amid the gray cloud, Finn sees Wayne leaving the room, seemingly untroubled by the fumes, the folder from the *Fantasia* box tucked under one arm.

Maybeck pulls a ninja kick on the first broom, snapping it in half.

The second broom aims its bucket at Maybeck. Finn abandons any thought of chasing after Wayne and jumps the broom from behind. Some of the bucket's contents splash to the floor and ignite. Finn manages to wrestle the bucket away and douses the broom with its contents. The broom bursts into flame, runs, trips, and falls to lie cooking on the floor. The gas from the fire-suppression system puts the fire out an instant later, leaving only remnants, charcoal-black bits of wood.

Maybeck and Finn bury their faces in the crooks of their elbows to avoid the gas and flee the room. The lobby stands empty, its floor littered with archival records. The guard remains unmoving.

In the distance: emergency sirens.

Maybeck's the first to say what Finn is thinking. "We gotta return. And fast."

"Philby and Willa," Finn says.

"Present!" It's Philby's voice. He, Willa, and Charlene are running down the hall.

"Char—lene!" Maybeck calls out, overly enthusiastic.

"Hey, there!" Charlene's blue eyes sparkle at the sight of Maybeck.

The five Keepers hurry out of the building, running to the terrace. Behind them, four demons gather at the door.

"Those guys are nothing to mess with," Philby says. "Take my word for it."

"Ready?" Finn asks.

Wordlessly, they take each other by the hand. Routine.

Finn pushes the button.

9

CONTEMPLATING THE AFTERMATH of the destruction caused to the temple grounds by the earthquake, Tia Dalma identifies a series of sinkholes where the earth has caved in to reveal dark pits, some of which expose a section of the labyrinthine tunnels that claimed her colleagues. The air from these holes smells of dust and decay. Rats with blind oversize eyes flee to the surface, darting out over the unfamiliar terrain. At the sight of these vermin, Tia Dalma's eyes narrow; she moves to a patch of smooth ground, collects sticks and debris, and then sits, cross-legged, clearing a space before her. With the sticks, she builds a small teepee enclosing a pile of brown leaves in the center. She holds another stick upright and begins spinning it between her palms down into a tuft of dried moss that she has placed on a log before her. She hums a mystic's melody, her eyes clamped shut, patiently working the stick.

A puff of smoke. She stokes the ignited tinder with a whisper, blows the burning moss off the log and into her teepee construction. The leaves catch fire. Soon, the stack is burning. She feeds the teepee more twigs.

Eyes squinted, Tia Dalma continues to hum. She adds a steady, repetitive stream of strangely accented French words, a chant, a looping incantation. It sounds vaguely religious— something a priest might murmur from the altar.

The leaves of nearby mangrove trees stir in a wind centered on Tia Dalma and her flickering, flashing fire. The mangroves' lower branches are supported by aerial roots, connecting limb to earth. Soon, the limbs appear to swell and bulge, as if they have swallowed something too large for consumption.

As the lumps that are swelling the tree limbs collide, the roots break free from the ground. The surface of the bare brown wood becomes scaly. Some lumps begin as ovals, then form into diamond shapes. Neither roots nor runners, the lumps now reveal themselves to be the heads of six-foot-long pythons, draped languidly from every branch. They fall to the ground and slide silently toward Tia Dalma, stopping short at the fire. The snakes seethe and coil, intertwining in an unruly mass.

Slowly, the witch doctor lifts her arm and points at the rents in the earth. The snakes separate, moving in pairs and groups of three, sliding away from the fire like the spokes of a wheel. They slither over the edges of the holes and disappear. They are Tia Dalma's antennae, each a scout on a search-and-rescue mission.

The fire flickers and dims; the swirling wind calms. But the crouched figure remains unmoving and silent, her eyes closed, her head hanging down slightly. To the uninitiated, she might appear to be asleep, but such an assessment would prove a grave mistake. She is far from asleep; to the contrary, she is unusually attuned to her environs; she knows the location of every creature down to the smallest insect. She can hear the plants breathing, the giant stones of the temple still cracking in the aftermath of their heavy falls. Were you to approach uninvited, those steps would be your last.

An hour passes. Two. Or perhaps it is but a matter of minutes, for the fire still glows. What begins as a rumble quickly grows. The massive temple stones quiver like terrified children.

First come the bats, escaping from the holes amid the fallen stones in a fluttering veil of black. Next are moths, rats, and mice, swarming up in desperation as an ungodly sound chases them to the surface. Spiders, centipedes, roaches, and every creeping, crawling thing move like a slurry from the pits, fleeing for their tiny insignificant lives from the enemy: the source of that horrid sound.

Tia Dalma's eyes flicker open. She uncurls her body from its corpselike posture and turns her head to see the pythons she has summoned now streaming from the depths. She hears what no other could, their hissing voices announcing in a unified chorus, "He comes!"

Indeed, the triangular tip of a black wing rises like a tattered sail from one of the many holes. The enormousness of the protrusion gives an inkling of the size of the Beast below. ⋇Like the twisted, gnarled roots of the surrounding trees, Chernabog's claws emerge. A mixture of veins, skin, and muscle depleted of nourishment, the four bent and bony appendages belie the power lurking within. Despite being trapped for three years in the temple underground, living a brutal existence devoid of light, sound, and souls, this creature is not to be forgotten. Nor ignored.[3]

A high-pitched voice pierces the air. A woman's voice. A witch's. The Evil Queen clambers from the same hole. Her robe is tattered and crusted with mud, her once gorgeous face as pale as the pink skin of a newborn mouse. She is in disarray, starved to half her former size, her lips blistered and bubbling with insect bites and disease, for she has fed on the very creatures that have just fled. Her voice is more that of a trapped animal than a woman. "Beware!" she calls to Tia Dalma. "He is of foul and perverse spirit, for the three years he has spent in this dungeon. Ripe with distemper and ill-will, a sorry soul

---

[3] Pirate_Amanda

56

of misery and malice." The Evil Queen speaks in an ancient tongue. Beleaguered by three years in the tombs with nothing but a distempered bat god for company she has succumbed. Gone is the action figure; hello malevolent soul fueled by hatred, bent on revenge. Tia Dalma flinches. The Evil Queen's blood has turned to venom.

"Our lord is more powerful than ever before. A god among those that live below, brother of Hades, lord of the dark."

Horns appear. A pair of angry yellow eyes. A massive bull's head.

Tia Dalma folds forward in submission, her arms outstretched in meek homage. If she possessed a human heart, it would be beating out of her chest. She offers but three small words before the Beast's growl thunders through the jungle and rises into the sky: "Welcome, my lord."

10

ALL THE KEEPERS AWAKE almost simultaneously in the back of the van, which is parked alone in the hotel parking lot. Maybeck sits up with a start, looks around for Charlene, then sinks back down and lies with his eyes open, staring up at the van's ceiling.

"It's going on four in the morning," Brad says from the front seat. "Your parents have been notified and are on their way."

"Wait . . . what?" says a groggy Willa. Fatigue remains a challenge for all the Keepers. Their activity while DHIs hardly counts as rest. On nights like this they must get by on three or four hours' sleep if they're lucky.

"The Archives are compromised," Brad says. "We need you in Burbank."

"What about graduation?" Philby says. He sounds perfectly Philby—alert, awake, ready for a physics quiz. The others look at him inquisitively. "What?" he says, seeming honestly to have no idea how he's coming off. "I'm not missing my graduation. I'm summa cum laude. I'm giving a speech."

"It's been taken care of. You're going to Burbank. That is, unless you want to drop out of the group and leave Wayne in the hands of the Overtakers."

"He—" Finn blurts out. "We— The thing is, we don't even know if that was him, right? It could have been a DHI."

"The security cameras . . . we watched it all. You were all terrific, by the way. But listen, there are so many reasons Wayne couldn't have been a DHI. First, you destroyed the

58

OTs' only server during the cruise. Second, they stole *your* data, not Wayne's. Third: Why hasn't he come forward to warn us that they might have his data?" Brad asks.

"You've never been in DHI state," Philby answers. "It's not that simple. Servers can be programmed. Data can be compromised. A little thing called identity theft." Philby becomes belligerent when he knows he's right—and he's right most of the time. "He may think he had a horrible nightmare or something; he may not realize the breach at the Archives even happened. Not until he hears about it and it matches his dream. The same thing has happened to all of us before. Crossing over . . . you don't know what it's like until it happens."

Brad has known Philby for many years now. He respects the Keepers individually and as a group. That respect is reflected in his level tone. "Wayne has a pattern of dropping off the grid. He was in the company of the Overtakers. But Wayne . . . the old man was directing things."

"Possibly his DHI," Philby said.

"Not projected from our servers. And this was *inside* the Disney local area network, don't forget. Our LAN is behind a dozen firewalls. If that old man was a DHI, then we've got an insider working for the OTs."

"Don't call him an old man," Finn says testily. "He's a legend. A genius. And that wasn't him!"

"You have to distance yourselves from your emotions, Finn. All of you have to. The evil is out and among us, okay? This was a violent, destructive breach at the heart of the company. The Archives are like our bank vault. They hold all our knowledge—our institutional knowledge—of how we got to where we are. Our history. We can't have the OTs picking things off the shelves like it's a grocery store."

"Wayne had to be a DHI," Philby repeats, but it sounds

as if he's trying to convince himself, not the others.

"And when you can prove that, we'll be happy to review your evidence," Brad says.

Silence.

"In the meantime," he continues, "your parents are on the way with a suitcase for each of you. You will say your good-byes. We're off to Burbank before sunrise."

"Why can't we just work from here?" Willa proposes. "I mean, sleep is sleep. We can be DHIs from wherever we go to bed. I'd rather stay home, if it's all the same to you. Graduation's important to me. I worked hard for this."

"Exactly," Philby says.

Brad glances back and forth among them. "It isn't 'all the same to me.' This is Wayne. You were there, boots on the ground. You tell me: You think this can wait a week?"

"I'm just saying we don't need to be out in Burbank. We can do this from here." Willa checks out the other Keepers to make sure they understand her position. "I'm not wimping out. I just don't see the point in physically traveling out there when we can be DHIs from here."

"Willa, right now the facts say that Wayne has betrayed us. I don't believe that. You don't believe that," Brad says, working his smartphone. "You did not see this. You understand? I never showed you this. Neither I nor the company has access to military satellite imagery. Is that clear?"

Heads nod.

"Is that clear?"

"Yes, sir!" the Keepers say, nearly in unison.

All but Maybeck, who rolls his eyes and says, "Crystal."

Brad turns his phone to face them. The images run as a slide show. From above, a jungle. The next slide zooms in lower, showing more detail: rocks, rubble, jungle floor.

Finn sees it first. "That's the sacrificial table. That's where . . ." His voice trails off. Willa places her hand on his shoulder affectionately.

"You didn't know, Finn. None of us knew," she says. Then through the dark she stabs Brad with her eyes, furious at him for raising memories of Dillard's death.

"The temple grounds," Brad says.

Professor Philby speaks up. "But they're— It's destroyed. Most of it anyway."

The slides keep moving in tighter on the temple grounds.

"You can see the signs of an earthquake," Maybeck says. "Those black slashes in the ground are where the tunnels caved in."

"The tunnels?" Philby sounds panicked.

"The labyrinth?" Finn says. "But if the labyrinth caved in, if those are the tunnels—"

Brad stops the slide show and pockets the phone. "If you don't come with us," he says to Willa, "no one's going to fault you. We all have lives to live. I'm the first to acknowledge that. You can go home with your parents when they arrive. Whoever's with me"—he glances at his watch—"we're out of here in fifteen minutes. Say your good-byes."

Headlights stream into the parking lot from several entrances, aiming at the white van.

The Keepers exchange glances. In their eyes are fear, grief, confusion, worry. Philby looks stunned. Willa looks sad. Finn's face is a mask of pain; he can't let go of what happened to Dillard. Three years have passed, but to look at him, anyone would think it had been only a matter of days.

"It's Wayne," Finn whispers harshly, sounding ready to cry.

"It's happening," says Philby.

11

THREE FIGURES SKIRT THE LIGHTS, moving between the eighteen-wheel trucks parked side by side, backed into the shipping docks. Heard over the groan of straining gears and hissing air brakes, cicadas shrill in the damp night air. Trucks come and go at a rate of more than one a minute. Weary drivers stroll to and from the dispatcher's office, some smoking, some yammering in Spanish into cell phones. Nearly all sport tattoos or a potbelly or both.

The smallest of the three figures, a female form, stops the others, peering out into the painful glare of the bluish arc lights, which blast the loading dock with artificial daylight. The woman shields her eyes from the brilliance as she squints to read the paperwork clipped to the wall behind the open truck. A pair of black leather boots appears from within the truck trailer, shocking her back into the shadows. As the booted man exits into the warehouse through a doorway of hanging plastic slats, another takes his place, pushing a trolley loaded with wire baskets stuffed full of live chickens. The worker is just a boy, seventeen at the oldest, covered in sweat. Stuck to the sweat are chicken feathers. There are more feathers in his black hair; one appears glued to one earlobe like an earring.

"Boy!" the woman calls softly. The light reveals her skin as dark cocoa, her hair as matted dreadlocks. Tattoos of tears and ancient pictographs adorn her rounded cheeks. As the boy looks around distractedly and spots her, the woman focuses on him intensely.

⽊At first he looks confused. He stands still like a doll waiting to be played with. The woman calls him to her with a curling finger. He walks toward her.[4] He moves reluctantly, straining with each step as he abandons his cart of clucking fowl. His hands fly to his throat and begin clawing at his flesh, as if trying to eradicate an impossibly stubborn itch—or to get at some unwanted force within. Suddenly, he collapses. The woman admires her work, and then, with a sharp hiss, extends her hand toward the sufferer. He falls eerily still as she speaks through her cupped hand into his ear. The woman raises her victim to his feet, where he stands, somewhat at attention. His eyes are devoid of any human life or expression.[5]

The boy-doll nods into space like an obedient child, a boy soldier. He returns to the milky plastic curtain that screens the loading dock from the warehouse and pokes his head inside. He comes back out, looking left and right. He nods again.

The woman struggles to climb up onto the high dock, but the biggest of the three figures hoists her effortlessly, like a mother cat with a kitten. Behind her follows a robed woman, and finally a creature—neither man nor ape. More a bull with giant wings and a gorilla's body. They hurry into the truck trailer and the boy follows behind with the trolley.

"The manifest," says a man's voice, "lists the destination as Long Beach, south of Los Angeles."

* * *

The voice snaps Finn's attention away from the flat-panel screen, away from the events on the loading dock that he's been watching, and back into the luxurious private jet carrying him

---

[4] Clouds_Willatree
[5] Keepers_Puzzle

and the other Keepers from Orlando to Burbank.

"So, let's talk about what we know and don't know," Brad says.

"Let's," Maybeck quips. Of all the Keepers, Maybeck has the most difficulty with Brad—and the feeling is obviously mutual. Brad tolerates Maybeck's sarcasm and cynicism for the sake of team harmony and because his bravado at times provides the leadership necessary for the group to tackle dangerous situations. Youthful arrogance has its place.

"What we know is this: the Evil Queen and Chernabog survived the tunnels. Obviously, Tia Dalma is present as well. Three years ago she performed a ceremony at the temple that may have restored Chernabog to his former . . . *glory's* not the right word, but you get the point. A ceremony you, the Keepers, interrupted. Now they're on the move. Eleven hundred trucks pass through that depot every day. So, do we know their intended final destination? No. But Long Beach is nearly due west of Anaheim. Any guesses?"

"Ha-ha." Maybeck sounds just too bored.

"Something else we don't know," Brad adds, "is what they have planned, what resources they possess."

"This is like tracking terrorists," Philby says, a little too eagerly.

"Down, boy," Maybeck says.

"We don't know what shape they're in," Willa says. "Three years underground, eating what, bugs? Worms? Rats? Living in filth, surviving on whatever water trickles through the rocks . . ."

"It does more than trickle," Finn says, speaking from experience. "But yeah, you're right. They can't be in great shape."

Brad says, "You know how to start a riot? Starve the population."

He lets the words sit there, filling the air.

"So," Maybeck says, "they've got a jacked-up monster beast and a ticked-off evil queen."

"We also know," Willa says, addressing Brad, "that Maleficent is dead. One of their strongest, most active leaders is gone. Some of us saw her struggle to hold the OTs together. They've lost her. And we all know Chernabog's not a candidate for the debate team. So it's going to fall on one of the ladies to try to unify the OTs."

"We know," Philby says, picking up on Willa's line of thinking, "that they got on the Disney *Dream* for a reason. They didn't just want to jump-start the Beast; they wanted to get to Disneyland."

"Exactly," Brad says. He's awkward as usual, uncomfortable treating kids so much younger than he is with respect, but clearly he values their opinions, understands that this is how they operate. Without them, he's got nothing. "We don't know what it is that they're planning."

"Our destruction," Maybeck says, instantly sobering the group, "for one thing."

The jet engines whine outside the windows. Blue sky. Brown terrain forty thousand feet below.

"The end," Finn says softly. "They're planning the end. Of us. The parks. The magic. They have Tia Dalma's black arts, the Evil Queen's conjuring, and Chernabog's evil. We've got . . . Without Wayne, what have we got?"

No one dares answer, not even Brad. "We've got to get to Wayne. Figure this out."

"No movement relies on any one individual."

"Since when do five people make up a movement?" Willa asks.

"A basketball team," Maybeck says. "Enough for a basketball

team. Barely. We can't even field a baseball team. We're pathetic."

The conversation has gotten away from Brad. He drags a wrist across his lips as he tries to sort out how to herd the Keepers back into positive territory. His eyes are bloodshot from fatigue.

The pilot instructs his passengers over the intercom to prepare the cabin for landing. The private plane's one flight attendant, a wiry but small man with a bad toupee, collects drinking glasses and plates, returns backpacks to storage. A moment later, they experience the smoothest landing in aviation history. Through it all, Maybeck looks terrified.

"You've never flown before," Brad says, challenging him. They can't avoid picking on one another.

"I—it's—" Maybeck stutters.

"Everyone's first time flying on a private jet," Finn says, coming to Maybeck's defense. "And it's very cool."

"Very!" Philby chimes in.

Maybeck shoots Finn and Philby a look of thanks. Finn's expression says, *I've got your back.* The plane taxis and slows. Maybeck peers out the window.

"Charlene!"

* * *

The air tastes different. Willa hadn't noticed it as a DHI the night before. Her attention had been on things flying. It's fresh. Brown hills rise out of the green of palm trees. All that talk of Los Angeles smog, and yet even at the Bob Hope Airport there's a hint of citrus and sea in the breeze.

Or maybe the hint of lemon and sea salt is Charlene's perfume. She seems to float across the tarmac to greet Maybeck with a hug. He picks her up and twirls her off her feet. Her giggles carry over the roar of a jet taxiing in the distance. Finn and Philby close in to welcome her as well, leaving Willa to deal with the backpacks being handed down the plane's collapsible stairs by the flight attendant. Willa is transformed into a Sherpa: two backpacks slung over her right shoulder, another clutched in her left hand, her purse somewhere she can't see it.

A white extended SUV waits to pick them up. Its driver's door is embossed with an image of a red-robed Mickey wearing the sorcerer's cap and waving his magic wand over the words WALT DISNEY IMAGINEERING.

Willa feels chills, despite the afternoon heat. She's always wanted to be an Imagineer, ever since she learned about the creative team responsible for the attractions in the park. It was seventh grade—some book she read, or maybe a documentary, or maybe someone just told her. But that had been the dream. Now here she is, stepping off a private plane and being chauffeured by the very same people. Pinch me.

Philby glances back. It takes him longer than she would have wanted, but at least at some point in that boy's brain of his, it occurs to him he's a jerk for forgetting about her.

He tries to make up for it by helping her with the backpacks, but he just makes a mess of things. All the bags tumble to the tarmac; he and Willa bang heads as they bend to retrieve them. And it hurts. Really hurts. The tears that threaten to spill from Willa's eyes have little to do with the collision, but Philby would never consider the alternative.

"Sorry, sorry!" he says. "I've hurt you! I'm so sorry!"

He doesn't understand what he's saying.

Yes, you've hurt me, Willa thinks, but hears herself say, "You can be such a blunt instrument sometimes."

That stops him. She has two of the backpacks now and she's headed for the SUV's open hatchback. The man waiting there wears the offbeat outfit of a creative type: sandals, cargo shorts, a Hawaiian shirt, extremely cool eyeglasses, a French beret. But he has the leathery skin of someone older than her parents, and the long hair of someone from another era.

Philby is trying to catch up as Willa shakes the man's hand.

"Joe," the man says. He has a smile that makes her relax. He's intense, but laid-back. Probably brilliant, but dude-who-lives-next-door normal.

"You surf?" Willa asks, having no idea why and wanting to hide.

His smile is so genuine she relaxes yet again.

"The web," he answers, "but not the ocean."

She giggles. He joins her with a chuckle. "You're Willa."

She nods.

"This whole thing. What you've got going," he nods toward the others. "It's awesome."

"It is," she says.

"It's important."

She doesn't know what to say.

"We're at a moment of critical mass."

"Brad was telling us."

"Yeah, but now I'm telling you."

She nods.

"Critical mass," he repeats.

"Hi! I'm—"

68

"Philby," Joe says.

"Right."

Joe studies Philby. Sizes him up as they shake hands.

"You're smaller than I thought," Joe says.

"Am I?"

"Your voice is higher."

"They made it lower for my DHI. A Disney host thing."

"I'm a fan," Joe says.

Philby blushes.

"Of all of you."

"Of course!" Philby attempts to recover.

"I'm blown away by Wayne."

"We don't believe it ourselves," Philby says.

"Who said I believe it?" says Joe. "Brad sits in front. The rest of you in the back."

"Yes, sir," Philby says.

Willa can tell that just slipped out. Philby's time abroad, living in England, shows up at the strangest times.

Joe points to the private terminal where the pilots are headed. "There are cameras everywhere," he says. "We'd better get you all in the car ASAP."

"Cameras," Philby says.

"Smile," says Joe.

* * *

Having had no time to talk the night before, the Keepers inundate Charlene with questions about life in L.A. and what it's like to be a television star. Mostly they've been communicating this past year on Instagram and by text, so the excitement of all five of them being together as themselves and not as DHIs is infectious. Charlie is humble about her success on television, perhaps overly so, not wanting to create distance from her closest friends. A slight tension hangs in the air, nonetheless—she is making money, real money, and is on her way to fame, and she carries some of the trappings: her jeans, jewelry, shoes—even her haircut speaks of a lifestyle none of the others can afford. Her attempt to make her life out to be normal isn't working.

By the time the van pulls through the security gate and the Keepers look out at the Legends terrace where, the night before, all heaven and earth seemed to implode, a brooding silence shrouds them.

They are dropped off. They take their backpacks—their duffels and Rollaboards will be delivered later—and follow Joe as a group.

"I'll give you the dime tour," he says. But it's more a dollar than a dime. The studio lot is laid out like a town, as it appeared the night before to their DHIs; it's cut up into small village blocks that are home to bungalows, three-story office buildings and, occasionally, a giant soundstage. Finn spots the barnlike Mill at the far end of a street. Everywhere the grass is mowed perfectly. The streets are clean of oil stains and dirt. It's quiet and there aren't any people around. Joe points out the commissary where they will eat meals with other Cast Members, takes them inside one of the office buildings, and walks them down a hallway of extraordinary Disney art. The images of Maleficent give them all chills.

Joe explains the history of the studio and Walt Disney Pictures, detailing the lot's role in dozens of Disney film classics. The Keepers are captivated. They listen. They try to absorb all the information. They laugh. Philby and Willa seem to keep up, to the consternation of the other three. Soon, Charlene is no longer special; she's just better dressed.

As they descend a set of stairs, Joe explains how the Animation group came to be physically linked by tunnel to the Ink and Paint building. His explanation is lost on every Keeper: they are no strangers to tunnels—the most recent encounter was in the jungles of Mexico. This tunnel is well lit and well organized, but it hardly matters. Finn fights off the ghost of Maleficent transfiguring into a dragon; Philby recalls the server room off the Magic Kingdom's Utilidor.

"Speaking for the group," Maybeck says, winning Joe's attention, "I think it's safe to say we're not big fans of tunnels. Creepy dark places seem to attract creepy dark creatures, and note to self: creepy dark creatures are the bad guys."

"That attitude may need to change," Joe says.

They reach a thick metal door that hangs on rollers like the door to a horse's stall. He slides it back, revealing a storage room containing a mishmash of street signs and other Disney memorabilia. He waves the Keepers inside and motions for Maybeck to slide the heavy door shut. Maybeck does so with Charlene's help.

Against the far wall lean several colorful doors, seemingly left over from movie sets. Two, a red one and a black one, have no hinges and overlap. Beside them lean a purple and a green door, both on hinges and hung in their door frames. Next is a dark blue door. On it is painted a white star with the words MR. DISNEY below it.

Like the others, the blue door leans against the wall at an angle. It is blocked by a stack of furniture atop a heavy-looking library desk with a leather top. Joe prattles on about the history of the storage room, but no one is paying attention. The rolling door thunks into place.

Joe's tone changes instantly, all the levity and familiarity gone. "Watch your step. And don't touch anything until we're inside." He walks around a large desk and straight through the pile of furniture it appears to be half supporting.

"Holograms," Willa whispers.

Maybeck reaches out. The library desk is real. The furniture atop and behind it? Three-dimensional projections.

Joe pulls the blue door's handle up on an angle to open it. "Well, hurry it up! As long as this door is open, the outer door to the hallway can't be opened. We don't like that condition to last too long. It can raise questions that are hard to answer."

"What the heck?" Maybeck asks.

Joe waves them through. "Quickly, please."

One by one the Keepers move through the furniture hologram, step over the raised and angled doorjamb, and slip through the opening.

Joe calls from behind them, "Welcome to the Crypt."

ᴊᴋThe Keepers find themselves facing filing cabinets that stand sentry like soldiers at attention around the room's perimeter. Long fluorescent lights buzz urgently overhead, as if striving to keep the contents of the room an absolute secret. Each cabinet has a smartly printed label indicating what precious treasure is locked away inside. There is only one door in and out, which has locked immediately behind the Keepers.[6] They can feel the history permeating the walls. They are told Walt Disney built the Crypt with money earned from *Snow White and the Seven Dwarfs*. It's a kind of Disney museum: each wall is plastered with concept paintings, storyboards, even production art featuring the Overtakers. A corner table bears models of attractions from each of the Disney Parks worldwide, some instantly recognizable; others represent ideas that ultimately went unbuilt. The wall farthest

---

[6] Keepers_Puzzle

from the door features two gigantic pictures: a painting of Disneyland Park commissioned by Walt Disney in 1953 and an enlargement of a satellite image of the park today. Note cards flag similarities and differences between the two.[7] On the wall to their left is an emblem, a shield split into quadrants, each depicting one of the four parks at Walt Disney World: the Sorcerer's Cap, Cinderella's Castle, Spaceship Earth, and the Tree of Life. The same emblem adorns the floor where they are standing.[8]

The Keepers all have varying opinions. Philby appreciates the technology. Finn likes the "magical" side of Disney better— some things are best left unsaid and unseen. Maybeck's artistic eye is drawn to the models; for whatever reason, he instantly distrusts the place. Willa, the calm of the group's storm, withholds any comments. As always, Charlene just wants to get started with the debriefing; she's a girl of action.[9]

Pale-skinned Cast Members face computer monitors, eyes awash in the glow of the screens. The attendants are moving. It's hard to track them, giving the Keepers the sense there are more than eight people here. Maybeck taps Finn on the shoulder and points to an adjacent room that houses a long black table. Brad has moved into this conference room. Finn steps inside and takes a seat in one of the ten swivel chairs surrounding the table. The other Keepers file in.

Brad takes the chair at the head. "Okay. So, let's get down to business,"[10] he says. "What we know and don't know," he adds, returning to his favorite theme.

"What is this place?" Maybeck asks.

---

[7] Wish_Changerob
[8] Levitate_Monorail
[9] Nightfall_Cruise
[10] Hyenas_Adventure

"Ah, that!" Brad surveys the Keepers individually, expecting someone to volunteer the answer. He resigns himself to the fact that nothing is forthcoming. "What? You thought you were the only ones?"

"The only . . . ?" Charlene asks warily.

"Kingdom Keepers." Brad allows this to sink in, though it's apparent to all in the room that it's going to take longer than a few seconds. "Cast Members—Imagineers, in this case—dedicated to the defense of the realm, if you will."

Again, he studies each of the Keepers. "Think it through, people. This battle has been going on for—"

"Decades," Philby gasps.

"Voilà!"

"You said Walt Disney built this . . . bunker—" Willa says, reminding everyone.

"A long, long time ago," Brad says. "For a very specific purpose."

"Defense of the realm," Finn says.

"No way," Maybeck says.

Brad nods. "Over fifty years and counting. You, my friends, are but the latest."

Finn feels light-headed. Why this possibility has never occurred to him, he can't say. But it never has. He thinks back to Wayne's introduction of the DHI technology as they sat together on a bench at Town Square in Disney World, Finn unaware that he was a hologram. At the time, he thought he was in a dream, part good, part bad. He feels that same way now. On the one hand, he and the other Keepers are not unique; on the other, they're not alone. They've just been made aware of a support group that has been in place for decades. Finn says, "The Overtakers have been active—"

"Since the start. More or less," Brad replies. "Sometimes

more, sometimes less. Mr. Disney was a visionary, as we all know. He saw it coming. Others were skeptical. There is a fine line between genius and eccentricity. One mustn't forget that the villains, regardless of their origins in folklore, were the product of Mr. Disney's imagination. He knew them better than anyone. Knew what to expect. He had the wisdom to build the Crypt long before it was needed."

"The Crypt," Finn says.

"I'm sorry." Brad waves his arm theatrically to encompass their surroundings. "Mr. Disney named a room down the hall 'the Morgue.' It houses retired materials that may be useful to the company in the future."

"Well that's intriguing," Philby says.

"It's believed the Crypt was named because he had a theme going," Brad explains.

"Cryptology," Philby says.

"There's that too—the science of codes."

"The Overtakers were sending codes," Finn says. "They were intercepted and Walt knew he had a problem."

"Who said you were 'just kids'? Very good, Messieurs Philby and Whitman. Very good indeed."

"An underground movement," Maybeck says. He joins the others as they laugh.

"Quite literally," Brad says.

"Unified against a common enemy," Finn says. "No one knew that enemy better than the man who created them."

"The director of the Crypt is . . . how should I put it? The parks are the company's heartbeat, the thing that the public associates most with the name. So to assume the position of director, to accept the mantle of defender of the realm, is among the highest callings within the company. To date, only two people have held that title. Mr. Disney and—"

"Wayne," Finn says.

"Mr. Disney's protégé. Just a kid at the time. About your age, Finn. But as you know, Wayne had a nose for it. Among Mr. Disney's many remarkable skills was the ability to spot talent and put it to good use. Mr. Kresky was identified at an early age. He was carefully groomed, I'm sure."

"So there is no way the Wayne we saw last night is the Wayne you're describing to us," Finn says. "He must have been a DHI."

Professor Philby cannot resist a lecture. "But the first thing the . . . Crypt . . . would have done—should have done—is run a data filter through the DHI projection server, blocking Wayne's data and screening him out, if you get what I'm saying. If he was being projected, that filter would act like antivirus software. At the very least, Wayne's DHI would have been corrupted; it would have sparked, become transparent, decayed. Or, if entirely successful, he would have vanished, confirming he was a hologram and not a human being."

"You really are made for this work," Brad says. "All of you. Precisely, Mr. Philby. And of course, you're right: that was indeed among the first protocols implemented."

"And nothing happened. No change," Finn said. "Wayne stayed right where he was."

"Easily explained," says the Professor, "if the OTs have their own server."

"Finn destroyed it," Brad says.

"A server, yes. But the only one? We don't know that," Finn says.

"A server coming online should have been detected," Philby says. "Bandwidth drawdown, pixilation anomalies . . . there are ways to detect such renegade servers."

"Maybe the antivirus protocol was never run?" Willa says.

Charlene chimes in. "Because there's someone on the inside. A spy. A double agent."

Brad's expression never changes. "You all are so adorable."

"Impossible?" Finn asks.

Brad doesn't—or can't?—answer right away.

"Funny, because Wayne always told us that nothing is impossible," Finn says.

"It's the Disney anthem," Willa adds. "'Believe.'"

"We all have our jobs to do," Brad says. "You need to confine yours to the need at hand. You may be interested to know the data screen is in place, and it's screening your data as well as Wayne's."

"Our data?" Philby is not pleased.

Brad responds to Philby's accusatory tone. "You want the truth? Have it your way! Twice we have data-screened for Wayne, preventing his DHI from being projected. Twice he has reappeared within days, the second time last night."

"That's impossible," Philby fires back.

"Why? What?" Maybeck asks Philby.

Willa answers. "With screens in place to block existing data, the subject's data would need to be replaced with new information. That means they would need to green-screen Wayne for a second—"

"And a third—" Brad adds.

"Time," Willa finishes. "Meaning he would have to cooperate."

"Impossible," Finn says.

"I thought you were just telling me nothing's impossible," Brad says.

It stings. Finn settles back in his chair, wishing they'd never agreed to come out here.

"Wait!" Charlene is the least technology-minded among

them. "You're saying that for Wayne to be projected after you screened him out, he would have had to do all the green-screen stuff we did to become DHIs?"

"Twice," Philby says, disappointment heavy in his voice.

"So even if he was a DHI last night—which we don't know for sure," Charlene says, "he'd have had to be a traitor anyway? We're talking about Wayne!"

Silence. Finn hears a copier running out in the Crypt. "Well, I don't believe it."

"None of us believes it," Brad says. "But if it isn't true, then there's an explanation, and we need it."

"Torture," Maybeck says. "He could have been threatened or drugged or whatever into doing the green-screen work."

"Or it was never done at all," Philby says.

Brad directs his attention to Philby. "Go on."

"The OTs have found themselves a programmer who can take existing data and codify it. He or she reworks all the ones and zeros into a new set of ones and zeros, creating images so similar to the first that it's impossible for the naked eye to detect the difference: a change in skin tone and color, a slightly shorter limb, a body that's thinner, fatter, wider."

"Very good," says Brad. "That's what our people arrived at as well: a single set of data revised just enough to make a new set of data."

"An algorithm," Willa says. "Billions of pixels. That kind of thing would need to be automated."

"So it's possible," Finn says more brightly, "even probable, that Wayne had no part in this."

"Voilà!" Brad says again. "But we need proof, and we need Wayne back. And . . . well, there's more, but that's nearly enough for now."

"Nearly?" Charlene says. She likes things neat and clean.

"How many of you are up on your history?" Brad asks.

Willa raises her hand sheepishly. Philby, proudly.

"For the benefit of the rest of you, history is filled with examples of technologies developed for good that go bad. Fireworks in China's night sky three thousand years ago eventually become missiles destroying London in World War II. A search for nuclear power becomes the atomic bomb."

"This is our problem because?" Maybeck says.

"DHI 2.0," Brad says. "Seemed like a terrific advancement at the time. Now, come to find out, it's a projected hologram that can't be hurt by bullets or Tasers or fire. It's an indestructible soldier."

"Being used to combat evil!" Finn says emphatically.

"One man's evil . . ." Brad says. "We have unconfirmed intelligence that there are parties seeking 2.0 in order to amass an indestructible army—an army that can suffer no casualties."

Finn wonders if he should mention that he and the others have discussed this before but decides not to. Brad might believe they gave someone the idea, that one of the Keepers leaked or sold the idea. That there was a traitor among them! There's been too much discussion of impossibility tonight, Finn thinks. "Wayne is not involved in this!" he says instead.

Brad ignores him. "The result of this intelligence is that a decision has been reached—and this comes from the top, so don't shoot the messenger—to permanently shut down the 2.0 servers and return to a slight upgrade of version 1.6 we're calling v1.6-plus. To this end, you will all need to green-screen again. That studio work commences at oh-eight-hundred. Report to studio six."

"You're downgrading us?" Philby says. "How do you expect—?"

"I expect, we expect, you to be team players. To do the

best with what you're given. And what you're being given is a chance to set things right. To clear Wayne's name. To stop whatever's going on—which apparently includes Chernabog, the Evil Queen, and Tia Dalma."

"What we're being given is weakness," Maybeck says.

"Vulnerability," Willa adds. "In v1.6, our fear makes us solid, makes us suffer if we're injured. It isn't close to 2.0."

"Deal with it," Brad says, getting to his feet. "We know it's a game changer, and we know you're good at adapting. So we expect you to adapt."

12

THE BLACK HELICOPTER from the Air Mobile Unit of the U.S. Border Patrol Special Operations Group rakes noisily across the night sky above the Calexico East border crossing. If the pilot hadn't flown this route every night, the line of semi-trucks on the Mexico side might have surprised her. Five parallel lines of vehicles stretch back a third of a mile from the secure inspectors' booths. Another twenty or so are grouped in a pullout area to the right, a large, well-lit parking lot where trucks have been randomly flagged for closer inspection.

Among these eighteen-wheelers is one from southwestern Mexico bound for Long Beach, California. The manifest lists its cargo as "Live Chickens."

As the helicopter flies over, the three men arguing about who's going to inspect this one are forced to pause. The aircraft flies east, the rattle of its rotors softening to a cicada's buzz, then a mosquito's whine, and finally a gnat's whisper before its white flashing belly light vanishes.

The three Mexican Customs officers continue to bicker bitterly in Spanish.

"I am allergic to the chicken."

"You are not going to eat it! Get in there!"

"It stinks."

"You stink! Besides, the poo falls through the cages and the grate in the truck bed and down onto the highway. It's not that bad."

"Then you do it."

"I am the senior officer."

"I would do it," says the third officer, *"but I am afraid of chickens. Deathly afraid. When I was a child, my grandmother . . . Well, we were out at her farm and she wanted to cook us all tinga de pollo. We kids didn't know that meant she was going to—you know, with a hatchet? I think I cried for a week."*

"You're twenty-eight years old."

"A moment like that does not ever leave you."

"You two are pathetic," says the senior officer. *"I will do the chickens, but then I will take an extra break and both of you will work two extra trucks."*

"Fine."

"Fine."

Having come to an agreement, the two younger officers leave quickly before their chief changes his mind.

жкThe short, pot bellied immigration officer lifts the dirty, rusted, oddly cold metal handles on the back of the eighteen-wheeler's door.[11] The officer shines his flashlight into the darkness and startles as he sees chicken feathers wafting down. He has never seen snow, but he imagines that this is what it must look like. He sets his flashlight on the truck bed and pulls himself up into the confined area. As he bends to retrieve his light, something rumbles in the bowels of the darkness.[12] He has been well trained. He knows almost all the telltale signs of smuggling. He has seen blood spills, torn clothing; he is well familiar with the stench of unwashed bodies. But the massive hoof marks on the metal grate confuse him. Baffled, he creeps deeper into the trailer, peeking into every sliver of space among the cages of chickens. The cages can be arranged to create hiding places.[13]

---

[11] Castaway_Fred
[12] Keepers_Puzzle
[13] Shadows_Crossover

What he sees next: where the hoof marks tighten, he spots jagged lines scratched into the metal grate. How heavy must an animal be to damage steel? Looking closer, he spots what appears to be animal hair snagged on a hook. Chickens don't have hair. It's his job to keep things like this from happening. His pulse quickens—it's been a while since he's seen any real action; his two subordinates will be jealous when they realize they passed up some excitement.[14]

Then, through the cages, the officer glimpses what can only be described as a crown. As light from the parking lot's lamps penetrates the unnatural black of the trailer, rainbow prisms of color sparkle off the crown's jewels. The officer is taken aback by a sudden rush of foul-smelling air—an eerie wind from inside the cages.[15]

His eyes adjust. The officer rubs a sweaty hand across his mouth and shuts his eyes tightly, hoping to un-see and un-hear what he's just witnessed. He takes a quick, one-eyed peek and then whips his flashlight's beam toward where he saw the crown. A scream lodges in his throat. He staggers backward.[16]

He hears a voice but is unsure if it's a man's or woman's. It sounds vaguely French. It sounds . . . inviting. He knows he should fear it, should pull his gun or radio for help, but he wants to get closer.

His legs feel as if they're moving on their own, though he's in such a fog he can't be sure. Why can't he think clearly? Do the chickens carry some kind of virus? Should the whole truckload be quarantined? And why won't his legs stop moving? He's suddenly afraid, more afraid than he can ever remember being—petrified, although he's not frozen in fear but marching

---

[14] DHI_Sorcery
[15] Castaway_Fred
[16] Keepers_Puzzle

like a stiff-legged soldier into the heart of danger.

He looks up. There, through the fluttering wings of nervous fowl, he catches repeated glimpses of . . . a pair of yellow bowling balls, each in its own cage. What the heck? No . . . it's behind the chickens, behind the cages. And not bowling balls, not unless bowling balls can somehow move in unison as a synchronized pair.

It's two large yellow eyes he sees staring at him through the stir of chicken feathers. Yellow eyes like melons cleaved in half. The involuntary movement of his legs suddenly grinds to a halt. Moments before his world goes black, the terrified officer notices two other figures lurking in the farthest corners of the truck, and if he didn't know any better, he would swear one is wearing a jeweled crown. It wasn't his imagination.[17]

In that instant he feels his body no longer his own—it's as if he's under a spell—and the chickens begin screeching; the wall of cages begins to shift, then suddenly splits open, sending cages full of panicked, squawking chickens tumbling to the floor. The guard can't breathe; his body has shut down; he's going to faint.

Those eyes belong to a monster! The thing steps forward, causing another blizzard of feathers. A giant open mouth appears, a black tongue as long as a human arm lolling out. The guard's head is engulfed. His world goes black. . . .

Tia Dalma steps forward from behind the cages, observing the headless corpse lying on the grate. She looks up at Chernabog, back at the guard's body. She shakes her head.

"Now, that's a problem," she says.

---

[17] Keepers_Puzzle

13

SOMETHING ISN'T RIGHT. Finn quietly shuts the door of the greenroom off Stage 6, trapping Charlene inside with him.

"What's going on?" she asks. She's chewing a protein bar, and indicates the closed door with her chin.

"Am I the only one who thinks it's strange that they're keeping us so busy we never leave the studio?"

"Hmm."

"You hadn't noticed?"

"Not really. But I guess you're right."

"As in: no trip to Disneyland?"

"It's not as if it's next door. It's an hour's drive or something. Besides, they need us for this mission, right?"

Finn looks out through a set of interior windows into the cavernous soundstage. The hangar-like structure is wider and longer than two football fields placed side by side, with a flat ceiling sixty feet overhead rigged to hold cinema lights and equipment of every kind. The soundstage's floor is gray-painted concrete, the walls black. The corner closest to the room he now occupies is cluttered with tripods bearing lighting panels, digital video cameras, and sound equipment. Behind is a wall of sturdy road cases on wheels, the type he's seen at rock concerts. Thick cables run in an orderly fashion to a control room adjacent to the green room.

What makes the soundstage special is what Finn thinks must be the world's largest green screen, a sheet of stretched fabric seventy-five yards long, suspended forty feet high. It curves forward at the bottom to meet the floor seamlessly so that, standing in front of it, the actor is entirely surrounded by a green background that editors can replace with any image they choose. It is here that the Keepers, wearing special motion-capture suits, gloves, and hoods, act out physical movement. Gymnastics equipment and wires support unusual motions such as flying or jumping long distances. At the moment, Maybeck is walking and squatting, walking and squatting. The work is repetitive and can be tedious.

Seeing Maybeck, Finn says, "I forgot how many motions our bodies make that we take for granted."

"It's *so* boring," says the gymnast. "I only like it when we get to the wires and trampolines. And we're at least a week away from that."

"Speaking of which." Finn lowers his voice. "We acted out three-quarters of this during shoots in Orlando. Why do we have to do it again?"

"Come on, they explained that—we're bigger, older. You know." She blushes. "We aren't exactly kids anymore."

"Yeah, I know what they said."

"What's bothering you, Finn?"

Charlene places her hand on Finn's shoulder, and he feels the contact all the way down to his toes. He's aware that she and Maybeck like each other; it's impossible to miss. And for him, it's all about Amanda. But Amanda isn't around much, and when they are together, Amanda can overpower him. She's intense, which is something he both likes and dislikes about her. Moments like this with Charlene remind him what a good listener she is. She's thoughtful and caring, joyful and energetic. The truthful answer to her question is that not much bothers him when he's with her. And the meaning of that used to confuse him.

But as he's gotten older, he's learned that his feelings—his true feelings—need to have rounded corners, not the sharp absolute edges he saw as a kid. You have to pad those corners, Finn thinks. Growing up means learning to fit the situation, to soften. Hard truth can embarrass, wound, or start avalanches.

"I think we're prisoners," he says, knowing Charlene can handle it. Maybeck would throw a fit. Philby and Willa would turn into Mr. Spock from *Star Trek*, analyzing Finn's conclusion six ways to Sunday.

Charlene appears to consider Finn's words only briefly. "I know what you mean."

"Except, I'm serious. I think they're holding us here. Why, I don't know."

"We're green-screening around the clock to get our 1.6-plus DHIs onto the servers."

He appreciates her pragmatism.

"Have you asked to leave?" she says.

"No."

"See? You have to ask."

"I'd need a good reason. Otherwise, they're smart enough to know I'd be testing their authority."

"But that's the point. Right? There is no good reason to leave. We have work to do."

"I suppose."

"I know that voice. You think I'm stupid."

"Not at all. Never!" He turns and faces her. They're too close. Finn takes a step back. Charlene takes a step forward and he doesn't know if she's trying to tell him something about her feelings or if she wants to stand closer as they talk. "This isn't random, Charlie. I wanted to speak to you about it first." He can see flattery, confusion, even concern on her face. It passes faster than a fleeting shadow.

"Finn . . ."

She's read things into his words. Things that are probably there, things neither wants to confront. He's opened some box; now he slams it shut as quickly as possible. "Because you're levelheaded," he says, clearing the air. "You don't overthink this kind of thing or overreact."

"Like some people we know."

She's blushing scarlet, Finn notices. There are too many levels of meaning to the simplest of words; Finn sets traps unintentionally and then walks into them himself. "Exactly!" he says. "But you and I get each other."

"It's true."

"I don't want to freak anyone out."

"You mention this, and you will."

"Exactly!" He's nodding so vigorously his neck hurts. "That's what I mean!"

"Still, you need to come up with a plan," she says bluntly. "It's what you do, Finn. If you're going to get all conspiracy theory on us, then you need to tell us how to figure it out."

Her words hit him like a slap across the cheek. It started with Wayne telling him he was the natural leader. A lot has changed since then. Philby was a Wayne favorite for a while, but never exactly the Keepers' leader. Finn never asked for the role, but has to concede he's stuck with it. "I suppose."

"A plan," she repeats. She finishes her protein bar, wipes her hands on some tissues.

"If we're going to find out the truth about Wayne, we're going to have to do it ourselves."

"That right there is what I call a good place to start. Maybe you keep this whole prisoner thing to yourself and we start by helping Wayne. Everyone's going to support that."

"Even if it means breaking the rules?"

Her forehead wrinkles but her eyes brighten. "Since when has that ever stopped us?"

* * *

"We're going to Disneyland," Finn says.

For their lunch break, they've gathered in the Morgue, a space not unlike the Crypt in that it's accessed via the same underground tunnel, has a similar oversize metal door on tracks (currently closed), and is cluttered, floor to ceiling. The Morgue floor plan includes file cabinets and standing wooden racks that hold oversize artwork. It's like an art museum archive left unattended for decades, the walls a collage of everything from watercolors by famed Disney illustrator Mary Blair to sketches by the veteran animators fondly known as the Nine Old Men.

"We're going to find Wayne. On our own. Starting tonight, if Philby and Willa can manage to cross us over."

Philby and Willa engage in a rapid conversation, all whispered. Philby acts as their spokesperson. "We can't engage our own server. The Imagineers have every conceivable security measure in place to detect new servers coming online."

"Leaving us to work with what we have," Willa says, clearly irritating her partner.

"The existing servers are currently in use to project our DHI hosts within Disneyland." Philby takes over, but he goes on too long, trying to convey how tricky and difficult this will be. Only Willa has any idea what he's talking about, and even she looks dazed by the time he stops.

"We can or we can't?" Finn asks once Philby winds down.

"The server runs a full virus scan every night. It takes a little over ninety minutes, auto-locks, and shuts down, powering back up two hours before the park opens. I can make it look like it's running its scan when it'll actually be running a limited version of v1.6 in the background over a proxy. Our old imaging, not the new stuff. And likely a low-res version at that. We can be full bandwidth for those ninety minutes. If we're still crossed over when the server auto-locks, we'll be SBS until sometime around six in the morning."

"They don't wake us up until six-thirty anyway," Maybeck says.

"Yeah, but if we're in the syndrome, then we aren't moving. We aren't responding. Willa and I," Charlene says, gesturing to her roommate with a flick of her head, "heard someone come in around three in the morning and check up on us."

"Let's hope they don't challenge you to a game of cards," Maybeck says. "Sleep of the dead—that about describes what we're like when we're crossed over."

"I'm just saying," Charlene says.

Finn doesn't want his plan defeated and has to fight back a rush of emotion. Confronted by Charlene's honesty, he feels betrayed.

Philby says, "If the Cryptologists figure out we're crossed over, the first thing they'll do is shut down the DHI server while they prepare to code in a subroutine to allow for manual override."

"English, please!" Maybeck says.

"We'll be stuck in 1.6 SBS," says Willa, looking to Maybeck, "same as you were in Space Mountain."

"That was not pretty," Maybeck says. "I got so . . . So tired. I don't know if I could have fought off OTs the way I felt."

"We'll find out," Finn says.

"What makes you think we can find Wayne?" Willa asks. Of the five Keepers, she seems the most skeptical about Finn's plan.

"You do, actually," Finn says.

Willa looks at him quizzically.

"You made a friend in Hollywood Studios who I think could help us."

"Ariel!" Willa and Charlene say nearly in unison.

"For those of us who believe in empirical evidence," Philby says, "I'd suggest we search for the demons and wraiths from the other night, because they were directly connected to Wayne."

"A Halloween shop!" Maybeck snipes.

Philby stares him down. "Close." Of all the Keepers, the pragmatic Philby struggles the most with Maybeck's irreverent attitude. "Home of the dead and house of the supernatural wraiths and demons."

"Haunted Mansion," Willa says.

* * *

The afternoon green-screen work for the Crypt involves only Maybeck and Finn, which gives the other Keepers the afternoon off. At dinner, taken in the commissary, a buzz passes among the five of them. It's nearly as palpable as static electricity—they dare not get too close. Thankfully, no one but Brad knows them well enough to see this change, and Brad is working in the control room on Stage 6 compiling source code.

One of the changes is glaringly obvious: the Keepers hardly speak to one another. It's all glances and giggles, burbles and snickers. The promise of adventure feeds their appetites (larger than usual), colors their cheeks (rosier), and fills their eyes (brighter). Later, as Maybeck, Philby, and Willa dig into strawberry shortcake while Finn takes on carrot cake, Willa looks over at Charlene disparagingly before speaking— Charlene is skipping dessert.

"Interesting, don't you think?" Willa remarks. There is Willa the somewhat awkward girl attempting conversation, and then there is the brainiac Willa, analyst and fellow conspirator. The one speaking is definitely the latter.

Philby follows her gaze.

"The topiary?"

"That's what it's called!" Charlene blurts out. "I can never remember that word."

"Plant sculpture," says Maybeck, the artist.

"Mickey," says Finn. Willa's head snaps in his direction. "What?" he asks.

"I don't know exactly," Willa says, "but remember when Brad told us there was more to discuss? That we'd get to it later?" Finn and the others nod. "When I saw Mickey out there on the lawn, it reminded me of when Ariel rescued me from Echo Lake at Hollywood Studios. She and I had climbed the Earful Tower and we were talking about stuff."

"Fascinating," quips Maybeck.

Philby silences him with a laser look.

Willa restarts, more tentatively. "We started talking about leaders. She said something funny, ending with 'We lack only a leader.' I said, 'What about Mickey?'" Willa looks out at the backside of the five-foot-high topiary mouse. "Ariel did this faraway trance thing and said we'd talk about it another time."

Maybeck stabs the strawberry shortcake. "Which leads us exactly where?"

"Maybe I'll get a chance to have that talk with her tonight," Willa says. "Maybe, since we're going there anyway, we could change the plan a little and Philby and I could add Ariel to our mission—"

"While we go after the spooks," Maybeck says. "That sounds fair. P.S.: News flash! We always change our plans."

"What do you think Ariel meant?" Philby asks, trying to calm things down. He focuses on Willa; no one else is in the room.

"That something's going on. She said she and the others assumed that was why we had come. Her words! To lead! For her to say that about us? I mean . . . that's bizarre."

"You still want to be leader, Witless?" Maybeck asks Finn caustically.

"You're tired, Maybeck. This is how you get when you're tired."

"True story. We all know each other way too well."

"Get some sleep before we cross over," Finn says. "Could be a late night."

"I think I can handle ninety minutes."

Finn lowers his voice. "Everyone to bed by ten. Dress accordingly. Philby—"

"With any luck," Philby interrupts, "Finn will cause a slight diversion; meanwhile, I'll slip a thumb drive onto the server that'll automate the crossover and the return. We don't have a fob, so it has to be automated. Total run time could be anywhere from an hour and a half to two hours. The bad part: we won't know when it's going to return us."

"Wait a second," Maybeck says, abandoning the shortcake. "We what?"

"That's right," Philby says. "We should cross over sometime around two in the morning. We return when we return—when the scan's complete."

"And if we're about to be creamed?"

"We hunker down and wait it out."

"Hunker down?" Maybeck says. "Seriously?"

"Seriously," Finn says to Maybeck, "you're way tired."

"Let me get this straight," Maybeck says, glancing at

Charlene, concern in his eyes. "We're going into Disneyland, a place where some of us have never been, trying to find an old dude who may not be there. We can't control when we arrive or when we leave, and the best clue we have is a bunch of demons who nearly smoked us the other night?"

"Well," Finn says, "yeah."

Maybeck nods. "Well, good. Glad to hear it. I'm in, by the way. Have a magical evening." He pushes his chair back and heads for the commissary doors.

14

FINN AWAKENS AS A HOLOGRAM ON Central Plaza beneath the statue of Walt Disney and Mickey Mouse. For an instant, the experience feels so familiar, he thinks he's in Disney World. But the castle—Sleeping Beauty's castle, not Cinderella's—alerts him to his surroundings: Disney*land*. Beauty's castle is pink; it's considerably smaller, oddly wider, and its roofline is less sharp and pronounced. Central Plaza itself feels smaller, the area around it more compact than the corresponding locale at Disney World.

If all this isn't enough, the night sky would give it away. Walt Disney World's sky can be dark, even starlit. Disneyland's glows sepia, the megawatt lights of Southern California seeping into the marine haze layer and obscuring the heavens.

Finn lifts his arm and feels a wave of nostalgia wash through him when he sees the thin blue line that shimmers at the edge of his DHI. Software version 1.6. He wants to find a mirror and see what his face looked like when he was three years younger. There's a body of water in front of the entrance to Frontierland. Finn kneels and looks down, studying his glow.

"Mirror, mirror?" Maybeck's voice, coming from behind. Finn spins, realizing anew how much his friend has matured through high school. Two different kids.

"Whoa! You should see yourself," Finn says. His voice sounds . . . odd. Mechanical and distorted.

Finn stands there transfixed at the sight of Maybeck's

partial DHI. This crossover is like none before. A dull hum fills the air, making Finn feel as if he needs to clean his ears. A grainy image of Maybeck sputters in and out, rimmed by a blue line characteristic of v1.6. Philby tried to upload as much data as possible onto the thumb drive, but clearly his scheme isn't perfect. Finn stretches his arms out and they briefly disappear, then re-form.[18]

There's a slight lag in Finn's actions; it's like he's trying to move through syrup. He wonders if all of the Keepers' functions have been slowed as a result of rollback to their incomplete version v1.6.[19]

"What the—?" Maybeck sounds troubled.

"We'll have to wait for Philby to see this. My guess? Some of our movements uploaded okay. Others, maybe not."

"Well, that makes it interesting," comments Maybeck.[20] "Now you see me, now you don't!" He laughs as he hops back and forth, his DHI unable to keep up to speed.

Finn shakes his head. No use in yelling at Maybeck to cut it out, seeing as his own voice currently sounds like Rice Krispies cereal in a bowl of milk.[21] "Bizarre, isn't it?" Finn says.

"Crazy!" It's Charlene, approaching from behind Maybeck.

Willa appears to Charlene's left. "Philby? Anybody seen Philby?"

The Professor is curiously absent.

"He might have been too wired to sleep," Maybeck says. "Of all of us, he was the one who had the most work to do."

"Or maybe he stayed behind to try to help us return," Finn says, whispering. "Here's what we do."

---

[18] Visitors_Brave
[19] Imagineering_Sorcery
[20] Visitors_Brave
[21] Amanda_Hologram

The other Keepers collect around him.

"In case we were overheard or something—which would mean we have hardly any time—I suggest we divide into two teams. Willa and I will take Ariel's Undersea Adventure because she has a history with Ariel. Maybeck, you and Charlie will take Haunted Mansion. Reconnaissance. That's all we're after. If we can spot either the demons or wraiths without them seeing us, maybe we can follow them to Wayne. Maybe Ariel knows something."

"And if she's got nothing on Wayne," Maybeck says, "what then?"

"We don't know," Willa said, coming to Finn's defense. "But we have to start somewhere."

"There's Walt's apartment." Charlene is quick to side with Maybeck. "Wayne had that place above the Firehouse. So maybe in Disneyland he lives in Walt's apartment or something."

"We can't go all over the place," Finn says. "There will be other nights. Our time is limited."

Willa walks back to get a good look at Central Plaza, obviously bothered by Philby's absence. The other Keepers follow.

"He's okay," Finn says.

"We don't know that," Willa replies.

"We don't know otherwise." Finn wraps an arm around her and gives her shoulders a reassuring squeeze. "He may have had to cross us over manually. Maybe he had to hide in the Crypt after installing the thumb drive. Maybe he got locked in there for the night."

"Maybe he drank a Mountain Dew and can't get to sleep," Maybeck says, winning a laugh.

Finn catches Charlene studying her outstretched hand.

"Isn't it strange how 2.0 makes all of this feel so retro?" she says.

"Keep free of fear," Finn says, reminding the group of the devastating effect fear can have on their DHIs; fear triggers their temporary transformation into a partially or even entirely solid material state, and therefore makes them more susceptible to harm. "Remember, in v1.6, we don't have nearly the same control. We get too sideways and we can't even grab hold of stuff. We're a lot more limited. Things can get sketchy."

"Talk to me." Like all of the Keepers, Maybeck got into his fair share of trouble as a 1.6 DHI—kidnapped, locked in Sleeping Beauty Syndrome. His SBS-induced coma kept his aunt on a round-the-clock vigil.

"Just remember," Finn warns, "we all have fewer skills and abilities. We're more vulnerable."

"And we can't pick when to return," Willa says. "But we need to be together when we do. Here, in the Plaza. Ninety— more like eighty-five—minutes from now."

Version 2.0 makes returning easier too. Willa's reminder shakes Finn. "We're going to return when we return," he says.

"Profound," Maybeck says.

Finn makes eye contact with Charlene. "Good luck with that."

She grins. "I'll get him back on time."

"No heroics," Finn says.

"Yeah, yeah," Maybeck says.

Finn addresses Maybeck. "I wasn't talking to you."

* * *

The simple act of walking helps Finn settle into his 1.6 skin. It's funny how being inside an empty, darkened park affects him so strongly each time he crosses over. It's as if he's never experienced this before; though technically, because they're in Disneyland, he has not. Finn's reaction is mainly triggered by the overall impression of the empty park's grandeur, shadowed by a cloud of mystery.

"Do you miss her?" Willa asks. No need to elaborate on whom.

"It's not like we're married," he says.

"It's a simple enough question, Finn, jeez."

"Yes, I miss her. Okay? But don't read too much into it. She helps us out. She and Jess both. So I miss her on several fronts." He wonders if she's fishing. "Are you worried about him?"

"A little. Of course."

"Me too," Finn admits.

"But you said . . ."

"Comes with the job."

"He's okay," Willa says. "You said he's okay and I'm going with that."

They are careful to take the long way around—holding close to the park's perimeter before crossing and avoiding the open terrace that separates the entrance to Disneyland from the one to Disney California Adventure.

Once inside the sister park, Finn and Willa start to jog. If asked, they would claim they're trying to make the best of the precious minutes remaining; in fact, their unfamiliarity with the park breeds fear of every shadow. And there are many shadows.

Willa is panting as she speaks. "Can't forget about how fear affects us."

"It's not exactly like we can all clear." By mentioning the condition, Finn reminds them both that he's the only Keeper who has perfected the ability to all clear in real life, transforming from a normal kid into a DHI. The process is different

99

when a Keeper is already in DHI form—it amounts to keeping fear away. He casts a glance over his shoulder at Willa. She'll be okay.

They jog past the rising mountain wall that composes the back of Grizzly River Run. The entrance to Radiator Springs appears on their left. Some restaurants. Water. As they arrive at a circular plaza with a tower in its center, Willa points out the entrance to The Little Mermaid—Ariel's Undersea Adventure.

"How will we find her, do you suppose?" Finn asks.

"I have a feeling it will be like that time she rescued me in the Studios. Remember? I was drowning?"

He does remember. But he doesn't like leaving things to others. Maybe, he thinks, that's what defines a leader.

They slip through the entrance and into the attraction, hurry through the empty waiting line, and reach the loading walkway with its clamshell people movers. Finn leads Willa by the hand through one of the oversize clams onto the edge that runs alongside the track. They pass a silent Scuttle, perched on a nest of sea grass.

Then the tunnel they've entered goes belly-of-the-beast black. A few glowing LEDs offer the only waypoints. Several times, Finn smacks into one of the upright clamshells or bangs a shin. Willa tightens their grip each time he collides.

Neither speaks.

They should be used to this: an attraction in the dark, no music, no projected images. But it's as disconcerting as ever. Finn's spooked. He wishes he knew the ride better.

They reach the first Animatronic of Ariel, wondering if somehow she'll come to life. The Animatronic is only somewhat visible, illuminated by a stray light source Finn can't pinpoint. He can make out her mermaid tail and her flowing red hair. The rest of the scene is lumpy with shadow.

"That's creepy," Willa says.

"Sure is." After a few more difficult steps, Finn stops.

"This is the big room," Willa says.

But the abundance of small LEDs has revealed that already. It's half the size of a gym, filled with an octopus, clams, dancing fish, musical fish, coral, and seaweed.

"No fear," Willa whispers.

Easier said than done.

"Ariel?" Willa calls out. Nothing.

Finn points ahead through the sea of creatures and coral formations. "If she's in here, she'll be someplace the guests don't go."

"That can apply to OTs as well." Willa looks around and shivers. "We're going there, aren't we, Finn?" Willa sounds terrified.

"We are."

"Because we're insane."

"Because we need to find her. We need to help Wayne." He adds, "Why don't I go and you stay here as lookout?"

"Because we're not letting go of each other."

Finn leads Willa into the scene, stepping carefully. The v1.6 DHIs glow brighter than the v2.0s, which is a real help given the ride's darkness. Finn navigates using his own glow.

"We're like anglerfish," Willa says. "Phosphorescent, so we can see our prey."

"Show-off," Finn says, hoping to lighten the mood. The deeper he leads them into the vividly painted scenery, the higher his level of anxiety rises.

Willa whispers. "What are we supposed to do if we actually encounter OTs? Run?"

"We keep away the fear, maintain clean DHIs, and we see if we can find Ariel." He pauses. "Or if she can find us."

"That's it? That's the plan?"

"I'm open to suggestions."

Finn continues to step gingerly through the set because his DHI is not all clear. He's guessing Willa's isn't either. And if they're not pure projection, a material part of them remains, making them vulnerable to attack and susceptible to injury. They reach the back of the set, and Finn ducks behind staging that holds a waving turtle. His hologram casts a bluish light into the void.

Finn kneels, trying to concentrate his projection. Cold whips through him.

"Look at your arms," Willa says.

Finn's left arm looks chopped off; it's degraded by DHI shadow, as the projectors don't reach behind the staging. His right arm is grainy and half-disintegrated because of the limitations of the outdated software being run on up-to-date servers.

"DHI shadow," she whispers.

"That could help us," Finn says, "if it turns out we've got the wrong kind of company." He sweeps his arm about, trying to gauge the degree of degradation of his DHI; the closer to the backdrop of the set, the fuller the DHI shadow and therefore the more invisible they are. "If we get into trouble, we make for this wall. We'll disappear. Move in that direction." He points deeper into the darkness. "Away from the projectors. No talking. When we bump into each other, we'll know the other is safe and we'll move on from there."

"Got it," she says softly.

It feels good having some sort of fallback plan in place. Finn takes a deep breath. "We need to separate now, spread apart, so we don't make for an easy target."

"I don't like that word," she says.

"Just remember the plan," he says.

"Yeah. I got it. I still don't like that word."

Finn lets go of her hand, but Willa fights to stay connected as long as possible, her fingertips tickling his palm, then the tips of his fingers.

He doesn't like it. If he's ticklish, it means he's feeling. And if he's feeling, then he still isn't pure DHI.

And if he isn't pure DHI . . .

* * *

"I've never been a big fan," Charlene says. Hidden behind a table in the Mint Julep Bar across the open expanse of terrace from the Haunted Mansion, she moves closer to Maybeck so that their arms touch. He doesn't seem to notice.

"It's so different," Maybeck says, his artist's eye at work. "The tall columns. The whole New Orleans antebellum look. It looks like a plantation home."

"Same as Florida."

"Not at all. In Florida, it looks more like a museum. It's brick and up on a hill. This is just . . . creepy."

"That's the point, I think."

"You're funny." But he's not amused. The hologram of his arm is partially degraded and sparking. His left side from his hip down is much the same.

"You don't look so hot," she says.

"You're missing half your face, Sleeping Beauty."

"What?" Charlene takes great pride in her looks. People have been telling her how pretty she is for as long as she can remember. There's a mirror behind the bar.

"Don't you dare," Maybeck says. "Take my word for it: You look like the mayor in the second Batman movie."

"The guy with the rotting face? Oh, way to help out!"

"We'll fit right in," he says. "We look like zombies, right?"

She looks him over. "I see what you mean."

"We're perfect. Trust me."

"I do trust you."

She wins Maybeck's attention. For a moment he seems to be on the verge of saying something serious to her—a rare event for him. But what comes out is, "You look so disgusting."

She wishes he wasn't so predictable, but then again that's what she finds reassuring. You never know what's going to come out of his mouth and yet you can count on it being sarcastic and amusing. "I guess if we're going to do this . . ."

Maybeck follows her as she hugs the wall of the train station and cuts through the cemetery. Charlene ducks under a waiting-line tape.

"What's up?" Maybeck says.

"In Disneyland the stretching room is actually an elevator. It won't be turned on. We have to go around."

"How can you possibly know all that?"

"I do what's impossible for you: I read."

"Ha-ha." He's not laughing.

She hurries up the small rise through the trees and around the house, cutting in to the exit. They enter the ride from this side, walking the mansion backward. This approach means they start out in the hitchhiking ghost tunnel, dodging their way through the frozen Doom Buggies, before entering the climax of the attraction: the graveyard. Charlene, in the lead, slows down, walking tentatively.

There's no music and virtually no light beyond the glow of their DHIs. Before them are crooked gravestones (some topped with carved heads), freestanding tombs, cobwebs, skeletons, and corpses. Nothing moves. There's not a spit of wind or a click of sound. It's as if the world has died and they have walked into the gray heart of it.

"This is freaking me out," she says.

"Yeah, okay." He sounds concerned. "There!" he says, causing Charlene to jump.

"Terry!"

"A tomb." He points out a square stone structure low to the floor. "Check out the stones. The coloring."

Charlene steps closer. "How'd you see that?"

"Because I respect the artwork that goes into these things. Wouldn't mind being a Disney artist someday."

He's spotted a feathering of black soot spread in long fingers across the stones. The fat ends of the flares form a straight line where the stones intersect. Charlene studies the pattern more closely.

"It's like a wind or something."

"Or . . . a door," Maybeck says. "Something came out of there with a wind behind it. A strong wind that carried the dust." He wipes his fingers on the stone, cutting a line through the feathered soot as if he's dragging a finger through colored writing on a white board at school. "A trapdoor."

"A hidden door," she whispers.

"Agreed." Equally soft.

"As in: maybe we leave it that way."

"Maybe not," Maybeck says. He eases her aside. Their imperfect DHIs sputter and turn grainy and transparent.

"I—am—not—liking—this," Charlene says.

Maybeck hoists his one decent hand. It moves more slowly than he intends, making the motion awkward and unpredictable. He opens his palm—slowly—against the tomb's stacked stones and feels for a hidden trigger to unlock the door.

All at once the ride turns on: lights, motion, music. Charlene lets out a yip of terror. Maybeck falls back and bumps into a gravestone. It's the bumping he doesn't like—the shock and associated scare of the ride coming alive knocks him out of pure v1.6 DHI and into the mix of human and hologram that makes v1.6 so dangerous.

An eerie song blares from unseen speakers. A row of ghost heads sings. The explosion of action and noise makes it difficult for Maybeck and Charlene to recover.

"Terry! The—"

"Trapdoor!" Maybeck says.

Add to the music the sound of grinding stone.

The tomb door is coming open.

* * *

Finn hears what sounds like wind through branches. But there are no trees here, no breeze.

"Finn!" Willa calls breathlessly.

"I hear it," he says. Whatever it is, it's coming toward them. "Don't let it scare you."

"Oh, sure!"

Not a wind. Not exactly. More like . . . *slithering*.

"Version 1.6," he reminds them both. "Keep yourself pure."

Finn calms his thoughts. As a projected image, no harm can come to him. But in the back of his mind lurks a more virulent thought: they are not fully 1.6. Philby managed to cross them over, but with obvious design flaws, improperly rendered movement, and lower resolution. What if these inherent problems with their current projections also prevent them from being fully transparent? What if, no matter how hard they try for all clear, it's an unattainable condition?

Eels! The oddly colored pinprick eyes of Flotsam and Jetsam penetrate the dark. The twins are *on land*, moving like a combination of python and cobra.

The eels move closer. Easily four feet long and thicker

than Finn's arm, the two creatures look perfectly comfortable out of water. Finn never liked them in the movie; in the flesh, he realizes they were given a makeover for film. They're green skinned, reminding him of Maleficent, but scars and poorly healed wounds cover their slimy hides. They're mouth breathers; their ugly lips turn down in disgusted frowns to reveal rows of spiked narrow teeth, sharp as needles. Their eerie, serpentine movement is deceptive and hypnotic.

Finn imagines himself in deep space: no sound, no gravity. He tingles all over, suggesting all clear. He's safe—for now. He steps forward, putting himself between the eels and Willa.

Flotsam strikes at Finn's ankle, deceptively fast, his jaws opening wide. The eel chomps down, with a clap of teeth as they bite into nothing but light.

Willa lets out a shriek.

For Finn, the trick is control: when to be transparent, and when to solidify to grab or touch or . . . *kick*. Flotsam works to make a second attack on Finn.

Willa's high-speed brain computes Flotsam's course. She kicks the eel as if it were a lawn hose and sends it flying.

Faced with fight or flight, Jetsam flows the short distance across the floor, aiming himself at Willa. Finn turns to intercept it, but too late. The green moray unlocks its jaw, aiming for Willa's knee. She hasn't had time to make sure she's pure hologram. She's going to lose her leg from the knee down. Worse: injuries sustained as DHIs typically transfer back to bed with you. If she loses her leg here . . .

The eel's teeth mere inches from Willa's knee, Jetsam's head slams to the floor with a loud report. Willa has sagged, nearly fainted with fear, but Finn catches her.

The bent tines of a trident pin the eel's head to the ground.

Finn follows the shaft of the trident to a girl's hand, the hand to an arm.

"Storey!" he whispers with such gratitude that the name sounds worshipful.

* * *

Wraiths!

The ghostly aliens flow from the opened tomb like smoke. The music, lights, and ghoulish sounds overwhelm Maybeck and Charlene, who are briefly transfixed.

The smoky trail coils high above, circles, and turns. The lead wraith dives for the Keepers.

In a flash, Charlene scoops up a pile of cemetery soil and tosses it high into the air, blinding the lead wraith. Its dreadful screech is louder than the attraction's theme song. Maybeck pivots and pulls on a smaller tombstone, heaving it forward and back until it's dislodged. Lifting it in both hands like a swimming pool paddleboard, he swings it with perfect timing. The lead wraith loops overhead and dives; Maybeck connects. It vaporizes into black dust. He takes out the second wraith with his backhand, and the third with another forehand strike.

Charlene remains collected and strains to pull the tomb's stone door further open. Despite his early successes, Maybeck is losing the battle behind her; the wraiths separate and attack from all directions. One attaches to Maybeck's back; his DHI drains of color. Charlene picks up a brick and lays into the hooded head of the parasite, clobbering it and winning a glass-shattering cry. It lets go of Maybeck and thrusts its skull face out of the shadow, smack into Charlene's face.

She screams, swings, and splits its skull with the brick. It decomposes to powder and rains down on her like charcoal ash.

"In here!" she hollers, widening the gap in the door with one heroic tug.

"You—have—got—to be kidding!" Maybeck vaporizes two more wraiths, but it's a losing battle.

Charlene grabs Maybeck by the arm and hauls him through the square black hole. She hears him land a good distance below. With a mighty heave, she pulls the tomb's trapdoor shut. Sudden silence. They can hear nothing but the dull thumping of the music.

"Terry?"

Her foot catches on a ladder's rung. She climbs down.

Maybeck's glowing DHI lies prostrate on the cellar floor.

"If I'd been fully myself," Maybeck says, "I'd have broken my neck with that fall, and you would have killed me."

"If you'd been fully yourself, that wraith on your back would have killed you, and I'd have been hauling your corpse through that door."

They're both out of breath. Charlene wipes sweat from her eyes.

"I always thought this place was haunted for real," Maybeck says.

"We're in the cellar of the old house."

"Yep."

Stacks of antiques clutter the whole space. Civil War artifacts, tintypes, hat stands, and a boar's head are piled in heaps beneath the rusted pipes suspended from the overhead floor joists. A pale light bleeds from a rectangular shape—a doorway?—a good distance away.

"Suppose that leads outside?" he asks.

"Worth a look."

Charlene helps Maybeck to his feet. He takes the lead, breaking some cobwebs for her. The two pass an antique vanity with an oval mirror. On the vanity, a pair of scissors glints in the light. There's an ivory-handled hairbrush, a box of face powder. A collection of pearls and other jewelry hangs from an ornate stand. Along the wall is an army cot, and next to it an old steamer trunk.

Charlene approaches the vanity. Touches the hairbrush. She pulls a strand of hair away.

"It's black."

"Save the estate sale shopping for another time."

"That would be Leota."

"Who?"

"In the Haunted Mansion. The story. Madame Leota was in love with Master Gracey. She killed Constance, his blond bride, and stuck her in a trunk in the attic, hoping that with Constance gone, Master Gracey would love her instead. But it backfired. Gracey hanged himself. People think Leota died of old age and returned to haunt the mansion."

"Don't talk like this is real."

"Because?" Charlene asks. "It's obvious a bunch of kids can't become holograms. A bunch of Disney villains couldn't possibly be responsible for *killing Dillard Cole*."

"Okay . . . okay! Sorry."

"There's no dust on the vanity. The mirror has been wiped clean."

"Listen to you! You're trying to freak me out—*and it's working*."

Charlene points to the trunk. "That's a trunk. It's big enough for—"

"Now you're just being mean," Maybeck says.

A woman's laugh coos out of the dark. It grows to a cackle.

Charlene whispers hoarsely, "What if the wraiths *wanted* us down here?"

"What if ghost stories are real?" comes the voice from the dark. "You clever girl."

"I know that voice!" Charlene says in a hush. "It's Madame Leota!"

Maybeck's DHI stretches out, reaching for what was once a wall decoration of two crossed Civil War sabers. He concentrates, allowing his DHI to physically grab the handle of one of the swords and wrestle it free of its scabbard. He hoists it two-handed, prepared to do battle.

An emaciated form with an ancient, withered face appears out of the dark. The deeply creased skin is sucked back over high cheekbones like fruit left too long in the sun. The eyes are the gray-blue of lake ice, the nose withered to a black hole beneath what appears to be a shriveled red chili pepper. The specter's cracked lips have been smeared with red greasepaint, forming a hideous cavity absent of teeth but occupied by a black tongue that ticks back and forth like a clock's pendulum.

"That's . . . her." Charlene can barely speak.

With fingers like her former nose and a neck like a turkey's, Madame Leota is the single most hideous human, female or male, the two have ever seen.

"Wait! He didn't want to marry *her?*" Maybeck says to Charlene. "Go figure."

The ancient Leota glides forward. "We always have room for two more."

"Get some original material," Maybeck says.

Charlene is apoplectic, unable to move. She stares at Maybeck in awe. Grunts, but cannot speak.

Seeing this, Leota turns toward the girl.

"No you don't, sweetheart." Maybeck swings the sword down. It swipes right through the ghost's arm and clangs onto the stone floor.

111

Leota reaches out for Maybeck while stepping toward the paralyzed Charlene. The ghost's arm passes through Maybeck's DHI. Leota looks at him, puzzled.

"You ain't the only ghost in the kingdom, gorgeous," Maybeck says.

Leota's jaw disconnects as her chin drops to her collarbone. She shrieks and directs herself at Charlene, only inches from the girl's face.

After several seconds, Charlene's hair begins to blow back; Maybeck realizes she's lost her DHI.

"Dance with me?" he says, closing his eyes and running his entire DHI body through Leota's ghost. Leota spins twice before Maybeck steps out of her. It takes her only a fraction of a second to reorient herself.

In that time, Maybeck reaches for Charlene, who's gone ashen white—Leota has scared the life out of her. Her DHI fades to gray, pixelating and beginning to lose form. Charlene is melting before his eyes.

"All clear, Charlie." Maybeck says the words as warmly as he's ever spoken two words in his life.

Leota is in his face, wailing her tortured cry. He feels himself slipping. He feels cold but to accept the cold is to welcome death.

He has no idea where it comes from—abject fear, a lack of doubt—but he returns Leota's cry with an agonized howl of his own that blends in an eerie harmony with hers. But as his shriek bends downward at the end and begins to clash with her sound, Maybeck sees Leota tremble. So he slides his pitch down further into a dark, grating dissonance, making her shudder. *No fear!* he chides himself.

He moves himself to feel no ill will, to push away his desire for vengeance and a sense of disgust. In all the noise, he finds quiet. The pixelated particles pushed by the ghost's bellowing draw back into his projected form and he feels stronger. Louder.

Leota backs up a step.

"Duck!" shouts Charlene, and he obeys, having forgotten about her. For a few moments, until he forced himself to wake up, Leota owned him.

Maybeck drops to the floor and looks up to see Charlene holding the vanity's oval mirror up to Leota's face.

The screeching stops in that instant. The ghost's eyes narrow and flare. She swoons at the sight of the horrid face looking back at her. Emitting a series of pitiful groans and complaints, Leota sheds black tears and slowly backs up, returning to the shadows. Maybeck has never heard a sound so miserable and heartbroken, so full of grief and loathing at the same time.

"She hates herself," Charlene says before Maybeck can ask. "Hates what she did to Gracey. Hates what she's become."

"But how could you poss—"

"I'm a woman, Terry! That's something you're going to figure out one of these days."

He stares at her, dumbstruck.

Charlene grabs his hand and pulls him toward the beckoning light.

* * *

"I thought that was you!" Storey Ming says to Finn. She seems to ignore Willa entirely.

The Keepers met Storey aboard the Disney *Dream* cruise ship during the Panama passage. An elusive girl the Keepers believe is allied with Wayne, she came to their aid on multiple occasions. Finn has come to rely upon her. Charlene, Willa,

113

and Amanda are less generous; they claim that there's something "off" about Storey and believe she's after Finn. He thinks back to their kiss on the *Dream*, but immediately pushes the thought away.

"What are you doing here?" he gasps instead, looking down at the writhing Jetsam.

"Me? I headed here the minute we docked. This is it. The ultimate destination. Disneyland. Where it all started. Where it all ends . . . if *they* have their way."

"How did you find us?" Willa asks.

It seems to take Storey a great deal of effort to turn toward Willa. "You found me," she says.

Storey squats to address Jetsam. "We've had our run-ins before, haven't we, you ugly green leech?" She wiggles the bent trident, choking down on the eel. "Now, get back into your scene and stay away from this area, or I'll skewer you and roast you for supper." She pulls a fragment of a sandwich from her pocket and throws it far into the dark, then lifts the trident. With one shake of its tail, the eel vanishes into the dark. A moment later they can hear it feeding.

"I've been hiding in here the past few days—since that newspaper story about the earthquake down in Mexico." Storey motions them deeper into the dark. There's a mattress on the floor, a bowl of water, and a wrinkled face towel. "Staying out of the park because of the security cameras. Luckily, there's a Dumpster backstage and plenty of perfectly good food is thrown away with all the ugly stuff. I remembered what you said about how dangerous the parks could be at night. I've been hoping to see you all. And here you are!"

"Here we are," says Willa. "Oh, joy."

"You saved us," Finn says.

"I think of those two as rats with very long tails," Storey

says. "All they're after is food. So I carry some around." She empties another pocket to reveal a chicken wrap. "Pretty harmless once they eat, as long as Ursula isn't here to order them to do stuff."

"Speaking of which: have you seen any OTs?" Willa asks.

"Have you seen Wayne?" Finn says, adding enough emphasis to make it sound like the more important question.

"Two sides of the same coin," Storey says. "Wayne and the Overtakers. No, on both accounts. That is, I don't know exactly which characters qualify as the bad guys. I haven't seen anyone from the ship, if that's what you're asking." She hesitates deliberately and lowers her voice in a conspiratorial manner. "There was this guy. Older. Could have been a Cast Member. Like cleanup crew or something."

"Go on." Finn's eyes tick to Willa. On a balcony deck aboard the *Dream*, there had been an older Cast Member working near the Keepers who turned out to be—

"I saw him . . . just a silhouette, a shadow on the wall *inside* the opera house."

"Main Street," Willa says, easily slipping into Philby's professorial role.

Storey nods, her first real acknowledgment of Willa. "I can't say for sure, but it felt . . . mysterious. I don't know how else to put it. And whoever it was didn't come out. I stuck around to make sure."

"That's Wayne!" Finn says. "I've had that same feeling about him. Mysterious, like you said."

"Wayne's here?" Storey sounds intrigued. "Here, in Disneyland? Where?"

"It's possible," Willa says. "But we don't know where."

Storey swipes her hand through Finn's DHI. "That is

so cool." She jokes, "I couldn't hold on to you if I wanted to."

"That would be Amanda's deal, anyway," Willa says.

Finn can practically hear the cats hissing.

Storey says, "Glad you're here. I haven't had anyone to talk to."

"We're on a mission here," Willa says testily.

"Well, pardon me! Sorry if I inconvenienced you *by saving your lives!*"

"We're holograms. We weren't in any danger."

"Didn't look that way to me."

Finn intervenes. "We've got to go. But it's good to know where to find you."

"I'm around," Storey says, making sure to direct her words at Willa. "Don't go stepping on any eels."

Finn and Willa both jerk their heads down to look at their feet.

"Gotcha," Storey says. And they all laugh, releasing pent-up tension.

* * *

"Well, if we'd hoped to spot the wraiths," Maybeck says, "then you can consider our mission a success." He looks at Charlene sympathetically. "But we didn't exactly follow them to Wayne, if you know what I mean. . . ."

"And we didn't find Ariel," Finn says, "but Storey Ming was there and basically—"

"Saved us." Willa purses her lips and nods. "Seriously."

"The OTs are certainly active," Finn whispers. He and the three others are hunkered down in shrubbery on an island of landscaping between the Astro Orbiter and the castle. Technically they're on Central Plaza and believe they will therefore be returned when Philby's server stops whatever process he described. Waiting for the return is unnerving compared with having the fob in hand and controlling the process themselves.

"We could spend a long time in here and never find Wayne," Maybeck says. "Talk about a needle in a haystack."

"Better idea?" Finn asks.

"You know the skywriting they do at Disney World?" Maybeck suggests, to the others' amusement. "'Wayne, please call—'"

"Shh!" Willa reminds them as they all laugh more loudly. "Let's remember we're trying to hide."

"So, we return, and then what?" Charlene asks.

The resulting silence brings all their attention to Finn, whose stony face is caught in mottled light.

"Philby works to improve our DHIs. We try to figure out why the Cryptos want us out here, yet seem so desperate not to allow us to do anything. We keep trying to find Wayne, because he'll tell us what's really going on."

"Maybe we should ask to go home," Charlene suggests. "Maybe then the Cryptos will include us more."

"I wouldn't count on it," Maybeck says. "I think that could backfire."

"I hate just sitting around," Willa says.

Everyone nods in agreement.

"We got stuff done tonight," Finn reminds them. "Storey's here. She can help us."

"We've also confirmed that the wraiths came from the Haunted Mansion," says Charlene.

"So the attack on the Archives was organized here in Disneyland," Willa says. "That's got to be important."

"Wayne's here somewhere," Finn says softly. "I can feel—"

But before he completes his sentence, their holograms dissolve and vanish.

15

*Y*OU UNDERSTAND THE RISKS? Charlene remembers Philby asking after she volunteered to be his guinea pig. She remembers it again as she opens her eyes beneath the Legends statue—it's just like the night of the wraith attack. She was alone then and she's alone now, despite Finn's vehement attempts to pair her with another Keeper.

Philby's counterargument was simple enough: "If I get it wrong, it's better to limit the damage."

"Then let me be the one," Finn had replied nobly.

"Charlie's our jock. She's the best to test it because she can move at speeds and in ways that will put the tweaks I've made in the source code to the test. We need better modeling than you guys had inside the park. There's a bunch of stuff to accomplish, Finn, and if it messes up and we trap Charlie in SBS for a day or so, we'll find ways around that. If we trap you, *oh fearless leader*, then we're in trouble. Besides," Philby said with added emphasis, "if you get hurt, everyone will think I did it on purpose so I could take over. And believe me, that is *not* my intention, my wish, or my desire."

"So what happened to all the paranoia over the Cryptos watching us so carefully?"

"Technology," Willa said. "Philby and I hacked the hallway camera feeds and replaced them with iPhone videos of empty corridors. That's all the Cryptos or Security will see."

Maybeck couldn't hide that he was impressed.

The mission objective was for Charlene to cross over—

119

which she has now accomplished—and to meet Philby on Stage 6, where he'll put her through her paces in an attempt to improve their DHI effectiveness. If and when her v1.6 DHI fails to execute correctly, Philby will make real-time fixes to the software, like a doctor operating on a patient who is awake while parts of her body are anaesthetized.

The always-protective Finn plans to be on the soundstage with them. Maybeck and Willa will remain outside as scouts. The Keepers are under curfew and are not allowed on the studio back lot after midnight—an hour at which Stage 6 is almost certain to be unoccupied.

Charlene went to bed at 11:00 P.M. She checks her phone, which reads 12:02 A.M. Philby isn't wasting time.

Stage 6 is located directly behind the Frank G. Wells Building, a straight shot: Charlene can see the southwest corner of the hangarlike structure down a long alley past a courtyard. She takes off in that direction, moving among the Legends Plaza towers for cover.

At the end of the terrace, she crosses the sidewalk and bounds down the stairs into the sunken courtyard. White lights suddenly sweep across the wall of the Wells building—lights connected to a golf cart operated by studio Security. She sees the two guards in the cart before they see her, allowing her time to duck behind a large concrete tub holding a tree. But she's trapped; one of the guards climbs out of the cart and heads for the steps behind Ink and Paint. He's briefly screened from her, and Charlene reacts instinctively, ducking low and cutting across the patio toward the entrance to the Wells building. At this point the only place to hide is inside.

The door is locked. She can hear the guard approaching.

Charlene reaches out. Her open palm makes contact with the door's cool glass. She closes her eyes, exhales a deep breath, and calms herself, quieting her thoughts. *No fear!* It feels as if she pushes the door open, but she knows that is not the case. With her eyes still closed, she steps forward, her DHI following her arm through the locked door and into the lobby. She dives and rolls behind a chair set out for visitors just as the beam from the guard's flashlight washes across the wall behind her.

When she's certain he has passed, she takes off down the hall in the direction of Stage 6.

"Sorry I'm late. I know how important this kid stuff is," a man's voice says from above her. His last words are muffled as a door shuts behind him, but her ears pick up "kid stuff" nonetheless.

Charlene only gets a few steps farther before deciding the voice is Brad's. What 'kid stuff'? she wonders. Which kids? Us? And important? *How important.* To whom?

She stops, tempted to stay with the plan to meet Philby at Stage 6. But her curiosity wins out. In other circumstances, she might not give such a banal comment any weight, but it's Brad doing the apologizing. Which means it's her and her friends he's talking about, and it's insanely late at night to be having a meeting.

She has to have a look, can't tear herself away. How can a one- or two-minute detour hurt anyone? Philby can wait.

Climbing the set of stairs is awkward in Philby's hacked version of 1.6: her idea of how quickly her feet arrive at the next tread is not matched by the projected image, and she falls forward onto her face more than once as she stumbles uphill.

Finally, she arrives at the balcony overlooking the lobby. She didn't get a good look at Brad, but his voice sounded clear enough to suggest this general area. She proceeds cautiously, step by careful step. She catches sight of her reflection in the glass of an office wall: her face is that of a younger girl, a freshman well before the Panama Canal cruise, a figure she remembers but doesn't recognize. Her sight line shifts, and she sees that her right arm and hand are half their proper size, shrunken and deformed. *Philby!*

She flexes her hand repeatedly as if it has fallen asleep; her arm thickens, extends, grows back to normal. It's one of the most discomforting effects she's suffered as a DHI. She takes another careful step forward, not wanting to pass in front of a conference room and be spotted. The horizon shifts, angling lower to her left. She tilts and falls over.

Her left leg is half size. It looks more like an arm than a leg. It's Philby again, messing with her DHI software, probably believing she hasn't crossed over yet. She wiggles her ankle as she did her wrist a moment before; again, her entire limb swells and returns to its original proportions. She doesn't dare stand still for fear he'll capsize her again—she can't stay lying down in the middle of the concourse, so she hurries forward on hands and knees, her attention on her own limbs as much as her surroundings.

Philby has sabotaged Charlene, throwing up distractions and injecting fear into her, rendering her as much human as DHI. As she closes in on the only glowing windows, she reads a plaque identifying it as a conference room. Pulling up short, she leans her ear against the glass panel fronting the office closest to her and makes out the low murmur of voices, male and female. She's in the right place, but the fidelity of her DHI hearing isn't good enough to overhear the conversation. She strains to listen, chafes at her limitations—in v2.0, sight and sound are hi-def—thinks again how far the software has evolved.

Blinds are lowered inside the conference room, but there's

122

an edge of exposed glass that could reveal her if she tries to press her ear against it. She's so close to being able to eavesdrop. It drives her crazy.

I can't just stand here. For one thing, she's out in plain sight in the hall. Anyone could arrive at any moment. It's a risky place. She considers alternatives. None are promising.

As a skilled climber, Charlene looks overhead for a way into the conference room from above, but there are no options. The high vaulted ceiling over the lobby atrium offers nothing. She follows the slanting ceiling to its intersection with the office wall. She knows what to do. She moves her DHI through the wall and into the office that's adjacent to the conference room.

Inside, Charlene moves to the far corner and stands facing the wall shared with the conference room. She settles herself, knowing this is where the real risk taking begins. Looking down, it registers just how pathetic her DHI is—granulated, spotty, with poor color, its refresh rate lagging badly. When she moves her leg, her sneaker looks more like a blob that grows and then refocuses than a shoe.

The degradation of v1.6 reminds her of her time with the Keepers in Walt Disney World and Orlando. She wonders for the first time in a while about the trade-off she's made for her television career. Involved again as a Keeper, she realizes how much she has missed her friends. How will she feel when they go back to Florida without her?

Thinking clearly and without fear, she leans partially into the wall, head first. It's not entirely dark inside—light trickles in from the tiny gaps around the electrical boxes and wall switches. The walls are hollow, about five inches thick, constructed of metal studs and drywall. Wires of various thicknesses and colors snake through. Her head is now half in, half out of the wall; she inches her feet forward and sees her DHI toes enter the narrow space. The front of her thighs pass inside the wall, though her bottom and her heels are still in the office behind her.

She remembers that a single black hair adhering inside his DHI's pants' pocket once prevented Philby from crossing through a stateroom wall—the two worlds of material and projection don't always behave according to theory. She hopes she doesn't encounter any surprises. There are inherent dangers in what she's attempting; it's one thing to step through a wall quickly, but quite another to do as she's doing now—to expect the two states to exist separately and together in one moment. If Philby should mess with the code now, anything could happen.

Her focus must remain on purity, on maintaining a lack of fear or concern. She has no idea what might happen if she slips, and she doesn't want to find out.

What she thought was poor lighting inside the wall turns out to be some kind of barrier on the back of the office-side drywall. Charlene tests it by slowly pushing her finger through the drywall up to the barrier layer, and through it.

Her finger disappears on the inside of the wall.

She tries again. Same result.

It's a layer of mesh—copper maybe. Willa or Philby could probably explain its purpose—some kind of security screen to prevent wireless transmission and bugging devices—but it visibly eliminates her projection, delivering her finger into DHI shadow. Invisibility! She pushes further, more fingers, her hand up to her wrist. Invisible. She tries the other hand and arm. Nothing of her DHI will be visible in the conference room, on the other side of the mesh.

Inching forward, Charlene puts her forehead and chin

through the vertical plane. She daringly angles her head and places her right eye to the back side of the drywall that lines the conference room. A portion of her invisible head and face pops through, and she finds that she can see and hear—not perfectly, but pretty well—everything that's happening inside the room.

ᴶᴷCharlene flashes back to the moment when she first went into DHI shadow: she and the other Keepers had been hiding in a teepee in the Indian Encampment, overlooking the Magic Kingdom's Tom Sawyer Island. She laughs silently at the memory, at how young and naive they all were. None of the original five Keepers could have imagined back then how much they would have to go through to arrive at this moment—three thousand miles away, the stakes impossibly high.[22]

Three of the attendees around the conference table have their backs to her. Of the other four, she recognizes only Joe, who showed the Keepers around when they first arrived. He sits at the head of the table; Charlene assumes that this means he's in charge. He looks tired and older than he did a few days ago. His left eye twitches uncontrollably behind his glasses, while his lips form a knot of impatience.

Two women flank him, both of whom are Charlene's mother's age. Two chairs at the table are empty. The backs of the heads are all men: one balding, one gray-haired, and one with well-groomed dark hair.

Before she hears another word spoken, she can tell the mood is solemn and glum.

"It's an insidious suggestion," Joe says.

"It requires consideration," says the balding man. He has a high, feminine voice and a habit of rocking wildly in his

---

[22] Twilight_StageB

office chair. "We would be doing everyone a favor, the children included, if we prove ourselves right."

"An enemy within their ranks?" It's the voice she heard speaking earlier from the hallway. *Brad?* she wonders, but she can't be sure. The combination of v1.6 and DHI shadow is badly affecting both her hearing and her eyesight. She doesn't dare stay long given how unstable it all feels—she's experiencing a sensation that most closely relates to extreme fatigue, but isn't. It's more like when the sun goes behind a cloud or when Terry offers a rare compliment—then falls silent and becomes uncommunicative.

"It could be unusually destructive," says the gray-haired man, speaking in an eerily calm, disassociated voice. "These children are emotionally resilient and codependent allies. Suggesting we withhold an operation—an important operation involving Kresky—based solely on the *possibility* of a traitor seems drastic, don't you think? The unforeseen consequences could be . . . disastrous. We don't want them turning against us."

"I tend to agree with that," Joe says, "but the counterargument is that we have definitive proof that a Mexican Immigration officer had his head bitten off—"

※Charlene gasps and immediately regrets it as several heads turn toward her. She's invisible, not noiseless. To her ringing ears, her gasp sounded as loud as thunder.[23]

She pulls her head back inside the wall and stands absolutely still, though frightened. As her limbs and body become more solid, her muscles and bones find steel studs and drywall within her flesh. The burning magnifies to an unbearable pain. Worse, the mingling of flesh and projection locks her in place.

---

[23] Adventure_Willa

She's stuck. If she moves her left leg, she's going to take a steel stud with her.

At the moment when she's about to give up and scream her lungs out, Maybeck's voice fills her memory. He's joking about growing pains and shin splints, holding the Keepers enraptured as he spins tale after tale. Her imagination, or a memory? It doesn't matter: the image floods her with mirth and humor, countering the fear. Warmth returns—not burning heat—and her legs move freely, allowing her to back out of the wall and into the empty office.

Now Charlene can process what she has just overheard. If a head was bitten off, it has to have been by Chernabog; he is said to devour humans and feed on their souls. She takes a deep breath.

The Overtakers aren't just villains anymore: they're murderers. This realization brings with it an unwanted memory of Dillard's death. What are she and the others getting themselves into? Who will die next? Charlene takes a deep breath. She can't believe her ears. After all the Keepers have gone through, after all they've sacrificed, it's almost too much. They've given up so much to protect the Parks—sleep, graduation, all sense of a normal life—they've put their lives in danger for the sake of the Disney magic. Now the Cryptologists and Imagineers think that one of them could be the enemy? It's completely unacceptable. For a moment, she wants to leap through the wall and tell them exactly what she thinks.[24]

But Charlene controls herself. One of the great benefits of being a DHI has been to learn such powerful self-control, to be able not only to push anger to the back of your head, but to let it go completely. To be free of it.

---

[24] Adventure_Willa

As she regains her composure, Charlene hears a series of sounds back inside the meeting room: a chair bumping against the common wall, voices, the clank of a glass door thrown open too quickly.

Her entire body aches; her DHI has absorbed too many of the materials inside the wall. It's like a tooth has been yanked without Novocain. But there's no time for pain. She knows the thoroughness of the Disney Cast Members and people like the Imagineers—they never leave a job half finished. Her gasp troubled them and they are coming in search of her.

For Charlene the skill—the practiced skill—is to remain unfazed, fearless. The melody of a Taylor Swift song swims in her head: *Fearless*. With her back to the wall, she steps into it once more, double-checks her toes and heels, and finding herself almost fully within, stands still.

Perhaps it's her level of excitement, or maybe Philby is tweaking some computer source code over at Stage 6, but she could swear her hearing is better, her vision sharper.

The one place to hide is obvious: *Where they aren't looking for me.*

She takes one more step backward, through the mesh, through the second layer of drywall, and into the conference room. Into full DHI shadow. She stands, her nose pressed against the conference-room side of the wall, her bottom nearly touching the back of one of the chairs. Doesn't want to look. Doesn't want to allow even a smidgen of fear or concern into her DHI. Stands like a wall ornament. An *invisible* wall ornament.

After a moment, she gathers the courage to take two giant steps toward the end of the conference table, moving away from where Joe sits. She doesn't know if he's still sitting there, because she won't turn around. Won't risk it.

128

"Well, that was weird," says Brad.

From the sound of his voice, she can sense that Brad is going to run into her when he returns to his chair. She takes one more giant step to the left. Freezes again as in her peripheral vision Brad reaches out his hand, aiming directly for Charlene's shoulder.

"Earth to Brad," Joe says.

The hand stops. Brad turns and sits.

"Nothing in the office," Joe says. "And there wasn't time for one of them to get down the hall without me seeing."

"You're saying six of us imagined the same gasp at the same time?" One of the women does not sound happy.

"I'm saying sound is the least dependable of the senses. We can touch, taste, smell, and see far more accurately than we can hear."

"You're saying . . . ?" The same woman.

Brad intervenes. "The HVAC, the air vent, could have coughed. It happens."

"Of course it does," Joe says. "Of course it happens."

"It's late," says the woman, disgusted. "Let's end this."

"What do we tell them?" asks the other woman.

"We tell them what we know," Brad says. "I'm a firm believer in the best lie being the truth. We lay out the orders with no wiggle room: Cross over. Do some quick spying. Cross back."

"And if they don't obey?" The first woman again.

"They lose our trust. We use them less frequently," Joe says. "Consequences breed proper behavior."

"They're getting far too powerful for their own good," says the first woman. "More powerful than most of us in this room."

"Which is exactly why we brought them here," Joe says, reminding her. "Why we need them."

16

THE NIGHT AIR SMELLS SALTY and tastes sour, like a marina at low tide. Dozens of steel cranes reach up toward the pale, glowing clouds like skeletal fingers beckoning evil spirits to descend.

Rows of shipping containers stacked eight high stretch for nearly a half mile. The containers are in two groups: those being loaded off trucks and into the stacks, and those being loaded out of the stacks and onto trucks.

Along the docks, behind this bustle of activity, cranes on steel frames overhead move containers on and off the ships. The Long Beach, California, container yard is the model of efficiency; engineers from a dozen countries have studied it. This, in part, is because of its enormous size. A person standing among the chaos of containers looks comically small and insignificant; it seems entirely a place of robot cranes and multicolored, trailer-size metal boxes, a child's gift assembled alongside the Christmas tree.

Tia Dalma handles the switch far more carefully than in Mexico. No more missing heads! First, she scouts the yard for a truck heading to Disneyland. This effort alone consumes more than an hour. Having located her quarry, she leads the Queen and Chernabog on a daring dash *under* truck trailers for some hundred yards and into the back of a truck's trailer. Its load consists of hundreds of brown cardboard boxes holding plastic tableware: forks, sporks, knives, plates, and cups.

She gets Chernabog settled, ensures that the Queen will

look after him, and climbs into the truck's cab. Hiding herself in the narrow sleeping cabin behind the two air-cushioned seats, she lies in wait for the driver.

Her hands cuddle a woven raffia figurine, discolored by perspiration and nearly constant rubbing, worn shiny like an old brass doorknob. She used one just like it to manipulate the oil rig operator in the jungle. Knowing her dark magic is far more effective when she holds a personal item—the more personal, the better—she smears tobacco chew, discovered in a Styrofoam cup, onto the doll's leg. The foul-smelling goo is the man's spit laced with the tobacco's brown juice.

She hears a man's gruff voice outside and catches her hair in her grip to keep the beads adorning her dreadlocks from clattering.

The cab's door opens. She hears the driver seat's suspension hiss, listens to the clicks and taps as he secures his phone in a cradle and snaps on his seatbelt. She peers through a crack between blackout drapes with an unblinking eye, grateful that the only mirrors are mounted outside the truck's cab. He'll have to turn around to spot her.

Her lips move in a silent incantation.

It's no easy task, what she has in mind. It requires study and concentration, and the most elusive element of all: memory. She observes and mentally records the movement of the driver's every limb: left leg rising and falling in concert with his right arm, which is doing the shifting; right foot on the accelerator; left hand on the wheel. He's a moving marionette, a tap dancer, a drummer. Such shifts come effortlessly to him, as does the coordination of all these actions, but not to Tia Dalma, who takes additional time to understand the patterns.

When she is confident in her knowledge, she begins speaking the curse again, this time in a soft whisper, like wind through a screen door. With each repetition of the verse her voice grows infinitesimally louder. She is in no hurry. All in good time.

It's not long before the driver shakes his head as if fighting off fatigue. Rubs his eyes. Pinches the bridge of his nose. Checks the cab's air-conditioning system. Rolls down his window, ruffling the blackout drapes. Tia Dalma leans back. She does not interrupt her chant, which she now speaks in a normal voice; he can hear her well enough, yet he does not react. By now her voice is like music in his head, a song he's never heard but can't get out of his thoughts. A song that owns him.

Tia Dalma owns him. Her fingers have begun working the doll, testing her control—little gestures such as bringing a hand to his cheek or tapping his fingers on the steering wheel. Soon she's the puppeteer, the one driving the truck. She accidently weaves the big rig out of its lane on the highway, drawing honking horns; she grinds a few gears, but gets the hang of it.

"You will do as I say," she tells him, and is pleased when he does not respond. "You will do as I wish." She allows that a moment to sink in. "Acknowledge."

"I will do as you say. I will do as you wish."

"Drive on," she says, willing him into a semiconscious state that allows him to follow his course yet question nothing. He utters no complaint, offers no resistance.

"Drive on," he echoes.

She seeks this control not for the mundane business of driving a truck, but for the opportunity to take over once the driver has delivered them inside Disneyland's backstage area. She must be able to cleanly start the truck from a stop, drive to a different destination than the one he intends, and pull over in an area less populated by Cast Members. An area that will allow her to unload her precious cargo.

132

For now, she sits back and lets him drive. Everything in good time.

* * *

Back inside the container on the truck's trailer, things aren't going as smoothly. The Evil Queen grows concerned.

ᴊᴋChernabog is clearly impatient. He keeps fidgeting, trying to get comfortable, growing frustrated by their confinement. Without warning, he lets loose a hideous roar and slams his elbow into the container wall. The metal screeches in protest.[25]

"Calm down!" the Queen says. But they both know who's in charge. Chernabog doesn't speak; his communication seems to involve a combination of telepathy, body language, and facial expressions. She hears or senses his desire for her to mind her place; hears or senses that he's tired of the backs of trucks; understands he's tired, and likely hungry and thirsty too. She watched him in the temple tunnels, feeding on rats and mice like they were finger food, drinking gallons of water at a time. For such a massive beast, he has lightning reflexes.

But patience is not his most salient quality. The Queen doesn't appreciate being locked in a warm container with him.

ᴊᴋHis power may be a great asset, but it is also a problem. He does not know when or how to stop killing. Death is his solution to everything. Tia Dalma is right to worry about the consequences of his actions. There's no telling when he might decide that one or another of the Overtakers is a threat, no telling what he might do in that instance. But they need him. He is the chosen one, the most evil of Walt Disney's creations. His judgment can be compared to that of a child, swift and

---

[25] Power_Accelerator

often emotional, not logical. This dangerous combination of attributes is enough to cause concern; but his power so transcends that of any mortal being that it more than makes up for his deficiencies. Her job is to humor him.[26]

"It will not be long, my Lord," the Queen says. "Upon arrival there will be much to feast upon. Your kingdom awaits!"

His eyes glow yellow, then red, signaling rage. In the months of their confinement she has learned to read him—knows him better than the Black Mamba, better than he knows himself. In this way, the Queen has her own powers, powers she has chosen not to reveal just yet. She covers her ears. He lets out a roar loud enough for others outside to hear.[27]

She wants to tell him to shut up, but she likes having a head on her shoulders. She knows better than to rile him.

Her problems are compounded when the truck encounters stop-and-go traffic. The starting and stopping throw her and the Beast repeatedly off balance. It's uncomfortable and bruising. His impatience builds. She tries to console him.

"It is the others, my Lord. The iron horses. They form long lines. We are but the tail of the snake, never able to reach the head."

We are the might and power above all else, he somehow communicates—so clearly, like a voice in her ears. *We are the head of the snake, the heart of the lion, the teeth of the jackal. We part the clouds and shake the earth. Who dares challenge such claims?*

The Queen wonders if she's simply imagining his thoughts, if fear triggers such impulses. The brooding look in his oversize bull's eyes assures her that she has understood him correctly.

---

[26] Holographic_Imagineering
[27] Kingdom_Willatree

"Only fools, my Lord," she answers. One doesn't contradict a twelve-foot-tall bat god. She has seen him in this state before—irreconcilable, unpredictable, unstoppable.

She wills the truck to start moving, begs him to stay calm, but this monster knows no such state. Since Tia Dalma restored him to power in the ceremony at the jungle temple, Chernabog is an entity unto himself—forthright, impatient, and inconsolable.

ЖHe growls, takes several steps to the back, and dents the container wall with a blow of his massive fist. He tears through the truck's back door, not minding the possible consequences.[28]

"My Lord, to reveal oneself to the enemy prematurely is not a decision to take lightly."

As she speaks, he tears the hole wider.

ЖThe car trailing them pulls over to the side of the road. The driver has his window down and phone out, videoing the strange occurrences in the truck ahead.[29] The Queen would like to throw a curse onto the driver, but it's more important to keep Chernabog off the video. She dares to reach out and tug on his folded wing. Her Lord does not appreciate such contact.

His wing extends, throwing her into the boxes. He pivots, prepared to strike.

"The mortals have magical memory," she says, crawling away from him. "The metal bricks they hold capture our every movement."

He clomps toward her. Snorting, he glances back toward the gaping hole. She can feel him contemplating whether or not to confiscate the driver's phone. She can see that cloven hoof, so close he could stomp the life out of her.

---

[28] Kingdom_Willatree
[29] Kingdom_Willatree

"Better not to be seen just now, don't you think?" Depending on what the driver does with the video, they could already be in serious trouble. Life is a stage—immortal life a vast stage indeed.

"They can make stories with these bricks. Stories like ours, yours, and mine. We do not need such stories—incorrect ones—poisoning thought prior to the beginning of the End. They will only serve to challenge our position."

He blinks his strange inner eyelids. She perceives that he understands, though can't explain to herself how it might be so.

"Best we surprise them." She knows he understands surprise.

He grunts.

The Evil Queen accepts the small victory showing absolutely no expression.

17

$\mathbf{I}$NSIDE THE TOWERING CONFINES of Stage 6, one boy sits alone, cross-legged in a sea of green. He seems small and insignificant, drowning in all the color.

A tired Finn Whitman glances at his watch for the umpteenth time, shoots a look at Philby in the control room, and shakes his head in disappointment. Adjusting the microphone of his headset, Finn says softly, "You think she can't fall asleep? The excitement or something?"

"I told you: she crossed over thirty-five minutes ago."

"Makes no sense."

"I see her!" It's Willa's voice, crackling over the headset. "The back of the Frank—"

"I've got her!" says Maybeck over the airwaves. He and Willa can't see each other, but between them, they're able to keep watch over the three back lot streets with access to Stage 6.

"Finally!" Finn says, standing.

"Go easy on her, Finn," Maybeck says. "If she's late, there's a reason."

"The reason being, she's your girlfriend?" asks Willa.

"Shut . . . up!" Maybeck says. Three peals of nervous laughter fill the headsets.

Charlene enters the cavernous space. Like Finn, she appears to have shrunk; she looks tiny and insignificant against the enormous soundstage. She gracefully crosses to Finn, excited and with a palpable sense of urgency, rushing her words as she spills out the news of what she has overheard in the conference room. Her report is delivered in broken sentences punctuated by purposeful pauses as she collects her thoughts, trying but failing not to color her tale with emotion. The others hear her breathlessness over Finn's headset microphone; she sounds like a young child whose closet door pops open of its own accord, awakening her in the middle of a deep sleep.

"Once again," Finn says, once Charlene has finished.

"'An enemy within,'" Charlene repeats. "A mission for us, but they don't trust us, and they fear our power."

"The OTs murdered some guy?" Finn's hopeful tone begs her to correct him, to tell him he's heard her wrong.

"She's nodding," Finn tells the others via the headset. "She's nodding and she's scared."

"Took his head off," Charlene gasps.

"So it's come to this," Finn says, his voice full of unmistakable desperation and profound disappointment. "First Dill. Now some complete stranger."

"Don't go there," Willa says through the headset. "Tia Dalma tricked you, Finn. You can't go on blaming yourself. It wasn't your fault. It's—"

"They're *murderers*," Finn says bitterly. "They've killed two people, maybe more. For all we know, they'll kill us without a second thought."

Philby's voice: "'An enemy within.'"

"I caught that the first time," Maybeck says. "That's trash talk, and we all know it."

Finn says, "A secret midnight meeting to talk about a *rumor*? I don't think so. If they're going to that kind of trouble, they must have evidence. Right or wrong, they think it's at least a strong possibility."

Collective silence floods the airwaves. In the silence, sparks of spitting static echo like fireworks.

"We can talk about this later," Philby says. "I've got to get the bugs out of v1.6. If we're facing murderers, we need every advantage we can get. Besides, I've got a surprise for you all." He pauses. "Maybeck?"

"Here."

"Get your butt over to the Legends statue. Make sure no one sees you. Bring back our guests."

"Guests?" Finn says.

"That's my surprise," says Philby.

* * *

⽊"Well, what are you waiting for? Go say hi!" Jess says, nudging Amanda.

A flood of emotions ripples through Amanda: the rush of crossing over as a DHI; of vanishing from her bed in Mrs. Nash's house in Florida and appearing in Walt Disney Studios in California; the idea of helping the Keepers take down the Overtakers; and more than anything, seeing Finn for the first time since the prom. They are magically within reach of one another.[30]

The group, standing scattered around the green-screen stage, waits awkwardly, sensing the moment between Finn and Amanda.

⽊Finn can't read her, has no idea what she's feeling. Is she happy to see him? Angry because of his ditching her at the prom? He resists an urge to hug her; doesn't know how she'll react; can't risk it.

After several tense seconds of staring, Finn rubs the back of his neck, trying to disperse his nervous tension. He can feel the eyes of each of the other Keepers on him; his stomach

---

[30] Amanda_Hologram

twists into knots, and he can't make himself talk. He is so pleased to see Amanda, but he doesn't know how to express himself. First, he tries a grin. Seeing disappointment on her face, he summons a burst of courage and steps in for a kiss. On the cheek.[31]

Maybeck, who has returned to his lookout, groans and says over the headphones, "I heard that."

Amanda awkwardly glances away as fast as possible. Throughout her time as a Fairlie, she has struggled to remain independent. She's only given her full trust to Jess, and only then after a long, testing friendship. She feels she can trust Finn; they have an undeniable connection. But their pasts are so different. Is it possible they are more than the closest of friends? After all this time, can she still be unsure? *Sometimes life is about learning to surf the waves you can't stop.* She can't recall who told her this, but it seemed important at the time. Should she heed the advice now?

"Hey!" Finn's voice breaks apart her thoughts. This is it.[32]

She finally allows her face to break into a giant, lovely smile. He grins back with that same sweetness she always sees in him. She knows she's supposed to say something, but a lump catches in her throat. Memories flood her: the prom, the cruise. Tears spring up in her eyes.

"You okay?" Finn asks.

Butterflies swarm in her stomach. She hears fireworks in her head. She wants to hug him, to burst into honest tears and tell him how much she has missed him.[33]

"Doing great," she says, lying.

Philby exits the control room and enters the stage area.

---

[31] Imagineering_Sorcery
[32] Amanda_Hologram
[33] Popcorn_Seek

After confirming that Willa and Maybeck can hear him over their headsets, he addresses Jess.

"Tell them what you told me in your e-mail."

"Another dream," she says, reaching into her pocket with a rueful smile. "The more things change—hey, guys?"

She attempts to hand Finn a folded piece of paper, but his fingers pass through its projected light, and it sticks to Jess' hand like flypaper, a part of her hologram. She and Amanda are less experienced as DHIs; Jess seems uncomfortable with her present state of immateriality.

Philby eyes the sheet of paper, still impossible to disassociate from Jess's DHI. "There's an interesting bug. The fob has never had that problem." For a brief flash, he sounds like Professor Philby. "I can work on that as well. We need to get started."

"Hold on a second!" Finn says, a little too loudly.

Jess holds up the unfolded sheet of sketch paper for all to see. It shimmers, framed by a thin blue line. Like so many renditions of her dream visions, this is a collage of images and words, some faint, some bold. They mix and combine on the page in a sprawl of abstract confusion. Her visions are more foretelling than fortune-telling; they often lack specifics or misread entire parts of a message. Jess is no Rembrandt, but she's capable of telling stories with images. She's a good enough illustrator to capture her recollections of her dreams and depict them boldly.

Then again, sometimes Jess's dreams are nothing more than night-bound fantasies, fears, and hopes taking flight in an overactive imagination; sometimes her dreams probe deeply into a crystal ball, defying all understanding of time's hold on human consciousness. Only Einstein might be able to explain Jess's supernatural ability to see around the curve of the present into the blur of the future.

But she has repeated this feat too many times for the Keepers to consider it mere luck or diagnose it as the result of some chemical or hormonal imbalance. Her vision makes her more than special; it makes her unique, important. She is a lens through which the Keepers can anticipate the ambushes of the Overtakers.

The collage is busy and requires thorough study, for which none of the Keepers presently has time. It contains, among other images, a ski lift gondola; the bolded words **If Cars, Ice**; a long climbing flight of stairs reminiscent of what the Imagineers have dubbed "Escher's Keep" in the Cinderella Castle; the horns of a monster that all recognize as Chernabog; a doll; and the Mexican temple where Dillard died at Finn's hand. In the center of this confusion is a magic lantern—an ancient oil lamp—puffing a series of translucent steam clouds from its curved spout. It's beautifully shaded and realistic. Among the clouds of steam float words *A wry snake is the key*, partially obscured by shading. Shoe prints and cat paw prints wind confusingly like a net around and across the other images.

"What does it mean?" Finn asks.

"In my dream, the lantern was important. I saw you, Finn, out of breath and facing it. You rubbed it and—"

"I rubbed it?" Finn says.

"And then disappeared," says Amanda anxiously.

"Yeah," Jess says to her sister, as if continuing an argument, "but maybe I awoke then, before I could see what happened."

"You did not awake. You saw a snake."

"But it could have been a different dream."

"You were scared. You woke up scared. You told me that. Finn was in trouble."

"Finn is *always* in trouble in your dreams, Jess," Willa says.

"Not *always*," Jess replies disagreeably.

"In a large percentage of them then."

"Explain the words," the Professor says. "The 'Cars' thing, the snake thing."

"Cars Land," Willa says into the headsets. "California Adventure. Ice? Maybe the mountains in the scenery?"

Finn repeats her words for the sake of Amanda and Jess, who don't have headsets. Heads bob. Only Philby ever beats Willa to such instant analysis. It's a competition between them.

"The snake," Jess says timidly. "It's true what Amanda said: I did have a nightmare involving this humongous snake and Finn. But the words . . . I don't know. I draw what I see. You know? That's where the words—those exact words—belong on the page. I know that sounds stupid—"

"It doesn't." The Professor is the final arbiter of what is and is not considered stupid. He has passed judgment. "The brain's subconscious functions cannot—"

Maybeck makes a loud snoring sound over the headset. Charlene covers her smile. Philby reddens, highlighting his ginger complexion, but recovers quickly.

"Any explanation for the articles and the verb being less important? Only 'wry,' 'snake,' and 'key' are shaded."

"You're killing me here, Philby," says Maybeck.

Jess levels sympathetic eyes on Philby as she shakes her head. "I draw what I see."

"Why so urgent?" Philby asks. "Your text—" He pauses, then explains to the others, "Jess texted me, saying that they needed to cross over, needed to see us tonight."

"Actually, I asked you first what color shirt Finn was wearing," Jess says.

"True. I forgot that part."

"And you said a blue polo." Jess nods to Finn, who is, in fact, wearing a blue polo. "That did it for me. I was dreaming

143

about . . . I saw Finn in my dream," she says, lowering her head demurely, "in a blue shirt."

"But Finn isn't crossed over," Charlene says bluntly, "I am." She reaches one arm through the other to demonstrate her current state as a DHI. Jess looks hurt by Charlene's combative tone, and averts her eyes to the ground. "Philby is debugging version 1.6."

Finn addresses Philby. "Tell me you weren't thinking what I was thinking, after what Charlie told us."

"I admit, it crossed my mind," Philby says.

"Whoa! Wait a sec," Charlene says. "If he's going, I'm going."

"I need you here," Philby says. "I'm in the middle of coding. We won't get chances like this. If Finn goes, it's with someone else. You and I are busy."

"That would be me," Maybeck says over the intercom. "A magic lantern? A giant snake? I gotta see this."

"That's an effective team," Philby says.

"Can we go?" Amanda asks too hopefully. "Jess and me?"

"I can't reroute you once you're crossed over in this version. That's what Charlene was saying. I'd need to return you. You would then need to wake up, signal me, and go back to sleep. It's complicated. And most of the time—for us, anyway—it's pretty rugged trying to get back to sleep after crossing over. I'm usually wired. I think we all are."

"But we could try," Amanda says. "As long as it doesn't slow you all down."

Maybeck's voice fills the headphones. "It would be awesome to have Amanda's ability to 'push,' and Jess's future vision along for the ride."

Willa calls out a warning: a Security patrol appears to be making the rounds, including a door-to-door check. Moments later, Maybeck confirms. Philby runs for the master light switch on a control board. "Behind the green!" he shouts.

As a group, the kids move toward the immense green screen, which hangs a foot in front of the back wall. They slip behind it single file.

When the lights pop, the building fills with the kind of darkness found only in outer space or inside intestines. "Not you!" Philby's winded voice calls. "Mandy, Jess! I can see you back there!"

The glowing DHIs look like one large luminescent blob behind the green screen cyclorama. Philby hurries, stumbling and tripping in the dark. He meets up with the Fairlies, opens a protective case on wheels, and directs them to climb into the virtual coffin. He locks them inside, twisting the last butterfly clasp shut as he hears the door to the soundstage open. He drops face down and belly crawls around and behind the wheeled case in which he's hidden Amanda and Jess.

"Cover up!" Philby hisses to Charlene. She wraps a soundstage quilt around her to mute her glow.

The guard's flashlight sweeps the cavernous space. The man is sniffing the air, a hound following a scent. Perfume? Philby wonders. The aroma of theater lights as they warm? Human sweat? Because by this point Philby is a geyser.

The guard moves across the soundstage toward the green screen concealing the Keepers.

The door sounds like a brush sweeping the floor as it opens.

"You with me?" a gruff male voice calls.

"Coming," says the guard nearest to the green screen.

"We got the Wells and the TDB to do, floor by floor. You want me to die of nicotine starvation?"

"That's your curse, not mine. And it's against the rules, FYI."

"Yes, *Mom*. Sometime *this lifetime* would be nice."

"Ha-ha."

"Food! Turkey sandwich?" the gruff voice calls. Philby hears the sound of him sniffing as well.

"See? I'm not insane. And it smells fresh!"

"It's probably the lights. This look like the commissary to you?"

"Exactly."

"Exactly, what?" The gruff voice is unhappy and impatient.

"It's warmer in here. Did you notice? Noticeably warmer, like the lights have been on."

"So they shot something in here today."

"They did not," the closer man answers. "Nothing scheduled."

"You work too hard. Gotta get a life."

"Or you, not hard enough."

"That stings."

"Fresh food. Warmth, from the lights. What's that add up to for you?" The guard has not stopped moving. Philby, lying on the floor, can see the man's black running shoes through the gap beneath the case. He's getting closer.

"I have no idea where you're going with this," the gruff man says. "You want me to turn on the lights? Or can we get out of here?"

The flashlight's beam paints an arc across the gray concrete next to Philby's left leg. Philby pulls into a ball behind the case, losing his view of the man's shoes.

"I'm telling you: someone's been working in here tonight! I walked this stage not three hours ago. It wasn't this warm in here and it didn't smell like Chick-fil-A!"

"Probably Joe and his team. It's their job. How about we do ours and walk the Wells?" The gruff voice pauses. "What's with you, anyway?"

146

"Joe and his bunch had the conference room booked in the Wells. Do you read *any* of the memos?"

Talk about smell: Philby can make out the man's cologne or deodorant, a sickly combination of fruit and musk. He's that close.

The guard bumps the case. A girl's muffled voice emits a cry of surprise.

Then: silence. Total silence. The kind of silence that runs shivers up and down Philby, who twists his neck to look up at the back of the case. If he needs to run, he wants the benefit of a head start.

He hears the *click, click* of the case's butterfly clasps coming unlocked.

Not good. The girls are in there.

"You hear that? Come over here!" the guard calls to his partner. At the same moment, he lifts the lid of the case warily, only an inch or two.

The DHIs of Amanda and Jess erupt out *through* the lid of the box, waving their arms overhead and bending from side to side, cooing and wailing in eerie tones. As the shocked guard jumps back and yelps, dropping the lid, the girls continue to writhe, visible only from their waists up, glowing, swaying.

The man cusses and swings a nightstick at the girls— Philby sees the end of the stick overhead—but hits nothing but air.

"*Gho-o-o-o-osts!*" he yells at the top of his lungs.

In theory, the two men must have run from the sound-stage, but in physical terms, Philby thinks it must have been closer to flying. The time between the guard's cry and the slamming of the door clear across the vast building approaches the speed of light.

The two DHIs hug and giggle.

Philby stands. "That was brilliant!" he says, sounding more British than usual. His childhood accent—a consequence of his having grown up in England—comes out when he's nervous.

Charlene and Finn emerge from behind the green screen. When Finn asks what happened, Amanda and Jess break into hysterical laughter.

Over the next few minutes, Philby preps Charlene for her green-screen work; Willa repositions herself, climbing a ladder on the back of Stage 6 in order to reach its roof, where she becomes the only lookout; Finn returns to his dorm room and climbs into bed, well accustomed to calming himself in order drift off to sleep and cross over.

Amanda, determined not to be left out, and giving everyone the sense she and Jess are keeping something to themselves, pressures Philby into returning the two, which will put them in their beds in Mrs. Nash's house. Then she wants Philby to cross them over into Disneyland. Philby makes no promises.

Willa, who operates on the same cerebral plane as Philby, has requested he photograph Jess's illustration and text it to her. She promises to "begin analysis" immediately from her rooftop perch, using her smartphone.

In a ten-minute period, the Keepers have delegated the needed responsibilities among them, assumed those responsibilities, and taken steps to spread themselves across a continent in order to rejoin forces in Disneyland, where, if all goes well—and too often, it doesn't!—they will seek answers to questions that have yet to be asked. All they have is Finn's blue shirt somehow telling them they must go tonight, and a magic lantern emitting steam-driven alphabet soup phrases that mean nothing to anyone.

Just another night as a Kingdom Keeper.

18

MAYBECK AND FINN CROSS OVER at the Partners statue on the plaza in front of Sleeping Beauty Castle. As soon as they're stabilized, Maybeck drags Finn by the arm into the shadow of the Jolly Holiday café.

"Cameras," he whispers. "Philby's worried about the cameras."

Disneyland's already protective Security team may be on a state of heightened alert, given that recent activities point to Overtaker movement and interference. Park Security wouldn't target the Keepers, but they aren't about to overlook a couple of kids inside the park after closing, either.

"Got it," Finn says, shaking loose Maybeck's strong grip. He looks down at where Maybeck's hand was. "Don't do that again, okay? It pulled me out of all clear."

"I scared you," Maybeck says proudly.

"Startled. The only advantage we have, Terry, is staying pure DHI. If we go even a little bit solid . . . not good."

"Yeah. Sorry about that."

An apology from Maybeck would typically be cause for a national holiday, a parade, and fireworks. The glee on Finn's face expresses this. Maybeck shifts closer to the street leading into Adventureland.

"We're close," he says.

"Yeah."

"So, let's get going."

"Not that way. We're going to head toward the front gates."

"Why?"

"Because if anyone saw us as we crossed over, we can't afford to lead them into the Bazaar. We'll be trapped. It's called the art of deception."

"But if they can follow us on camera, how does deception help? What does it matter? That's stupid, Whitman. The enemy here is time, not park Security. We've got to hurry. The only thing your deception does is waste time."

"We head away from our destination," Finn explains. "Then we get backstage where there aren't cameras following our every move. Look, arguing about it wastes even more time. Follow me."

Finn sets out down Main Street. Maybeck keeps a step behind, grunting his displeasure. Finn cuts to the right, staying in shadow; arriving at a white wall, he walks through it, Maybeck right behind him.

"How cool is it to be one of the Keeps?" Maybeck says, forgetting his earlier aggravation.

They're in the woods of the Jungle Cruise. Finn heads off to the right, in the direction of the docks.

"Okay, I get it," Maybeck says. "You could have said we were going to sneak around back of the Jolly Holiday. Good idea."

"What have you done with the real Terry Maybeck?" Finn asks.

"Ha-ha. Very funny. Credit where credit's due."

"Since when?"

"Charlene," Maybeck says. "Since Charlene."

"Yeah," Finn says. "Changes things, doesn't it?"

"You, too?"

"Oh, yeah."

"I can be a real jerk," Maybeck says, seeing Finn's reaction.

150

"Have been, at times. But my life has been radically different from any of you guys'."

"Understood. No argument."

"Charlene accepts me for who I am. You know? And I don't exactly get it, but that makes me want to be different from who I am. Better. Not sure that makes sense."

"It does."

Maybeck feels exposed, like he's lost his pants or something. In that moment, a thread connects him to Finn, and it's as though electricity is being exchanged between their DHIs, as though something strange is happening. He senses it's a moment he will not only remember but treasure for a long time. Friendship is an elusive, gooey thing; it shrinks with the cold, expands in the heat; it has ways of vanishing right before your eyes; or of appearing out of nowhere. This is a moment—right now—in which it proves sticky.

"Let's do this thing," Maybeck says. "Let's go rub ourselves a genie!"

Finn doesn't speak, but despite his silence, despite the v1.6 software and projection, despite the fact that they come from different worlds and were thrown together only by chance, he shows excitement, acceptance, and . . .

Finn takes off across the open concourse, glows briefly, and then is absorbed by the darkness of the Bazaar. Maybeck follows at a run.

Inside, Finn can see by the glow of his own DHI. A newcomer to the Bazaar, Finn moves to his right, arriving at shelves of hammered brass plates, cups, and pitchers. He might be able to convince himself that the pitchers are the lantern he seeks, but there are a dozen of them and they're tall and narrow, nothing like Jess's sketch.

Maybeck passes behind him. "This way," he says, though

he has no more clue where he's going than Finn does. Yet, he leads them to a small alcove, more like an open closet containing a low table. A bejeweled lantern sits atop it. On the wall above it is a sign, but the area's too dark to read it.

"You suppose I just rub it?" Finn asks Maybeck.

"There's something not right about this," Maybeck says.

"The jewels? I don't remember any jewels in her drawing."

"Something else, I think."

Finn's hand pauses over the ancient oil lamp. He lowers his palm and rubs it. Nothing happens.

"Try again. Are you thinking of something you want?"

Finn removes his hand, pauses. He rubs it again.

Nothing.

"Well, that's awkward," Maybeck says.

"It isn't real. It's a tourist attraction. Nothing more."

The voice does not belong to Maybeck.

Finn turns to see Jafar, Aladdin's nemesis, standing with his legs spread wide, arms crossed, his red-lined robe flowing, scepter in hand. His parrot, Iago, perches on his left shoulder, shifting its head back and forth inquisitively.

Maybeck gives in to his bad habit of swearing at such moments.

The Keepers have faced Jafar before to bad results. Finn wants nothing to do with him. With Maleficent's death, Jafar is among the most powerful sorcerers in all the Kingdom, capable of levitation, fire breathing, and transfiguration; his scepter can hypnotize with the barest gesture from its master. Even his parrot is smarter and more dangerous than he looks.

"Keep clear," Finn says, reminding Maybeck to keep fear out of his DHI.

Easier said than done; Finn's hands and feet tingle, causing him to wonder how vulnerable he might be to attack.

Most troubling of all, Jafar, an expert at impersonation, has not bothered to put on any disguise. He apparently has no use for such a ruse, which suggests he has no reason to attempt to manipulate the two boys.

Which suggests he intends to kill them.

"No way I'm clear," Maybeck whispers in a rare admission of weakness.

It's a complication they didn't need. Finn had hoped to make a run for it, possibly through the wall to his left into the hat display beyond.

"I wonder what it is you wished for," Jafar says. His inquisitive eyes bore into Finn, as if Jafar is attempting to read his thoughts.

As long as Finn can keep the sorcerer's mind active, he can buy time for himself and Maybeck. "I killed Maleficent."

Turns out not even a sorcerer can keep surprise from his face.

"I tore her heart out." Finn reaches over to Maybeck and demonstrates, sliding his hand into Maybeck's DHI shoulder. "I'll do it to you if you make me."

"I don't believe you."

"Yes, you do. Our mission is to end you. We didn't understand that at first—we're just *kids*, after all," he says sarcastically. "No one has ever told us straight out. They didn't hire us as assassins. We think of ourselves more as bounty hunters. Capture you. Bring all of you to justice. But it's not as if you'll go willingly. It's not as if there's any other justice for murderers."

Maybeck has stopped breathing. Still as stone, he stares at Finn as if it's the first time they've met and he's not sure he likes this guy.

"Tia Dalma tricked me into killing my friend," Finn confesses. He struggles to get his words out. "I will end her for it."

The tingling has receded; Finn knows he can endure any amount of magic or ill intent this wizened old man can dish out. He has Dill on his side; he has Lady Justice.

He takes a step forward. Jafar involuntarily takes a step back, and Finn knows he has him. The sense of power he experiences is its own poison; it's how the Overtakers must feel, and he wants nothing to do with them, nothing to do with the assumption of personal power. He makes it about Dillard, about working toward a greater good—not vengeance, but liberation. He's a freedom fighter, not a hired gun.

The slight bluish glow from his DHI reveals a set of muddy prints on the concrete floor, a trail Finn hasn't seen until now. He does not dare to take his eyes off Jafar for another millisecond, but he processes what he's seen and counts his blessings that Jess and the Fairlies are on their side. Her drawing showed cat's paw tracks going in two directions. Another glance at the floor confirms it: there's a concave arc of prints traced on the concrete.

How to communicate what he's discovered to Maybeck?

He addresses Jafar. "There is a song—music—my parents play. One of my dad's favorites." He shoots a look at Maybeck to make sure he has his attention. Maybeck has not moved. All good. "Turn, Turn, Turn." Another glance to Maybeck; this time Finn sweeps his eyes to include the floor. Is Maybeck paying attention? He appears to be in a trance. "Iago!" Finn calls to the parrot. "The band was called the Byrds." He pauses and quotes, "'To everything, turn, turn, turn.'" Another hot glance at Maybeck and then the floor.

"Why should I care for such a song?" Jafar says irritably. Finn has rattled him with the news of Maleficent's death. But he and the remaining Overtakers must have assumed such an outcome. Or has Tia Dalma been in touch and assumed control but withheld the truth of the tragedy from them? Will she, could she, cause division in their ranks?

Perhaps there is a way to defeat the Overtakers other than violence.

Maybeck speaks. "Was it vinyl?" he asks Finn. "A vinyl album?"

"Yes!" Finn says.

"Played on a turntable?"

"Yes!"

"Quiet!" Jafar strikes the floor with the base of his scepter. The eyes of its snake's head glow.

"Don't look!" Finn admonishes, lowering his gaze, knowing Jafar has the advantage now. The snake's head can and will hypnotize them if they slip even fractionally out of their DHI state. Unable to see Jafar, he cannot possibly anticipate what might come next. He must remind the sorcerer that he is still of substantial value alive.

Finn says, "My wish is a powerful one."

"And I will hear it before you die," Jafar says.

"Unlikely," Finn says.

"We'll rip your lungs out," Maybeck tells Jafar. "We'll watch you suffocate." Maybeck knows such bravado will win a telling and condemning look, Finn realizes, watching his friend take a step toward the lantern. Maybeck reaches for it.

"Unhand that!" Jafar roars.

"It's just a tourist attraction," Finn says, moving to screen Maybeck with his body. Maybeck isn't rubbing the lantern, but wrestling it back and forth in an attempt to turn it right or left. He lets go.

"Zilch," Maybeck says.

Finn can hardly believe it. "But it must—!" he gasps.

"No," Maybeck says.

"*Silence!*" Jafar thumps his scepter again. Behind him, pieces of jewelry fall from the displays, and as they strike the ground, the necklaces break and stretch and morph into black snakes. Slithering into a writhing knot, they roil on the ground at Jafar's feet, hissing and striking at each other, so eager are they for a kill.

"Relieve yourself of the trinket!" Jafar instructs Maybeck.

"Was the song *rock* or folk?" Maybeck asks.

"Ah!" Finn says.

The snakes unwind, fan out, and approach the boys. Finn steps back, bumping into the table holding the lantern. Maybeck smacks into the wall, and he and Finn start poking and pulling the stones that comprise it.

"*Stop!*" Jafar opens his mouth and spews a stream of molten fire. It hits the wall next to Maybeck and begins to spread. Maybeck falls, reaching for a tassel hanging from the sign to catch himself. He grabs hold of it, his fear giving weight to his DHI. The tassel pulls down and stops.

The concrete floor spins beneath their feet.

Maybeck jumps away from the snakes, landing on top of the table that bears the genie's lamp. He and Finn, along with the lamp, table, and wall behind them, have spun 180 degrees. They're on the other side of the same wall, the Bazaar and Jafar safely behind them. They find themselves in a tunnel, with flaming torches like sconces lining its stone walls.

"Took me a second," Maybeck says. "Turn, turn, turn. Turntable. The floor. How'd you know? I must be tired."

"Nice job with the tassel." Finn is propped on the opposite end of the short table, looking down at the snakes that made the trip with them.

"Yeah. That was certainly my first choice."

156

"Jafar'll be—"

"Whitman!" Maybeck stabs the air, indicating something behind Finn. It's the head of a cobra, pinched in the crack in the moveable wall like a shoe keeping a door from closing. Its head is the size of a football, its body like a fire hose. To the naked eye, it appears stationary, but the head is *moving* away from the gap in the wall. The cobra is pushing through to their side.

"—right behind us!" Finn cries, finishing his thought while leaping away from the wall. Half the small snakes immediately swim toward him in an undulating wave of shiny skin. "Come on!"

"Finn, I hate snakes."

"Hate them down here with me before that thing has you for lunch." He points to Jafar's transfigured snake shape. "It's *him*! We've got to get out of here."

Maybeck lands next to Finn, and they run. The tunnel arcs to their left.

"If he gets stuck, we're in luck," Maybeck says.

"Since when have we ever been lucky?"

"Point to you."

From behind them comes the sound of the partition closing. Jafar, the cobra, is through.

Finn gets another look at the floor, illuminated in flashes by the flickering torchlight. The same muddy prints are there. Too big for a cat. His brain is in the act of processing this difference when a bone-chilling roar sounds from the flame-lit dusk.

"Oh!" Finn says, skidding to a stop. "*That* kind of cat."

"What?"

"Never mind," Finn says.

A Bengal tiger the size of a Smart car appears out of the

darkness. Its rumbling growl resounds to the depths of the cavelike tunnel.

Sighting the boys, it lowers onto its front haunches, ready to spring.

Maybeck looks back. The giant cobra is moving toward them faster than the boys can run, catching up to the smaller snakes that are also hard on the boys' heels. "Pickle!" Maybeck says, citing a baseball term, though he doesn't have much patience for the sport: when a runner trapped between bases is run down by the opposing team's players, who are trying to tag the runner out, that's a pickle. The runner rarely, if ever, escapes.

The tiger leaps. Maybeck's far-too-solid DHI is knocked to the ground. His life flashes before his eyes. He feels the jaws tear into his shoulder, can picture the pool of—

"Come on!"

Maybeck opens his eyes. It's Finn's face; and it's Finn's fingers tearing into his shoulder, not the cat's teeth. Maybeck is paralyzed—he can't move. The tiger snaps up two of the black snakes like a robin feasting on worms. Then it skids to a stop, facing the giant cobra.

"Hurry!" Finn says, giving Maybeck a hand and pulling him to his feet. The boys flee down the tunnel. "That's Rajah, Princess Jasmine's protector."

"I think I missed that movie."

"Rajah must know we're the good guys, or at least, that a fifteen-foot cobra can't be."

The cat roars. The boys stop and turn to watch. Rajah and Jafar face each other, first moving counterclockwise, then doubling back. Counterclockwise again. Testing. Challenging.

The cat's claws swipe the snake, which hisses and rears up. It flares its hood and strikes. Rajah jukes to the side; Jafar misses. But Jafar is wily; he's slowly turning Rajah, pushing the cat's tail up against the stone and limiting Rajah's movements. Turning Rajah like this also provides the cobra with an opening down the tunnel toward the boys.

"He's coming! Let's go!" Maybeck says.

"I can't!" says Finn, edging closer to the duel.

"Are you *crazy?*"

"He saved us."

The cobra has pinned Rajah back onto his rear haunches. Rajah paws at the snake, but Jafar's too clever by far.

"Go! Find out where this leads!"

"As if!" Maybeck says.

"Find a door. Hold it for me and the cat. Be ready to close it the second we're through!"

"Finn—"

"Do it! Now!"

Maybeck shakes his head, takes in the scene. "I—"

"Move!"

Maybeck runs.

Finn gathers himself as he has a dozen times. He silences the noises of the battle, quiets the doubting voices in his head, imagines a pinprick of light in a sea of darkness. Normally, he need not do this routine when in his DHI state, but he's terrified, and it takes several long seconds to calm himself. His DHI glows a shade brighter.

Rajah's in trouble. Finn has no time to test his transparency. He runs toward the cobra, skidding to a stop. "I thought you wanted me, you withered old man!"

The cobra's head snaps toward Finn, its black tongue licking the air, tasting his scent. Without further warning, it strikes.

Finn closes his eyes.

The cobra soars through his DHI. Finn dares to peek; he spreads his legs to straddle the reptile.

Rajah sinks a claw into the body of the cobra. The snake rears up in pain. Finn, allowing panic to steal into him, rides the snake backward and is crushed against the overhead stone ceiling. The world goes black.

Finn comes awake bouncing, feeling what must be warm blood oozing over him. It takes him a second to realize he's in Rajah's mouth. The big cat has him in his jaws. The liquid he feels is not blood but cat drool—Rajah is carrying him as if a kitten.

A rectangle of artificial light glows ahead. Finn shifts slightly to adjust his vision: it's not a window, but a doorway. Maybeck is holding a door open twenty yards ahead.

Fifteen . . .

Ten . . .

Finn steals a look behind Rajah. Jafar in cobra form is coming for them as fast as a freight train. Fluid leaks from his fat tube of a body where Rajah tore him open. He's one unhappy cobra. His black eyes glitter with vengeance. He'll kill them both and revel in it.

Five . . .

The cat's head swings left, snaps right and releases Finn, who flies through the air—and through the door. Finn crashes to the pavement and rolls.

Maybeck slams the door, but too late. Once again, the cobra is half in, half out. It writhes to lengthen itself, its tongue lashing out at Maybeck. It rears up, puffs out, and strikes at Maybeck for a deadly blow—and comes up just short, its dripping fangs no more than an inch from Maybeck's face.

Jafar's snake eyes bulge. Rajah has hold of him, his sharp claws steadily hauling the snake back into the tunnel.

160

"Run!" Finn hollers.

At that instant, the snake vanishes, replaced by an ugly, long-bodied weasel with a bad cut in its back. The weasel's paws scrabble against the stones, and an instant later, it's gone.

The cat's head is visible through the gap in the door.

Finn waves. "Thank you, my friend!"

Maybeck looks back and forth between Finn and the eyes of the cat. "This, they're never going to believe," he says.

19

GETTING INTO THE CRYPT after hours isn't easy. Philby knows the routine involving the sliding door to the underground storage area, the deception created by the holograms of furniture, and the correct door to take. But it's locked. Joe must have used a key to enter the Crypt—and Philby has no key.

The one Keeper capable of lock picking is Willa, who learned the art from her younger brothers. Willa leaves her rooftop surveillance duty to take care of that task—a convenience for Philby, who appreciates the extra time with her.

Philby is an expert in all aspects of technology. He's a decent rock climber. His confidence is typically quite high; but at the moment he's glad he's not a DHI, because he's scared. His fear has nothing to do with sneaking into the Crypt.

"How are you doing?" he asks Willa.

"You mean other than—"

"This. Yes."

"I miss home. I'm sad to have missed graduation. I didn't bring enough clothes with me, and I'm beginning to feel like a prisoner. Other than that, it's all good."

"I meant . . ." Philby wonders why he can't seem to finish his sentences.

"Us."

"Well, yeah."

"Good, I guess."

Guess. She doesn't know.

He says, "I wish we had more time . . . together, I mean."

"We're together all the time," she says. "When *aren't* we together?"

He feels like an idiot. "Never mind."

She gets the door unlocked and Philby is in. She tells him to remember to lock it from the inside when he's through. Then she's gone, leaving Philby thinking that no matter what people say about him, he's really not so smart.

In the midst of data-mining the Crypt's servers for information that he is not supposed to access, Philby receives a surprising text from Amanda, saying that, as agreed, she and Jess are heading off to sleep in hopes of crossing over. The surprising news is that the Fairlies *must* cross over: Jess dozed off, had an elaborate and alarming dream, and has sketched the whole thing out—the Keepers are in danger.

Philby responds, grateful for the distraction, wondering if he can think up an excuse to bring Willa back down with him. He'd like the chance to start all over.

* * *

"It was the wrong lamp," Maybeck says. He's out of breath, bent over, clutching his knees in the shadows of the Jungle Cruise dock.

Finn, who's assumed a hands-on-hips pose similar to Peter Pan's, is also gulping for air. "What are you talking about?"

"The lamp."

"We should be talking about calling Philby so he can return us, not fake lamps. The nearest pay phone is over there." Finn points beyond the Bazaar. "The exact direction that weasel headed."

"Fake lamp? You think? You rub the thing and Jafar shows up and you're saying it's a fake?" Maybeck huffs derisively, trying to breathe. "It wasn't fake, it just wasn't the one from Jess's dream. If there's one thing I, personally, have learned about the parks, it's that *nothing* is fake. And by *nothing*, I mean: no thing, as in 'No Thing Fake!'"

Finn's DHI face twists with frustration. He closes his eyes. A moment later, his DHI strengthens and he's no longer out of breath.

Impressed, Maybeck tries closing his eyes. Nothing. He's still acting like a runner at the end of the four-by-one-hundred-meter relay. Through gulps of air, he speaks. "Jess rarely gets stuff wrong. There's a second lamp. Trust me."

"Since when are you all Mr. Positive?" Finn asks. "I like it."

"Part of my turning over a new leaf, in case you haven't noticed."

"We want to remember: that was Jafar. Snakes. A giant cobra. That wasn't negotiating tactics. He was trying to kill us."

"We're DHIs. "

"And if we slip up and we're snake bit as DHIs, then when we return we're still snake bit. As in: dead." Finn is trying not to sound scared.

"I got that. But he didn't bite us. And there's a second lamp somewhere. Look, we have to focus on what we can trust—and that's Jess. The Cryptos are talking bad stuff behind our backs. We're basically on our own."

"Do you know another attraction with a magic lantern or a genie lamp?" Finn asks. "'Cause I don't. Maybe Philby does. So let's get to the pay phone."

"We should have brought our own phones. This is why, FYI."

Philby forbade them from crossing over with their phones, believing the Cryptos were using the devices' GPS signals to make sure the Keepers didn't leave the Studio. The solution was for Finn or Maybeck to place a call from a park pay phone and request to be returned.

"Still. I don't love that Jafar headed that way," Maybeck says.

"The longer we wait, the more time he has to recover from those wounds. Being a sorcerer, I doubt it'll take long."

Finn pulls coins out of his pocket, marveling at the DHI experience; there are still so many unexplained elements surrounding the phenomenon. At times it feels as if the Keepers have barely scratched the surface of the possibilities.

"You keep watch," Finn says. "Hoot like an owl if you see something wrong."

"How 'bout I just scream?"

"If you give yourself away, we're in deep trouble. I may need you."

"You always need me," says Maybeck. "It's me, after all."

"I thought you said Charlene had taught you things."

Maybeck grins, unfazed.

"Once I make the call," says Finn," we run for the Plaza—we need to return together."

"You don't trust Philby?"

"I don't trust the technology. We're partial 1.6's. He's trying to fix that tonight with Charlie, but we don't know what works and what doesn't, how well it works or doesn't. I don't love being a guinea pig when someone like Jafar is hunting us."

"Point taken," Maybeck says. "I guess I should say 'Good luck,' even though I'm more of the school that says you make your own luck."

Finn rolls his eyes; Maybeck laughs, and then Finn takes off across the open walkway, aware of the whirl of humanity outside the park: a jet on final approach somewhere overhead; the underlying buzz of electricity, humming like a creature that wants to break out of a cage; the creepy feeling of closed-circuit cameras watching him. Although they do not fully understand why, there are times when only the Keepers are able to see the Overtakers. That is one of the positive features Wayne deliberately sought to achieve in creating the DHI technology in the first place. It's doubtful that the OTs will show up on security cameras, rendering useless any justification Finn and Maybeck might make to the authorities for their being here. Ironically, at night their allies—Disney Security—also become their nemesis.

Finn is nearly across the path when he catches a flash of color in his peripheral vision. It comes from his right—the Plaza—and is *moving* toward him. He runs faster. Maybeck hoots like an owl, confirming that what Finn thinks he has seen is not only in his imagination. Someone is back there and coming for him—fast. The pay phone is lit by a lamp. It looks so normal, reminding Finn how *abnormal* his own situation is. Maybeck hoots a second time. Finn remains focused on the task ahead. A pure DHI is the best defense he can mount, so he refuses to look back and see which OT is chasing him. Fear is the real enemy within, no matter what the Imagineers might think.

Finn heads toward Frontierland, creating a challenge for his pursuers: he doesn't go around obstacles, but runs through them—a stone wall, a copse of trees—creating enough of a lead to lose his pursuers. How much of a lead, he can't be sure. The trick will be getting back to the Plaza in time to return. He skids to a stop at a pay phone and lifts the receiver.

It only takes credit cards. No coins. He'll have to make a collect call. He dials zero for the operator.

In the next instant, Finn is lifted off his feet and smashed backward into the wall, the phone's receiver torn from his hand. The terror of the moment leaves pain radiating through his body; he feels as though someone just dropped him from a roof. Drawing a painful breath, he dares to look back and confront his attacker, steels his mind to face whatever OT it may be, including Jafar.

It's Amanda, with Jess beside her.

It takes Finn a moment to realize that Amanda "pushed" him. He's been on the receiving end of her paranormal power before, but it didn't feel like this, a powerful wind blowing directly in his face. The last time it was more like being pulled by cable from behind. She went easy on him. Despite this, he feels like he's been in a car wreck and is slow getting up.

"You were able to cross over," Finn says.

"Yes. Jess discovered a game changer. The lamp in the Bazaar—"

"Backfired on me and Maybeck." As Finn speaks his name Maybeck appears, coming up the lane at a jog as if summoned. "I didn't get my wish, unless I secretly have a *death* wish. Believe me, I'm beginning to wonder."

Finn motions for the four of them to slip out of sight. They move near the exit of Thunder Mountain and tuck into the shadows. The glow of their v1.6 DHIs makes hiding fully difficult.

"I have an idea," Jess proclaims. "Which direction did the lantern face in the Bazaar?"

Finn considers. "The spout faced right. But it's mounted. It's not like you can move it."

"The lamp in my . . . dream . . ." Jess doesn't experience them as dreams, more like "visions" but has never dared call them that, "faces left."

"There's a genie lamp in Storybook Land," Amanda announces. They look at her curiously. She says, "You think

Philby's the only one who *reads*?" She pauses for emphasis. "Trouble is, it's small, and the only access is up steep, tiny stairs, so reaching it and rubbing it—"

"Ain't gonna happen," Maybeck says, his voice filled with defeat.

"Actually," Amanda says, "Charlene already went through this. Philby messed with code before Charlene reached the stage. And he continued until he crossed you over. He resized selected portions of her DHI. Turns out it worked: at one point her leg shrank to the size of an arm and she fell over."

"Get to the point," Maybeck says.

"A picture's worth a thousand words," Jess says. "Time?" she asks Amanda, who checks her watch.

"Three minutes! We'd better hurry!"

"To?" Finn asks.

"The Plaza! We've got to be at the Plaza by half past."

"To return!" Finn says, excitedly.

The girls look at each other and speak nearly in unison: "Not exactly."

* * *

Three minutes later, Finn, Maybeck, Jess, and Amanda skid to a stop next to the Partners statue in the shadow of the Sleeping Beauty Castle.

"Did you know Walt Disney named the castle after Sleeping Beauty because the movie was in production and he wanted the extra publicity?" Jess says.

"Seriously?" Maybeck says. "Crass!"

"You can't survive as an artist," Jess says, "if you don't understand business. Vincent van Gogh died broke and unknown. Now his paintings sell for a hundred million dollars *each*."

"Think what you could get for his missing ear," Maybeck says.

"Eew!" Amanda groans.

"Bogies!" Finn warns. "Nine o'clock!"

Finn's grateful for the training and experience they've all had. No one breaks his or her neck straining to get a look. The three others manage to turn to pretend-speak to one another and, in the process, sneak a peek.

Jafar is hunched over, a result of wounds inflicted by Rajah. Even from a distance, he looks older, angrier, even less patient. Oddly enough, he resembles a python ready to strike. On his shoulder perches Iago. Iago's parrot head and parrot beak are lowered below his parrot shoulders, transforming him into a parrot assassin with all the cuteness of a sixty-year-old crow. The bird takes flight; a target-seeking missile.

Finn feels his DHI slipping. Jafar taps his scepter, and sudden light fills the eyes of its serpent head.

"Caution: evil hex." Maybeck voices what they're all thinking. That scepter is nothing to mess with.

Through it all, Jess keeps her cool, her full concentration on her wristwatch. She calls out: "Three . . . two . . ."

A bird chirps.

Everything around Finn begins to grow to a comically large size, as though he has stepped into a world inhabited by giants. Then pain hits him and he screams. Every molecule in his body vies for his attention as bone, muscles, and organs shrink against his will. This must be some kind of dream state or hallucination. Finn's voice goes from his normal deep tones to a squeak that sounds like he's sucked a breath or two of helium. He hears other such squeaks and thinks that it must be his friends crying out.

Iago tucks his wings, dive-bombing Finn's head in what

is sure to be a kill strike. Finn tries to accomplish all clear, but before he can, the pain ends as quickly as it started, and the world stops growing. Iago misses, attacking a full-size Finn who is no longer present. Finn takes deep, heaving breaths of relief.[34]

The bird chirping turns out to be not Iago but Amanda, crying out for Finn to duck. She shrank before Finn, her voice jumping several octaves as her DHI grew smaller. Now that Finn grasps what's happening, he begins to understand some of the hallucinations he's experiencing. It's not easy having the world grow to ten times normal size around you.

Iago turns to attack again but miscalculates a second time as Finn continues to shrink. The voices of Amanda, Maybeck, and Jess transition from high, ear-piercing squeaks to their normal pitch as Finn's size matches theirs.

"If he gets us this time," Maybeck says, glancing at the parrot, "he'll have us for lunch!"

Finn spins fully around, taking in the mountainous size of the Partners statue, the towering walls of which were no more than knee high before the group shrank. Now Finn and the others are no more than five inches high.

"What happened?" Finn gasps.

"Philby . . ." Jess says, pausing. "When I . . . The thing is . . . The second lamp—"

"The tiny one," Amanda says. "The only way to get to it . . ."

"Oh my word," Finn says.

"*Honey, I Shrunk the Keepers,*" Maybeck quips.

"I should have warned you better," Jess says. "Like I said, Philby practiced on—"

---

[34] Jelly_Monorail

170

"Quick!" Maybeck grabs Jess's arm and runs toward an enormous bench that looms overhead like a high-rise building. He leads the group under the structure as Iago—who now resembles a 747—makes another approach. The overhead slats of the bench seat form a protective cage, forcing the gargantuan parrot to veer away at the last second.

"Look!" Amanda calls, pointing.

Timon and Pumbaa are prancing along the street between the castle and the plaza. Not characters in plush costumes, but the real character animals. Timon, a meerkat, has a long narrow body and stands about two feet high; Pumbaa is nearly three feet long and almost as tall.

Amanda hurries out from beneath the bench. "Pumbaa! Pumbaa!"

The warthog turns in her direction.

Maybeck's and Jess's attention is on Amanda, but Finn feels compelled to look overhead. Iago, his giant wings spread, has turned and is coming for Amanda. Finn sprints, shouting her name. Amanda pivots, looks up—and is paralyzed. Pumbaa lowers his tusks and charges. Finn dives to tackle Amanda, knowing in advance that he's failed—Iago will simply eat both of them instead of only Amanda. In a blur of alarming speed and unexpected agility, Pumbaa springs up.

Finn thought he'd seen everything, but an airborne warthog is new. Pumbaa looks like a flying butterball with horns and a shaggy mane. Turns out he's more a flesh-and-bones cannonball with two curling tusks. He collides with Iago just behind the bird's orange beak, a blow to the head that not only pushes the feathered dive-bomber off course, but knocks the parrot into Tweety-land—seeing stars, hearing whistles, out cold. To the miniaturized Keepers, Iago's subsequent belly flop and skidding tumble across the concrete looks like the crash of a jetliner.

Pumbaa hollers at the fallen bird, "Go ahead! Make my day!"

Timon catches up. "He watches too many movies!" He shakes his head and tail and drags a paw across his eyes. "He can be so in-*fur*-iating!" Self-amused, he doubles over with laughter.

Jafar moves toward the Plaza. To Finn, it looks like the Empire State Building going for a stroll.

"Could you help us please?" Amanda asks Pumbaa, allowing Finn to help her up.

"I've never met a doll that can talk!" says Pumbaa.

"You have now," Maybeck says. "Four of them, actually."

"We need a ride to Storybook Land," Amanda says, "before Jafar gets anywhere near us."

Jess catches up to them. "Like right away!" she says. "Better make that the Casey Jr. Circus Train."

"No," says Amanda, "I think you mean—"

"I've got this," Jess says. "It was my dream, remember?"

Jafar is now only yards away.

"All aboard! I've not met any two-legged creature that can catch a warthog," says Pumbaa proudly.

"And if he gives you any trouble, I'll run circles around him and climb him like a tree. He won't forget that, believe me!" Timon proudly displays the razor-sharp claws on his forepaws, which he waves around like hands.

The DHIs climb aboard and Pumbaa proves as good as his word, taking off so quickly that Finn, in the lead, has to grab the warthog's mane to keep from falling off. Amanda grips Finn around the waist, then Jess, with Maybeck sitting astride near the point where Pumbaa's mane ends. Timon, down on all fours, circles them playfully.

"That old goat stayed back with the bird!" Timon hollers.

Pumbaa skids to a halt. "First stop, Casey Jr.! Will you be needing a return fare?"

"How do we find you?" Amanda asks.

"We're always up for a good laugh!" The two chuckle and bound away, gone in seconds.

"Whatever that means," Maybeck says.

"Quick," Finn says. "Before we're seen."

"We're the size of clothespins. Who's going to see us?" Maybeck asks.

"Shrinking us is part of Philby's plan," says Jess, "to avoid our being seen by the security cameras. That's why he was testing it out on Charlene in the first place."

"Is that what he told you?" asks Maybeck. "You gotta watch out for that kid. The Professor is prone to exaggeration."

"Look who's talking!" Finn hollers.

"Hey! Are you all coming or not?" Jess has a lead on them.

The perspective of his newly massive surroundings overwhelms Finn. For a moment, he loses his balance to vertigo. It takes him twenty paces to cover the distance of a full-size human stride. He feels as if he's walked miles by the time Jess leads them onto a paved path; they pass a blue-roofed structure that looks like part of a fruit stand. Jess climbs over some pieces of gravel that resemble giant boulders; it looks like she's mountaineering. Finn follows, careful of every hand and toe-hold. Once up, he leans back to help Amanda but lets Maybeck take care of himself, a gesture he knows the other boy appreciates.

Jess leads the way through dense planting; they pause at a railroad track that to creatures their size looks as wide as a twelve-lane highway. There's a solid steel wall to cross over, supported by inordinately large wooden beams—the railroad ties, Finn realizes.

"This will not be easy," Jess says. "The metal is superslick."

Maybeck lays his hand on the rail. "It's vibrating. News alert: the train is running."

The Keepers have encountered such unexpected anomalies many times before: segments of an attraction operating after hours. The train running implies the work of the Overtakers. Finn and Maybeck understand this fact and acknowledge it with an exchange of glances; for now they keep it from the two Fairlies. No reason to scare them if their fears are unfounded.

"Heads up! Stay alert!" cautions Finn, as close as he'll get to an all-out warning.

They stand in front of the steel rail, their DHIs shimmering.

"In my dream," Jess says, "we climbed over. It was hard."

"You sketched a locomotive," Amanda reminds her.

"Yes."

"Not good," Amanda says, "if it happens to be coming right at us."

"That occurred to me. Yes."

"Occurred to us all," Maybeck says. As an artist, he clearly grasped more of the meaning of Jess's sketch than Finn, who barely remembers more than the lamp in the middle of the confusion.

Jess removes the sheet of paper from her back pocket. Again, it sticks to her fingers like flypaper, but remains a projection. She unfolds it, and they study the locomotive.

"It's coming right at you. That does not look so good," Finn says.

"It looks fatal," Maybeck agrees.

"So we walk through it," says Amanda. "Right?" she asks Finn, turning to him and meeting his eyes.

174

"Absolutely." The connection between them intensifies. For a moment, there is only this girl, a castle rising up behind her. She is the princess of that castle. She is everything.

"So . . ." Maybeck is clearly about to complain.

"Company!" Jess cries.

Two scruffy feral cats, one a tailless Manx, have spotted the four chipmunk-size DHIs. Lowering their heads, bodies frozen in place, the cats sense a late-night snack.

The train rail's vibration intensifies, approaching a clatter.

"Push *all* thought away. Focus instead on blank nothingness. Close your eyes if you have to. Here we go. Jess, you first. Then Terry. Amanda and I'll go last."

Amanda keeps her eyes locked with Finn's. She looks frightened. He shakes his head and forces a caring smile.

Jess turns toward the rail. Her eyelids flutter shut, and her DHI's blue outline appears to shimmer. She steps forward and passes through the metal barrier.

The Manx cat stalks toward them, seeming seductively motionless, and yet somehow moving. Finn edges away from the others as Maybeck follows Jess. He vanishes. The metal rail is jumping as the locomotive approaches.

"Made it!" shouts Jess, excitedly.

The Manx focuses on Finn, lowering its massive head to the concrete.

"Go!" Finn tells Amanda without taking his eyes off the Manx.

"No. Back up toward the rail. We go together."

"Since when do you give the orders?" Finn asks, still enmeshed in a stare-down with his would-be attacker.

The cat springs. Its outstretched paw, claws extended, aims for Finn's face. Finn's feet betray him, unwilling to move. Five claws like sharpened meat hooks whir through the air; Finn is about to have the flesh of his fear-frozen face ripped from the bone.

He's struck by a ferocious wind. The paw moves up as if yanked hard by a rope.

Finn cocks his head to see Amanda, arms outstretched. She has pushed, throwing Finn over and altering the course of the cat's paw.

"We . . . go . . . now!" she shouts. She takes a step forward.

Finn rolls, passing through the rail. Sits up. He can see the train coming at him.

No Amanda.

A few feet away, Amanda bangs into the rail, unable to get through. Her strength has lessened because of her telekinetic push, limiting the power and clarity of her DHI. She's disoriented; Finn rolled and disappeared, but she can't follow. The cat with no tail turns its attention on her. She senses she's about to be lunch meat. She bangs her balled fists against the metal.

The cat takes a step toward her. Another.

Her ability to push something so big is lost; she used everything she had to save Finn. "Finn!" she hollers.

* * *

Finn moves well before he hears her call his name. Forcing his mind—and his pounding heart—to still, he dives at the rail, arms out, head first, and passes through it, arriving at Amanda's feet.

He catches the movement of the cat out of the corner of his eye, somehow knowing there's no time to think or calculate or plan. He wraps his arms around Amanda's knees and lifts, pushing her from below up and over the rail.

176

As the cat strikes out, Finn somersaults. With a *whoosh*, he finds himself on the other side of the rail, nearly on top of Amanda.

The train is bearing down on them. Twenty yards . . . Fifteen . . .

Finn grabs Amanda by the hands and swings her around; once—twice—and he releases her, sending her over the far rail. . . . But not quite. She lands on the rail and stands. The train is a only a few yards away.

"Fi-i-i-i-inn!"

Finn sees he's taken too long. He looks toward the rail, thinking: Never gonna make it. He closes his eyes, imagining a pinprick of light. Amanda jumps to safety. Finn turns to the train and opens his arms wide.

It runs him over.

* * *

Responding to an urgency fueled by Amanda's hysteria, Maybeck is the first to vault atop the rail to look for Finn.

Nothing.

Reluctant to tell the others, he calls back, "Just a second—still looking!"

"What's wrong?" Amanda calls out.

His tight voice has belied his confidence. "I . . . ah . . . Just a minute." He jumps over the rail, landing on a railroad tie, unable to face telling them the truth.

Maybeck wonders what he's looking for. What happens when a *partial* hologram is struck by a moving locomotive? Your pixels are scattered, he answers himself. Your projection stops and your human self is trapped in SBS for eternity. He hopes that *for once* he's wrong about something.

Idly, brain whirring with shock, he wonders at all the

thousands of people who have fallen into comas over the centuries, never to wake up again. Is this strictly a medical condition, or does it have something to do with a similar phenomenon? How long have groups of determined individuals battled the supernatural villains of the world? In Europe, such folklore stretches back for centuries. In China, for millennia.

He searches the tracks for bits and pieces—a sparkle, a jewel of fading color, evidence he has no desire to discover. He wonders if Philby can possibly reconstruct what was once a compromised DHI. No person could face an oncoming train without fear—to do so would be superhuman—so what happened to the *human* percentage of Finn when the train hit?

The thought of telling the girls is devastating. But not knowing will hurt them even more. He hears Amanda's sobs, hears Jess comforting her, and realizes he is in charge. He wonders what he's supposed to do.

Lead.

It's not something Maybeck's comfortable with; at times, he can barely keep himself together, much less others. He hears his snide remarks to Finn and Philby replay in his head, sees himself as an idiot for making them. How's he supposed to comfort Amanda? Shouldn't he get word to Philby? What's next in the quest for the lamp? He's overwhelmed.

For a moment he wishes it had been him and the train instead of Finn, but only for a moment, as again he ponders Finn's fate and a lump lodges in his throat. He wishes he could take back a lot of things he's said to his friend over the years. The thought, *friend*, overwhelms him with grief.

Until the Keepers came along he was a loner, limiting his time at school and spending every other minute with his aunt in her pottery shop, Crazy Glaze. He only auditioned to be a Disney

Host Interactive because his aunt needed help with building his college fund, and the winners of the audition were being offered college tuition. Now, years later, he has more than friends. He has a family. And though his natural inclinations tend toward sarcasm and cynicism, Charlene has explained to him that this is anything but natural; instead, it is a kind of defense, a wall he put up to avoid being hurt by *other people's comments*.

Family. And in a weird way, for all his faults, Finn was the head of the family, the older-brother figure, while Wayne served as grandfather.

Maybeck drops to his knees. He doesn't know a lot about prayer. His aunt takes him to church, but it's mostly singing. He doesn't believe, but he doesn't disbelieve, either. He's still waiting for some kind of message, one he suspects will never come. His aunt says faith is a decision. A person must decide if he or she is the end all or if there might be something bigger at work, that belonging and standing on one's own are not incompatible ideas. He raises his eyes to the sky and pleads with whatever is out there to throw a thunderbolt or set a bush on fire, send him some signal or give him a random thought of what he's supposed to do. "Bring Finn back!" He finds himself mumbling repeatedly. "And if you can't do that, tell me what I'm supposed to do."

He catches himself kneeling and jumps to his feet. Has no idea where that came from, why that, of all things, was his first reaction. He feels foolish and is glad no one saw. He's got to get the girls to the lamp. He's got to continue what they started. A flicker of realization flutters in his mind—*I know what I'm supposed to do!* He takes another glance at the night sky. Says, "Nah . . ." And passes to the other side of the rail to meet the crying girls.

"We can't assume the worst," he says, having just done

precisely that himself, and wondering if this is what Finn and Philby do on a daily basis. "The good news is: he's not spread all over the place."

He regrets phrasing it like that, realizing there are some adjustments he needs to make—fast. He marvels at this moment of insight, wondering if he knows the real Finn and Philby, if their Keeper selves might be entirely different from their normal selves.

"But—" Amanda starts.

"You don't want to go there," Maybeck says, cutting her off. "It serves no purpose. 'A lazy mind assumes the worst. Optimism fuels possibility.'" He has no idea—none!—where this comes from; he must have picked it up from his aunt. She's constantly laying out aphorisms for him, maybe hoping they'll rub off. And they have, he supposes, because here he is, regurgitating them.

"We keep going. We follow Jess's sketch—get to the lamp. The train was there, in her drawing. The lamp's in the center. The lamp's important. It's why you crossed over in the first place. Finn—"

At the mention of Finn's name, Amanda breaks down sobbing again.

"Okay. My mistake! No more mentioning . . . *him*. Okay? By any of us. We're going to 'fuel possibility,' right? We're going to make this happen. We need to get to the lamp and do whatever it is you do with a lamp like that and then get back to the—"

It dawns on him that he has no idea what to wish for. Finn was going to do the wishing. A new pair of running shoes won't do the trick. They'd be nice, but they won't exactly help the Keepers. Kill Maleficent? That's been handled. What was Finn going to ask?

"You okay?" Jess asks. Except for a few snail trails left down her cheeks by digital tears, she has remained remarkably composed.

"I . . . yeah . . . the lamp," he says.

"This way." Jess pulls Amanda to her feet and leads them down an embankment to the edge of a manmade waterway. The canal looks as wide as the Mississippi River to the group of shrunken DHIs. She points out the waterfall on their side of the Storybook Land canal. "Through that and into the cave."

"A shortcut!" Maybeck cries, realizing they've bypassed a mountain village, the Sultan's palace, and a half dozen other obstacles. "If we can max out the v1.6, we won't have to get wet in the waterfall."

"Speak for yourself," Amanda groans, sorrow weighing down her words like stones.

Jess is careful with her footing, testing both the substance of her DHI and how stable the rocks are underfoot.

The girls are hardly DHI novices, Maybeck remembers, though they lack the crossover experience of the Keepers. In any other setting, Jess's tentativeness would be cute, but Maybeck is on edge, worried for the three of them as he's never worried before. This leadership stuff isn't so great, he thinks.

As Jess hesitates before the waterfall, Maybeck's unease demands he look behind them. His heart sinks as he spies a pack of dogs cresting a hill from the direction of the Alpine Village. Big, angry dogs, running extremely fast. It takes him a fraction of a second to realize that the dogs are scaled to his size, not monster dogs of the real world, but dogs that live in Storybook Land. And not dogs at all: wolves. Big, black wolves.

A shot rings out. A gunshot. Amanda and Jess spin to take in what Maybeck's witnessing: a miniature man in lederhosen and knee socks brandishing a musket. He stands on the ridge, reloading his single-shot musket. A wolf has fallen behind the pack, hit by the bullet. The animal rolls and the pack turns instantly, retreating to feed on the fallen animal.

"Go!" Maybeck says, pushing Amanda in the back and shoving her into Jess, who is forced through the waterfall. Amanda is next.

The clatter of an approaching train rises. It has lapped the circuit and is approaching again.

Maybeck can't keep his eyes off the pack. It devours the fallen wolf in seconds. Musket Man has the gun raised up to his shoulder. Maybeck sees a puff of smoke; hears the dull report a fraction of a second later because of the distance. Something tells him to drop; he falls like a marionette with its strings cut. A chip flies out of the rock behind him: Musket Man is aiming at *him*. He's not on their side. Maybeck scrambles backward as Musket Man stands the gun up on the stock to reload. The wolves are far faster than anything Maybeck has seen. They're nearly upon him. He's not going to make it.

The sound of the train grows louder, deafening Maybeck. The train passes. A blur of color tumbles from his right. It's like a wheel or a rock or a . . . person doing somersaults.

"Finn!" Maybeck screams at the top of his lungs.

The girls jump back through the waterfall, nearly stepping on Maybeck's head.

"No!" he says to them, grabbing Amanda by the ankle. *"Go!"*

So much for his leadership qualities. Neither girl moves— they're transfixed by the sight of the approaching wolves.

A tumbling Finn somersaults directly across the path of the wolves, distracting them. The pack turns toward him.

Amanda drops to her knees in tears.

Musket Man pulls a long rod back out from his gun and hoists the weapon to his shoulder.

Finn reaches the edge of the canal, the lead wolf nearly upon him. He stands up. "Come and get it!" he says, opening his arms invitingly. He steps back and falls.

Maybeck scoops Amanda up under the arms and drags her forcibly toward the waterfall as a shot rings out. A musket ball penetrates the dirt where Amanda was kneeling.

Finn hangs from the ledge by his fingers. He taunts the lead wolf. "Tasty young boy!"

The lead wolf loses control on the slick concrete. Trying to slow, he instead slides off the ledge and into the water; the other wolves follow their leader. Paddling wildly, the wolves are carried off by the current.

Finn's ability to maintain his DHI state makes pulling himself up nearly effortless. He hurries through the waterfall and into the dark cave.

Maybeck and the girls rush forward to meet him. When all the hugging and gushing settle down, Finn explains that he managed to fully control his DHI. His hologram never moved; it was absorbed by the locomotive as he maintained his clarity of purpose. As the first tingles of compromise teased his fingertips, "I jumped up and grabbed some piece of the undercarriage. In seconds I was too far away, so I spent a lap inching to the outside of the train car. When we got here, I swung off, spotted the wolves, and . . . well, I improvised."

More group thanks and Amanda's tears fill the next minute. Through the waterfall, Maybeck sees the Musket Man charging down the hill.

"This guy must think we're bandits or something. He seems determined to shoot us."

"Let's go!" Finn shouts, his voice echoing through the canal tunnel. "This way?" He points up a set of narrow stairs cut into the tunnel wall.

"Yes," Jess says. "This way."

She takes the lead. Finn follows. Close on his heels is Amanda; she and Finn are awkwardly holding hands. Maybeck is last, marveling at how effortlessly Jess takes control, how Finn doesn't challenge her, how tempted he was to assert himself and claim the lead for himself. How all of this is so confusing. Maybeck wants another turn, another chance as ringleader, is sorry he relinquished it so soon. Opportunity is so temporal, he thinks.

A shot rings out.

"Pick it up," Maybeck says. "Move! I think I've been shot."

Amanda rises to the occasion, overcoming her grief and joy at Finn's return to take a stand and challenge the Musket Man. As she drops out of their line, squatting, Finn turns. "Go on!" she cries. "Let me do this!"

Finn hesitates. Maybeck reaches him and pushes him up the stairs, getting him running again.

Amanda stays behind, her knees not entirely stable beneath her, her eyes blurred by drying tears. She has regained some of the strength she lost with the earlier push, but by no means all—the process always leaves her drained for a while. She's counting in part on the trail of water shed by their DHIs, which has left the stairs slick and precarious. She's also counting on surprising Musket Man and catching him in midstride, and counting on whatever force it is beyond the hologram projectors that make this all possible, that make it happen. Something bigger and unexplainable. She summons it, the way she assumes all Fairlies do.

The top of Musket Man's Bavarian hat appears. The guy

must have been a caretaker or innkeeper in Alice's village. What's he doing here? Amanda holds her breath, pulls in her arms, and shoves. Musket Man is struck by an invisible force, skids across the slick stair tread and, dropping his musket, flies off and falls into the canal. Amanda races up the stairs. Her last image of the man is of him swimming for shore.

He's the evil Bavarian Energizer Bunny: he just won't quit.

* * *

The stairs rise steeply. It's too dark inside the long, cavelike stairway to see Musket Man fall, but the splash is heavy enough to signal that it's not Amanda's DHI going down. In the lead, Jess carries the burden of possible failure in her every step. Philby and the Keepers have gone to great lengths to follow her simple sketch of a magic lantern with its spout facing to the right. What if her dream was a mirror image? Or what if she was simply having an "Aladdin dream"—imagining herself as a character in the movie? It wouldn't be the first time. There's no way she's full DHI: her thighs are killing her. They must have climbed several hundred steps by now. Whoever built this stairway made it more of a ladder. Endless. Straight up.

"Terry!" she calls back, his name echoing throughout the cave. "Are you okay?"

"Define 'okay,'" Maybeck responds. And she grins. Jess knows better than to make waves—and she doesn't want to challenge Charlene—but she's recently come to like Terry in ways that go beyond casual friendship, ways she doesn't fully understand and is afraid of. She and Amanda are with the Keepers for a reason. She must not allow *anything* to get in the way of that; Amanda's open feelings for Finn already pose a challenge for their mission.

"Your leg?" she calls back.

185

"I believe I am now a *hole-y* man, if that's what you're asking."

"We can stop," Finn says.

Finn always seems to think of others, Jess thinks. It comes so naturally to him. She and Amanda have discussed how, of all the Keepers, Finn seems different—not better, but like a different species, as if Wayne had planned for him all along, and the Keepers would not exist without him.

She has so many questions yet to answer. As the world of the Keepers seems to be building to a make-it-or-break-it moment, Jess knows their survival is at stake, their lives. Something horrible is coming. Her dreams show her flickers of it: flames, chaos, ruin. Death. There are sketches she has not dared show even Amanda.

Reaching the top of the stairs, Jess sees it: the brass lamp sitting on a pedestal where the stairs terminate.

Finn and Maybeck arrive. Maybeck's calf is bleeding real blood, meaning he is not now, nor will be, pure projection any time soon. Finn drops to one knee to examine Maybeck's wound.

Maybeck says, "It's a through-and-through."

"Meaning?" Jess asks.

"The bullet didn't lodge," Finn says. "In one side and out the other."

"No bones were hit," Maybeck says. "I can walk."

"That's your DHI speaking. It will be worse when you return. We don't experience pain as fully when we are crossed over. You know that!" Finn studies the wound more closely. "It caught the edge of your leg. The wound is two inches deep. We can't mess around here. It needs tending."

"You're the designated worrier, Finn. It's barely bleeding at all. Rub the lamp. We'll deal with me soon enough."

One of the big problems with the boy Keepers is their heroism, Jess thinks. What makes them great is also their weakness. Maybeck would sooner bleed to death than admit he needs help.

Amanda reaches them panting, out of breath. "I . . . he went in the water . . . but I think I only delayed him."

Only now does she notice Maybeck's wound. For a moment, there is much discussion. Then Jess says, "Enough!" silencing them. She's so worried that she has brought them all here for nothing, that she is responsible for Maybeck's wound, for the risks they've taken.

Finn stands, facing the lamp. "I guess this is it."

A voice pleads inside Finn, raw and aching as hunger: *Save Wayne!* He twists and turns internally, wanting so badly to use his wish to this end. He doesn't open himself up to the possibility that the lamp won't work; if it doesn't, it doesn't. Instead, he focuses on what to ask of it, believing his wish might actually be granted. Selfishness needles him: he could wish for personal wealth, for Amanda to be in love with him for life—but these aims are counterbalanced by his being a Keeper. He has no idea if a personal wish would be granted, yet he knows intuitively that if his wish is correct, if it is selfless and for the good of all, it stands the best chance.

Wishing for Wayne is too small. Wayne himself would forbid it. So what to ask? Is Maleficent actually dead? Can Dillard be brought back to life? Is the battle of all battles about to take place? The wish can't be too specific, and it will fail if it's too general.

The others are practically holding their breath, waiting for him to do something.

Amanda peers over the edge of the top step. "That guy's coming. He's pulled himself out of the water."

187

"His musket?" Maybeck asks. "Tell me you threw it into the water, too."

"I . . . ah . . . well . . ."

"Got it," Maybeck says.

"I think we should hold hands," Finn says. "What happens to me happens to all of us."

"What wish are you asking for?" Maybeck inquires.

"I'm not going to speak it aloud." Finn extends his left hand. Amanda accepts it. She takes Jess's. Jess reaches out for Maybeck.

"This could be really stupid," Maybeck says to the girls. His humor is lost on them.

A musket shot rings out. The Bavarian is firing up the flight of stairs. Given the confines of the cave, the shot sounds like a bomb going off. The bullet ricochets all over the place; overhead the plaster explodes, chips flying everywhere, leaving a white gash exposed by the musket ball. Dust floats down onto the lamp and Finn.

"Push him," Maybeck orders Amanda.

"I need a minute. Maybe more. Besides, he's too far away."

"I'm going to do this," Finn says.

He closes his eyes. Focuses. His right hand blindly finds the lamp, and he rubs in gentle circles. His lips move silently. He squints: Nothing. He closes his eyes, continues reciting his wish in his mind like a mantra. He feels heat coming from the lamp. A low tone, like a hum. He squints again: steam or smoke, maybe both, emerge from the spout. The gas collects rather than dissipates. Forms into three circles of differing size. Inside the cloud an image appears.

Jess gasps. "I dreamed that, too!" she says.

Within the lamp's swirling steam and smoke appears a

row of tall columns and reddish stone walls that immediately identify themselves as the decor at the entrance line for Indiana Jones Adventure: Temple of the Forbidden Eye.

The steam and smoke disperse.

"We're still here," Finn says.

"You were expecting something else?" Maybeck says. "What did you wish for, anyway?"

"Get down! I've got this!" Jess shouts, winning the others' attention. The soaking wet Bavarian presents himself, brandishing his musket, then raising the gun stock to his shoulder. He's too close to miss.

The others drop. Jess remains upright. She marches calmly straight toward the man and right up to him, halting only a few feet away from the barrel of his musket. "You don't want to do that."

"Witches! Sorcerers!" the man shouts, lowering one eye to the gun sight.

Amanda draws a breath, about to call out. Finn squeezes the hand he's already holding, stopping her.

"My friends and I—" Jess begins calmly.

The musket fires, the bullet passing directly into Jess's chest and out the other side, then ricocheting off the wall. She never breaks stride.

"—are neither witches nor sorcerers. We are— goblins of good, sent to save the kingdom from those of whom you speak."

"I . . . shot . . ." Musket Man says, in a thick Bavarian accent. He looks to be on the verge of fainting.

"No harm can come to us," Jess says. The Keepers exchange a knowing glance; Jess managed to remain pure DHI, and the musket ball passed through her without injury.

Finn is in awe. Until this moment, he believed that only

he possessed such absolute courage under fire. It cannot have been easy looking down that barrel; he's not sure he could have managed it. Finn wonders once again about the origin of the Fairlies, marveling at the "coincidence" of their arrival in the lives of the Keepers, and the powers they clearly possess.

"We intend you no harm," Jess says. "You would do us a great favor by putting aside your firearm and your animosity toward us and going back to your village—to all the villages of Storybook Land. You must spread the word that the time for an uprising has come. We goblins of good have been sent to drive back the wolves and restore order, but we cannot do it alone."

Musket Man sniffs the flintlock on his gun. He seems satisfied that the powder ignited. He studies the thing as if it's foreign to him, as if someone has just dropped it into his hands. He looks at Jess, then back at the musket. He steps close to her, stabs the gun at her but, making no contact, gasps and withdraws it from her abdomen.

He garbles a confused sentence in a thick Bavarian rural dialect.

Jess grabs the musket, pulls it from the man's grip without effort, and tosses it down the staircase. Musket Man's eyes follow his prized possession as it clatters down the stone steps. There is a loud splash.

The Bavarian turns and races down the stairs, stumbling and slipping. He regains his balance and continues running until the sound of splashing in the distant waterfall signals his departure.

"We'd better get going," Jess says, addressing her friends. "He won't believe me yet. He'll call for a militia. Our best bet is to leave quickly."

Finn is the first to stand. He moves toward Jess reverentially, studying her as if seeing her for the first time. He then does the same to Amanda.

"Who are you?" he asks them.

* * *

Back outdoors, the Keepers don't see Pumbaa anywhere.

"We need to get to Indiana Jones. And fast!" Finn says.

"'We're always good for a laugh,'" Amanda says. "Remember?"

"Yeah? So?"

"So we need to laugh," Jess says.

First Amanda, then Jess, and then the two boys begin faking laughter. Louder. Louder still.

Pumbaa and Timon come racing around a corner, also in hysterics.

"Only in Disneyland," Finn mumbles. He makes eye contact with Amanda, and there's an unspoken thank-you in his gaze. She nods. Her smile is wide, her eyes knowing.

The wacky warthog carries them to the entrance of the Indiana Jones attraction. They slide off his back and down his tail like experts.

"Will you wait for us, please?" Finn says.

"I'm waits for no man!" Pumbaa says.

"It's not 'I'm,' it's *time!*" Timon says, correcting his friend.

"Time for what?" Pumbaa says, laughing hysterically at his own joke.

Timon slaps him. "We will wait," he says. The two trundle off, Pumbaa still chuckling.

"What did you wish for?" Maybeck asks Finn again. The group is a few yards into the vacant queue, making time.

"I'm afraid I'll jinx it by telling you."

191

Philby must have tracked their DHIs moving across the park, projector to projector, because all at once the world spins and they all lose their balance and fall. When they stand up, they are full size again. They won't be using Pumbaa again.

"Philby really should warn us," Maybeck says, holding his bleeding leg.

"Finn, you won't jinx anything by telling us," says Amanda, with uncharacteristic harshness. "The lamp told us to come here. Why?"

Finn sighs. The group collects around him. "My wish was to learn how we could stop the OTs once and for all."

For a moment, no one moves or breathes.

"Well," Maybeck says, "at least it wasn't anything big."

"Why here?" Jess says. "My dream . . . I don't remember. . . . Not this place. Not exactly."

"And yet," Finn says, "here we are."

"'Once and for all,'" Maybeck says, quoting Finn, his sarcasm replaced by hopefulness.

"How amazing would that be?" Amanda says dreamily.

"*Will* be," Finn says.

"Of course," she says. "That's what I meant."

They pass a cordoned-off generator marked HIGH VOLT-AGE. A cooking area. A small temple; two large gold cobras guard the stairs. Finn pauses below a stone lintel carved with an all-seeing eye and hieroglyphics.

"Suppose this is trying to warn us?" He points to his eyes, indicating that the others should remain vigilant, and silences them again with a finger pressed to his closed lips.

The seriousness of their purpose hangs in the air; it's not as if the Overtakers are going to let them walk in and end the conflict once and for all. It's never been that easy. It never will be.

Contradicting himself, Finn speaks softly. "'Beware the eye of Mara.' Translation: maybe we're being watched. Subtitle: we're outnumbered. Let's make this a reconnaissance mission. If anything goes wrong we meet up at the Plaza. Stay clear. Stay safe."

"Nice. I like it," Maybeck says.

Amanda speaks. Her voice sounds distant, trancelike. "Mara's a goddess said to grant the seeker riches, eternal youth, or . . ."

"Or what?" Maybeck asks when she fails to complete her thought.

"Visions of the future."

All eyes turn to Jess.

Finn speaks first. "Maybe this isn't the place we defeat them. It's the place *you* see *how* we defeat them." Jess shrugs. Finn can see in her eyes that she does not want this burden placed on her.

"Maybe it's not visions of the future. But granting eternal youth isn't necessarily any better," Jess says. "Death is eternal. And *we* are young—as in 'youth.'"

"It could mean SBS," Amanda cautions.

"There's a cheery thought," Maybeck quips.

"Are we sure we should do this?" Amanda says.

"We're never sure of anything," Maybeck says. "We never got around to writing that Keepers handbook we always talk about. . . ."

The deeper they move down the narrow red-rock throat of the queue, the creepier it gets. Sound echoes, causing the Keepers to jump. As they reach a small circular room with an artifact at its center, Finn turns to Jess and mimes writing: she should take notes. He points to the artifact—a pyramid-shaped stone with animal forms chiseled into its sides—and to the

193

oversized pale blocks of stone that make up the curving walls, some of them also incised with scattered hieroglyphs.

More hallway, more carvings, more hieroglyphs. They round a corner and moonlight streams in from overhead. The area opens up. Rustling stalks of tall bamboo serve as a wall to control the would-be lines.

"We're in too deep for a quick retreat," Maybeck says.

Finn nods, a feeling of dread overtaking him.

The ceiling gives way to stalactites that take Maybeck back to the island of Aruba and a near-death encounter with the Overtakers. The walls appear increasingly molten, like cold lava, flowing stone frozen in an instant.

The shapes remind Finn of animal horns and skeletons. He and the others pass a giant millstone upended on its edge, seemingly ready to roll or tumble.

"Remember," Maybeck says, breaking the silence, "Indy had to avoid all sorts of traps and tricks meant to kill him. We're in here after dark, after closing. There's no telling what we might encounter."

"How reassuring," Amanda says.

Finn shoots a look at Amanda. Her face is white.

"Sheesh!" Maybeck says. "Freaky."

The ceiling opens up to vines and a rickety-looking bamboo ladder hanging from a platform. The lighting is dim and casts confusing shadows. The room grows even wider. The path meanders.

Finn nearly says *This feels wrong*, but he knows better. He's learned to temper his fear, both for the continuity of his DHI and the sake of his partners. But it feels wrong, just the same.

"How can this possibly take down the OTs?" Maybeck says, verbalizing what's on everyone's mind. "This ride came light-years after the opening of the park. The OTs had been around forever at that point. I mean, what if the OTs somehow made Jess's dream happen, tricked us into coming here?"

"One word," Finn says. "*Wayne*. The things he's helped us with have never relied on a timetable. This attraction, all the attractions, were dreamed up and built under the direction of the Imagineers. Maybe there's no big showdown in Indiana Jones, but there's treasure, right? Indy's always after treasure, and so are we. It makes sense. 'Visions of the future.' That's got to be it."

"I saw some of this," Jess reminds them, reminding them of their purpose. "This is part of our search. Part of something bigger."

"The Eye on the Globe screen," Maybeck says, pointing to a dark wall ahead. "We're nearly there."

"Where?" Amanda asks.

"Where it all starts," Maybeck says. He changes his voice to sound like the Sallah character in *Indiana Jones*. "The Chamber of Destiny. Eternal youth; earthly riches; visions of the future."

"We need to get Jess into that Chamber," Amanda says dryly.

Finally, they pass a caged office full of artifacts and arrive at the cars. The emergency lights are on. An electronic hum suggests that the ride is running.

"Just like the dolls in It's a Small World," Maybeck says. "Ride is turned on. No one here."

"Let's hope not," replies Finn.

"You need to close your eyes," Amanda whispers to Jess as the first car rolls forward.

Finn and Maybeck have taken the outside seats of the vehicle's front row, bookending the sisters, who sit in the middle.

"Not going to happen," Jess says.

"You'll stay clearer," Amanda counters. "Maybe with your eyes closed, you'll see whatever it is you're supposed to see."

"We don't know if I'm supposed to see anything. Finn asked to be shown how to bring down the Overtakers. The answer to that could be anything. Terry and I are the artists here," Jess says, raising her voice.

"Darn right," Maybeck says.

Stress darkens Jess's voice. "We might see something the two of you could miss."

"We're not going to see much," Finn says as the first door swings open, admitting the car into the blackness ahead.

"The treasure of Mara," Jess hisses.

The way is lit only by harsh emergency lights. Sharp shadows cast the normally gleaming displays into gloom through which the shimmer of gold can be seen.

"Riches!" Amanda calls out. "The first of Mara's three promises."

Jess takes Amanda's projected hand—they both feel the contact, which is a bad omen. They aren't fully crossed over.

Above them, the heads and necks of six golden dragons coil together in a writhing mass. Ahead, the face of Mara stares blankly down through hollow eyes.

Amanda grips Jess's hand tightly, expecting the dragons to peel away from the wall and strike them.

Nothing happens—at first. Then, as they close in on Mara's huge golden mask, smoke and light pour from her eyes. The car swings left and into a tunnel of—

"Light . . . ning," Jess mutters. She looks to be asleep already—or in a trance. Amanda rubs her hands hard against her jeans to dry her palms.

The hallway is nearly pitch-black.

"It starts and ends in lightning," Jess says, her eyeballs dancing behind her closed lids.

On cue, the walls are suddenly alight with feverish blue-and-white bolts of electricity. The flashes partially illuminate more dragons—these are made of stone—and a frozen Animatronic Indiana Jones, which the Keepers are fast approaching.

"Eternal youth," Amanda says. "Lightning is the universe's energy. The Big Bang. The final clap of thunder waiting at the end of it all. It starts and stops everything."

"It starts and ends in lightning," Jess repeats, her sleepy voice sounding more confident.

The ride gives the Keepers no time to think. They are tossed and jostled as they struggle to secure their seat belts.

Turning abruptly left, they bounce through the dark. A horrid face, fifteen feet high, rises up before them, all cheeks and teeth. A beam of energy fires from its left eye and explodes into a fireball so close to Maybeck's arm that he feels the heat.

"Not liking this," Maybeck cries. "Just saying. Fireballs. You know who."

"She's dead," Finn says. "I killed her."

"Yeah. Right." Maybeck doesn't sound convinced.

Left again. Always left. The car picks up speed, flying recklessly toward a horrible demonic face from which all the Keepers instinctively avert their eyes.

Amanda cries, "Help me!"

Maybeck reaches toward her, fighting along with Amanda to keep Jess in her seat. Jess seems to be under a spell, or somehow sleeping through the car's ragged movement; she's flopping around like a puppet, her neck bending so far back and in such an ungainly, otherworldly way that Maybeck in terror pulls her into his shoulder and secures her in a kind of improvised headlock. He softly strokes her hair.

"Not . . . supposed . . . to . . . be . . . this . . . rough," Finn manages to croak.

The car has taken on a life of its own.

"They don't want us getting visions of the future." Maybeck's voice sounds half strangled, like he's about to throw up.

"Hold on!" Finn cries.

The car swings left yet again. Finn presses against Amanda, and Amanda to Jess and Jess against Maybeck's shoulder. Maybeck's ribs are crushed, stealing his breath.

Maybeck gags on his words. "You hear that scratching?"

"Scarabs," Jess whispers.

"Beetles," Amanda says as the three—all but Jess—slap at their arms. Thousands, tens of thousands, of the things are crawling across their skin.

The girls *and* the boys let out screams of horror.

It's Finn who first thinks to brush them off Amanda instead of himself. He's more efficient at it this way. Amanda, spitting and groaning, catches on and attacks the bugs crawling all over him, sweeping the beetles off his arms, pushing them out of his hair and face, digging through them at his mouth and nostrils to keep him from smothering. He gasps for air.

"Disgusting!"

Maybeck hollers, *"Get them off—"* But his words are choked to silence.

As Finn clears Amanda's mouth, she calls out roughly to Maybeck to keep Jess breathing. Only then does it occur to her and Finn that if Maybeck's helping Jess, there's no one to help him.

198

Finn lunges across the front row, lying atop Amanda and over Jess, and digs at Maybeck's face, scooping the seething mass of beetles away by the handful. Maybeck coughs and gasps for air.

As quickly as they came, the beetles are gone, running over the sides and off the back of the vehicle like a black blanket being pulled off a table.

It's at that moment that the vehicle stops, halting so abruptly that Finn nearly flies out.

"Snakes!" he says.

"That's no ordinary snake. That's more like a giant sea serpent!"

They're facing a cobra three feet thick and thirty feet long. Forty, if it were laid out straight.

"That ain't no Animatronic," says Maybeck. "And it has bloody scars on its back. Jafar?"

"Who else, with those scratches?" Finn says, his voice sounding fragile and dry.

"We had help last time."

"I'm aware of that."

"Check out Jess," Maybeck says.

The girl, eyes closed, skin pale, trembles in the front seat as Amanda attempts to console her.

"She's way under," Amanda mutters. "We're not waking her when she's like this. She'll surface when it's time."

"When is that, exactly?" Maybeck asks, his voice tense with anxiety. He never takes his eyes off the impossibly large cobra, its head the size of a refrigerator. The snake's tongue unrolls and flickers past Maybeck's bleeding leg.

"It smells your blood," Finn says.

"Oh, gre—"

The cobra snatches Maybeck into its mouth so quickly that

Finn never sees it move. The snake is right back where it was, towering over them, but now Maybeck is clamped in its jaws, prone, his feet sticking out one side of the huge mouth, his head the other. The snake works to rotate Maybeck to make him easier to swallow, but Maybeck holds tightly to its lower jaw, refusing to budge. Covered in slime and goo, he kicks at the opposite side of the cobra's jaw, dislocating it; but not to his advantage. The reptile can easily dislocate his jaw to swallow large prey; Maybeck has only accelerated the process.

"Finn!" Maybeck cries.

"All clear!" Finn shouts.

"Oh, sure! Get real. *Help me!*"

Finn dives across the snake's body and slams a clenched fist into an open wound oozing green pus. Jafar—the cobra—startles and wrenches his swollen mouth toward Finn.

Finn strikes the wound again. And *again.*

The cobra rocks forward to bite Finn, nearly losing Maybeck in the process. But then the snake's tail lurches up out of the dark, aiming for Finn, but missing, and swats its own back, striking the open wound. The cobra reels in agony; Finn has the presence of mind to slide off just in time.

Finn snatches a burning torch from the wall and waves it toward the cobra's eyes. The snake reels back, afraid.

"Eyes shut. Long tunnel. Pinprick of light," Finn instructs.

"Not going to happen: big teeth, long throat, strong tongue!" Maybeck calls, his voice distorted with pain and terror.

The snake's tongue winds around Maybeck's leg, then stretches out and turns the boy in advance of swallowing him whole.

Finn races up the rocks around which Jafar is coiled and shoves the burning torch into the serpent's right eye. The snake rears back, throwing Finn off balance. Finn drops the torch.

Jafar nearly drops Maybeck, but swallows instead.

Maybeck is gone.

The cobra strikes out for Finn with his fangs, each the size of an ax handle, outstretched and dripping with fresh venom.

Then its head smacks into the rocks, missing Finn completely. Amanda teeters in the front seat of the vehicle, her arms outstretched, her body weak from her telekinetic effort.

Finn seizes the burning torch, jumps atop the snake's body, and stabs the flame into an open wound. The snake issues a horrid sound, half cry, half gurgle, and regurgitates a slime-covered Maybeck, who smashes down onto the ground. Finn stabs again and again, his eyes spilling tears.

As the cobra sits up tall to strike again, Finn does not flinch. He grips the flaming stick with both hands, one high, one low. He closes his eyes.

The cobra attacks.

The burning torch, held up vertically like the Statue of Liberty's, punctures the snake's lower jaw and right through the roof of its mouth. The flame is not extinguished but continues to burn, dancing barely one foot from the snake's horror-stricken eyes. Finn's DHI sticks out of the reptile's mouth too, motionless. As the snake's jaw opens in pain, Finn falls out.

The cobra rises, waving its massive head from side to side, crying out and struggling in agony to free the torch as the heat sears its flesh. The creature slithers off into the dark, a long, anguished hiss trailing after it.

Finn rushes to Maybeck, meeting Amanda at his side. They clear the sticky goo from Maybeck's face as he gasps for air.

Behind them, the truck's engine rumbles back to life. Finn had not realized it had gone silent. Slumped in the seat, a dazed Jess opens her eyes.

"Quick," Finn says, "into the truck."

"Lightning," Jess murmurs. "It starts and ends in lightning. . . ."

20

AVA GARDNER SUFFERS. Though named for a long-ago glamorous movie star, she is unhappily burdened with a mannish face and the shoulders of an infantryman. It seems she was destined for security work: having dropped out of school in the tenth grade, she spent the rest of her teens collecting change in an East Coast highway tollbooth.

Working night shifts as a backstage Disneyland Security guard is a dream job. Ava belongs to a family now, and she makes it her goal to never let a single Cast Member or guest down, to pull her weight and protect the company at every opportunity. Just last week, she refused a delivery of frozen goods for improperly executed paperwork. Her superiors and coworkers agree: Ava Gardner is no slouch.

Deliveries come at all hours of the night, though few arrive after 2:00 A.M., so Ava perks up as a truck approaches—something to relieve the boredom of manning the small booth solo. Her partner's off napping, though he claimed he needed a bathroom break; not much escapes Ava—including sixty-thousand-pound trailer trucks with enough horses under the hood to start a stampede.

Ava fluffs her hair as she notes the color and make of the truck. She recognizes the rig, and the driver too. Some of the other drivers can really be a pain, but a few, including William, add a few skips to the beat of her heart.

But something's odd here. It isn't like William to grind the gears and stop short of her window, and make her step out to greet him.

203

"Well, hey there, sailor, whaddaya got for us tonight?" she says.

William moves mechanically on the other side of his window—a window he hasn't rolled down so he can say hello and throw her a compliment, as he usually does. Ava feels self-conscious about her flirting; she's never had good timing with guys and tends to hop around with one foot in her mouth. Maybe she's gotten lucky and he didn't hear her.

The window finally lowers. William pivots stiffly to hand her the bill of lading. She and William often share a game of acting out various celebrities or rock stars, leaving the other to guess who they are impersonating.

"David Bowie!" she exclaims excitedly. "No, no, no! It's that other guy. You know, the one with oversize suits and spiky hair, David Something. . . ."

They're always talking music. His tastes run toward early rock 'n' roll and rockabilly; he does a pretty decent Elvis imitation.

William doesn't even look at her; he stares overhead with lifeless, unexcited eyes.

"The robot thing," she says. "You're moving all jerky like that. David Whateverhisnameis."

Nothing.

"Dang, William, you could at least say, 'Hey, darlin' or something."

"Hey, darlin' or something," the driver says, his voice sounding a single flat note.

"More with the robot thing, huh?" Ava plays along, doing her best to make her movements look mechanical as she inspects the delivery manifest, flipping pages. "Plasticware, huh? Captain Kirk to Mr. Spork." She waits for him to acknowledge the joke. "Mr. Spork?" she repeats. Still nothing. "You okay, William?"

"I . . . am . . . fine. Busy."

"In a real hurry to drop off some plastic knives, are we?" Zero reaction. "Did I do something wrong, William? Something to upset you? I'm just having a little fun."

"I . . . am . . . having . . . fun too."

"You don't have to mock me." Ava swallows hard, telling herself she's not going to cry in front of him. "Go on. Make your delivery. What do I care?"

She steps inside the booth and hits a button, lowering the massive concrete-and-steel barrier until it sinks level with the roadway to allow the truck to drive through. The barrier has been tested against a tank. The tank lost.

William's shifting of the gears makes it sound like he's forgotten how to drive. The noise causes Ava to step out of the booth once again and try to catch sight of him in the truck's side rearview mirror. What the heck is he thinking, driving like that? The truck is barely moving as he grinds the gears for the fourth time.

Ava's walking behind the truck now as it rolls across the barrier, while William is still searching for a gear—any gear, it would seem. Looking at the back of the trailer, Ava starts to run to catch up. She reaches out and grabs hold of something stuck to the back door just as William gets the truck rolling.

The vehicle pulls away, leaving her with a handful of what she mistakenly thought was a Davy Crockett or Tom Sawyer raccoon cap. Turns out it's not a cap at all, but a thick tuft of animal fur, which seems somehow to have gotten snagged on the trailer door and torn off. But it's enough hair to fill a plastic sack from the supermarket. It's disgusting, and smelly, and . . . *wild*, Ava thinks. Long hair, like that of an abominable snowman—something freakish and scary.

She drops the clump of fur. It gets caught in the draft of

the truck and scurries along the pavement like an unleashed rodent. It finally stops, and Ava retrieves it.

The existence of the fur bothers her. It's the kind of thing she feels compelled to report. She's already composing her report as she returns to the security booth: "Small chunk of fur—likely that of abominable snowman or yeti—found stuck to delivery trailer."

If she wrote such a thing for any other company they'd have her locked up in a loony bin. But not in Disneyland!

She loves this place.

21

FINN, PHILBY, AND MAYBECK share an actors' trailer as their dorm room. It's twenty-two feet long with a double bed in the back, a small galley kitchen, and a shower/toilet. The trailer has two televisions, one in the bedroom and another in the sitting area, where a bench converts into a narrow bed. Refusing to sleep in a double bed together, the boys rotate places, with one of them sleeping on the floor or—in Finn's case—a narrow loft at the front intended for storage, but just big enough to hold him.

This storage area also plays host to stereo speakers connected to a below-average radio–CD player, its sound so pitiful the boys use their iPhones and earbuds to play their tunes instead.

After the return from Indiana Jones, the Keepers gave immediate attention to Maybeck's leg wound, which looks better now. He is sleeping soundly on the converted bench; Philby has the bed tonight. It's late, extremely late, the kind of late that is no longer fun. Finn's head is gooey, his limbs restless, his mind too active to allow him to drift off. Dawn looms like a ticking clock in his head; he wills it to go away, to give him more time, to spare him the fatigue that weighs him down like wet clothes.

He misses home. He misses Dillard. The events of that fateful day replay in his memory, preventing sleep even if he could feel tired, which he cannot. It's a lousy night in paradise.

Involuntarily riding a roller coaster of semiconsciousness and poisonous nightmare, Finn hears voices.

Actually, only a single voice: Wayne's.

Convincing himself he's fully awake, Finn traces the source of the voice not to his own driven-toward-insanity-exhaustion but to the stereo speakers. It's not Wayne, but the radio. Stupid Maybeck must have bumped the radio's on/off button in his sleep—it wouldn't be the first time; the console is right at the foot of his bench.

Fury at Maybeck sweeps through Finn; he's mad at Philby too, for having the bed tonight after he, Finn, was nearly killed in the Indiana Jones ride.

For an instant, the haze lifts and Finn realizes it's the fatigue making him think of his friends this way; it isn't the *real* him. But at the same time, that also feels like a lie; it's increasingly difficult to distinguish the angry Finn who killed his best friend from the well-intentioned once-innocent kid who wanted to help save the Disney kingdom. Noble aspirations, he's learning, disperse fast under the pressures of reality. What's at stake are no longer only fairies, princesses, and sword-wielding heroes but human lives, his own included. The Keepers must confront wounds and pain, frustration and confusion, and complicated relationships that aren't anything like they look in TV and movies. He and Amanda hurt each other's feelings, usually unintentionally, and that hurt doesn't go away when a laugh track kicks in.

How many times has his mother warned him, saying things like, "I know you're in a hurry to grow up, but believe me, cherish your childhood. You won't get these days back," and "Growing up isn't all it's cracked up to be"?

Being a DHI has spilled over into his other world as well. His mother hasn't fully returned to herself after the weeks she spent under Maleficent's control. Like Finn's, her nights are restless; unlike Finn, she battles unpredictable headaches and endures times when she hears no one, locked in a damaged space she has yet to describe or explain. She gets a faraway look sometimes that terrifies her husband and family. Finn worries for her, for his fellow Keepers, for Wayne and the kingdom. His former not-a-care-in-the-world self has been contaminated by his worrier-warrior self. His brain won't quiet, his heart can't stop aching.

Finn hopes beyond hope that this is not what being an adult is like. If it is, he understands why Peter Pan thought better of it.

As he suspected, the radio is on. Worse, Maybeck's feet smell so bad that getting close to the console to turn off the radio is an act of self-torture. Worse yet, the radio's on/off button now appears to be broken and won't switch off. Pinching his nose with one hand, Finn resorts to turning down the volume. Of course that knob is also broken.

By this point, Finn half convinces himself that he's fallen asleep after all—the thing may be cheap, but when does a radio not turn off or turn down? He must be in some kind of waking nightmare. He tries changing stations, which also has no effect. It's the same voice on every channel, prompting the inevitable question: Is he sleepwalking? Can people think clearly when they're sleepwalking? Do they think they think clearly, or do they not think at all? To outside observers, they march around like zombies, but if a sleepwalker can make himself a peanut-butter-and-jelly sandwich, isn't some cognitive activity going on?

But Finn knows he's not a zombie, just a tired kid trying to turn off a radio that won't stop blabbing in a voice that sounds incredibly like an old guy he admires and wants badly to please. Wait. Dream or not, Finn pays enough attention to the voice to determine the identity of the speaker, and it really is Wayne's voice—distorted, made thinner and higher by the horrible stereo, but Wayne Kresky's voice, no question. Perhaps *that* explains why it will not turn off, turn down, or change channels.

For a moment this simply confirms what Finn has been suspecting—that he's dreaming. But maybe, he thinks, if he pays attention to the voice rather than trying to eliminate it, the dream will pass and he can get on with his much-needed sleep. Whether it's the correct decision or not, he doesn't see much choice; the voice doesn't appear to be going away.

"What has two hundred and sixty-four legs, consumes more than thirty pounds of meat a day, and has only one head? At nine o'clock Friday night, hide where ears never listened."

The same question repeated over and over. How had he missed that? He wonders if the message changed at the instant he decided to listen, or if he was deaf to its content during his efforts to silence it. The sound of Wayne's voice has the unexpected effect of bringing tears to Finn's eyes; it's like seeing a lost family pet appear at the door. A flood of happiness and relief engulfs him, and he hears himself saying aloud, "Thank you. Thank you," having no idea to whom he's speaking.

The thing to do is write down the riddle. Finn takes to the task like it's his dying wish. He considers waking Philby— it would be unfair to wake the injured Maybeck—to help him determine the riddle's authenticity, but elects to get it down word for word instead. Wayne has a thing for words; he's careful and conservative in his use of language. Overall, he's impressive, not someone to question. He has answers to nearly every question, but often only poses the questions—a frustrating trait that has something to do with what he calls

210

"making one think for oneself." The expression baffles Finn; as far as he knows, thinking is an intimately personal act that you could not share even if you wished to. And he often does wish to.

He scribbles out:

What has one head, two hundred sixty-four legs, and consumes more than thirty pounds of meat a day? At nine o'clock Friday night, hide where ears never listened.

Wayne has offered up some doozies over their time as DHIs—the Stonecutter's Quill was among the most difficult puzzles to solve—but not only does this riddle seem to make no sense, it's as though there's a sentence or two missing.

The old Imagineer uses riddles to prevent the Overtakers' understanding any messages they intercept. He presumes the Keepers will figure them out, thereby establishing their superiority over the Overtakers and receiving information critical to their mission.

Yet this particular message eludes Finn. He wants badly to solve it himself, to be able to deliver the solution to the others; he wants to reinforce his leadership position even while he's wondering why it's his to begin with. Leaders don't kill their best friends. Leaders don't allow their mothers to be placed under spells. Leaders don't endlessly question their own decisions and their value to their team. At least, Finn doesn't think they do.

With a shiver, he forces his mind back to the task at hand. A message from Wayne is top priority. Grudgingly, Finn admits temporary defeat and wakes Philby for a consultation.

The groggy boy emerges from the trailer's only private

room, scratching his head of red hair and contorting his freckled face like a cartoon figure. The California sun has brought out Philby's freckles in ways the Florida sun failed to do, an effect the Professor feels needs scientific explanation—but that will have to wait. Philby fiddles with the radio, faces the front of the trailer, and gazes into the sound of Wayne's voice, repeating its inscrutable words in an endless loop.

"You're not dreaming," Philby says. "It's him. Have you written it down?"

"Yes. We need to wake the others. We need to solve the riddle. Now."

"Agreed. Here's another riddle: Why does this stuff always happen in the middle of the night?" Philby asks. "I was actually getting a decent night's sleep."

* * *

⊁KWilla feels a chill run down her back. She trusts Philby and she cares about him—really cares about him—but she can't believe what he's done. For a guy who typically thinks he's the smartest in the room, he's made a foolish and dangerous decision. Ever since Maybeck was captured and hidden in Space Mountain all those years ago, the Keepers have never, ever worked alone. Philby knows that. True, they're more experienced now. But what if this is a trap? Without any backup and an unstable DHI, Finn could be easy prey.

What if the Overtakers plan to capture him? What if, knowing that Finn killed Maleficent, they are out for revenge? Willa imagines Finn trapped, surrounded by villains, unable to go all clear because his DHI is malfunctioning. The villains approach him, getting closer and closer, and there's nothing Finn can do. . . .

"What were you thinking?" Willa gasps. For a moment,

212

she remembers the Cryptos' warning of an "enemy within." Philby has always wanted to be the Keepers' leader. His decision and its possible consequences terrify her.[35]

"Cross me over," Willa says. It's taken the Keepers a while to solve the first part of Wayne's riddle. Finn's impatience has caused a Keepers rule to be broken, and Willa can't believe Philby went along with it.

"No way."

"Why, because it's too dangerous? You realize how this is going to look? We're supposed to work in pairs. But you sent Finn off *alone*. Everyone knows you've wanted the leadership role. If anything should happen to Finn, how do you think it's going look?"

Philby looks panic-stricken.

"Yeah," Willa says. "That's what I thought. So I repeat: Cross me over! As in now!"

---

[35] Adventure_Willa

22

^{ЖК}**A** YOUNG GIRL, no older than six, clings to her mother as they board a Doom Buggy in the Haunted Mansion. A teenager's taunting in the Stretching Room scared the little one, causing her to question her earlier excitement over a first-ever visit to the "grown-up" attraction.

The Doom Buggy creeps forward. Sitting with her mother at her side, the little girl sees nothing as scary as the teenager suggested was in store for her. She relaxes—just a little—and begins to enjoy the ride.

Mother and daughter round a corner into a room in which a large glass ball floats like a giant bubble. A woman's head floats within the ball, her face pale, her lips red. A chant echoes eerily. The girl feels a chill. Her mother wraps her arm around her, and the girl cuddles close.

"You know the glass snow globes we have at home?" her mother asks. It's a rhetorical question; the snow globes are her daughter's favorite souvenirs. "That woman—Madame Leota, they call her—is like that."

"But she's alive!"

"It's a trick. An illusion. It does look real, doesn't it?"

The girl knows her mother's voice well enough to understand that even she is surprised by what she's calling "an illusion"—whatever *that* means.

Their buggy lunges forward as the ride comes to an abrupt stop. Around them, a few park guests scream. The girl, having never been on the ride before, assumes this is all just part of the show. Even so, she's prompted to complain. "I don't like this so much."

Her mother says nothing, only clutches her more tightly, making the little girl uneasy. Theatrical smoke spills into the room. It tastes funny, like the air in the laundry room at home.

"This is new," her mother says. She's a veteran of the ride. She doesn't sound too thrilled.

From out of the swirling smoke emerges a woman in a flowing nightgown.

"Look, Mommy, it's a vampire!"

Her mother squeezes her daughter's shoulder all the harder.

A hideous Madame Leota approaches, not at all the headless woman in the glass ball. But it's her. Somehow, there's no denying it. The young girl screams. Trapped in the Doom Buggy by the safety bar, the girl and her mother can do nothing but squirm away as far from Leota as they can get. Leota finishes her chant and raises her arms as her eyes roll back in her head. The girl's mother screams louder than she ever has before, prompting her daughter to release a shriek so shrill that a ripple of cries arises from the neighboring buggies in response.

A flash of lightning explodes only a few feet away from their buggy. Madame Leota is gone. Vaporized. A foul-smelling pocket of brown smoke spirals up from the spot on which the ghost stood.

"Who's that?" the girl says. But her mother's eyes are clamped shut. The person the girl has spotted holds something that looks vaguely like a gun, but thin wires emerge out of its handle. The wires are attached to a plastic comb, which is lying on the floor where the ghost was. As quickly as this person appears, he vanishes.

The buggies buck and start to move. Emergency lights replace the show lights. A calm voice tells guests, "Playful ghosts have interrupted our tour. Please remain seated in your Doom Buggy. We will proceed in a moment."

The buggies move faster than before, whipping along the track in the patchy glare of the emergency lighting. The scenes around them look like their family attic: scattered, dust-covered junk.

"That wasn't fun," the girl says. "Mommy? I said, 'That wasn't fun.'"

"No, sweetie," her mother says, looking terrified in the harsh white emergency lights. "That wasn't fun. It went too far, even for me. But we're safe now. We're fine."

"What about her?"

"Who, sweetie?"

"Her."

The girl points up. In the shadow of one of the rafters, a woman's burned face is just visible. It's Madame Leota, tucked into a ball, her singed arms clutched tightly around her legs. The little girl's mother screams.

Thirty yards away, the guests are quickly exiting with the help of Cast Members. They all turn as one in horror as the woman's anguished cry flies up from inside the ride behind them, spurring all to run in panic for the exit, despite futile calls from the Cast Members to remain calm.[36]

---

[36] Bridge_Shadows

23

FINN CROSSES OVER INTO THE PLAZA with only a minor incident. He knows where to find Club 33 and is feeling more familiar with Disneyland. As a result, he is more confident and relaxed. The issue is one he's faced before: the problem of how to deal with the astonished guest.

This time it's an eight-year-old boy who's familiar with the Keepers from *Disney 365* on the Disney Channel. The boy witnesses Finn's materialization—a shadow forms, particles of light sparkle, and the three-dimensional projected image of Finn Whitman appears—as real as any boy he's met before. Finn's celebrity is all that registers, not his being a hologram; in fact, it never occurs to the boy that he's looking at a hologram. He's seen so many special effects in his short life, he can no longer distinguish reality from the movies and shows he sees. Tell him Iron Man can't fly and he'll scoff at you; try to explain that Percy Jackson is just a story and he'll dismiss you as stupid and ignorant. This is Finn, the Kingdom Keeper.

"Is it really you?" the boy asks.

"It is." Finn steps up to the boy and kneels down onto one knee so he can look him in the eye. "And I'm on a mission," he whispers, "so I need you to keep a secret. You can't tell anyone you saw me. Can you do that?"

The boy nods, now unable to utter a word.

"Attaboy. Thanks!"

Another nod, this time sheepish. The boy looks back and Finn follows his line of sight to a woman busy with a toddler in a stroller; he takes her to be the boy's mother. Finn spots an autograph book sticking out of a pocket on the back of the stroller.

"The thing is," Finn says, "if other kids see me sign your autograph book, then maybe they're going to want my autograph too, and that means other people will know our secret, and then it won't be our secret any more. So let's do this: you sneak over there like the best Kingdom Keeper Insider spy we've ever had. Okay? Do your best to hide the autograph book as you bring it over to me." The boy is now nodding so hard, it looks like his head might pop off. "I will pretend to tie my shoe. Don't forget a pen! Bring me the book, place it by my shoes and I'll sign it and you can sneak it back. Deal?"

"Deal!"

"Great. You'd better tell me your name now."

"Phillip. My name's Phillip."

"Nice to meet you, Phillip. Okay. Start your mission!"

A minute later, the autograph book is signed, and Finn is on his way, wishing he and the Keepers had more interaction in the parks with the guests. The encounter will be something the boy remembers always—Finn is certain of that. The astonished eyes, the sincere excitement—that's what the parks stand for: the thrill of imagination, the magic of the mind. All that is what he and the Keepers are fighting for—quite literally at times: the opportunity to dream. Finn's brief encounter with the boy has satisfied some empty space in him that needed filling. The Overtakers want to blot out such thrills, destroy one of the few places left where mind triumphs over matter.

His head lowered so that his face will not be recognized, Finn follows the sea of running shoes, sunburned legs, ankle socks, canes, crutches, and wheels of many sizes and varieties. Reminded of his reason for coming here, he feels emboldened.

Might cannot be allowed to triumph over right.

Finn's destination remains only marginally uncertain. When the Keepers solve one of Wayne's riddles, they try not to second-guess themselves. The solution involved a battle of wits and demanded a combination of both knowledge and experience.

* * *

Hours earlier, the Keepers had gathered for dinner at the Studio Commissary, taking a table away from other workers. Food fueled their collective power of reasoning. They did some of their best group thinking at places like Cosmic Ray's or the Disney *Dream*'s cabanas.

What has one head, two hundred sixty-four legs, and consumes more than thirty pounds of meat a day? At nine o'clock Friday night, hide where ears never listened.

Maybeck began sketching almost immediately, first drawing legs: many, many people, each with two legs.

"Too many legs for any kind of sports team," he said, very quickly.

Willa stole the pencil from Maybeck and sketched out the curving arc of a choir.

"A choir!" she said. "A big choir has hundreds of legs and a conductor who could be considered the head. And a choir could easily eat thirty pounds of meat!"

"Or a band. One of those marching bands that visits the parks," Finn said.

"Or girls at a cheerleading contest. You do not want to see how much food cheerleaders can pack away!"

Philby had trouble keeping up with his iPhone. He was on the Disneyland Web site, checking out the nighttime activities. The others waited for him impatiently.

"It's a no on the choir," Philby said. "There *was* a band in the park today, from Alberta, Canada, but they were part of the afternoon parade and that's all over."

"Cheerleaders?" Charlene inquired.

"Nada," Philby answered.

Maybeck took back the pencil and drew an ugly centipede. As he sketched, the group fell silent. Maybeck spun the napkin he'd drawn on so that the creature faced each of them. They didn't need any encouragement to envision the centipede at a gargantuan size—with 264 legs, a single head, and a voracious appetite for meat—or human flesh.

"Yeah, okay," Finn said, "point taken. But what about the second part, the hiding 'where no ears listened'? How does a monster centipede fit into that? And why would Wayne tell me about a giant insect anyway?"

"A new Overtaker?" Maybeck said.

"Like Gigabyte," Charlene said, reminding them all of the thirty-foot snake that had attacked them in Epcot.

"Gross," Willa said.

"No ears," Charlene said. "Maybe the thing is deaf. Maybe Wayne's trying to warn us the bug is deaf."

"And I'm supposed to hide where the thing doesn't have ears?" Finn said.

"Furniture," Philby said.

"What?" Maybeck asks.

Philby slid his blank napkin to Maybeck. "Furniture has legs."

"At last check," Maybeck said, "furniture doesn't eat thirty pounds of meat."

"Math!" Willa said excitedly. She plucked the pencil from Maybeck before he could start sketching. "Two-hundred sixty-four divided by four—tables, chairs, doesn't matter, they all have four legs. It's—"

"Sixty-six," Philby said.

"Show off!" Charlene can't help herself.

"A head table?" Finn asked. "Like in Harry Potter at the end of the dining hall?"

"A headwaiter!" said Willa. "It's a dining room! A restaurant in the park."

"If there are sixty-six tables, there are hundreds of people," said the Professor. "Easily enough to eat thirty pounds of meat."

"But if it's sixty-six *chairs*," said Willa, "then we know the capacity of the restaurant. It's smaller. Easier to identify. Wayne's telling you," she said to Finn, "to meet him at a restaurant."

"Sixty-six people eating thirty pounds of meat?" Charlene said. "That's disgusting."

"That's a half-pound hamburger per person. It's logical," Philby said. "And the number of chairs is the key. Willa's right."

Willa blushed.

Philby was already busy surfing the Internet. His head snapped up. "Wait a second!" He took in the group. "The math doesn't work, but I'm not sure it has to. Sixty-six is the important number. That, and the name of a restaurant . . . if you cut it in half."

"Thirty-three!" Willa spat out, wanting to solve the math ahead of everyone else, but having no idea of the number's significance until Finn spoke up.

"Club 33."

"It's a private club!" Maybeck complained.

Philby's fingers flew. "I can't confirm the capacity, but I mean, come on! Club 33. Yes, a private club. But an old-time Imagineer like Wayne would probably belong, right?"

"What about hiding 'where ears never listened'?" Charlene said, clearly skeptical.

"I don't know," Philby said. "I admit it. But sixty-six chairs in Club 33? It's possible, right? It would be so Disney to make a play on the number, wouldn't it?"

"And if it happens to seat sixty-six people, then even the thirty pounds of meat makes sense," Willa said. But Willa tends to support Philby when it comes to such things, and by now each of the Keepers was trying to make sense of it for him- or herself.

Having gone back to his phone, Philby looked up and said, "Trust me, it has to be it. There aren't any restaurants close to that small in Disneyland. Not that size *and* with a headwaiter."

"I'll have to figure out the part about hiding 'where ears never listened' when I get there," Finn said. "But it's worth a try."

* * *

Now as a DHI, Finn makes his way with the teeming crowds, *trying* to move quickly enough not to be recognized; *trying* not to move too fast for fear of sticking out; *trying,* even now, to make sense of "hide where ears never listened." He notes the past tense. Wayne said not *listen* but *listened.* That's significant. Even the tiniest part of one of Wayne's clues is significant. The ears had failed to listen sometime in the past, meaning that whatever they had heard but failed to attend to had to be something *known,* something to do with Disney history or lore.

It takes Finn several minutes to find a pay phone, several

more to borrow a quarter to use it: he reaches Philby on the first ring.

"It's me. Who's the woman at the Archives?"

"Becky Someone," Philby says. "Why?"

"You need to call Becky. Make something up about us doing a report or something and ask her about any lore that has to do with Club 33 and something that happened in the *past*, an incident when someone didn't listen."

"Are you feeling all right?" Philby asks.

"Yeah."

"Because you sound a little strange," Philby says. "You want me to call some woman I've never met and—"

"We saved the Archives. She owes us. She will be happy to help."

"You know this, how?"

"Call her. I've only got twenty minutes. You've got to hurry. Now, Philby. I need this now. Disney history. Disney lore. Wayne used the past tense."

"You're going all language arts on me?"

"Mickey Mouse could be the 'ears' in 'where ears never listened.'"

"I'm on it!" Philby says excitedly. Finn has finally gotten through to him. "How do I reach you?"

"I'm on a pay phone, but it says it doesn't receive calls."

"So you'll have to call me back."

"That's a hassle. I don't have any quarters. It would help if you'd get version 1.6 stable enough that we could bring our phones with us."

"I knew you were going to say something like that. No matter what I do, it's never enough."

"Cue the violins. You're sounding like Maybeck."

"As if." Philby pauses, then blurts out, "Maybe I can

223

get the information to Willa before she crosses over."

"Wait! What?"

"Willa."

"I got that part," Finn says.

"She thinks I set you up to fail. She's crossing over as we speak."

"You can't do that! It could be a trap!"

"A point I tried to make. Live with it. She's coming."

"I'll call you back." Finn hangs up. He doesn't like sparring with Philby. It only seems to happen in moments of crisis; the rest of the time, they get along well enough. Arguing makes him suspicious of Philby, a feeling Finn doesn't like. He knows that Philby, with his superior smarts and keen sense of reasoning, feels like the real leader of the Keepers and feels denied by Finn assuming that role. For a long time Finn did not want the leadership position; he even let Philby have it. But for a brief period when Wayne seemed to favor Philby, Finn did not like it one bit. He realized how much he valued Wayne's attention, how much Wayne's faith in him mattered. He wanted to be the one getting assigned the missions, the one setting the agenda. He wanted to have the inside track, to know stuff before anyone else did. He knew how dangerous a road it was to walk—balancing your sense of self-importance against humility and what was truly important: ego versus reality.

But Finn can't shake the dread that surfaces occasionally, the fear that Philby might sacrifice him in order to lead the others. Not kill him—Philby is no murderer. But Philby is brilliant; he could easily orchestrate a situation that would make Finn look like an idiot or (and this was the worst thought of all) a situation in which a decision of Finn's might injure the other Keepers. What are Philby's goals and aspirations? Like all the Keepers, he must have his own reasons for staying in the group. How much is Finn in the way of his friend's ambitions?

Finn can't let Willa, DHI or not, put herself at risk by getting too close to him. He has to move fast.

"Excuse me? I've lost my family and I need a quarter to call my mom's cell phone. I wonder if you happen to have a quar—"

"Here. Use mine." Finn faces a girl who looks to be his own age, but slightly taller. Her arm extended, she holds out a cell phone. She has a toothy smile revealing a mouthful of braces. She can't quite bring her bright eyes to focus on him. It's then Finn sees she's wearing a Kingdom Keepers T-shirt. Maybeck had once shown them all a Web site selling the Keepers Kharacters shirts, but it's the first time Finn has seen anyone wearing one.

"Brooke," she says. "My name. It's Brooke."

"Finn."

"Yeah." She giggles.

Finn's embarrassed. "You sure you don't mind?"

"Think about it," she says, gesturing toward her shirt. "I mean . . . really? You can erase the number and everything. I don't care. Not that I'd ever redial it or anything like that, because I wouldn't. Can I just ask you something?"

"Please."

"Are you—*you*? You know? I mean, are you Finn or are you *him*?"

"I think I know what you mean," Finn says. He waves his hand and it passes through hers.

Brooke lets out a happy-sounding sigh. Something great has just happened for her, Finn realizes.

"Oh!" she says. "That is so-o-o-o-o-o cool. You can kind of feel it, you know?"

"You can?" First Finn has heard of that.

"Or maybe I'm making that up. Maybe I imagined it."

Finn waves his hand through her arm again.

She looks like she's either about to fall asleep or shout for joy. Her eyes are glassy, as if she might cry.

"You're sure you don't mind?" he says.

"What?" He's lost her; she's off somewhere else.

"Your phone?"

"Mind? *Do I mind*?" She does not mind.

Finn gets Philby's voice mail and asks him to send a text to Brooke's number.

"I gave Philby your number."

"No worries."

"You don't mind hanging here a minute?"

"Ah, no . . . I don't mind." She takes a deep breath. "So what's it like? Being you, I mean?"

"Same as you," Finn says.

She laughs loudly. It's a great laugh. A big, heartfelt laugh that Finn could listen to for hours. "I don't think so."

"Some of it's cool," he says, "but some not so cool."

"I don't mean to stalk you or anything."

"Not at all! You're doing me a favor."

Her phone buzzes. She avoids looking at it as she passes it to Finn, which impresses him.

a listening system was installed in Club 33 so an unseen host could answer questions or make fun of guests at tables. was never used. small closet with working equip still exists.

Finn reads the message twice, deletes it, and returns the phone to Brooke.

"You know the park pretty well?" Finn asks her.

"I do indeed. I am all about everything Disney. 'A walking

encyclopedia,' my mother calls me. She means that as a compliment."

Finn laughs. "Would you happen to know any way a hologram could sneak into Club 33 without being caught?"

"Angels," she says.

"Excuse me?"

"I just may know a way," Brooke says.

* * *

Ten minutes pass. An excited Brooke leads Finn into the Court of Angels, a dead-end alley. She points to a wooden staircase leading up to a New Orleans–style balcony. "I've seen waiters up there before. It's definitely Club 33—when the doors open, you can see the gold-and-white wallpaper."

"Like a service entrance."

"Maybe. I've never actually been up there," she says.

"You're just observant."

"I am." She pauses. "You can walk through walls, right?"

"I can."

"I heard you all can go invisible."

"Not really. It happens sometimes, but it's nothing we can control." He adds, "Sadly. How cool would that be?"

"I know, right?"

"It's more like a shadow thing. It has to do with the location of the projectors."

"Will there be projectors in Club 33?"

"Good question. Probably. The technology can use security cameras—don't ask me how!—and there would be security cameras in a place like Club 33."

"Can you wear an apron?"

"I could, but I tend to stay pretty much all clear, so it would probably fall off."

"Carry a tray?"

"Yes. Definitely."

"I've seen waiters come and go through that door to the right. You could check there . . . maybe."

Finn thanks Brooke. Their parting is awkward. Brooke offers to stay below and signal Finn if someone's coming up the stairs. He tells her that could be helpful, but he doesn't want her getting in trouble.

"I'll sing the Small World song. If you hear the Small World song, that's the signal."

"Got it."

"I'm a good singer," she says. "And a competitive skater. I'm enrolled at Pepperdine. Freshman year." She looks befuddled. "Did I just say all that?"

"Philby has your number," Finn says.

"Yeah, I guess that's right."

Finn thanks her again and heads upstairs.

Everything Brooke has told him is accurate: The door to the right appears to access the club. The door straight ahead is open, leading to a vestibule of some kind that contains some furniture but appears to lead farther inside. Disneyland and Disney World are like no other places, built like stage sets, with misleading corridors and false facades. Finn enters the club, head down. There are two main dining rooms separated by a wide L-shaped expanse of old wooden flooring. A sign to Finn's left reads MAXIMUM SEATING: 33. Another identical sign is mounted straight ahead. That totals sixty-six. Finn knows he's in the right place.

Just ahead Finn sees a tray of dirty dishes on a collapsible waiter's stand. He picks it up and starts moving.

The dining room that is now straight ahead is the closer of the two to the top of the staircase used by guests as they enter. There's a maître d's station with a computer screen. Finn moves toward this dining room, feeling conspicuous. He's saved by how busy the restaurant is. Waiters are practically flying in all directions, racing from one place to the next. No one has time to study a kid who might be a busboy.

Finn slips past the maître d's station, grateful that it is unoccupied, and continues past an empty coat check and, in the wall to his left, an oddly shaped cupboard or closet door mounted at waist height.

Timing is everything. *Three . . . two . . . one.*

Balancing the tray, he tugs open the cupboard door just a crack. The door is wide, and about two feet deep.

"Help you?" It's a waiter. He sounds genuinely caring, not suspicious.

"I'm good," Finn says.

The man mugs, nods, and moves on.

Finn sets the tray of dishes down on another folding waiter's tray stand just nearby. Inside the cupboard are two high shelves that hold some dusty electronic gear, including an ancient pair of headphones, and, below that, open space. Finn checks around him. He waits for a pair of waiters to pass, then climbs in and pulls the door shut.

He's inside.

A narrow rectangle of yellow light seeps in at eye level from some kind of small aperture in the wall of the cupboard that faces the dining room at the top of the stairs. There's just enough light for Finn to discover that he's in DHI shadow—but there's no way for him to know exactly where the boundaries of that shadow begin. If someone were to open the cupboard door, would they see all of him? Part of him? He hopes it doesn't come to that.

Remarkably, he fits well into the space, sitting with his

back against a sidewall and his knees bent. It's almost as if the cupboard had been made to hold a person—a thought Finn dismisses, until he begins toying with a small sliding piece of wood he discovers on the wall, which accounts for the rectangle of light.

The sliding cover moves on little tracks. Finn places his digital eye to the slot that the open cover reveals: he's looking into the restaurant through a peephole. He can imagine, but can't confirm, an oil painting or decorative mirror concealing the peephole on the dining-room side. None of the diners appears to be the wiser for his having opened the peephole.

Finn looks out on tables with adults eating and drinking, some deep in conversation, some quiet, others more animated. The tables are mostly deuces and four-tops; among them are two groups of eight, and one person dining alone: a white-haired man wearing an Imagineer's ball cap that must date back twenty years.

Finn knows the cap, and knows the man. He nearly screams with joy. *Wayne!* Seeing him in the flesh has far more impact than having heard his voice over the radio. Voices can be recorded, impersonated. Finn wants to shout through the little hole in the wall, wave a flag, wag a finger.

⚡Finn's heart is near breaking. To see Wayne—a man whom he respects and, yes, even loves, like a grandfather— after so long, creates a flood of emotion. Few people in his life can arouse such feelings in Finn: his family, Amanda, Dillard.

As Finn watches Wayne, he begins to question his own gullibility, worries he's being set up. Is Wayne a DHI, like the one at Fantasmic!? Can he trust this man?

Finn is considered the leader of the Keepers, though they've never formally chosen him as such. It has always just been the position that best suited him, just as Maybeck is the artist and Philby's the computer guy.

Wayne is the real leader. Finn considers himself just a representative. Anger mixes with sadness as he wonders if he can trust this Wayne, his mentor since the very beginning. If he can't even trust Wayne, then who can he trust? One name flashes through his thoughts: *Amanda.*

Cynics would say you can only trust yourself, but for Finn that makes *trust* too lonely a world. Paranoia threatens, but he holds it at bay. He must look for signs: human being or DHI? He will not allow himself to be tricked by the Overtakers again. This thought strengthens his hatred of the villains all the more.

A salient battle cry echoes through his head: *This needs to end. Soon.*[37]

Finn hears a squeaking sound. *Not mice!* he prays. *Anything but mice! Except cockroaches. Not them either! Please!*

Finn's wristwatch ticks over from 8:59 to 9:00. The squeaking continues.

Finn lifts himself up off the floor where he is sitting, fearful that the creature is under him. He's going to freak out if there's a mouse or rat in here with him.

Nothing.

More squeaking. It takes him a moment to identify the source of the sound as the beat-up old set of headphones hanging from a hook above one of the shelves. He pulls the set closer and holds an ear cup to his ear. Not a rodent; it's a human voice coming from one of the headphone set's two ear cups. A man's voice, whispering: Wayne.

"The microphone is on your right. Speak to me." Wayne

---

[37] Visitors_Brave

repeats this, his head canted down toward the table. To look at him, he's just an old man talking to himself.

Finn finds the microphone, which is like no microphone he's ever seen before. It's a metal diaphragm suspended by rusted springs at the center of a wire loop shaped like a lightbulb. If Wayne hadn't told him it was a microphone, he wouldn't have known. He takes hold of it, but because of the DHI shadow the microphone appears to float toward him.

Finn speaks tentatively. "Hello?"

"And to you as well."

"I can't believe it's you!"

"And yet you must."

Finn sets his eye to the peephole again. Wayne flashes a mirthful look his way.

"It's good to see you," Finn says.

"It's good to be seen," says Wayne. "We have a great deal to cover. Will you take notes?" Wayne adjusts what looks like a hearing aid. Whatever the original intention of the sound equipment Finn has discovered in the closet, Wayne seems to have adjusted the system to allow them a private conversation.

"I'm a DHI. I didn't exactly come equipped for school."

"Very well. Shall we begin?"

"No." Finn *never* says no to Wayne. It sounds wrong coming out of his mouth. "First, I need to ask you about the Archives. The break-in."

"A tragedy."

"You were there! The Cryptos said—"

"By 'Cryptos' you mean Imagineers manning the—"

"Across from the Morgue."

"Well, they're wrong, which doesn't happen very often. It wasn't me. I would never do that."

"That's what I said!"

"What you and they apparently failed to comprehend was what it means."

"What *what* means?" Finn asks.

"If it wasn't me, but it fooled you all, *what does it mean?*"

"They—projected—you." The words fall out of Finn painfully. His heart twists. Is he speaking to a hologram now?

"I thought one of you might have noticed that I was wearing the same clothes as my hologram in Fantasmic! I realize it was a long time ago, but that's hardly an excuse."

"But you were—"

"So lifelike? I didn't think you all would be fooled by one-point-six."

"The Overtakers projected you!"

"I've seen the footage. They needed me to get the door open and take care of security for them. We can't dwell on this, Finn. You're going to have to trust me."

"Yes. Okay." Finn has so many questions, so many concerns. He wishes he weren't stuck in a cupboard wearing a set of crumbling headphones and talking over a tea strainer.

Wayne's voice lowers further. It sounds like a desert wind.

"Very well, let us begin."

Finn hears people passing close by the cabinet where he huddles, hidden. On the other side of the wall, waiters in the dining room occasionally obscure his view of Wayne.

Wayne maintains a low, conspiratorial voice, ensuring that diners eating at nearby tables have no chance of overhearing him. Peering through the peephole, Finn feels as though he's watching a movie in which he is somehow playing a part. It's a strange, disassociated sensation, one that fills his belly with a tangle of snakes looking for a way out; he feels simultaneously as if he's about to vomit or needs to run for the bathroom.

Contributing to Finn's nausea is the idea of Willa

wandering the park alone, looking for him, while the eyes of Overtakers seek them all. He has violated the DHI partner rule. Now Willa's doing the same: anarchy.

"The best way to explain it," Wayne's voice whispers through the one working earphone, "is that Mickey has always been considered the greatest threat to the OTs. He wins over the villains every night in the Fantasmic! show. His sorcerer's cap and, to a lesser degree, his conductor's baton, are his bewitching tools—his weapons, if you will. You must understand the history involved. This goes clear back to the early days. I was a boy your age, or not much older. Walt was a young man—only in his fifties—with big dreams. The park was perhaps half built, but not yet open. Mickey Mouse was everything Disney. There was no Mary Poppins, no Winnie the Pooh in Walt's world. Not yet. It was this mouse, this silly little mouse everyone loved.

"Or nearly everyone. A divide emerged. A schism within the ranks of the villains. How, we don't exactly know. We don't even know when. But it was early. And it was real. Rebellion. Nothing short of it.

"For those who became the Overtakers, all they could see was that darn mouse, Mickey, looking back with his big eyes. Destroy Mickey, maybe you destroy Walt's dream. Maybe, if you're an OT, you're never again demoted to the status of class clown, rendered insignificant with the stroke of an illustrator's pen, made absurdly colorful, your features exaggerated, your personality stereotyped. Maybe, the reasoning went—at least, this is what we think—there was a way to stop Disney's magic before it ever began."

"But they didn't destroy Mickey," Finn says. "Disneyland's here. Walt built Disney World. All the movies got made. I don't get it."

234

"There's so much magic in the kingdom, Finn. So much magic." Wayne sounds tired, almost defeated. The aching timbre of his voice fills Finn with dread.

"But that's a good thing. That's what we love about Disney. Isn't it?"

"It can be."

Looking through the peephole, Finn has to wonder if the old Imagineer's head is slumped to disguise his speaking, or if it's a sign of unconscious surrender.

Wayne speaks carefully. "Good magic and dark magic."

"Understood," Finn says.

"It took them years, you see? Decades."

"The Overtakers," Finn says, attempting to clarify the point. Wayne no longer seems to be talking to Finn, but only to himself.

"They started by attacking the park's characters after hours. In Disney World, we built Mickey and Minnie their own homes. Not for the guests' sake, Finn, but for the characters' security."

"Those aren't there anymore. Fantasyland . . ." Finn is struggling to understand what Wayne is telling him. "You're saying they *got* him? The Overtakers *got* Mickey?"

He speaks too loudly. Wayne's head lifts as several diners look over toward the wall. Finn overhears two men's voices: "Who said that?" "Where'd that come from?"

Finn quickly sets down the headphones and the microphone. Believing that the nearest security camera, and therefore his DHI projector, is likely near the stairs and the maître d's station, Finn squats and flattens himself against the wall of the closet, hoping to force himself entirely into DHI shadow.

The cupboard door swings open.

Finn is looking into the face of a waiter. It's clear from the man's expression that he doesn't see Finn. The man's eyes drop downward.

"Get a load of that!" he says to the fellow waiter who now appears beside him. "A pair of running shoes."

Finn looks down: his running shoes are visible from tongue to toe. From the waiters' perspective, the depth of the cupboard's interior must explain why only part of the shoes shows.

"Since when did this become our lost and found?" The man eases the door shut and Finn heaves a sigh of relief.

He waits a few seconds.

"I'm back," Finn carefully whispers to Wayne through the ancient mic.

"I need not remind you that the OTs have ears *everywhere*, Finn. We wouldn't be meeting like this if it weren't necessary."

"Understood. I'll keep it down."

"The point is this," Wayne says gravely. "The last time you saw Mickey, the last time *anyone* saw Mickey, was very, very long ago. You don't kidnap someone as iconic as Mickey Mouse. You destroy him."

Finn finds it hard to breathe. "Come again?"

"You heard me."

"The Overtakers destroyed Mickey Mouse?"

"And nearly all the magic that goes with him."

⅏The news hits Finn hard, reminding him of his first time entering Escher's Keep all those years ago, when the idea of being a Kingdom Keeper was a novelty. He's unsure what is up, down, right, wrong, forward, backward. He reaches out mentally for something solid to hold on to. Solid. Yeah, unlike anything I, or the other Keepers are, he thinks. This news . . .

236

it changes everything. Everything we've ever thought about ourselves, what we've done, who we are, what becomes of us now.[38]

"Walt's pen," Finn says, remembering the power that instrument still possesses. *Something solid.*

"A pittance by comparison, but yes: you'd have to get up early to beat Walt Disney."

"But if the OTs got Mickey?"

"They didn't *get* anything. And, by the way, I hate that word. It's an ineffective word. You can do better!"

Wayne's always been petty about the oddest things; but more than anything else so far this comment convinces Finn that he's dealing with the real deal. No Overtaker would know how to fake the quirkier aspects of Wayne's personality.

"They destroyed Mickey. But what does that mean, exactly?" Finn can't see what Wayne's aiming at.

"Ever notice how *everything* in these parks, in the films, *everything* to do with the kingdom is symbolic? It's a magical world built on symbolism, whether it's Main Street, USA, a Fairy Godmother, or Hades himself. It started with a rabbit. Oswald. But it was Mickey who launched an empire. Mickey who carried this company and all it stands for on his back, and Walt never forgot that for a moment. He treasured that first sketch of Mickey like it was the Declaration of Independence or the Constitution. That was, symbolically at least, the start of everything *good* in the kingdom. A single sketch kept in a file in Walt's office, never far out of reach."

"Now you're giving me goose bumps."

"I must focus!" Wayne says. "It's about time. Do you hear me? Can you *see* me, Finn?"

---

[38] Keepers_Puzzle

237

Through the peephole Finn sees Wayne fiddle with his wristwatch.

"By coming here to Disneyland, Finn, the Overtakers have increased their powers exponentially. This is where it all began. You and your team made a valiant effort to keep them away. You, and Dillard in particular, sacrificed a great deal. No matter. They have returned. The incident at the Haunted Mansion is proof. This event justified my taking a chance to reach you. Here we are. And now it must be stopped. *They* must be stopped. Do not for a minute assume that earthquake in Mexico was a fluke. Be on guard to prevent it from happening again, and . . ."

Finn tries to take all this in, but it's overwhelming. He's supposed to stop *an earthquake*? Dillard's name distracts him, sends him plunging into his own dark memories, momentarily deafens him almost, like static buzzing in his ears. He's not sure what Wayne says next, but he knows better than to ask the man to repeat himself.

". . . So you must be vigilant. Betrayal is guaranteed—"

"'An enemy within.' The Cryptos warned us." Finn feels sick and knows he's lost his full DHI. Should anyone open the cupboard now . . .

"Without a doubt. You must trust: it is not me. It would never, will never, be me. But betrayal will come *from all sides*. These are the dark days, Finn. The final hours. All clichés, yes, but there's no other way to say it. It comes down to this: do or die. You and your friends must *do*."

"What exactly does that mean?" Finn doesn't like the sound of that. "If we 'do,' then who dies? No more dying! Please, no more dying!"

24

THE CAST MEMBER "WORKING THE BOARD," as it's known in Security, sees a code appear in the "hot box"—a normally blank box on the computer screen that posts one of a dozen codes to signal a problem. It might be a code for improper use of an emergency exit door, a spot power failure, a data interrupt—all signals that appear so commonly, the Security officer has them memorized. But this code puzzles her. Three years working the board, and she's never seen it.

More to the point, the first two of its six digits—54—tell her it's an old code going back to 1954, the early days, when Disneyland's security system was being installed during the park's construction. She suspects a computer error or a software glitch; an errant line of computer code must have spit out a false alarm. But her job is to be thorough. Earlier today, the Haunted Mansion was closed; an officer at the back gate reported a zombielike truck driver whose truck was later found abandoned, nowhere near its destination. Strange goings-on. Terrorism is on everyone's mind, and Security is trained to spot even the slightest indicator. She is prepared and trained for the worst.

She leafs through the three-ring notebook listing the various codes. As she suspected, she finds the number that's currently occupying the hot box handwritten in a two-column list on the first page. Some of the codes reference Walt's apartment above the fire station and the status of the light that glows in that window; others reference long-defunct attractions such as

20,000 Leagues Under the Sea and are highlighted in orange to indicate rides or spectacles that have been retired.

But the code she matches is not only retired, it's just plain ancient, a code from Club 33, one she doesn't even understand. A code she has to call her supervisor about. When her supervisor informs her that he must make a call in turn, she feels sure that it's a dead code, a computer misfire, as she originally suspected.

To her surprise, her supervisor comes back on the line and asks her to repeat the code slowly, like spelling for a two-year-old.

"Five-four-three-three-two-two." After she finishes, there's a long silence. It sounds as if he's hung up.

"You still there?" she asks.

"I'm here," he says, but it sounds as if he wishes otherwise. He asks if she's sure she has read him the code she is looking at correctly. She assures him that yes, she has.

"What's going on?" she asks.

"Darned if I know," he answers. "Do me a favor." He walks her through a series of tests she's never used before, followed by some she has: tests of data flow, of voltage and wattage on specific circuits. It takes her a minute, but she sees what he's doing. Her suspicions are confirmed as he instructs her to run an audio interrupt on a live audio feed from Club 33, which is sort of like putting a telephone call onto speakerphone.

"Do you hear anything?" he asks. It's a rhetorical question: the information she's gleaned suggests voice traffic.

"How is this possible?"

"What? Tell me what you hear!"

"Two men talking. We have a dining room bugged? Isn't that illegal?"

"We didn't do it. It was the Imagineers before they were

240

Imagineers." He sounds agitated and impatient. "Walt being clever way before anyone was ready for that type of cleverness. Every table in the room is wired for sound, for eavesdropping. The system allows guests to talk to an omniscient voice that comes out of the ceiling. And yes, there were legal issues. It was never used."

"Until now," she says.

"Until now," he echoes. "What do you hear? Who is it? What are they talking about? Why now, all these years later? No one even knows of that system's existence, much less how to use it. Am I supposed to think Walt Disney himself has been resurrected?"

"Which question would you like answered first?" she asks.

"Send a pair of guards to check it out," he says, ignoring her. "And you take notes, officer. You take notes like a stenographer. You got that?"

"Got it," she says, her head ringing with a dozen questions of her own.

25

PHILBY STUDIES HIS RINGING PHONE with apprehension. It doesn't identify the caller's number as either Brooke's phone or the pay phone from which Finn recently called him, and yet the first eight digits are identical to the pay phone's number—area code, central office code, and the first two digits of the station number. Only the final two digits are different, radically increasing the probability that the call is also coming from a pay phone inside Disneyland.

"Hello?" he answers tentatively.

It takes him a second to recognize the voice as Storey Ming's. She talks a blue streak, not allowing Philby a word—something about Finn being "busted"—and she mentions "Security" several times.

"Slow down!" Philby shouts into his cell phone.

"Listen! I *said*, I overheard two Security guys talking on their walkie-talkies. A bunch of them are headed to Club 33. If there's any possibility Finn is inside the club, you need to get him out now. If he's a DHI then you've got to return him. I'm hoping we can trust Security, hoping they support you guys—but if I heard about this, then others have too, and if they have, he isn't safe."

"First, he's not alone. Willa's there somewhere. Second, I can't return either of them until they're at the Plaza. Third, I have no way to contact him or her. No way to warn either of them. So I'm afraid it is what it is." Philby's mind is going like a washing machine. Suds of panic rise. Willa warned him of this. *Accused* him of this. If anything happens . . .

"There must be something! I'll go over there myself," Storey says.

"And walk into a trap? Inadvisable."

"This isn't theory, Philby. Security is going over there to get Finn or Willa or whoever it is they've realized is over there."

Wayne, Philby thinks. At first he feels a stab of terror, but it sorts itself out in his clinical mind and becomes a useful tool. *Wayne! Of course!*

"I have a possible solution. Stand by. Move to a pay phone closer to Club 33 and call me back from there. Don't do anything stupid, Storey. For one thing, you might unintentionally put Finn in more danger than he is already in. Are we good?"

"I'll call you," she says. She doesn't sound very good at all.

* * *

Incoming calls at Club 33 are rare: the restaurant's reservations come through the Disney Dining group and appear on the computer screen before the maître d' at his station, where he has to double as receptionist. So when the phone rings, he answers the phone with reservations of his own. "Dining . . ."

He doesn't identify the club by name because *common people* are always trying to discover the number and publish it on the Internet. He and the headwaiter are responsible for protecting the club: its storied history, its elite membership, and all aspects of its clientele's privacy.

"Hello." There's no mistaking the sound: it's a young man's voice. A mere kid. "I'm sorry to bother you, but I need to reach someone dining at the club tonight. Wayne Kresky. It's about his daughter, Wanda, or I wouldn't bother you."

The maître d' is not in the habit of confirming any particular guest's presence at the club, nor the identity of members.

"I am aware of Mr. Kresky, of course. One of our Disney Legends. I can neither confirm nor deny Mr. Kresky's presence with us here this evening. I am sure you understand. I am afraid you will need to find an alternate means of contacting him."

"It's an emergency!"

"Yes, well. I would love to help, but I'm afraid there's little I can do. Good evening."

The maître d' hangs up the phone, knowing there is something he can do. He crosses into what he and his waitstaff call "the old dining room," heading directly to the table where a white-haired man dines alone.

"Sir?" he says in a hushed voice.

The Legend looks up with piercing blue eyes.

"I am sorry to bother you. I've just received a phone call asking to speak with you. It was concerning your daughter and was said to be an emergency. I, of course, did not confirm you were our guest this evening but thought it prudent to communicate the message to you nonetheless."

"Thank you," Wayne says.

When the exchange ends there, the maître d' returns to his station, wondering if he has done the right thing: Wayne Kresky is still just sitting there talking to himself.

* * *

"You're Willa."

"Yes. Hi. I'm sorry, I don't mean to be rude, but I don't have time for this right now."

"I'm Brooke."

"Really, I—"

"Finn's up there."

"Who are you again?"

244

"He snuck in about ten minutes ago and hasn't come back out, so I think it's safe to say he wasn't caught. I'm standing guard, sort of. Keeping watch for him. And now you show up."

"Do I know you?"

"Kind of the opposite, but that doesn't matter. My signal is to sing, 'It's a Small World.' Should I start singing?"

"No. I mean, I don't know. Is he in trouble?"

"Doesn't seem like it. Not so far. But then you show up, so—is he?"

"I hope not."

"So no singing."

"Ten minutes?" Willa asks.

"Corr—" Brooke grabs for her pocket and pulls out her vibrating phone. She studies the screen. "I know this may sound stupid. But I think this is for you. I think it's Philby. You're a DHI, right? Can you hold the phone?"

"Speakerphone might be better, if you don't mind."

"I don't mind." Brooke answers the call on speaker. She turns down the volume so it doesn't blast around the Court of Angels, holding the phone at head height between them.

"Brooke? Is this Brooke?"

"Philby, it's me, Willa. I'm with Brooke."

Adopting his Professor Philby persona, Philby outlines the events of the past few minutes: the call from Storey about park Security, Philby's attempt to contact Wayne inside Club 33. "You two need to get to the Plaza so I can return you, ASAP. Brooke will call me to tell me when. Storey's on her way, but I wouldn't wait for her." He doesn't allow them any chance to reply. "If I don't hear from Brooke in . . . seven minutes, I'm going to manually cross over everyone else as backup. Do you copy?"

"Copy," Willa says.

The call ends. Brooke's face is a knot of confusion. "That's it? Just 'copy?'"

"That's it. Put the phone away and clear your throat," Willa says.

"What's going on?"

"Time to start singing."

* * *

Storey hurries through Central Plaza at a run disguised as a fast walk. She can't entirely hide; she needs to be able to be seen by the Kingdom Keepers. She moves to swing around a clump of family members when a boy is pushed to the pavement by his sister. Storey slips trying to avoid him. They are looking at each other at ground level when the boy's eyes go wide.

"I know you!" the boy proclaims proudly.

Storey scrambles to her knees.

"We were on the cruise! The Panama Canal. You taught my sister dance, or something. You were with the Kingdom Keepers!"

"Not really. Good to see you again." Storey turns to go.

"Hey, will you sign our autograph book?"

Storey keeps moving as if not hearing the boy.

"Finn did!"

She returns to the kid. "Today?"

"Yeah. Absolutely! Not that long ago."

"Did you happen to see where he went?"

"That way." The boy points toward Frontierland.

His older sister arrives bearing the family autograph book. Storey signs below Finn's scribbled autograph. Thanks are exchanged.

Storey heads in the direction the boy pointed. Philby

mentioned Club 33. Maybe the boy is a Kingdom Keeper, maybe an Overtaker.

She heads off, eyes wide open.

* * *

Philby can feel it all coming apart on him: Willa's accusations, Storey's message, the knowledge that Finn and Wayne, both critically important to the Keepers, are in the same building together and likely unaware of what's about to go down. However this ends, it's on him, and he knows it.

Power: Philby's well-protected secret is that he's addicted to it. Deep inside, he understands the driver of the bus, the pilot of the plane, the general of the army, the dictator of the country. For him, nothing comes close to the feeling of crossing over or returning the Keepers. He decides when it will happen. He makes it happen.

He has risked a great deal by sneaking into the Crypt during evening hours to cross over Finn, then Willa. Anyone could have walked in during either visit. Now, he's considering going back again. He's pushing his luck. He's allowing the godlike power of being in control of his fellow Keepers to dictate his actions.

His reasonable side tells him to let it be, to let the situation sort itself out, that it's dangerous to send the rest of the Keepers into what may already be a catastrophic situation. But the thrill of breaking into the Crypt combined with the rush of entering the computer code that will allow the others to cross over proves too tempting.

He can be the hero, the one to effect the rescue of Finn and Willa. Or by trying to be the hero, he can remind himself that no one person can do it all alone.

He won't know which until he tries.

26

Finn overhears the message the maître d' delivers to Wayne.

"Sir?" Finn says into the antiquated microphone, hoping Wayne will answer.

"Give me a moment," Wayne mutters under his breath. "Wanda has my number, you see?" Wayne has a phone out now, an old clamshell-style cell phone. "No calls, no messages—and yet an emergency. . . ."

Finn is as perplexed as Wayne appears to be. If there were a car accident or some other real emergency, wouldn't Wanda or someone else call Wayne directly?

"Besides, Wanda doesn't know I'm here. No one knows but you and whomever you might have told."

"Philby," Finn says at the exact same moment when he faintly hears distant voices singing "It's a small world after all. . . ." Two voices, girls'. "It's the signal. Trouble! We've got to go." Finn tries to sound calm. "We've got to leave now, sir."

Wayne stands.

Finn returns the mic to the shelf and headphones to their hook. He considers putting his ear to the cupboard door, but decides on doing things the DHI way instead. He eases his head into the wall, his right eye wide open, and keeps moving until he can see a slight glowing haze around his own eye. He moves incrementally forward, knowing that from out in the hallway, if someone looked very carefully, they might see an eye and a piece of his nose. Finn also hopes that such a sight would not compute; the brain would literally not see it, even if the eyes did.

What Finn sees troubles him: bounding up the stairs comes a man in khaki shorts and a white polo, a Cast Member lanyard around his neck—Security, more than likely—and, with him, a PhotoPass photographer, probably *undercover* Security. Philby claims there are hundreds of such undercover agents at work in the parks on any given day—one reason the parks remain so safe.

If Finn shows himself now, it will be trouble. He pulls back into the closet, peers through the peephole, and realizes that Wayne is gone. An exit sign suggests Wayne's avenue of escape. As he debates his options, Finn's mind is made up for him when the two Security men yank open the door of the cupboard. Finn immediately rolls out the other side, through the wall and into the dining room. In the process, the shock and surprise of it all degrades his v1.6, lending Finn partial materiality. He crashes onto a table where an elderly couple are enjoying their dinner. Food flies. Drinks spill.

So much for a quiet getaway, Finn thinks, as he dodges among the closely spaced tables and heads for the exit. He struggles to concentrate on three goals at once: first, to reach the exit before the two Security men catch him; second, to achieve full v1.6, as any degree of materiality will work against him; third, to catch up to Wayne and protect him at all costs. It's this third goal that fills Finn with unexpected anxiety, even dread. Why, he's unsure; Wayne can take care of himself. But it's not the first time that an idea, sometimes even a seemingly random idea, has gripped Finn like a hand squeezing his heart; he's experienced such feelings of premonition before. Finn had once dreamed about jumping from a factory roof with Willa in DHI form (complicating his dream exponentially). Bizarrely, an undeniably similar event happened only days later, leading Finn to wonder privately if he shared a premonitory power similar to Jess's. If so, could he learn to use it deliberately? To trust it?

So why the disturbing sense of panic concerning Wayne?

These thoughts do not occupy Finn's conscious mind, but grind away in his subconscious as he manages to attain a state of v1.6 all clear and run *through* the tables in the restaurant on his way to the exit. Not a napkin flutters, not a spoon is knocked out of place.

The dinner guests break into applause—by now, a not unfamiliar reaction to DHI special effects. Finn passes through the exit door without opening it. His immaterial state buys him time; his pursuers are forced to avoid the tables and chairs.

The exit opens into a hallway that leads out to the balcony and the stairs down to the Court of Angels.

Finn calls out to Brooke and Willa, "Wayne?"

The girls shake their heads in unison. Brooke looks slightly afraid. Willa appears ready for anything.

Finn tries to figure out where Wayne has gone, but he can't take the time. The two Security guys are already out onto the balcony.

"Go!" Finn shouts to the girls. He catches up to them on the run as the three land at the bottom of the stairs and enter the courtyard. "Right!" he instructs, remembering that to the left is a dead end. Brooke proves to be an incredibly fast runner. At the Golden Horseshoe restaurant, in the lead, she runs to the right toward the plaza. Finn lets her go.

"This way," he tells Willa, leading her toward Big Thunder Mountain Railroad.

"But this is the long way!"

"Exactly!"

"You want to take the long way?"

"Which way will those guys go?" Finn asks. One of the advantages of DHI v2.0 is endurance; Finn and Willa wish they could run at full speed indefinitely. Hopefully, they'll have more endurance than their pursuers even in v1.6.

"I suppose they'll separate."

"Divide and conquer. Yes. Only if they are very well trained. They will be betting on us to head straight for the gates, not the Plaza."

"Good point."

Finn glances back—no sign of either Security guy—grabs Willa's hand, and tugs. They walk straight through the fence and find themselves in thick greenery.

Willa collides with a tree and turns; she's lost her pure DHI state. Finn holds on to her hand and pulls her along with him, making sure to avoid obstacles. It's a setback.

"Do your best to get it back," he says.

"I know!"

The pressure of such a request doesn't help matters; Finn wishes he'd kept his trap shut.

Finn stops abruptly and releases Willa's hand, and the two spin their arms frantically, trying to maintain their balance; they are perched on the edge of the Rivers of America lake, about to fall in. Willa stops her forward progress first and steadies Finn.

"This way!" she says, taking the lead and keeping the water to their left.

Finn feels the urgency to run, sensing the Security pair behind them, even though he does not see or hear them.

"You hear that?" he asks Willa.

"I'm so far from all clear, I'm only hearing my heart about to burst."

"Feet . . . many feet . . . coming really fast."

"Those guys?"

Willa is leading Finn at a run along the water's edge, following a tamped-down path through the vegetation. Finn is thinking that the path must be the result of Cast Members maintaining the lake, but with the sound of steps growing closer behind them, a second thought enters his mind.

"Animals."

"What animals?"

"This path. Those feet. Animals, not people."

"Animals?" Her hand softens in Finn's grip as she draws closer to pure DHI state, but now it firms up again. She's scared.

As he achieves all clear once more, Finn hears animals panting and low, slurping growls. His body tingles as he, too, loses some of his DHI state.

"Dogs. Wild dogs."

"*Bambi!*" Willa calls back to him. She possesses Philby's encyclopedic intelligence, the ability to call upon her learned database of sometimes unrelated facts and assemble them firmly together, like playing with magnets. One word, *dogs*, and she's able to identify the right Disney film as source material. It wouldn't be *101 Dalmatians*, because all the dogs in that movie are good; the dogs in *Bambi* are quite a different matter.

"Refresh my memory!" Finn says.

"Bloodthirsty. Relentless. Nothing Bambi did could slow them down."

"Overtakers?"

"Well, they aren't on our side, if that's what you're asking."

Willa skids to a stop. They've arrived at the Indian camp with its teepees.

"Remember the Magic Kingdom?" Willa says.

The Keepers had used a similar Indian camp as a rendezvous point once before, long ago, having discovered that once they were inside the teepees, they were in DHI shadow, and therefore impossible to see.

"Let's go!" Finn says, taking the lead from Willa.

"Only one problem!" Willa calls out, halted back at the fence that surrounds the encampment. "In Disneyland, Big Thunder Mountain Railroad is haunted by Indian ghosts because it was built on a burial ground."

Finn skids to a stop. He can hear the dogs dangerously close.

"Willa! Those are only ghost stories! The teepees are our only hope! As in *now!*"

Finn and Willa glimpse the dogs' reflections in the surface of the lake an instant before the dogs themselves charge into view. Willa sprints toward Finn, her hand outstretched. She felt so much safer holding his hand.

Finn takes hold and together they run, not to the first teepee but to the one in the center of the camp. Finn climbs through the entrance into the teepee's interior and watches his arm disappear as if it's been hacked off.

The pack of wild dogs is bearing down on Willa as she dives into the teepee behind Finn. They are scraggly, scruffy, drooling, ugly dogs with matted fur and savage eyes.

Willa lands face-first on the sand floor and rolls to her left, into the darkest corner of the tent. By the time she's sitting up, Willa looks down at herself and sees nothing: DHI shadow. She knows to shut her eyes and focus on an imagined pinprick of light in a void of total darkness—a technique learned from Finn that helps her obtain all clear. She presses her invisible hands to her invisible ears, and the world goes quiet. Not quite silent, but better. Willa imagines the bottom of a deep well—cool, quiet, and absolutely dark. . . .

The horrifying growl of a dog startles Willa, making her open her eyes involuntarily.

The dog is inside the teepee, nose in the air, red-and-black gums displayed in a nasty snarl of broken teeth. But the animal is lost. It doesn't know where to strike.

"Shoo!" an old lady's voice says—*from inside the teepee*!

Willa lets out a terrified yip. She hears Finn brush against the canvas wall of the teepee as he startles too.

The dog's head is shoved down into the sand, clearly not of its own volition.

The disturbance of the sand spreads a fine dust up into the air; caught in the unnatural bluish light that emanates from Disneyland at night, it swirls inside the teepee. Like a photo developing in a chemical bath, the dust exposes a shape. Then, detail by detail, the figure of a Native American woman is revealed. She's as old as dirt, with brown skin shriveled like a raisin; she's covered in animal skins decorated with eagle feathers, wooden beads, and a single piece of turquoise.

She's a ghost. Or is she?

It's unclear if she can see Finn and Willa the way Willa can see her, but she looks directly into Willa's eyes, sending a flash of heat down the girl's spine.

Willa just *knew* that the stories of Indians haunting Thunder Mountain had to be true. The longer she's been a Keeper, the more she's come to realize: *It's all true!*

The woman hits the dog a second time. It snaps at her, but, chomping down on air, ends up only biting its own tongue.

"Shoo!" the old woman says again, her voice as dry as the sand underfoot.

The dog whines, backs up, and leaves them.

"Where are the spirits of the children that have joined me? Show yourselves!"

Willa marvels at the woman's confidence in dealing with the dog and in demanding that she and Finn show themselves. Her courage begs the question: Do ghosts have anything to fear?

Clearly, the ghost of the Indian woman is afraid of nothing. So why should Willa be afraid? In DHI form, she can't be bitten, stabbed, or hurt in any way. What, other than her own fear, takes hold in her and compromises the purity of her DHI? Willa realizes that, in a sense, she *is* this Indian ghost, only a lot younger and with the advantage of leading an alternate life as a living, breathing human being—something she can't help imagining such a ghost must long for. She has nothing to fear. This, she realizes, is what Finn has been telling the other Keepers for several years now. But what a difference there is between hearing it and discovering it for herself!

This is what "growing up" means. For the first time, Willa gets it. However briefly, she owns it: *she herself* is the only thing standing in her own way. Regardless of how long it may take to perfect this insight, if she can just keep moving, keep growing, there is nothing to stop her, nothing that can hurt her. The discovery leaves Willa feeling so elated that she wants to let loose a scream of happiness. She wants to celebrate! But she controls herself.

"Here," she answers calmly, scooting forward just far enough that her crossed legs and her face return to visibility.

Finn doesn't trust this woman—he doesn't trust any ghost. He wishes Willa hadn't shown herself. The Overtakers have come after them as wild dogs, yet here's Willa, playing hide-and-seek with some ancient grandmother.

"I'm a human child," Willa says, "but I am not in human form."

"A shaman!" the woman exclaims.

"I am beyond your understanding, but I'm not a shaman. I work for the side of good."

"Whose good?" the woman asks suspiciously.

As the Indian woman's hand moves to the beaded necklace she wears, Finn tenses. Willa has lost sight of the reason this woman and her people haunt these grounds. Her question to Willa sums it up: *"Whose good?"*

Willa's face reflects awareness of her mistake, but there is something else there that Finn doesn't recognize. Self-assurance. Willa now projects a power he's not seen in her or any of the other Keepers before.

"There is only one good," Willa says. "Make no mistake. You are an elder and therefore wise. You must know there is only the spirit. All else is dust and rock."

"It is so," says the woman.

"I and my friends do battle against those dark forces that fail to recognize this spirit. Those who would dim its flame to darkness."

Willa doesn't sound like herself. She must be channeling a history book or documentary film, or maybe she's just empathizing with this wavering ghost. Whatever the case, Finn's impressed. He finds himself scooting forward, allowing himself to become visible.

"Take this message back to your people," Willa says, "from the children of light."

Willa nods toward Finn. The ghost drinks him in with her wise gaze; she smiles.

"We come to bring change. Anyone and anything that stands in our way will feel the great force of the spirit like a wind of fire on their heels. We will drive them to the edge of the earth and throw them off into a great void."

Finn's jaw hangs slack. "Willa?" he gasps.

"Willow?" the ghost echoes uncertainly. "Are you the one they call Willow?"

Each of the Keepers struggles with being considered part of Disney lore, with accepting that word of their exploits has traveled among Characters and Overtakers alike for several years now. Stories about them are told, embellished, and exaggerated, tales that involve children of light, heroes who beat the odds, drive back the villains, defeat the powerful, slay the dragons.

"I am," Willa says. "And this boy is Finnegan."

The ghost smiles cruelly. "My, my," she says.

That doesn't sound good.

"I did not believe the stories—you must forgive me, child."

The woman throws red dust at Willa. Where it comes from, Finn can't be sure, but he thinks that her necklace likely concealed it. To his astonishment, the dust falls through Willa's DHI, sprinkling the sand beneath her. Finn has always known Willa to startle, to scare easily. Like the other Keepers, she loses at least a small percentage of her hologram's qualities when cornered or pushed to the wall by the dark powers.

But not today. Not here. *Willa?*

The ghost looks puzzled by the ineffectiveness of her magic, like a kid with a firecracker that doesn't light. Confusion fades from her face, to be replaced by anger. From that anger comes a change. Her features sharpen, her neck thickens, her hackles raise, and she transfigures before their eyes into a creature with a woman's body and a massive wolf's head.

Finn backs toward the teepee's open entryway.

"Willa!" he calls, and she starts moving too.

The transfiguration isn't instantaneous; the process buys the two Keepers time to join together at the mouth of the teepee, but not quite enough time to escape completely. The wolf-woman lunges and snaps her powerful jaws.

Finn makes a fist and delivers a roundhouse blow to the wolf's chin. As its teeth snap together, it takes a huge bite out of the canvas wall. Finn and Willa stumble back through the teepee's entrance. As they fall to the sandy ground, they hear horses' hooves charging. Finn expects to see more Native American ghosts, this time on horseback. What he sees instead makes him scream aloud.

Not Willa. She rises to her feet, grabs Finn by the collar, and helps him up. Coming straight at them rides the Headless Horseman, his glinting sword raised to strike.

"Run!" Finn shouts at Willa.

The Headless Horseman gallops toward them. Finn calculates that he's riding too fast to maneuver among the teepees.

"There!" Finn directs Willa, pointing between two teepees toward the water. No way the horse can make that turn.

To Finn's surprise, Willa runs, but in the wrong direction, directly toward the decapitated equestrian, who carries his own head under his left arm like a soccer ball. Finn lunges, trying to grab her around the waist, but fails to stop her. This is a Willa he doesn't know. But it's a Willa he loves to see. Something transformative has just occurred inside the teepee; it's as if she has graduated to another level, grown in a way even he hasn't managed. He was there to witness it, but has no idea what he witnessed. *Some red dust. A lot of nerve.*

Willa remains on the rider's right—his sword hand side—until the last possible second. Then, jumping directly in front of the steed, she tosses a handful of sand into the air with perfect aim and timing. The sand blinds the widened eyes of the Horseman's disconnected head; the blinded rider reacts, tugging the reins sideways and directing his horse straight into a teepee.

The wolf-woman is standing only yards away. She fixes her gray eyes intently on Willa.

As the horse digs in its hooves to skid to a stop before it crashes into the teepee, the Horseman is thrown. His head rolls in the sand; his sword lands tip down, standing upright, vibrating like a small tree in the wind.

Willa runs for the head and kicks it to Finn as if she's trying to score in the last minute of the World Cup. Finn bounces the head off his knee, sending it facedown into the sand. Then he stomps on it.

The wolf-woman charges.

The headless body starts to spin in aimless circles as the black horse rears back, whinnying. The noise startles Finn, who steps back and kicks the head again, inadvertently making it rotate just enough for the eyes to roll back up out of the sand.

The Horseman grabs his sword with the effortlessness of a ballerina and swings for Finn.

Finn knows he's lost a good deal of his DHI integrity. The events of the past few minutes have rattled him to his core—and none so much as the feeling of that man's head bouncing off his knee. Finn might be able to achieve all clear if a deep-bellied wolf's growl did not erupt behind him, but the rumbling menace turns his knees to water.

The sword whistles as it swings past Finn's neck; clearly, the Horseman intends to include Finn in his headless club.

Finn feels himself shoved aside. As he falls to the sand, he turns to see Willa standing in his place, a serene smile on her face—the self-satisfied expression of a martyr willing to sacrifice herself for a greater cause.

Finn lets loose an anguished cry. "No-o-o-o-o!"

The blade severs Willa's neck so cleanly that her head remains in place, then the sword stroke's follow-through swipes the wolf-woman's snout clean off.

Finn crawls forward, tossing sand in front of him as if trying to splash a buddy in a swimming pool. He hits his target, once again burying the Horseman's fallen head up to the eyeballs.

Willa ducks and steps *through* the Horseman. Her head is not detached! Somehow, she has managed to maintain her all clear. She gets two steps in front of Finn and kicks the fallen head once again, lofting it high into the air. It lands in the water, where it rolls briefly, sending up a few bubbles before sinking out of sight.

The wolf-woman rushes the Horseman just as the wolves arrive. While the two Keepers avert their eyes, horrific slobbering, crunching noises turn their stomachs. They run.

"OT fighting OT!" Finn shouts to Willa. "What's with that? And while we're at it: What's with *you?*"

"Things are changing." That's all she says. It sets his mind spinning.

CHARLENE MOVES FROM ONE DREAM to another, not really knowing what's happening, because that's the way dreams are. This one has her sitting in the Disneyland Central Plaza; she's wearing the dark-blue boxer shorts and Beijing Olympics T-shirt that she counts as her pajamas. She has her retainer in, and her hair is held back in a French braid. Park guests gawk at her as they pose for photos by the Partners statue. Charlene pulls herself up to kneeling.

"I hate it when he does this!" Maybeck's voice, just behind her. He's limping slightly, wearing black boxer shorts and a faded purple T-shirt that reads: I'M A MAINE-I-AC! ART MAINE-IA FESTIVAL, FREEPORT, 2008.

Charlene immediately crosses her arms. This isn't a dream. She rubs her face vigorously with the sleeve of her T-shirt, remembering that she put on zit cream before going to bed. This cannot be happening! Stealthily, she pops the retainer out; unable to pocket it—because she has no pockets!—she clamps it between the elastic band of her shorts and her waist, hoping it will stay put.

Seeing that Maybeck is barefoot, she realizes that she's barefoot too.

"What the heck?" she says.

"You got me," Maybeck says. "I didn't hear anything about this." He indicates his boxers as evidence.

Charlene crosses her arms, nods.

"We'd better not stay here."

"No," she agrees, struggling to stand without the use of her arms.

She and Maybeck move to the perimeter of the Plaza, keeping watch—but for what, they don't know. Are they expecting other Keepers? Overtakers? Are they here by mistake?

"Do you remember the last time we crossed over *without knowing* it was going to happen?"

"It goes way back," Maybeck says.

"For me: constantly! You know how many times I've been caught in my nightgown? Sheesh!"

A small flurry of applause from guests across the Plaza draws their attention to Amanda, Jess, and . . . Philby!

"Now I'm really confused," Maybeck says. "Don't we need Philby in order to return?"

"And if not," Charlene says, "then who crossed *him* over?"

※Amanda awakens in the Plaza, wondering why Philby has crossed over her and Jess. She thinks immediately of Finn, who could be only feet away from her. So near, yet so far. She wishes she could run to him, make sure he's okay, but Philby must have something planned! Philby always has something planned. Finn! Her mind screams. What if he's hurt and unable to call for help? She pushes away the negative thoughts and in so doing, maintains all-clear.[39]

"Pixie Hollow," Philby says, walking past the two. "Keep your distance. See you there."

Amanda and Jess stay with him. Maybeck huffs, struggling with his painful leg. Heading toward the Matterhorn, he and Charlene take the path to Pixie Hollow, a forest hideaway off the main path where park guests experience what it would be

---

[39] Heightened_Crossover

like to shrink down to the size of Tinker Bell and her fairy friends.

Philby and the two Fairlies come around from the Matterhorn side. It's a good call on Philby's part: Pixie Hollow is deserted.

Philby huddles them up. "The long and the short of it: Finn and Willa are probably in trouble. They need us."

"But how did you—?"

Philby cuts off Charlene's question. "I found the Return in the Crypto lab." He produces the small black fob from his pocket, then stuffs it back in. "I was able to write code to cross us over. All of us. Like setting a timer. The only trick was for me to get to sleep quickly. It's never easy. Currently I'm asleep in the Morgue. I mean, my body is . . . Just the sound of that gives me the creeps, so no comments, please."

"What kind of trouble?" Maybeck asks. "And where'd they come from?" He nods his head toward Amanda and Jess.

"I . . . it was my call to bring you with us," Philby says to the sisters. "Your talents may be helpful." They, too, are in shorts and T-shirts, and both are barefoot. Only Philby is dressed in the street clothes he's been wearing all day. "The trouble is this: Finn convinced me to cross him over solo to meet Wayne."

"Without the rest of us?" Charlene complains. "Without a plan?"

"Alone?" Maybeck asks. "Since when?"

"You two just decided this?" Charlene says.

"It was a mistake, okay? My mistake," Philby says, genu-inely contrite. "Finn knew the park would be busy. He was worried that, since so many people know who we are, the more of us were there in the park, the more trouble there'd be for him. If he went alone, he could slip in and slip back out."

"That's stupid!" Maybeck says.

"It is," Philby admits, his head lowered. "Willa chewed me out for it already."

"And now they're both in trouble," Maybeck says. "*There's a surprise!*"

"We all are," Philby says. He watches his friends' faces as this registers. "Storey overheard that Secur—"

"Storey?" Charlene practically barks.

Philby says, "She's here trying to warn them."

Maybeck huffs derisively.

"Not as a DHI." Philby briefly summarizes Storey's phone call. "And there's a girl named Brooke with Finn."

"Let's just make it a party," Charlene snaps sarcastically.

"We pair up—I'll stay with Jess and Mandy—and we find Finn and Willa. We reconnect at the Plaza, I hit the Return, and everything's good."

"You make it sound so simple," Charlene says. "It's a big park. And it's busy."

"I got that," Philby says. "They were at Club 33 to start. We'll go there. You two search for them behind the castle: Toontown, Small World. Come back through Fantasyland and into Frontierland, where we should meet you. We'll take Main Street, Adventureland, and New Orleans Square."

"And if we find them?" Maybeck sounds discouraged.

"*When* we find them," Philby corrects him. "No matter what, we all hide until the fireworks. Then we meet at the Plaza during the show. That's when we'll return—the grand finale."

"But how do we communicate if—*when*—we find them?" Charlene asks.

Philby isn't often stumped, but her words give him pause. "We don't."

"Where's Storey? Can she help?" Charlene is clearly stressed.

"No idea," Philby says. "She said she was on her way to the club."

"I feel useless," Jess says.

"You helped us in Epcot, remember? You weren't asleep for that," Charlene says.

"Besides, you're a DHI and an extra set of eyes. You're completely helpful!" Philby is trying to reassure to her.

"Fireworks. Plaza," Maybeck repeats.

"It's probably best if we're on the defensive," Philby cautions. "If the OTs realize they have a chance at Finn . . . well"—he looks to Amanda—"I don't mean that the way it sounds. But the thing is—"

"They'll stop at nothing," Maybeck says, more bluntly than Philby would have. "So if we want to stay healthy, if we want to help Finn and Willa, we'd better stay all clear."

They separate into two groups and head away from each other, moving in opposite directions.

Charlene feels an uncharacteristic shiver overtake her. "I don't like this," she says to Maybeck.

* * *

"That's it!" Finn says, spotting the railroad tracks. He and Willa skid to a stop. "We jump the train and ride it around to the entrance. The OTs think we're over here somewhere. Security is expecting us to *leave* the park."

"But if we get to the front entrance, we'll be *entering* the park to reach the Plaza! And going in the direction opposite to the one they expect. That's brilliant!" Willa pauses. "But guests will see us getting on the train."

"Only if we get on the train."

"I'm assuming you're going to explain that," Willa says.

"You assume correctly."

* * *

"You okay?" Jess asks.

"No," Amanda says.

Philby stays several yards ahead of them, walking quickly toward New Orleans Square. Maybeck and Charlene are headed for Fantasyland; from there, they'll circle back around into Frontierland.

"The park's too big. We'll never find him." Amanda sounds like she's going to cry.

"Maybe Willa's seen him. Maybe she's with him."

"She can't help him the way I can." Amanda clenches her fists, knowing the power she has locked away in her palms. It started so small, moving a toy an inch or two every so often. She never thought anything of it, had no idea others couldn't do the same thing. It wasn't until she was eleven years old that inches became feet, that a few ounces became many pounds. Then many, *many* pounds. Once she got angry at her foster mother and slammed the door to her room without touching it. That's when she'd scared herself for the first time, and knew other people couldn't do *that* for sure.

"We have to stay positive," Jess says.

"You shouldn't be talking to me," Amanda snaps. "You're supposed to see what's coming. You're supposed to help me find him. Do that, will you please? Help me find him!"

They walk in silence, passing the Mark Twain Riverboat docks.

"I'm sorry." Amanda interlaces her fingers behind her head, leaning back into the space of her palms. "Ugh! I'm about to explode."

266

"Save your energy," Jess says gently. "We may need it."

They navigate around an approaching family, the kids carrying helium balloons.

"They're all so *happy*, you know? I can't stand that. They have no idea what's going on!"

"Don't go blaming the magic."

"No, I suppose not."

"You care about him, Amanda. There's nothing wrong with that."

"It goes so far beyond that. . . ." Amanda says, her throat tightening. "I've let this get out of hand."

"Your feelings are genuine. They can't hurt anyone. They're part of the magic. Maybe they *are* the magic. It's good you care—having something to care about is the best. That's why we're here, you know? And I don't mean Disneyland."

"I know what you mean."

"Then trust it. Go with it."

"As if I have a choice!" Amanda says. She stifles the laugh that wants to escape. "I've tried not to care about him. Believe me, I've tried."

A train whistle sounds, floating over the park. Jess stops. She stands absolutely still and closes her eyes, squinting.

Amanda opens her mouth to speak, but recognizes what's happening. She takes several steps toward Jess and extends her arms, forming a protective barrier around her, keeping her from being bumped by any park guests. How badly she wants to say something, to encourage Jess to "see" visions that will help them find Finn.

But all she can do is wait.

* * *

Charlene feels a chill as she and Maybeck pass through the castle's interior. It's not a Maleficent chill, not something from outside, but from inside. The passageway is overcrowded; it smells of people, food, and sunscreen, but the cold is the cold of suspicion, the awful sensation of a lack of privacy.

"Someone's watching us," she says.

"Well, that's plain creepy," Maybeck says. "Why would you say that?"

"Because it's true. Someone's watching us."

"Heard you the first time."

"Maybe from inside the walk-through," she says.

"The what?"

"We don't have a castle walk-through in the Magic Kingdom. It's only here. It's a hallway that starts on one side, goes over this passage, and comes out the other side."

"I don't love the sound of that."

"It's Sleeping Beauty Castle. That means Maleficent."

"Well, she's gone. Finn took care of that. So we can scratch her off the list."

"Would you take me seriously, please?"

"I take you way too seriously."

"Really?" Charlene says hopefully.

"No," Maybeck cracks.

"Then why did you say that? What do you mean by 'seriously'?"

"Leave it, would you?"

"Of course I won't leave it! This is important to me."

"What happened to our being watched?" he asks.

Charlene steals a glance at the castle wall, still feeling eyes on her. "I just know these things," she says. "Someone's watching me."

"Then I'm going to punch them in the face."

She yelps a tiny laugh, a bubble bursting from within her.

Maybeck reaches out, but his hand passes through her DHI arm. "Okay," he says. "I feel it, too."

"Don't mess with me!" She's angry.

"I'm not messing with you. But Maleficent's gone, Charlie."

"We don't know what she's capable of. What *gone* even means with her. Besides, the Evil Queen's attraction is right next door."

"Say what?"

"Snow White's Scary Adventures. It's up on the left there," Charlene says, pointing. Maybeck stops walking, and she stops beside him. "Guess who wouldn't seem out of place at all if she were seen around here?"

"As in, cruising the castle walk-through and spying on kids?"

"The Cryptos are convinced that the Queen and Tia Dalma and . . . you know, the Beast . . . escaped the temple. Right? If they're back in the park, where will they go? Tia Dalma to Pirates, the . . . *big boy* to Fantasmic!, and the Evil Queen to the next door on the left."

"She'd bring Finn here if she caught him," Maybeck says. "We're going to look for her in the walk-through."

"That's crazy."

"Maybe so. After that, we're going to her ride, and to Pirates and Fantasmic! if we have to." He takes her by the arm, confirming she's no longer pure DHI. "You stand guard. I'll go through."

"No way! What if you get into trouble? How am I sup-posed to know?" Charlene asks. "It's a bad plan. Besides, no offense, but I'm the action figure here."

"Seriously? You're going to go there?"

"We stay a team," she says. "That's the whole reason we're

in this mess—Philby shouldn't have crossed Finn over alone."

Maybeck nods, and they start off again in the direction of the attraction. "She uses witchcraft, conjuring, and transfiguration," he says. "The body changes, but not the eyes. The eyes are always the same."

"You might be able to see something like that, but I can't," Charlene says.

"You'd better trust me if I do." He steps back, allowing her to lead him to the door of the walk-through.

* * *

"The train," Jess says, opening her eyes.

Amanda calls out for Philby, who backtracks begrudgingly, dragging his feet as he returns to them.

"What?" he says.

"I saw them running for the train," Jess says. "They're together. Finn and Willa."

"Brilliant!" Philby says. "It's the perfect way to get around the park—the least exposure by far."

"I'm not always right," Jess reminds him.

"This time you are," he says.

"The train whistled a minute ago," Amanda says, pointing in the general direction of Big Thunder Mountain. "Over there."

"You sure?" Philby asks.

"No. But I think so."

"Are you always so honest?"

"Yes."

"No wonder he likes you," Philby says. His professor brain engages as his DHI eyes fix on a distant point, one only he can see. "The next stop is Toontown. If we hurry, we just might make it."

* * *

An oak-trimmed glass case holds a large leather-bound book open to the page upon which the Sleeping Beauty story begins. It's colorful, all simple drawings and fine calligraphy.

"'In a faraway land, long, long ago,'" Charlene reads aloud.

The walk-through is an authentic castle passageway: thick stone walls, dim and shadowy lighting, and narrow windows set back in deep embrasures. Charlene's words bounce and echo in the narrow space. One small window is positioned just above the bookcase. No light streams through; the glass is pitch-black, giving Maybeck a bad feeling.

"Let's keep moving. I don't think we want to stand in any one place for too long." Charlene nods. She closes her eyes and takes a deep, cleansing breath.

Maybeck performs a similar exercise, attempting to maintain all clear. Being stuck in v1.6 is like being held back a year in school—something Maybeck knows about from personal experience. The limits frustrate him; he's constantly forced to remind himself that he's not in 2.0, that he's bound to the restrictions of the new system's predecessor.

They move on, passing more leather-bound pages that advance the fairy tale, as well as small stained-glass windows.

A few minutes later, they find themselves back outside.

To their right, the lights in the Castle Heraldry Shoppe flicker repeatedly, pulling them in that direction.

Charlene leans her head through the door. "Weird . . . there aren't any Cast Members. It's empty."

Maybeck takes a look, then steps inside with her. "Hello?"

"You think it's closed?" Charlene says.

Maybeck eyes a vertical glass case with a red velvet backdrop; it contains a shield emblazoned with a lion crest and a multitude of swords and axes. At the top of the case is mounted a dragon gargoyle holding two drinking goblets in the claws of its forefeet. Its lower right talons grip a curled snake. Maybeck finds the image disturbing; he feels certain it must be symbolic but has no idea what it might mean.

"Cups can signify punishment being doled out," Charlene says over his shoulder, startling him. "The Bible is filled with references to cups and God's fury. The contents are bitter, not fit to drink. Sometimes blood."

"Cheery!"

"The snake represents the underworld. The fact that the dragon has killed the snake probably means the dragon is good, that it's conquered the underworld."

"*She*, not it. We know who the dragon is," he counters, "and she's not good. *Was* not good." He pauses, staring into the darkness, and then speaks again, slowly. "If Maleficent conquered the underworld and was the judge handing out sentences in this one, what does that mean, now that she's dead? More important to us: if she had control of the underworld, could you actually kill her, or is it more like mole whacking? You know, is she just going to pop up somewhere else?"

"It's just a symbol, Maybeck."

"It's Disneyland," Maybeck says, resolutely. "Nothing is 'just' anything. Everything has meaning, including this."

They continue along the corridor, down the stairs.

"You think the Queen took over her powers," Charlene says. A statement, not a question.

"After seeing this, I'm not sure anyone took over anything. How can you kill something that's already dead? If you've conquered the underworld, you're playing on their field, not ours."

"So Finn killed her, but not really?" Charlene gasps. "Are you *kidding* me?"

272

"I'm just saying . . . it's possible. Anything's possible."

A crash of breaking glass knocks Charlene and Maybeck to the floor and sends them scrambling backward. A full set of armor—about five feet tall and of Japanese design—hauls a samurai sword out of the display case, loosing it from its scabbard. The Asian Warrior breaks his trailing foot off from his pedestal and lumbers forward, taking giant steps despite his diminutive height. He brings the sword down onto Maybeck's arm with such force that the blade chips a piece of the stone beneath the boy's holographic limb.

His failure to sever the arm catches the Asian Warrior by surprise. His helmet rocks from side to side in curiosity, the gaze of his invisible eyes trained first on Maybeck, then Charlene.

Maybeck is slow to move, hindered by his injured leg, but not Charlene. She springs to her feet and cartwheels in front of the warrior, distracting him. Arriving at the shattered display case, she takes hold of an Arabian sword; it's smaller, lighter, curved—more to her size and liking than the long samurai sword would be.

In the time it takes the Asian Warrior to hoist his sword, Charlene connects with a blow, knocking him off balance and causing him to stumble. Maybeck crab-crawls backward out of danger.

Charlene wields the sword nimbly, slicing left and right. The warrior blocks the first of her attempts, but the samurai sword is too long, too slow to defend the next stroke.

Another crash to their right. A four-foot tall set of armor with a white plume on its helmet marches stiffly toward Charlene, a sharpened lance in its hands. Charlene feels suddenly, uncomfortably aware that she is wearing next to nothing. The Asian Warrior regains his balance, raising his samurai sword. Charlene turns, facing an empty space between the lancer and the warrior.

A blur from the display case—Maybeck; he's in midair, a sword in hand. He slices off the end of the lance and collides with the smaller knight, knocking him to the floor. The creature breaks apart: arm and leg armor in scattered pieces, breastplate.

Charlene spins to face the Asian Warrior, blocking a sword strike intended for Maybeck. She and the warrior go at it, swords clanging, the warrior advancing confidently with each contact. Charlene loses ground one step at a time; she's backed up toward the wall. Another few steps and she'll be trapped, with too little room to maneuver her weapon in front of her.

She catches a glimpse of movement behind Maybeck.

"Terry!"

Maybeck spins, and lucks out—he's holding his sword exactly where it's needed. A six-foot-tall set of knight's armor wearing an elaborately decorated helmet has broken loose from the corner. Armed with an ax from the Lionheart case, the knight is prepared to reduce Maybeck to mince pie.

Swish! The ax slices the air.

Maybeck's limbs tingle; there's no way he's all clear. He makes sword contact with the ax, defending himself and trying to hold his ground, but the knight is big and strong and entirely encased in heavy armor. The one or two blows Maybeck manages to land seem to stun him only briefly. It's like chopping at a tree trunk with a kitchen knife.

"We ... get—get them," Maybeck stutters to Charlene, "to ... to hit each other . . . and, and maybe . . . we get out of this."

She's fighting for her life. The Asian Warrior advances steadily, its joints loosened up now, the samurai sword swinging effortlessly.

Maybeck adjusts, moving back in order to stand shoulder to shoulder with Charlene.

"Can you all clear?" Maybeck asks.

"No idea," she answers. "Doubt it."

"We have to!"

They each block a blow, metal clanking on metal. Maybeck's no match for the behemoth. An attempt to decapitate him mercifully strikes the Lionheart case as Maybeck ducks, or the boy would be talking from the floor.

"How quickly can you . . . can you—all clear?" He's stuttering, struggling to calm himself and drive the needles from his limbs.

"Don't know."

"We . . . it'll have to b-b-be . . . basically—instantly. Can you do that?"

"Can try!" she says between parries. "When?"

Maybeck uses his artist's eye to measure the timing of the blows from each set of armor. Charlene's opponent is faster than the knight confronting him. Maybeck defends two blows in the time Charlene defends three.

There will come a moment when both swords strike at the same time once more. That is the moment at which they must dematerialize.

"Wait for it . . ." he says. "Steady . . ."

The two sets of armor draw back their swords in unison.

"Now!"

Charlene closes her eyes and takes a calming breath.

She hears her sword and Maybeck's sword clank simultaneously onto the floor. In achieving pure DHI state, their hands could no longer hold them. Partners, she thinks.

The warrior and the knight swing their weapons fiercely. But the blades swipe right through the projected light of the holograms. The clap and clangor ring and sing in the narrow confines of the room, loudly signaling their mutual destruction. The ax cleaves the Asian Warrior's chest; the samurai sword finds a gap in the knight's chain mail, slicing into his throat. The two collapse and fall bloodlessly, a mingled pile of empty steel and leather. Mere pots and pans banging down on kitchen tile.

Charlene throws her arms around Maybeck in a full-fledged embrace. It's a hug of victory, of rejoicing, of thanks.

Maybeck doesn't know how any of this works, not really. But he knows that a moment earlier they were pure DHI, invulnerable and undefeatable. They're far from that now, for he feels her, holds her, and revels in the armor's defeat while a nagging voice—his own—whispers gravely in his ear.

"The Overtakers are stronger here."

28

$\mathcal{T}$HE TRAIN'S STEAM WHISTLE sounds for the second time. Finn and Willa grip the transom of the last car, tuck their legs up, and ride along.

The track bends to the right. Finn had hoped to ride to the park entrance, but his plan is foiled by the occupied rear bench, which keeps him and Willa from climbing over and into the car. They can't very well be seen holding on to the back of the last car as the train pulls out of the next station, Mickey's Toontown, so they'll have to get off. Hopefully he and Willa can find a way to sneak out of Toontown and work their way back to the train tracks farther up the line, Finn thinks. The stop he wants is without question the park entrance.

As the train slows, Finn and Willa lower themselves and get their feet moving to match the train's speed. They finally let go and move to join the disembarking passengers with no one the wiser, and Finn leads Willa under the train bridge and onto the entrance path for Toontown.

Seeing the gigantic It's a Small World entrance to her right, Willa cringes. "I'll never look at that ride the same way again," she says.

"None of us will."

"I'm afraid to go in there."

"No kidding."

"You, too?"

"Not exactly *afraid*," Finn answers honestly. "Apprehensive? Cautious? I don't think I've been back since the dolls came alive."

Willa says, "Hey, Toontown should be closed for the fireworks by now. What's with that?"

"No idea."

"You think they'd change that? They *never* change that!"

"I think we need to forget about it and get behind Small World if we're going to get back to the train. We can cut over by Roger Rabbit's Car Toon Spin and disappear into the woods."

"That makes sense. But the thing is, Finn, Toontown should be closed."

"Forget about it!"

"It has so many character attractions, it's like an army base for the good Disney characters."

"A place the OTs would keep under watch."

"Exactly."

"Hadn't thought of it that way," Finn says. "You're right. So, let's make it harder for them to spot us. But we can't lose sight of each other." Finn gradually moves away from her. Her concern about Toontown has set him on edge. He knows better than to think that any Keeper is ever completely safe in the parks. And at a time like this, they are at a heightened risk.

The ambush comes from behind, led by a strange-looking guy and a group of six gangly weasels costumed like people and walking on their hind legs. The guy acts like he owns Toontown the way a sheriff owns a Wild West town. A bizarre figure with a pale, rubbery face and oversize eyes, the man wears a black undertaker's suit. His weasel-bodied minions aren't much to look at either.

Willa, the Keepers' foremost Disney historian, spots them and signals Finn. After a few moments' reflection, she recognizes the man as Judge Doom, from *Who Framed Roger Rabbit?* He's an obscure character, but his role as a sadistic executioner is well documented. He must have emerged from the Car Toon Spin, or maybe he's been following them since Toontown station. Near the station is the tent hosting the Mickey's Magical Map show. Its original plotline included Judge Doom and other Disney villains, all of whom were eventually scratched from the storyline. There's nothing more troublesome than an out-of-work villain.

Willa moves closer to Finn.

"You know who that is?" she says.

"Negative."

"Well, I do!" She gives Finn a capsule biography. "His arrival can't be considered coincidence. He's on a mission. He's the closest thing the kingdom—and the Overtakers—have to an assassin. He loves money, and will do anything for it—including kill a pair of sometimes holograms."

It's the "sometimes" part that has Finn worried. If he or Willa loses their all clear, it'll be a disaster. The idea of a known killer following them turns his stomach sour. If something horrible were to happen to any DHI, there's no telling what might become of the associated kid asleep back in the studio. The idea of being stuck in a permanent coma is so chilling for Finn that he misses a step, stumbles, and has to recover.

"Get out of here! Head for the train tracks," Finn says. "I'll meet you."

"What if Wayne's here?" she cries. Most everyone in Toontown is a friend to the Kingdom; it would make a good hiding place for Wayne. "Judge Doom may not know about us. He could be after Wayne!"

"Not know about us? He's looking *right at us!*" Finn contemplates their predicament. "I know we're supposed to be in pairs, but we've got to separate. You get to the tracks!"

Finn moves more deeply into the Toontown cul-de-sac, keeping Goofy's Playhouse on his left. His plan works: Judge

Doom follows him. But Finn only counts three of the wiry weasels.

Inside, it's a madhouse, a press of bodies with the smell of soiled diapers and perspiration hanging in the air. Families jostle and hurry to reach attractions before the park's imminent closing. Impatience, fatigue, and foul tempers show on the parents' faces, while the kids look half asleep and ready to cry.

Finn has a choice to make; he decides to err on the side of self-preservation, knowing the Cryptos won't like hearing he has made a show of himself. The Disney Hosts Interactive have been shut down for the night. The appearance of any DHI will raise eyebrows.

Finn focuses on remaining all clear as his DHI passes through the guests like a ghost. Many are too self-absorbed to see him or, if they do, to believe what they've seen. Seconds later, he's put a physical wall of park visitors between himself and Judge Doom, a human shield. Finn is relieved to have Doom's visage shielded from him; the guy's rubbery face is so horrid, a mask of creepily too-flexible flesh with high cheekbones and fat lips.

And Finn just can't get Willa's mentioning Wayne out of his head.

Finn's DHI continues through the crowd, passing through everyone in his way. He wins some oohs and ahs, but is surprised by how little notice is taken. At twilight, he's more a shadow than a person, a spectral vision rather than reality.

Finn is approaching the Chip 'n Dale Treehouse when he feels a powerful force turn his head to his right. Mickey's House looms before him. *The missing Mickey*: Wayne's primary concern during their covert meeting in Club 33.

Finn glances back quickly: no sign of Judge Doom. He walks between the house and its separate garage, passes a CAST

MEMBERS ONLY door, and, walking around back until he's out of view of the guests, steps up and through the building's exterior wall and into a passageway.

He's inside.

* * *

Willa is not about to let Finn fend off Judge Doom alone. Slowing, she glances back. Of the six weasels she counted before, three are now following her. For now, she'll have to think with her feet, hoping to outmaneuver or outrun them.

The three weasels resemble walking cartoon figures and, as such, cannot avoid attracting attention. Quickly, they draw a small crowd. Is this something she can use against them?

Willa stops, turns, working to retain her full DHI.

"Hey, fellas!" she calls out. More guests turn. Parents grab their children by the hands and spin them, making sure they don't miss what appears to be part of the Disneyland show.

Willa remembers these six more clearly now: they are Judge Doom's Toon Patrol. In the movie, they are indestructible in battle, but end up laughing themselves to death.

She focuses on Finn's pinprick of light at the end of a dark tunnel, inwardly superimposing the image across her vision. Taking a deep breath, she walks up to and *through* the three weasels, making them spin around as they try to follow the path of this strange being that has just walked right *through* them. She reverses direction and repeats the effect—now she has the Doom's minions literally spinning in circles. This wins laughter from the crowd, and from the Toon Patrol as well.

The stunt works against the creatures briefly, but the cruelest looking one, who she recognizes as Psycho, sees through her ruse.

"Boys!" he says. Psycho reaches out for her, but swipes his

paw right through her hologram. He looks at his own hand, eyes bugged out in confusion.

Willa doubles back through their group again. Two of the weasels bump into each other; she jumps clean out of the way, maintaining her all clear so that they bang their heads together, and watches as their knees wobble. Adults in the crowd gasp. The kids applaud.

Psycho remains standing. "Hey, little girl!" He charges her.

Willa steps out of the way; she's no Charlene, always itching for a direct confrontation. She kicks the weasel from behind. The crowd erupts in cheers. More people join the throng surrounding the four: now it's a full-on show.

Psycho pivots and backhands Willa across the cheek. He makes contact; her head snaps to the side.

The force of the blow shows Willa she's failed to maintain her all clear. She attributes this not to the violence, but to the look in Psycho's eyes. His name befits him: he's wild, crazed, ready to tear her head from her shoulders. She doesn't appreciate being called "little girl," either; the insult triggers her temper even as it reminds her of her mortality. She's vulnerable, and she has to remember that. She has to calm down. But that's impossible.

Psycho strikes her again—hard. The crowd is evenly split; the kids cheer loudly; the adults are uncertain of just what they are watching. Willa lowers her shoulder and hits Psycho in the gut, driving him back into the other weasels, who look dazed, still recovering from their head thumping. But none of them are laughing, and that's the only thing that can kill them— Willa knows they're otherwise indestructible.

Finn told her to head to the train, but plans change. How can he expect her to leave him? She has a choice to make. It's never really a choice at all.

29

"I DON'T RECOMMEND THIS," Charlene says as she walks alongside Maybeck from the Heraldry Shoppe to Snow White's Scary Adventures. "All it can be is trouble. Who do you think made that armor come alive?"

"And why would she do that unless we were getting close?" Maybeck says. "You stay out here. I'll go in."

"No way! We go together or not at all."

"Don't run so fast!" he says. "And lose the clichés."

"This is *me*," Charlene says. It's one of Maybeck's favorite lines; he grimaces wryly in recognition.

With the fireworks show approaching, the waiting line is mercifully short. They climb into one of the cars. Charlene nudges Maybeck; looking back, he sees that the Cast Member has her arm out, preventing other guests from boarding.

"Why would she do that?" Charlene asks. "Put us on here by ourselves?"

"Not good," Maybeck says. His arms sparkle. He looks over at Charlene, whose hologram is also degrading. "Partial shadow," he says.

Charlene studies them both, nods. "Honestly? I don't mind so much."

Doors open in front of them, revealing the cabin's cheery sitting room. Drying clothes hang on a line in front of the hearth. The seat jerks left; they face a chest of drawers and see Snow White, happily climbing a set of stairs, a flaming oil lamp in hand. The Dwarfs are playing and reading.

It's suddenly dark.

The Queen's voice: "Now to take care of Snow White!"

Next they're in the woods under a full moon; an instant later, the car plunges into the claustrophobic mines.

The ride stops. Maybeck mutters a word he should not. The music remains inappropriately happy, as if it's trying to balance the oppressive darkness.

"Visitors, I see!"

They spin around in their seats.

The Evil Queen. Not a character. Not a hologram. The real deal.

Maybeck and Charlene jump out of the car and take off running, their holograms sputtering and digitizing. They lose their legs, their arms—then regain them an instant later.

Alarms sound; a man's voice tells everyone to remain in their seats.

Maybeck pushes open the doors to the next scene. The Queen stands reflected in a full-length mirror. She turns, and the old hag stands before them. But not an Audio-Animatronic: a threat.

The hag throws an apple at Charlene, who deftly drops and slides on her knees. The projectile flies harmlessly over her head. They're surrounded by evil laughter and the sounds of crows.

The hag reappears in front of them. "Going somewhere?"

Maybeck skids to a stop, wondering where she came from.

"Shadow! Sides!" Charlene shouts.

She disappears, leaving Maybeck all alone.

* * *

Finn steps through a wall fashioned out of plastic grating and finds himself in a hallway, facing Mickey's laundry room. He

284

hurries toward it; he'll search the upstairs first. It's an area where guests are not allowed, and thus a likely spot for Wayne to take shelter.

In the laundry room, he skids to a stop, staring at the washing machine. His stomach turns violently: Mickey's big white gloves appear to be pressed against the machine's glass, buffeted by waves of water, as if the mouse is desperate to escape. Wayne implied that the mouse was missing. . . . Finn realizes that it isn't Mickey drowning, only his laundry being washed—but the effect is still disquieting. Finn pulls on the washer door, but it's fixed permanently, a part of the display. Finn's mission feels all the more urgent—he has questions only Wayne can answer.

Reaching the house's front entrance, where guests first arrive, Finn sees a child safety door with PLUTO painted on it across the stairway. He's so fixated on getting upstairs that he barely glances over his shoulder to check if he is being followed.

There's no one behind him, nothing but a broom from the laundry room leaning against the wall behind an old-fashioned radio. If it had eyes, it would command an ideal view of both the entrance area and the living room. Mickey and, to an extent, the Keepers, have an unpleasant history with Disney brooms dating back to *Fantasia.* Thankfully, this one just appears to be an ordinary old broom.

Finn studies the entrance area, looking through the doorway to the outside and, seeing no one about to enter, zips up the stairs, his DHI passing through the waist-high PLUTO door like wind through a picket fence.

Finn sees two more doors: one straight ahead down the hall, the other to his right, and therefore visible from the entranceway. He walks through the door to the right. And steps into . . .

Air. Finn is falling—the door turns out to lead into the vaulted ceiling of the sitting room below. He lands in front of the fireplace. A guest hurries forward to help Finn but reaches out and can't take hold of his projected arm. The man staggers back, astonished; he's never seen a DHI before.

"What's . . . going . . . on?" he gasps. *"Ghosts!"* he shouts, sounding like a little kid. His screams ricochet off the walls. Mickey's House clears as if someone yelled *Fire!*

Finn is left alone.

And in that instant he hears the sound of bristles brushing the floor. The sound grows more clear and specific: the bristles are moving in his direction. Someone scrubbing the floor? While guests are still in the park?

"Hello?" Finn calls out.

The scrubbing continues, coming toward him. Not scrubbing . . . more like sweeping.

Like a broom.

* * *

Maybeck and Charlene are in DHI shadow on opposite sides of the dark forest when a high-pitched man's voice rings out from behind the old hag.

"Always making trouble, you ugly troll."

Maybeck moves to see who's speaking. It's a very short, older man with a white beard but no mustache, and wire-rimmed glasses. Only when six similar-looking men emerge from the dark does Maybeck identify the leader as Doc, one of the Seven Dwarfs.

"Ugly, ugly, troll," Doc says.

The hag spins, furious. "Go away, little man! You're nothing but a nuisance! Another step and I'll—"

"What? Toss us an apple?"

One of the six—Happy?—bellows with laughter. "Toss us an apple!" he repeats, amused.

Maybeck steps out of DHI shadow, signaling Charlene to join him. His leg is better now, nearly back to normal; the exercise has helped it.

"You'll never be beautiful again!" Doc says to the hag. "How can we see any beauty in you when we've seen *that?*" He points at her wizened face.

Maybeck takes Charlene by the hand and leads her off; the Queen's too obsessed with the dwarfs' insults to notice.

"I hope they'll be all right," Charlene says.

Maybeck pushes through another set of doors; the ride is stopped, and Cast Members are consoling impatient park visitors.

"You there!" a man calls out.

Charlene pulls on Maybeck; together, their DHIs dissolve into and through the wall. The people they leave behind stand, gawking, wondering what it is they've just witnessed.

30

UNABLE TO RUN FOR FEAR of attracting unwanted attention, and intentionally avoiding the route Maybeck and Charlene have taken through the castle, Philby, Jess, and Amanda take a longer, slower route to Toontown Station, passing by Big Thunder Ranch and slipping through the heart of Fantasyland.

None of the three states the obvious: that they are taking a big chance, and following nothing more than Jess's vision. She's right more often than she's wrong, but that does little to console them. If this is a bad lead, they are wasting huge amounts of precious time.

"Fireworks soon," Philby says, recalling the rendezvous he established.

"We can't return without him," says Amanda.

"We'll regroup, switch around, change plans. Don't worry: we're not leaving without him."

"Them," Jess says, correcting him. "Don't forget Willa."

"As if Philby would forget Willa!" Amanda snorts.

Philby smiles.

"You should do that more often," Amanda says.

"Do what?"

"Never mind."

Philby asks several more times, but Amanda's dropped it; she doesn't want him to think she's flirting. Boys tend to misread such things. . . .

Approaching the Toontown Station is a disappointment.

The area's quiet, with just a few people milling around. There's a crowd outside It's a Small World and a number of guests leaving Toontown.

"This isn't right," Philby says. "Toontown should be roped off." Unable to stop himself, he blurts out, "Unless everyone's too busy chasing down Overtakers."

The train whistle sounds from far away.

"We missed Finn and Willa," Amanda says. "Not fair!" In anger, she throws both fists toward the ground, as if she's swinging hammers. She is lifted off her feet and propelled to the pavement flat on her back; she has "pushed" herself, allowing her anger to briefly own her.

Amanda stares down at her hands. Then she looks up at Jess, tears of frustration welling in her eyes.

"We're going to find him," Jess says. "Hold on to that energy. We may need it."

* * *

The commotion outside Mickey's House—shrieking parents running in all directions, their children held firmly by the hand—is the only signal Willa needs. Weasels on two feet cannot run nearly as fast as weasels on four feet. Willa has hidden herself among the crowds. The cries ahead of her are like a starting gun. Without hesitation, she makes for the front door of Mickey's House, stops, and listens. She steps inside.

No one. It's empty and silent and creepy because of it. Of all the attractions, Mickey's House should be roiling with childish laughter. "Finn!" she calls timidly, moving discretely into the living room. She stops abruptly and stands still, reaching deep to find her pure DHI.

There, just ahead of her, is a broom tiptoeing on its bristles.

As Maybeck and Charlene emerge from Snow White's Scary Adventures—a ride that has definitely lived up to its name—they spot a pair of Cast Members riding Segways; they're heading rapidly in the direction of It's a Small World.

"Security," Maybeck says. "They don't usually show themselves like that. Why aren't they backstage?"

"Let's find out!" Charlene says, jogging off, running hard to keep the Segways in sight.

* * *

Finn knows that his fear of the broom is degrading his hologram, despite his best attempts to mask it. The brooms could have killed Maybeck and Charlene in the Battle for the Base; they are skinny and fast, and he knows of no way to threaten or eliminate them. This one doesn't appear to have a bucket of the acidlike green goo that presented such a danger to Maybeck and Charlene, but that fact isn't enough to alleviate Finn's sense of dread. No matter how you slice it, it's plain disturbing to see a broom walking on its bristles as if it has two stubby legs.

When Willa appears behind the broom, a combination of anger and relief rushes through Finn. She's not supposed to be here, he thinks.

"What does it want?" Willa asks. Her voice spins the broom in her direction; a small puff of dust rises from the floor. She feels the hairs on her neck stand up.

"Me. Us, now, I suppose."

"What exactly is it supposed to do?" she asks. "Choke us on dust?"

"Don't make it ang—"

The broom comes at Willa so fast that she has no time to

move. It thrusts the top of its handle—its head? do they even have heads?—into her middle, below her ribs. As she bends forward, retching, its handle strikes her on the head, not once, but repeatedly. Her DHI is gone—she's feeling this brutally, as she would any such beating.

Finn runs and tackles the broom, pulling its handle to the floor with him. But the wiry wood bends like a pole-vault pole, then straightens, launching Finn across the room, a human projectile. Finn crashes into the stone above the fireplace and tumbles to the floor.

Willa covers her head with her hands as she writhes in pain on the floor.

"Stop it!"

The broom strikes again. And again.

"Hey!" Finn shouts.

The broom stiffens, then turns.

Dang, it's an ugly thing, Finn thinks. So common, you'd hardly even think about it normally; so dangerous, you just want to run. Finn has been in dozens of threatening situations; he has battled witches and dragons, monsters and pirates. He's faced dolls and crash-test dummies. Yet, once again he finds battling inanimate objects terrifying. How do you fight something that's already dead?

Willa points at Finn as if to say, *You.*

Finn bears the weight of that pointing finger. *Me.* Willa's in trouble; she needs him. But what does she expect him to do?

Thankfully, it takes Finn only a fraction of a second to realize he's being egotistical and self-indulgent. Willa isn't pointing at him; she's pointing at the fireplace behind him. Finn connects the fire to the broomcorn serving as the broom's two legs: Willa is pointing out a weapon he can use.

If this weren't Disneyland, if he weren't a hologram facing

a sadistic broom, Finn would accept that the red glow coming from behind him is only flickering electric light. But he knows better. *To dream is to believe.*

If he and Willa believe the red glow is the fire it pretends to be, then it's fire. The logs in the bucket on the hearth are not plastic, but wood.

Taking a deep breath, channeling his belief, Finn jams a log through the rubbery mesh screen into the fireplace. It comes out flaming. *I love this place!*

The broom reacts stiffly, but too late; in the midst of charging Finn, its forward momentum proves irreversible. Finn lights the broomcorn and watches the broom try to stomp out the flames burning up its "feet"—with its feet! Its efforts only fan the flames further.

Willa's up. Remembering that she alone can affect her current state, that fear is something that can be shed, she runs to the broom, grabs it, and hurries from the room. Finn follows.

In the laundry room, Willa drowns the fire in the broom's own bucket.

"Nails!" she cries, directing Finn to a can on a shelf above the drying towels. Nodding, Finn grabs a nail and the dust brush from the wall; he uses the latter as a hammer, securing the handle of the broom to the maple chest against which it leans.

"Not going anywhere," Willa says, breathless.

"Are you all right?" Finn asks, examining her head.

"No, but I'll live," she says, touching her bruises. "For the record? I considered letting him burn for a minute there."

"You're such a softie," Finn says, offering her a quick hug before they hurry from the house.

31

$\mathcal{T}$OONTOWN ACTS LIKE THE SWIRLING mouth of a tornado, drawing everything nearby into its turbulent funnel. First the Segways are swallowed up.

The conflicting currents within Toontown rotate clock-wise. A crowd mentality, spreading outward from the small number of families escaping Mickey's House, morphs the guests into a large group moving quickly toward the exit. Few know exactly why they're fleeing, but if five families are running, they think theirs should be as well.

On the opposite side of the vortex from Mickey's House are the Segways, Philby and the Fairlies—and a stream of Kingdom Keepers fans who have recognized their idols.

An instant later, Finn and Willa emerge from within Mickey's House and are caught up in the circular flow. Despite their DHI status, they instinctively work to avoid collisions, spinning and dodging what has become a panicked stampede. The heaving movement of the crowd spits them into the quieter center of the spinning mass, near the small fountain.

Emerging from within the crowd is a woman in an elaborately crocheted brown dress. She has a full head of long dreads and . . . *bare feet*. She turns.

It's Tia Dalma.

Finn's heart stops. His mouth goes dry. This woman, who has apparently followed him into Toontown, tricked Finn into killing his best friend, Dillard Cole. If she's here, does that mean . . . ? He tingles from head to toe, losing his DHI.

Tia Dalma is flanked by Cruella and Judge Doom, with the all-weasel Toon Patrol just behind. A murmur sweeps through the masses. The swirling storm stops. Philby and the other Keepers step into the empty center behind Willa and Finn.

There's a collective hush as the crowd awaits a street performance.

"Bring us the Legend!" Tia Dalma shouts, sweeping her arms outward.

Finn holds up his hand, halting his fellow Keepers. He steps forward.

Cameras flash. A child's voice from the audience rings out, "Give it to her, Finn!"

The top of the fountain is adorned with a statue of Mickey Mouse and his *Fantasia* conductor's baton. Finn's breath catches. *The Legend*. Does she mean Mickey—or Wayne?

Finn says the first thing that comes to mind. "Do you think these people are ever going to let you destroy the magic? No matter what you do to us, what you try to do to *him*, you will never win. It's the one thing you've completely underestimated: the power of good. This is their park," he says, gesturing to the crowd. "*Theirs*. Not yours, not ours."

"Do you pass out a collection plate now?" Tia Dalma says, her voice a mocking croak. "Those others with you, are they your choir? Take your preaching elsewhere, boy. We take what is ours. And if you believe it ends with this park, you have another think coming."

"Throughout history, evil self-destructs," Finn says. "It's an unsustainable force."

"Oh, really?" Tia Dalma shouts. "You bring him to us, boy, or we will walk over you to get him."

She glances at the oncoming Segways then, and does the

strangest thing: she sings. It's only a few lines, but they are unexpected—beautiful, soaring notes. Finn might respond more fully if he were not mostly DHI. To his dismay, he sees all the men in the large crowd turn toward the voodoo priestess, including the Security guys riding Segways, who immediately lose control and crash.

With a fierce cry, Charlene leads the Keepers into battle, Maybeck right behind her. She cartwheels, executes a back handspring, and lands atop Psycho, knocking him to the pavement. Maybeck blocks an attempt by two of the other weasels to grab Charlene, and the fight is on.

Jess hangs back as Philby and Finn march toward Tia Dalma and Cruella. Finn has no plan beyond focusing himself into full all clear. Cruella looks concerned. In contrast, Tia Dalma's internal confidence rattles both boys.

Doom and his Toon Patrol are fully engaged by Maybeck and Charlene. Willa joins in; never much of a fighter, she's battling as fiercely as she can.

Amanda walks steadily behind Philby and Finn, wishing there were a clear lane through which she could use her power to push.

Cruella shouts a single word, "Come!"

Tia Dalma's lips are moving. Finn spots two tiny, rag-limbed dolls clutched in her tattooed hands and a long row of similar figurines tucked into a crimson scarf tied around her waist. As she squeezes her hand, his knees give out and he drops. Philby spins, buckles over at the waist, and falls, writhing in agony.

"Must . . . go . . . all . . . clear . . ." Finn groans, squinting his eyes closed, searching for darkness and that pinprick of light. All he sees is red, the color of his anger.

Amanda never misses a stride. Head held high, her vision

locked on Tia Dalma, she raises her arms, pulls back at the elbows, and shoves.

Cruella and Tia Dalma catapult up and back, flying ten yards through the air before they crash hard to the ground. The crowd cheers, celebrating what they believe is a masterful special effect.

Finn screams. Philby throws up. Tia Dalma's right hand squeezes the dolls so tightly that her fingers are white and bloodless.

"Hands in your pockets, young lady!" she roars.

Amanda, whose hands are in fact raised and ready to heave the two witches into another zip code, sees Finn shaking, Philby retching. She nods slowly and complies.

Behind them, Maybeck, Willa, and Charlene are losing ground to Doom and his Toon Patrol. No matter what the Keepers throw at them, the weasels barely feel it. Doom's icy calm doesn't help matters. He strolls casually over to Willa and grabs her from behind, holding a knife to her neck.

Jess stands to the side, observing.

"There, there," Doom whispers. "You'll barely even feel it."

The cold pressure of the blade on Willa's throat causes her limbs to tingle, and she's afraid. Deathly afraid.

Amanda's eyes sweep forward again. Tia is badly shaken from her fall. Cruella doesn't appear to be moving.

The sound of rapid scratching comes like a powerful wind on all sides. The crowd screams, and chaos breaks out; park visitors scatter in every direction, revealing a rampaging horde of animals, mostly from the Jungle Cruise. Tigers, lions, leopards, monkeys, hyenas, and crows converge on Toontown from all sides, teeth bared, hackles up. They're responding to Cruella's summons, answering her call, *"Come!"*

Among them are the stray cats and dogs that must hide

inside the park all day and only emerge in the wee hours of the morning to hunt for food in the trash. They look prepared to devour everything in their path.

Among the shrieks and cries, the patter of running shoes slapping pavement surround the Keepers, stroller wheels spinning, lungs wheezing, feet flying. The retreat from Toontown is an exodus on an epic scale, a flight of all guests and Cast Members, scared off by the influx of wild animals, the flying witches, and the writhing boys.

Ignoring the chaos around them, Maybeck and Charlene are too engaged to see Doom's hold on Willa. Jess is screaming at them to pay attention, but heedless, they continue to fight.

The flow of human bodies fleeing parts and spreads into two distinct streams. In the center of the split, a caped woman appears. She carries herself with the stature of a queen. An Evil Queen, carrying a shoulder-high scepter.

Every living thing in Toontown seems to take a collective breath.

"Willa!" Philby moans, seeing the knife at her throat.

The flow of people is finally exhausted; the area is empty.

Maybeck and Charlene hear Philby's shout and stop fighting, even as the Toon Patrol moves toward them.

"All clear!" Charlene cries to Willa. It's her friend's only chance for survival.

Finn is shaking visibly, pain shooting through him, but still he sees the Evil Queen's approach. A pinprick of light . . . A pinprick of light . . . But it eludes him.

Philby, tucked into a ball, forces one eye open.

The Queen advances at a slow, eerily calm pace. A dark smile splits her beautiful features.

Jess steps up alongside Amanda. "Can you—?"

"No," Amanda whispers. "If I do, that creep's hand will move. I'll kill Willa." Her voice tightens. Breaks. "Jess, this time . . . I think we've lost."

32

"YOU WILL NOT WALK OVER ANYONE!"

The booming voice carves a path through the scene of battle and separates the crowd of Kingdom Keepers and Overtakers gathered in front of Mickey's House. It belongs to an unimposing figure: an old man with wispy white hair, wearing khakis, a polo shirt, and leather-topped deck shoes. He looks like he belongs at a marina or on a golf course. In his right hand, he carries what appears to be a pad of paper.

"We are tired of you and your kind," he says. "I find this all quite tiresome."

Finn can breathe again, and move. Color returns to Philby's face. Tia Dalma, an observer like the rest of them, has relaxed her grip.

"Some people know not when to give up," the Evil Queen says in her calm, regal voice. "Such a pity."

"And some nonpeople like you just plain take things too far," Wayne counters. "Pitiful." He holds up something in his left hand, a slender black object. "Looking for this, are we?"

The Queen cannot hide her surprise at the sight of the talisman. The other Overtakers seem to take their cue from her; clearly, they don't understand the significance of Wayne's offering, but they follow her lead just the same, with surprised expressions.

Finn's body tingles as he mentally focuses on and achieves all clear. The blue outline reappears around Philby and the other Keepers as well—all but Willa, who, with a knife to her throat, has a sputtering blue outline.

Tia Dalma's authority seems to have been usurped by the Evil Queen. The return to Disneyland appears to have rearranged the Overtakers' hierarchy, and Finn wonders how this might affect him and the other Keepers.

"And look! What have we here?" Wayne says, motioning to Jess to approach him. As she comes nearer, he whispers to her, *"The past and future are always present."*

"I dream *the future,"* she whispers back. *"But I've lived the past."*

"Correct. Listen carefully now, young lady, and believe it all."

As Wayne turns his attention to the Evil Queen, he hands Jess the pad of paper along with a black fountain pen, the mere sight of which runs chills through her.

"This young woman can see the future," Wayne says. The Overtakers are well aware of Jess's paranormal abilities; they have tried repeatedly to capture her and prevent her from aiding the Kingdom Keepers. Now they hiss angrily among themselves. "What she doesn't know," Wayne continues loudly, "is something you have feared all along. She cannot only dream it, but with this pen—*Walt's pen*—she can draw it as well."

Walt's pen! Jess studies the pen in her hand, wishing it weren't there, wishing he had handed it to someone else. She has no idea how to use it.

"Draw what you see!" Wayne instructs Jess.

Trembling, Jess uncaps the pen. Is this indeed Walt Disney's original pen, the same pen that saved the Kingdom after the Keepers solved the riddle of the Stonecutter's Quill? Wayne's declaration of her own powers is news to her. Is it a ruse to stall the Evil Queen? Jess has never considered herself a witch, but Wayne is talking about her as if she were one. She feels a burden she has never felt before.

Jess touches the nib to the paper, only to discover that the pen draws by itself. Ink spreads out into dozens of fine lines depicting the scene in front of her. As she lifts the pen from the page, the illustration animates. She can imagine Walt Disney seeing his mouse come to life.

A border forms around the illustration and the image splits in half, separating Willa from Judge Doom. The knife falls to the ground: in the picture, Willa is safe. But Doom seizes the knife and charges Wayne. . . . Jess jerks her eyes away from the image, unable to watch.

Her eyes meet Wayne's, who nods slowly and deliberately.

She shakes her head. "No."

Wayne nods again. "You must!"

"I . . . can't!" Jess complains.

The Evil Queen casts a sideways glance at Judge Doom.

Jess knows what's coming.

"Bring me that pen, Old Man!" the Evil Queen demands. As Jess steps forward, the Queen begins to rant. "Not you! Him, and him alone!"

Finn, Philby, and Maybeck exchange telling glances. Beside Maybeck, Charlene nods. Without speaking a word, they all know: inaction is not an option. They will not stand idly by while Wayne puts himself in danger.

Amanda's hands, now out of her pockets, shake as strongly, as surely, as if she's fighting back hurricane-force winds.

Wayne steps over to Jess and extends his hand, requesting the pen.

Jess reluctantly hands it over.

"You can stop this," he whispers.

"Silence! What did he say?" The Queen sounds childish.

"What did he say?" Finn makes eye contact with Amanda; with a glance, he indicates Willa—a silent command.

Wayne walks confidently toward the Evil Queen. As he passes Finn, he whispers, *"It's about time."*

He waves his left wrist and hand, casting his ice-blue eyes onto Finn in a way that freezes the boy in his tracks. Finn's emotions get the better of him. That look of Wayne's is a message; Finn's brain attempts to process and decode it, but he does not recognize the signal and helplessly delegates the job of translation to his heart. Finn has had dreams in which he is desperate to run but can barely move, his limbs heavy as buckets of water, his engine sluggish. Now it feels as if he is there again in such a dream, the wide-awake dream of his DHI existence, with the world swirling around him in slow motion. He shouts, but his words come out as gobbledygook.

Wayne reaches the Queen and proffers the pen. As she reaches for the pen with her thin, impeccable fingers, she looks again to Judge Doom, blinking once. Jess watches the muscles in the man's hand flex where he grips the knife. With one flutter of her eyelids, the Queen has sentenced Willa to die.

The Toon Patrol starts a slow-motion turn toward Maybeck and Charlene. It's to be a slaughter—all the Keepers will fall on this night.

Wayne snatches back the pen, spins, and tosses it to Jess, who rips the sheet of paper in two, exactly as she saw the drawn image tear moments before. Before her, Judge Doom and Willa separate. The knife sails from Doom's hand. Jess sprints toward Wayne to stop what she knows is coming, but it's like trying to run in the ocean.

As the knife falls, both Finn and Philby dive for it. But Judge Doom recovers it first and without hesitation plunges the blade into Wayne's chest.

With a scream, Amanda pushes telekinetically so hard that the Mickey statue atop the fountain bends. The Overtakers and Wayne lift off like errant leaves caught by an autumnal breeze.

Wayne lands near the gas station, flat on his back, the knife still stuck fast in his chest. Finn screams as he hurries forward, with Philby right behind.

The Queen, Cruella de Vil, Judge Doom, what's left of the Toon Patrol, and the savage herd of wild animals are pushed together by Amanda's power and driven down an alley that dead-ends in a closed gate—down but not done.

Philby takes Finn by the arm, but Finn tries to shake him loose.

Wayne's eyes are open and unmoving.

Finn sobs, "He's—"

"The most amazing man that ever was," says Philby. "He did it for Willa. He did it for us!"

Finn turns and shoves Philby to the pavement.

Finn remembers that first night in the Magic Kingdom, an old man sitting next to a statue of Goofy, his ice-blue eyes and scratchy voice, so calm and knowing. He recalls how it felt to be trusted with secrets of a kingdom that outnumbered him in years by nearly five to one, how this old man knew the beginning and feared the end. It feels as if they have lived whole lives in these few years, as if Wayne has been grandfather, father, and partner to Finn, all in one. Finn cannot imagine a world without him—*will not* imagine a world without him.

"Honor—that!" Philby chokes out, the wind knocked out of him.

Amanda is at Finn's side. "I'm sorry, Finn . . . I'm so sorry!"

Finn looks back and forth between her and Wayne. It's not her fault. Somehow, Wayne foresaw what was coming.

As the first *boom!* sounds and the fireworks begin, Finn screams into the night sky. Images of his mentor's face flash before his eyes; he is overwhelmed by memories of Wayne's kindness and concern, his humor, their shared history. This can't be true. First Dillard—now Wayne? The sounds coming from Finn are inhuman.

Jess joins Maybeck and Charlene. Willa seems steeled by her ordeal—a new strength resides within her.

Beneath the colorful flashes and blinding light, amid the deafening drumming of explosions overhead, Amanda reaches out to Finn and takes his hand. She holds on to him, as hard and fast as their DHI form allows, pulling him into a walk, then a flat-out run.

The Keepers race from Toontown, real tears running down their projected faces, real hearts torn from digital bodies, overwhelmed by real pain that dogs their heels as they hurry toward the Plaza, Philby in the lead, brandishing the Return as if it alone might represent salvation.

33

FINN COWERS WITH EACH EXPLOSION in the sky, slowing him and Amanda. The blue outline surrounding him sputters and sparkles. Amanda, who can't stop crying, pulls him along like he's an unwilling ox.

"We have to go!" she says.

Finn looks as if he doesn't recognize her, doesn't know where he is.

"We've lost them." Amanda stops, keeping Finn close to her. "Which way?"

Looking back toward It's a Small World, she sees the Evil Queen and Tia Dalma walking calmly in their direction.

"Oh, great," she says. Finn's unresponsive and numb, a sea anchor she must drag along. She doesn't know the park well at all. The proximity of the fireworks overhead only serves to confuse and frighten her. She steers him toward the Mad Tea Party, then, screened from the Overtakers by a pagoda, changes her mind and leads him past the entrance to the Matterhorn and in the direction of Finding Nemo. In doing so, she unknowingly takes the long way around, costing them more time.

"Come on, I need you, Finn!"

As they approach the Plaza, the crowd becomes obnox-iously thick, with everyone stopped and looking up at the bril-liant display of color and sound. The park guests give no quarter, their feet firmly planted; they have no interest or intention of moving out of the way for anyone. They act as a human wall.

Light flickers behind Finn's dazed eyes. He appears trapped in a state halfway between a material body and a DHI.

"Please!" she adds.

"I loved him." Tears spring from his eyes and splash onto the pavement, tears that have nothing to do with projected light. This causes Amanda to cry all the harder.

"I know . . . I know. . . ." She wraps her arms around Finn and pulls him in and feels his convulsive sobs as her own. It feels right to hold him. Each overhead blast matches a corresponding shock radiating through Finn. She spins him, takes him from behind at the waist and guides him through the crowds. It's slow going, like trying to push to the front of a parade. People complain and shoot impatient looks.

Finally, Finn stops. There's no going forward without making more of a scene. Amanda rises on tiptoes. The crowds are illuminated in flashes beneath the pulsating colors overhead. Hands are raised as cheers sound roundabout.

"We've lost them," she says. "Philby and the others," she clarifies.

From within the castle, flowing out of the central tunnel like billowing smoke, come the wraiths that attacked the Studio Archives. The crowd cheers their arrival, waving and laughing, ignorantly welcoming the corresponding terror.

Seeing the wraiths, Amanda turns Finn around once more and takes him by the shoulders. He hasn't seen them. "Listen to me, Finn Whitman. You need to do what you are so good at." She glances up to see the wraiths beginning to circle the Plaza; they are looking down, clearly searching the crowd. "You need to let this go and all clear. We *both* need to all clear, right now, right away. Are you listening to me?"

She shakes him. Still nothing. It's like a part of Finn has died with Wayne.

Several of the wraiths form a tighter circle over the path to the Royal Theater, spinning like a wheel. Amanda jumps up and down, trying to see, but it's impossible, what with the flashes of light and the arms raised in cheers all around them.

"The others are in trouble!" she shouts, reaching her own conclusions. "Philby will have no choice but to return them." *Boom! boom!* overhead. The wraiths continue in their wide circling, dipping and rising. "We're going to miss the return. We need to all clear. *Right now,* Finn. You have to erase it. Forget it. Leave it behind. If it disappears, so can you."

Finn stares back at her, his eyes blank and dull. Then he nods, and the last of his tears cascade down his cheeks. He starts to look up, but she grabs him by the hair—he must not show his face to the sky!

"We're going to keep our heads down, we're going to all clear, and we're going to get out of here before . . ." She doesn't dare tell him about the wraiths—he'll want to fight them all. "Before all the crowds start trying to leave. I've got you by the arm. Close your eyes. The minute I see your blue line, I'll try. And Finn, promise me, whatever you do, do not look up!"

He nods. Just before closing his eyes, he says, "I'm going to kill them all."

"You will," Amanda says. "You and me, both."

34

THRONGS OF PEOPLE have also opted to depart the park ahead of the massive flood of guests, using the distraction of the fireworks as a cover. Amanda joins them, steers Finn alongside families pushing strollers, the elderly, and those who are plain exhausted. As many people seem to be leaving Disneyland as there are staying behind. The crowd offers the two Keepers good cover.

A faint blue line sparkles on Finn's neck and runs down his shoulders in bursts. It's like he's being struck by tiny bolts of lightning. The blue worms of electricity crawl and sputter, but fail to join in any kind of continuity. Amanda can't remember witnessing anything like this partial all clear; it's more like Maleficent's fireballs, bundles of static electricity searching out a ground wire.

The pulses come more quickly now, flashes of pure brilliance. A small boy walking alongside them tugs his mother's sleeve and points. Amanda directs Finn away from them. They can't afford to be noticed.

Above the castle, the fireworks build to a finale. Some of those walking turn to face the spectacle. Finn and Amanda continue past, heads down. He is now outlined in pure blue; he guides Amanda, whose eyes squint shut as she exhales a long, slow breath. Her neck begins to sparkle.

By the time they reach the gates, Finn is too distracted by Amanda's crossing over and the crush of guests to notice that he's guiding them through a covered turnstile.

Seeing two kids move *through* the turnstile causes a Security guard to squint and lift his walkie-talkie to his lips.

* * *

Philby awakens in the Morgue, across and down the hall from the Crypt. He lay down in one of the aisles between the rows of file cabinets before crossing over; now it takes him a moment to orient himself. He has never asked the other Keepers if they suffer this same disassociation upon returning: he has no idea where he is or how he got there; he's not even sure *who* he is. It's horrifying, isolating, this sensation that he belongs to nothing, not the room he finds himself in, nor the body he looks down and sees.

But what troubles Philby most is that each time he crosses over, the disassociation upon his return lasts fractionally longer than the time before. Professor Philby is curious about the progressive nature of this sense of separation—what might cause it, what might prevent it. Philby the kid is plain scared by it, which is how he finds himself counting the seconds, hoping to identify where he is, who he is, and what he's doing there. *Seven . . . eight . . . nine . . .*

He's got it! The fireworks. Wraiths, spinning overhead. The search in all directions for Finn or Amanda. His finger on the Return, knowing what must be done. The look in Willa's eyes as it's apparent that they're not going to find Finn or Amanda . . . and that they can't stay one minute longer.

Philby peers into the tunnel in the direction of the Crypt. Stepping out, he hears voices and darts back inside the Morgue, sneaking a look as he goes. It's Brad and Joe. They pause to look in both directions. Philby leans back. When he next looks, they are gone, having entered the storage room that accesses the Crypt.

It's after 9:00 P.M., long past working hours. Their arrival suggests that someone reported seeing DHIs in Disneyland. Or maybe the wraiths, or the massive battle in Toontown. Joe and Brad are being held accountable for the chaos.

Philby looks down at his hand. He's holding the Return.

Finn and Amanda's only hope of getting back lies inside that lab down the hall. If he can't return them, they will be stuck in SBS until he does—comatose here in this world, in serious danger as DHIs in the other.

* * *

With only a matter of yards to go until they reach the entrance to California Adventure, Amanda calls to Finn. "Do you hear that humming?"

Finn says nothing.

"It's like summer, but louder," she says. "Like cicadas," she says. "Crickets."

"It's not crickets!" Finn grabs her hand and pulls her in the direction of the La Brea Bakery. A pair of Segways appears at the gate area, speeding toward them.

"How did you—?" Amanda asks.

"I remember that sound from Epcot. The Segways."

They run hard, dodging around a ticket house. "This'll slow 'em," Finn says. They pass some palm trees and jump over a low barrier into the bakery's courtyard, where they weave among umbrella-covered tables.

"That's the back of Soarin'," Amanda says. "My favorite ride."

The monorail sweeps past.

The Security guys on Segways, blocked by the planter island, move briefly away from the Keepers in order to get around the obstruction. They attempt to keep an eye on the pair, but that means looking in the opposite direction from the one they're traveling in. One Segway catches a wheel on the barrier, and its helmeted rider falls off.

"Now!" Finn says, leading Amanda up to the wall that serves as a boundary to California Adventure. "You're blue!"

"You, too."

It is a formidable moment for both, that instant in which one must trust the present, believe in the system, and demonstrate a total willingness to forget practical knowledge and commit. The commitment asks for an implied sacrifice: if they hit that wall running at full speed and are not one hundred percent DHI, they will go down in a bloody heap of broken bones, unconscious.

For safety's sake, the Keepers like to test obstructions—run a hand through, stick their hologram heads inside—but there's no time. Finn and Amanda need to vanish. The remaining Security guy will imagine they have run off, yet be fully aware that there's nowhere they could have run without his seeing them. Next, he will assume they're hiding. He and his fallen partner will kill time canvassing the area. They may call for backup.

Amanda and Finn aren't looking ahead as they reach the wall. They aren't squinting their eyes or expecting the worst. No.

At the moment of would-be contact, they turn their heads to each other. And they are smiling.

* * *

Finn and Amanda, now fully DHI, weave their way amid the pine trees at the side of Disney's Grand Californian Hotel, slip under the monorail, pass through a backstage wall and, soon after, alongside a parked single-engine airplane, emerge onto the path near the entrance to Soarin' Over California. To avoid the crowds, they remain on the perimeter. This proves to be their first mistake.

The second is not trusting their ears.

Taking long strides to cover as much ground as possible without breaking into an outright run, Finn and Amanda pass the twenty-foot-high bear standing outside Grizzly River Run. Behind them comes the sound of something breaking and crunching, followed by a steady *clomp, clomp, clomp*.

Amanda is focused not on these obvious sounds, but on the more disturbing drone of scratching and rubbing, like a thousand people running their fingernails along the teeth of a thousand combs in unison.

"That sound—it's still there, and it isn't Segways," she says. "Listen!"

"Bear!" Finn says, glancing back. He steers Amanda with him into the Redwood Creek Challenge Trail. He has no time to think about Wayne, pushes the thought away.

"Hide!"

The giant River Run bear, wearing a floatation vest and carrying a paddle and a raft, hardly seems like an Overtaker. Amanda pushes Finn into the tunnel through Big Sir, Disney's giant redwood tree.

There's a second bear, a six-foot-tall honey-colored grizzly just outside the area. Breaking loose from its pedestal, it looks mean, moves as if sore, and drools hungrily.

The Challenge Trail, an obstacle course of stairs and rope bridges mostly covered by a roof, offers the two Keepers a place of refuge. The griz runs like a much bigger creature, each stride covering two yards. Finn and Amanda power up the stairs. The bear is behind them, close enough to paw at what's left of their holograms. Their blue outlines sputter; their limbs tingle; they're losing all clear.

312

Finn is first onto the rope bridge, deftly dancing across webbing that springs like a trampoline. Amanda takes two steps and falls through, bouncing the net and dropping Finn, who falls on his back.

The salivating griz charges for Amanda and goes into the net face first, his front legs slipping through the gaping holes in the webbing. He bites angrily, attempting to take her arm off. Instead, he snaps the section of rope nearest his snout, and his head falls through as well. In his struggles to get free, he only succeeds in ensnaring his hind legs.

Finn extricates himself from the net and rolls toward the border of woven nylon, which serves as a path. He hurries around and, seeing the bear rising up on its haunches, dives for Amanda, shaking the net. The bear falls again.

Together, Finn and Amanda roll for the far edge and escape across another rope bridge to a lookout beneath a shed roof. The golden bear is up on two legs like a human being, coming for them, dancing across the webbing.

"Overtaker," Finn mumbles, recognizing sorcery when he sees it.

The golden is almost upon them. Finn pushes Amanda out of the way, stumbles backward, and is caught in the netting. The bear roars, lifts its ugly paw, armed with curving claws the size of kitchen knives—

And disappears.

Finn had shut his eyes before those claws took his face off, so when he opens them again and sees no bear, he's thinking, This is what death is like: now you see me, now you don't. He is somehow exactly where he was when the bear cleaved his head from his body. Amanda is exactly where she was too. He's glad that he can still see Amanda, that heaven includes his friends. He looks around for Philby, for Willa, Charlene, and

Maybeck. But it's Amanda who remains with him, and that fact carries significance. His heart even skips a beat. Although he supposes that technically he no longer has a heart.

Amanda looks paralyzed, staring off into the sky as if tracking his spirit's departure from his body. The thing is, he's not up there; he's down here, stuck in the net. Amanda isn't looking into the sky; she's looking at a twenty-foot-tall bear holding a golden bear by the scruff of its neck like a mama cat with her kitten. The River Run behemoth shakes her head at the golden and scrunches her face disapprovingly. The golden is all flailing paws and kicking legs.

Despite everything he's seen over the years, Finn can't believe that there's really a slight grin on the River Run bear's maw as she looks down at him and Amanda. But it's there, all right.

Park guests are flocking to the River Run bear, who places the golden back on its perch—where it freezes in place, instantly—and tromps up the path to her place outside the attraction, where she also solidifies. There is applause, cheering, and—no matter that people can produce video of the event—no evidence it ever happened. Just the word of a few dozen tired park guests who claim to have witnessed the coolest show ever, yet another Disney rumor that will circulate for years in the lore of the Kingdom Keepers.

Amanda helps Finn out of the net and they quickly join the path again, moving away from the astonished crowd. Only then, as the terror of the past few minutes seeps out of her and her blue outline reappears, does her focus return to the strange sound they heard earlier.

"Do you hear it now?" Amanda says.

"Yeah, I do."

"It doesn't belong in the park, a sound like that."

"No it doesn't. What do you suppose it is?"

"I don't know. It sounds like . . . summer . . . only deeper and louder."

"Oh, dang! You're right!" Finn says. "I hate it when you're right!"

35

GRASSHOPPERS—BIG GRASSHOPPERS, the size of dogs. Park guests fleeing in all directions amid shrieks of terror while other visitors a comfortable distance away applaud and start shooting video. The contrast between what they see as life threatening and what they see as entertainment creates two distinct groups in the world of California Adventure: those running for their lives and those grabbing for their cameras.

At the front of the runners' line are two people outlined in pulsing blue light: Finn and Amanda. Behind them, the grasshoppers seem to be multiplying. The insects don't exactly run; they leap several yards at a time, bounding forward, wings fluttering and carrying them aloft, then skid down to the pavement, where they recover and leap again.

Ahead, the night sky is alive with color, with glowing rockets shooting up and slicing the darkness. It's a sea of heads and bodies, camera flashes, and music that has gone virtually unheard.

"World of Color," Finn says before Amanda can ask.

The attraction is the single biggest spectacle in both parks; it comprises twelve hundred pressurized fountains, lights, music, and dozens of lasers, all computerized. More than ten thousand guests crowd together to watch, forming a human doughnut around the pond where the show takes place.

Amanda looks back. "They're closing fast! That's Hopper in the lead. From *A Bug's Life*. He'll kill us!"

The lead grasshopper's mandibles are the size of garden

shears. They look like they can cut through anything, including a neck or an arm.

"All clear," Finn reminds her, although his outline is sparking as much as Amanda's. They are forced to push their way through the crowd. "We're boxed in," Finn says. "Cornered."

Guests scream as Hopper and the other insects crash into the crowd. Finn and Amanda have a brief advantage; they're tightly surrounded, and Hopper can't see them.

"This way!" Amanda guides Finn toward Paradise Pier, then stops, reconsidering, and hurries toward a nearby food cart instead. "The umbrella!" she shouts. "Help me!"

The umbrella is made of sheet metal, one of four used to shield park guests from the blazing California sun. Amanda heaves its stem back and forth, wiggling it loose. Beside her Finn pitches in, but he's suddenly encumbered by his grief, despondent and barely moving. Losing Wayne comes back to haunt him.

"Why?" he asks.

"I'm going to get us . . ." With a heroic heave, Amanda tears the umbrella loose. "Out of here! Bring it!"

Finn does as he's told, moving mechanically. Amanda clears a path through the crowds. But Hopper and the grasshoppers are nearly upon them.

"We need to—"

"Hurry!" Amanda says.

Finn cradles the umbrella awkwardly, Amanda in the lead.

"Excuse us, part of the show!" Using a warm voice and a winning smile, she urges any intractable guests out of their way. Her blue outline continues to sputter. Finn's is sporadic as well—they are vulnerable to attack. If Hopper and company catch up with them . . .

"Where are we—?"

"The fountain!" Amanda calls back. "Grasshoppers can't swim. They hop on the water."

Ahead, plumes of water explode in hundred-foot-high bursts. The scene depicts Buzz Lightyear and Emperor Zurg from *Toy Story 2*. Amanda flashes Finn a smile over her shoulder, encouraging him on. Finn follows unquestioningly, obediently.

"First Dillard, now Wayne," he whispers.

"Not now, Finn!" she chastises. "Look out!"

A wet *snap!* from behind them sends Finn tumbling forward. Hopper is on his heels, mandibles snapping, trying to cut Finn in half.

"Faster!" Amanda calls.

Finn breaks out of his grief in time to swing the heavy umbrella at Hopper's mug, knocking the insect over and exposing the grasshopper's ribbed yellow belly. "Gross!"

Using one wing, Hopper rocks back up.

Amanda has carved out a path to the water. Before any curious Cast Members can reach her, she jumps the low guardrail and wades into the pool, Finn right behind.

Above them, Buzz and Zurg battle on a screen of misting water. Jets spout and music wails—until the chords are overpowered by screams.

A hundred or more giant grasshoppers have reached the pool's raised wall. Guests scatter, crawling and running toward the exits.

Confused and angry, Security officers shout after Finn and Amanda. "Stop! Stay where you are! It's not sa—"

One of the guards reaches for the radio at his waist, calling in to the control booth.

A life raft is hurled into the water by a Cast Member.

"They're going to shut down the show!" Finn calls to Amanda through the thick mist.

"Hurry!"

Finn and Amanda can see the hundreds of valves beneath the surface of the pool. Amanda turns sideways, trying to work her way through the maze as water explodes in fire hose–like bursts all around them. A shooting stream knocks the umbrella from Finn's hands. He bends to retrieve it and takes a blast to the stomach. Some of the water passes through his partial DHI; the rest knocks him over. He recovers the umbrella, holding it awkwardly so as to present the least amount of surface area, and carefully follows Amanda's lead.

"Look!" Amanda points up. Three wraiths survey them from above.

But then, caught by a power fountain blast, two are gone.

"We're cooked!" Finn said.

"No! Over here!" Amanda pulls Finn with her, grabs the umbrella, and carefully positions it top down, stem up.

The chaos in the viewing area scatters the Security team, buying Finn and Amanda more time. Amanda steps into the concave lens of the metal umbrella, holding on to the stem.

"Hurry!" she says.

"I'll never give in!" Buzz Lightyear declares over the loud-speakers.

"Finn!" Amanda catches him by the wrist and pulls. Together, they hug the umbrella's stem.

"To infinity and—"

Below them, the strongest blast of fountain water in the show goes off. The umbrella, and the partial DHIs along with it, is lifted ten stories—a hundred feet—in less than a second.

Fast as an eel, the remaining wraith stabs toward them through the mist.

Finn holds on, white-knuckled.

They peak out at one hundred and ten feet. The plume of water supporting the umbrella falters, and then stops. The wraith is six inches from Finn's face.

Through squinted eyes, Finn sees Amanda's hands let go of the umbrella.

Suddenly they are flying through the air at four hundred miles per hour, Amanda's legs still wrapped around the umbrella's stem. She has made an Amanda push, flying their umbrella-craft out of World of Color and over to Mickey's Fun Wheel. The same push throws the wraith against the roof of Ariel's Undersea Adventure, where it evaporates.

Amanda pulls Finn with her as she bails out of the umbrella, and they land together on the superstructure of Mickey's Fun Wheel. She easily climbs into an empty car. The ride is stopped because of the show.

They are safe.

"You okay?" she asks, like they'd waited in line for their seats.

"No. Not now. Not ever." Finn looks down at the fountain display, the thousands of guests, the symphony of color. In the chaos, the concern for two glowing kids is lost, and the show continues.

"We're going to make it," Amanda says.

"Not him."

"Finn, listen to me. I've dealt with that kind of loss—and worse. Family. You think you'll never get through it, but you will."

"Not me. Not ever."

"With the help of friends, you can. It took me a long time to figure that out."

"Jess," Finn whispers.

"Yes. Others, too. You can't do this stuff alone. We think we can, but we can't. Look, I'm just saying that I'm here. Okay? I'm here."

She wraps an arm around him and pulls him close. It's like holding a wounded puppy. Her eyes well with tears.

"It's not fair," she says. "It'll never be fair." She watches the show, still holding Finn's head to her shoulder. "We wait it out here. No one saw us through all that water. We're safe." Does she sound like she's trying to convince herself? "We'll make our way back to the Plaza later, when everything's shut down. Call Philby. He can return us."

Finn says nothing. The Finn Whitman Amanda knew is gone—she can feel it through her hand, holding his shoulder. She can hear it in his voice. Gone, like a leaf lifted and carried off by the wind. She knows better than to try to call him back to her. There is no fob, no Return for where he's gone.

Only time will tell who appears in his place.

36

F INN ATTENDS the morning meeting in the Crypt's conference room with Joe, Brad, and the other Keepers. He sees them looking at him. Their mouths move—especially Joe's—but all Finn hears are low rumbles and echoes, like someone speaking from the far end of a vast cave. He feels tears run down his cheeks and scrubs them away. He's calm for a few minutes. Then the tears start again.

He wishes Amanda and Jess had not returned to Mrs. Nash's, from where they'd been crossed over. They are as much a part of everything now as any of the Keepers.

Finn's hand starts moving indiscriminately, pen on pad. He can't recall whether or not Joe told him to do this, or if he's making notes about the talk with Wayne of his own volition.

> Mickey and Minnie homes "for their
>   own sakes"
> Sorcerer's Cap, conductor's baton
> You don't kidnap Mickey, you destroy him
> Nearly all the magic along with him
> Walt's pen
> It's about time

"Time," Finn says, breaking his silence.

Joe stops in the middle of a sentence and the room goes silent as everyone looks at Finn.

"Wayne said, 'It's about time.' He wanted to make sure I

got that. It was important. He kept shaking his watch at me to make sure I'd heard. He said the OTs destroyed Mickey. Not kidnapped, but destroyed. That's the word he used."

Brad and Joe exchange a look.

"What?" Philby asks. "What was that about?"

"What?" Joe says back to him. "We can't show our surprise? Are we supposed to know everything? We're on your side. We trust you guys. More importantly, we *need* you."

Despite his words, there's a palpable feeling of unease in the room, and all the Keepers feel it. Joe is trying to cover something up; Brad's face reveals that too. These two have a secret they are unwilling to share.

More secrets. At the thought—and at the talk of Wayne—Finn sinks back toward despair; he tries desperately to kick for the surface, toward the light, but the cold and dark engulf him. Water leaks from his eyes. He's drowning.

He barely hears Philby, who's talking about the Keepers missing something, saying that Wayne is always five chess moves ahead of his nearest competitor or teammate, that the OTs' raid on the Studio Archives precipitated everything—especially the theft of the binder. Philby reminds everyone that the wraiths were present again, just as they were during the raid on the Studio Archives, that there are no coincidences, that Wayne knew exactly what he was doing when he—

But he can't say it. Maybe it's because his heart won't let him. Maybe it's because he's afraid that he'll push his friend so deep that even the glow of the surface will disappear. Maybe, like Finn, he doesn't believe it himself.

Wayne is full of tricks. Finn has been chanting this in his mind like a mantra, trying to convince himself that the man's death was an illusion, a trick played at the highest level. But his heart tells him differently.

"The danger here," Joe says, "is that by showing themselves as they have, the Overtakers are signaling that they aren't afraid. They're back in Disneyland, where they started. That gives them a lot more power than they had in Florida. The kind of brazen behavior we saw in Toontown does not bode well. They are following a plan, and there's an endgame to that plan that none of us wants. With Wayne . . . with what happened to Wayne, they will believe they've . . . that they've gained the upper hand. Tipped the scales. We can expect more now, not less."

"I miss home," Willa says, drawing looks from everyone, some inquisitive, some disapproving, some sympathetic. "No one told us we'd be here this long. Why don't you let us out? Why are we treated like prisoners?"

Underground, there's a deep rumble the Keepers feel more than they hear: traffic. It never goes away here, never stops as it does late at night in Orlando. It's the only sound, along with a whispering drone from the air-conditioning system. A ribbon tied to the vent wiggles like a kite tail in the artificial indoor breeze.

Joe doesn't know what to say. He looks to Brad, who's equally speechless.

"An enemy within," Charlene says to Joe. "Until we solve that, you can't or don't fully trust us. Am I right?"

Joe purses his lips.

"What *aren't* you telling us?" Philby says. "Let's face it, there's something you're keeping from us, and at this point . . . I mean, we all want to go home. It feels like we've been here forever. Nothing good is happening. It's not like we're helping."

"Of course you are," Joe says. "You all contribute!"

"Right," Maybeck says. "Tell me how. We've been under attack since we got here."

"I know you don't want to hear this right now," Joe says, as tactfully as possible, "but Wayne knew from the start that you all were the key to preserving the magic. The raid on the Studios . . . what happened in Toontown . . . Wayne reached out to Finn, knowing that he took a risk in doing so. He would never have done that if it weren't important. Hugely important. Everything he said in that meeting is critical." Joe is looking at Finn. "You need to reconstruct that conversation as accurately as possible."

"What do you think I'm doing?" Finn says sharply. He spins the note around and slides it in Joe's direction.

Joe accepts it and reads. He says, "Thing is, no one knew about that meeting but you all. So how—"

"Not according to Storey," Philby says, interrupting.

"Who?"

"That's not important," Philby says. "She told me that Security knew about Finn and Wayne. That means they had to be listening in somehow. Maybe they recorded the meeting? You guys have authority here, right? Get that tape. Give Finn a break. Who can remember every word of anything?"

Finn thanks Philby with his eyes. Philby nods.

Joe points to Brad, who types a note.

"We can't make you stay," Joe says. "Your participation is voluntary. Always. We appreciate everything you're doing, but—"

"Come on!" Finn says, lifting his head, no longer trying to hide his sorrow. "You think we're going to let her get away with what she did? What comes next is this: you start to trust us. We need the Return. We need Philby to be able to cross us over whenever necessary, even if we sometimes can't explain why. And we need our software upgraded."

Maybeck says, "We're very needy."

Everyone laughs, even Finn, who hasn't felt anything but sorrow since the battle in Toontown.

"I can see that," Joe says, clearly contemplating how much to share. "As to your requests, we take them seriously and we'll study each one carefully, I promise. And we'll check with Security about the taping of the conversation in Club 33."

"If you bore us, you will lose us," Philby warns.

"Too much talk, and we walk," Maybeck adds. He and Philby fist-bump.

"That goes both ways," Brad says. "If you keep secrets from us, how are we supposed to properly evaluate your needs and figure out how we can help?"

Philby, Willa, and Maybeck make eye contact. Willa nods faintly. Maybeck casts his vote with a slight shake of the head.

"What's going on?" Joe doesn't miss much.

"Last night, as the three of us took off for the Plaza, Jess was with us. We got separated; she was maybe a minute behind."

"Less," Maybeck says.

Philby continues. "She shows up with the notebook . . . the binder that got stolen from here the night of the wraith attack."

"What?" Finn says, sitting upright now.

"Storey grabbed her. Just appeared and grabbed Jess and gave her the notebook, told her she had to get it out of the park. Said the OTs would kill for it."

"Of course they would," Joe says. "You're telling me this Storey person stole it?"

Philby shrugs. "How should I know? They were together for like five seconds. Boom: she hands Jess the notebook and takes off."

"Where is it now?" Brad asks.

"We hid it and the pen."

"What?" Joe is apoplectic.

Brad explains to Joe, "Though items that are on your person when you cross over, like watches and phones, typically make the jump, items you acquire while in DHI form don't return with you." He turns to Philby. "Where is it?"

Finn says, "The wraiths are connected to the binder. They'll have found it by now."

"Not a chance. We screened it from the skies," Philby says. "We stashed it behind the condiment station at the food stand by the horseless carriage stop."

"Brilliant," says Joe. "I'll send a crew." He pulls out his cell phone.

"You do that, and the wraiths will have it the moment it comes out from under that roof," Philby says.

"Your friend Storey was able to carry it around the park," Brad counters.

"We don't know when the OTs discovered it missing," Willa says. "Maybe she was so eager to get rid of it because she knew the wraiths had been sent to get her."

"Lovely," Joe mutters. "Okay, so we'll tell them to box it—something metal—and drive it up here."

"We want to see it too," Finn says. "With you. When it gets here."

Joe appraises him thoughtfully.

"Whatever's in there got Wayne killed," Finn says.

"We don't know that," Brad interjects.

Joe holds up a hand, stopping his colleague. "That's fair." He looks at the Keepers, nodding slightly. "Partners, from now on."

Finn answers breathlessly, "Partners."

37

"THIS IS HORRIFYING," Amanda says. She's in row 17, seat B, beside Jess. She holds Jess's journal in her lap. Jess, in the window seat, is half asleep, having been up drawing through the night.

"Do you think that's why Storey gave you the stuff from the Archives?" Amanda asks. "To touch it, so it would rub off on you and you'd see stuff like this?"

"I'm so tired," Jess moans.

"Are these flames?"

"I don't know. I think so."

"And is this a grasshopper?"

"Same answer. I really want to sleep. Please—"

"But you must have dreamed stuff happening. Right? You didn't just dream *pictures*."

"It could be nothing. You know how it works—or doesn't work, with me."

"If it was nothing, would we be flying to Hollywood?"

"Burbank."

"Same thing." Amanda makes a noise with her mouth, a long sigh like a tire losing air. "You really *are* tired."

"I am. So let me sleep. Please."

"Why do you suppose Mrs. Nash agreed to let us go?"

"To get rid of us for a few days."

"I'm serious."

"So am I. We're out of her hair for the next week."

"Someone made her agree," Amanda says. "Joe, I'll bet."

"I don't think it works that way. What's the one thing Mrs. Nash cares about?"

"Money. Wait, you think they *paid* her to let us go? Like a donation, or something?"

"Doesn't matter what I think. I'm going to sleep now," Jess says.

Amanda turns her attention back to the journal in her lap, running her fingertips over the picture in front of her.

"An octopus? Mickey's hat?"

"I don't know," Jess says, glancing at the page. "I drew them." The plane shudders through some turbulence. Jess grips her armrests.

"But why?"

"I don't know," Jess says, impatient now. "This stuff doesn't always make sense to me, Mandy."

"Come on, you know I don't love being called that."

"Unless it's by . . . *him*."

"Shut—up!"

"Sometimes it's better to admit the obvious. You like him. So what? It's old news," Jess says.

"So, everything," Amanda says. She opens the overhead vent and turns her face into the stream of cool air.

"Don't let it mess things up." Jess yawns.

"When have I ever?"

"There's always a first time." Jess leans her head against the wall of the plane and shuts her eyes—but she's trying *not* to sleep. She was lying to Amanda about wanting a nap. Going to sleep is no longer alluring for her; she fights her drowsiness with all her might, terrified of what she might see. She's become a kind of insomniac, something not even Amanda knows. Lack of sufficient rest leaves her hungry most of the time, wobbly on her feet, dizzy, and cold. It's the cold that's hardest. People look at you funny when the temperature's in the high eighties and you're wearing a bulky school sweat-shirt.

Jess struggles against the sandman, fights him back. But he always wins, eventually. She hates him for it, wishing she could kill him once and for all.

* * *

The girls' arrival at the Studios begins with a one-hour private session with Joe in a conference room. Amanda and Jess talk through their history with the Keepers, and Jess explains Storey's appearance "out of nowhere."

"Did she say anything?" Joe asks.

"She said the OTs would kill for it—the binder, I mean."

"She was scared?"

Jess tilts her head pensively. "Maybe. I don't know. I didn't really think about it—she was in such a hurry. She wanted me to get the binder out of the park."

An air vent whistles, distracting Amanda.

"Did you look at the binder before Philby and Maybeck hid it under that roof?"

"Open it? No. The place was crowded. Packed. There wasn't time."

Joe nods.

"Why?" Amanda asks. "What's in it?"

"Production meeting notes. Transcribed and typed. I promised the Keepers they'd get first crack. I think Finn has them now." He pauses. "I keep my promises."

"What did you promise Mrs. Nash?" Amanda asks.

"Amanda!" Jess snaps.

"It's all right," Joe says. "Mrs. Nash was made aware that foster care stops at eighteen, and you're both several months past your eighteenth birthdays. You're right about her misusing the system. We threatened an audit of her funds during your years in her care. You are now officially released from foster care."

Amanda says, "She threatened to turn us over to Baltimore."

"That isn't going to happen now," Joe says.

"The other girls?"

"I—we—gave her thirty days to get her act together."

"You can do that?"

"A little thing we believe in: doing good will never hurt you."

"Wait," Amanda says, astonished. "Are you saying we don't have to go back there?"

"We have an intern program," Joe says. "We have college scholarships, ways to take care of you. No one's going to force you to live where you don't want to."

"We're free to do what we want?" Amanda says.

"We get to work in Disneyland?" Jess practically shouts. "Let me get this straight: you're going to *pay* us to work in Disneyland?"

"If that's what you want," Joe says. "But honestly, we have bigger plans for you two. Much bigger."

* * *

"How are you?" Amanda asks Finn. Joe has allowed her to visit the trailer Finn shares, hoping she will rescue him from his sorrow. She doesn't believe in rescuing him; she believes in helping him through it.

She finds Finn sitting atop a yellow bedcover, a bunch of papers spread around him—the production notes, Amanda thinks. He looks up briefly, his eyes vacant.

"Is that you or your hologram?"

"My hologram might work in the hall, I suppose. Not in a private room. No projector in here."

"What are you doing here, Amanda?"

"It's nice to see you, too."

He tries to smile. It looks physically painful.

"They flew us here. Me and Jess. There's still work to do," she says. She briefly explains Joe's gift to her and Jess, their freedom from Mrs. Nash. "We're going to be interns in Disneyland and California Adventure. We're going to be your insiders!"

"I know I should be excited," he says finally. "But all I can think about is the memorial this weekend. Did anyone tell you about it?"

"No. But I'll bet it's more a celebration than a memorial. Wayne wouldn't want us—"

"Don't be like the others," he says. "Everyone keeps telling me what 'Wayne would want.' They don't know. Neither do you."

"Oh, and you do? Maybe if you got out of this trailer. California sunshine wouldn't hurt."

"Tough love? Is that what they said to try?"

"No one said to try anything. This is me, Finn! I *asked* to see you. I'm worried about you. I thought you might be happy to see me."

He looks up at her. Words struggle to come out. His head sinks again.

"Listen to me!" She raises her voice. "This was a crime! A crime that cannot, will not, go unpunished. You are either with us in that, or you're not. Joe, Brad, the rest of the Keepers intend to do something about it. Wake up, Finn. While you're in here moping, the people—no, the *things*—that did this are planning another strike. And whether you want to hear it or not, Wayne would not be feeling sorry for himself. He'd be doing something to stop it."

Finn closes his eyes more tightly.

Amanda takes a glass of water sitting on the nightstand and douses Finn. "Wake up!"

Now he opens his eyes. He is not happy. He spits water off his lips. Amanda realizes she's trembling. An apology leaps to her tongue, but she won't allow it to emerge. He deserves this.

"We—need—you. I need you!" She's about to leave when she sees that she's sprinkled water onto some of the pages. "Oh my gosh! I'm sorry!" She reaches across him, trying to undo the damage. Finn sees the problem and hurries to help, flipping the pages over and dragging them across the bedspread.

"Wait a second!" He holds one of the onionskin pages higher, so that it's backlit by the ceiling light.

Vague images, the outlines of hollow letters or characters, fade as the page dries.

"Did you see that?" he asks. His face is still dripping wet. "Those—"

"Yes! Invisible ink?" Amanda says.

"This is why the OTs stole the file," Finn says, his voice remarkably back to near normal. "They wanted whatever's written here."

"But maybe they didn't figure out that it was written in invisible ink."

"Which means we know something they don't." Finn sounds close to cheerful. "A message! Some sort of message or code."

He puts his hand on her arm. They've only known each other as holograms recently. The feel of her warm skin, the

334

"THE SORCERER'S APPRENTICE"   11/16/37

(Suggestions made during Story Meeting of Nov. 13th, not appearing in continuity)

Beginning (Up to time Mickey commands the broom.)

Suggestions: The things with which the Sorcerer works should
               not be too modern. They should be large, old
               battered copper retorts and transparent receptacles.
               Earthen-ware and copper would be good.

               If glass receptacles are used, they should be in
               containers that look very old.

               (As to what kind of character Walt sees in the
               Sorcerer is that of a stern, dignified looking
               man - fantastic looking as in Sketch 18.)

               On the first cut to Mickey, put over the idea
               he is very tired, have sweat falling off his brow.

               On another cut to Mickey, he pours a bucket of
               water, then wipes his brow; possibly getting a
               shot down from Mickey's angle showing the huge
               vat and the amount of water Mickey has to carry
               in to fill it.

               Another shot of Mickey, during the Sorcerer
               magic stuff, could be of him looking curiously
               at the Sorcerer and pouring water, missing the
               vat completely - the water going all over the
               floor.

               Walt made an incidental suggestion that after the
               Sorcerer has commanded his magic to vanish back into
               powder, there could be a little puff of smoke before
               it goes back into powder.

Mickey getting the broom to work for him. (Up to Mickey's dream.)

Suggestions: After Mickey's first command to the broom, get a
               shot of the broom coming to life - it stiffens and
               quivers, then it jumps off its hook. Mickey gives
               another command and the broom starts to walk, etc.,
               as in continuity.

               On cuts to Mickey working the hokus-pokus on the
               broom, show that he is working hard, sweat pouring
               off his brow, until he gets the broom working well.

               Get shots of Mickey directing and the broom reacting.

               When the broom comes to life (first part of this
               section), get a big smile on Mickey's face.

reality of it, lifts the corners of his lips and brings a light to
his eyes.

    "Welcome back," Amanda says.

335

38

THE CLAMSHELLS SIT unmoving inside Ariel's Undersea Adventure. The sign out front posts an apology for the inconvenience, suggesting that guests check back later in the day. The silence within the attraction, and the lack of any Cast Members attempting to resolve whatever the issue is, suggests some breakdown in communication. All the costumed Cast Members are on a break until notified otherwise, while the park maintenance crew has yet to arrive.

Storey Ming paces behind the wall that forms the backdrop of the attraction's final scene. This is the space where she has been living, waiting, watching for a very long time. The exit door, an emergency door, is locked, violating state safety codes. This would be reason enough to shut down the attraction, yet no one comes to repair it. The situation is highly suspicious.

Storey does not venture out into the attraction, does not show herself, but paces impatiently, treading silently even in her agitation. Even the smallest sound sends her to peek around the edge of the wall and look around. The unexpected sound of dragging feet draws her practiced eye.

Four workers in dark blue coveralls and low-slung baseball caps walk up along the track lined with stalled clamshells. The men move like first-generation Audio-Animatronics, not human beings. As Storey watches, the lead worker's head rises. He sniffs the air. Half his face is caught by the limited light, revealing stretched, gray, chalky skin sunken over sharp cheekbones. It's as if all the air has been sucked out of him. His upper lip and nostrils twitch as he seeks a scent.

Again, Storey searches the attraction expectantly with her gaze from the safety of her hiding place.

Suddenly, the worker swivels his head and looks directly at her. He has no eyes, only empty sockets below a shelf of prominent bone. His nose continues to twitch, and he licks his lips.

Storey withdraws, realizing that she has just seen a ghost from the Haunted Mansion: an Overtaker. A nuisance!

Her reaction is swift. She climbs a metal ladder attached to the wall, its rungs rising into the superstructure above. She has memorized the layout of the attraction's upper reaches. The labyrinth of catwalks runs like a crossword puzzle throughout the space, giving access to four emergency exits. She moves carefully and quietly.

The sound of zippers tells her the ghosts are shedding their outer layer of coveralls. One look confirms it: they're in no hurry, the explanation for which follows immediately as the leader floats off the floor and flies.

Storey stops in her tracks.

The ghost is transparent, which helps explain the need for coveralls—one can't be seen walking around California Adventure as a ghost. He arrives on the catwalk as fast as a gust of wind.

Storey backs up. She can see right through his smoky body and head. "Stand back," Storey says, loudly enough for her words to carry. She sounds eerily confident, her voice richer and more mature than normal. "One more step and I will consume you."

The ghost angles his head like a wild animal catching a scent. As two more ghosts land on the catwalk behind him, the leader takes a defiant but clumsy step forward. He brandishes a carving knife from the Haunted Mansion's dining table. His dry lips part, once again revealing his dead, black tongue—an attempt at a smile.

Storey lifts her hand. An inky cloud consumes him and the others.

"Stand back!" she calls.

The worker claws his way out of the cloud, but a bolt of blinding light strikes him, leaving only a wisp of black ash where the ghost stood.

Storey glances from the catwalk to the floor below. She sees a white-bearded man, his bare torso projecting up out of the blue sea of the set, the remainder of his body invisible below the sculpted waves: King Triton.

The lord of the oceans hurls a second bolt of lightning, dissolving a second ghost to dust. The third ghost flies off the catwalk and out of the attraction.

"Descend!" Triton calls in his strong baritone.

Storey returns to the ladder and has soon joined Triton on the floor of the attraction.

"You were expecting me," Triton says. "You were searching for me."

"I was . . . hoping. Yes. I don't like to rely on others, but I was sorely outnumbered."

"I—*we*—have observed you these many weeks," the king says. "You are comfortable here in the sea."

Storey does not reply, but only nods slightly.

"You like it here."

"I like water," she says.

"You must not disrupt our lives in this place. You must leave."

"I . . . ah . . ."

"Did you bring this upon yourself? Do not lie! Have you harmed those in the Mansion?"

"No. I come to assist the Children of Light."

"Easily said. More difficult to do."

"Determination is underrated," she says.

"Where have we met? You are somehow familiar to me."

"Am I? I was on the Disney *Dream*. Perhaps there?"

Triton shakes his head. "No. Long before that, I believe. From what element comes your line?"

"I would remember one so great and powerful as you, King Triton."

"Earth? Sea? Air? You are a friend of my daughter's, perhaps?"

"I am familiar with Ariel," she says. "I do not know her personally. While hidden here, I've watched how she thrills and excites the guests. You must be very proud of her."

Triton studies Storey with suspicious, questioning eyes. "Who are you?" He doesn't wait for her reply. "You must not disrupt our lives here," he repeats. "Should you bring more trouble to our attraction, you will be deemed most unwelcome. I will not come to your rescue next time no matter how your eyes may plead. Do I make myself clear?"

"Do you always take such a tone with your allies?"

"Why did the ghosts come after you? Do not lie."

"I am myself at a loss to understand why," Storey says.

"You possess powers. I saw what you did. A sorceress? A witch? You must be of the kingdom, and yet you fail to identify yourself."

"I told you: I am an ally."

"Telling and proving are two different things." He gestures out into the attraction with one mighty arm. The normally inanimate fish and other sea creatures have come alive and are all looking at Storey with glistening, inquisitive eyes. "We will be watching."

"No more trouble," she says. "Honestly, I don't know where they came from."

"The Haunted Mansion."

"I mean, I'm not sure *why* they came."

"To harm you."

"Yes—yes—of course. But why would they want to harm me? I—"

"Only *you* know. Not I." He stares her down. "Do not play games."

Storey hangs her head, her fists gripped so tightly, her knuckles look like miniature snowcapped mountain peaks.

When Storey looks up, Triton is gone, leaving behind nothing but the lingering smell of ozone from the electrical discharge of his lightning strikes and four sets of coveralls collapsed in pathetic little heaps on the floor.

39

W<small>HILE THE</small> C<small>RYPTOS INVESTIGATE</small> the possibility of invisible ink on the pages of the stolen Archives folder, the Keepers accomplish a preplanned Imagineer-approved cross-over into Disneyland. Amanda is paired with Charlene while Willa goes with Philby, leaving Maybeck with Finn.

Jess intentionally stays awake so as not to cross over. Joe has asked her to study her most recent drawings and write down every thought she has for each image she's drawn. He seems particularly interested in the grasshopper head, though when asked specifically about it, he denies any such preoccu-pation.

It is late afternoon. The Keepers randomly awaken from naps back at the Studio and find themselves holograms on the Plaza. Their DHIs, more than three years younger in appear-ance than they are themselves now, have been decommissioned for the night—with apologies to those families with reserva-tions for guides. The Keepers have been warned that this could cause some irritation in the unlikely event that a canceled fam-ily spots them; they've been told to use the excuse that they're currently undergoing testing.

Maybeck and Finn head off in the direction of New Orleans Square and the Court of Angels; Willa and Philby— the brains—are to gather any crime scene evidence that may remain in Toontown, while Amanda and Charlene go in search of Storey Ming. Total time of operation: one hour. No excuses. Philby carries the fob. In case of a missed return, manual returns will be performed at subsequent ten-minute intervals.

But neither Joe nor the Keepers wants to make a spectacle of kids vanishing from plain view. Once a day is enough. Repeats will only set the Disney blogs afire with speculation about the Keepers' escapades; that kind of publicity won't help anyone.

Finn and Maybeck work their way up the stairs in the Court of Angels, on the lookout for Storey. Better safe than sorry. They hurry up to the next floor and reach the location of Finn and Wayne's final meeting. Finn feels heavy-hearted as he is reminded of their last conversation, but is determined to come away with something—anything!—to help explain the events that followed.

"You remember the plan," Finn says, allowing Maybeck to walk in front of him to serve as a screen.

"I got it. No worries."

"You sure?"

"Whitman, this is me we're talking about. What do you think?"

Maybeck strides through the CAST MEMBERS ONLY door used by the waitstaff, Finn immediately behind. The two boys find themselves in the vestibule where Finn had hesitated and pretended to be a busboy, with the second dining room on their left and the "library" straight ahead.

"May I help you?" a waiter asks.

"You could help us find the men's room, my man," says Maybeck. "We ended up on some porch out there while we were looking for it."

"Sure thing. Down the stairs and turn left."

Finn keeps his head down, as if embarrassed by their mistake.

"No worries," the waiter adds. "Happens all the time."

Finn mumbles a thank-you but avoids lifting his head, fearing that someone might recognize the boy specter who had crashed through walls and raced through tables only days before.

Maybeck heads down the stairs, but instead of following him, Finn turns toward the dead-end hallway that houses the waist-high eavesdropping closet where he hid. The closet is newly padlocked. Finn has a choice to make: as an all-clear DHI he can jump or climb through the door, but he risks being seen on the way in or out. Unable to imagine there's actual evidence in the closet and unsure exactly what he's looking for, he reverses direction and heads to the table where Wayne sat in the library dining room. Wayne is—*was*, Finn corrects himself, registering a flash of deep pain—impossibly sneaky. There's no telling what the man might have left behind.

The table where Wayne sat is unoccupied. Finn slips into Wayne's chair. His chest tightens; his heart pumps wildly. Right here . . . so very alive . . . Finn grits his teeth, determined to get through this. He inspects the underside of the table with his fingertips: nothing. He leans forward to similarly investigate the underside of the chair seat: nothing. But looking down, Finn notices a small pile of wood shavings against the wall, apparently swept there by a broom; their red color contrasts with the dark wood floor.

"Are you waiting for someone? May I get you a something to drink?"

Finn sits up, feeling rattled and unstable, bumping his less-than-all-clear head on the table. As he rights himself, he glimpses, as clearly as if a spotlight were aimed at it, a scar of freshly carved wood on the table's understructure. That explains the shavings. Finn's head is spinning.

"No—I mean, yes. I'm waiting for someone."

"And the reservation is under . . . ?" The waitress is suspicious, or worse, perhaps she recognizes Finn.

"Kresky," he says, already tingling as he returns to all clear.

Word has spread through the Disney community by now. The waitress focuses intently on Finn. He wants her to recognize him, wants another minute or two at the table.

"Uh-huh." She sounds dubious.

He lowers his voice. "I need a blank piece of paper, small, and a pencil with a decent lead. I'll be out of here in less than a minute. Please . . ."

She looks right through him; he imagines her mind whirling as she considers her options.

"It's not for me. It's for him. He left me something."

"And you are . . . ?"

Finn's hand is palm down on the table. He drops his eyes there emphatically, trying to encourage her to follow his gaze. Deliberately, he moves his arm through the wood of the table.

Her eyes are wide as she gasps, "It's true, then."

"Yes," Finn says.

"Oh my gosh!"

Finn has encountered this response so often that he has become immune to it. It's nothing but a parlor trick, but it wins him allies and warns his adversaries, and thus serves its purpose.

"Paper. Pencil. One minute," he says.

"Which one are you?"

"I'm Finn."

She's impressed. "No way! The leader?"

"I get that a lot, but I'm not really sure we have a leader."

"And modest to boot!"

Finn has met with this response too: regardless of age, people he meets in his DHI form want to strike up a conversation and be his best friend. It's embarrassing for both parties, seeing as they've only just met. He won't be rude and shoo her away, so he purses his lips, nods, and waits, hoping she'll come back to earth.

"Cool. I'm on it!" she says.

He would ask her not to tell anyone, but that never works. People like to be viewed as special, and they take every opportunity to single themselves out from others. Some resort to shoplifting; some get 4.0 GPAs. Waitresses run back to the kitchen and tell everyone they've just met a Kingdom Keeper.

A pair of chefs in white aprons and tunics appears at the maître d's check-in table shortly thereafter. They pretend to be inspecting the reservation list, but Finn knows otherwise.

The waitress returns with a pad of paper and five pencils. This is another thing Finn has learned. People who want to help consider quantity a show of respect. He smiles wryly.

"Thank you."

"Hey, it's an honor."

Finn wants her to leave him alone; he doesn't want her to see what he's about to do, doesn't want to draw any more attention for fear the Overtakers might hear about his visit to the restaurant, putting an innocent bystander like this waitress in danger.

There is a clock running in Finn's head. There's plenty of time to make it back to the Plaza, he calculates, but he and Wayne were spotted in here by Security—and maybe by Overtakers too. What's to stop that from happening again?

Maybeck's arrival from downstairs sets off alarms. Maybeck draws attention wherever he goes; he's one of those guys people like to notice, one of those guys who makes sure people like what they see.

Finn's mental clock ticks ominously.

* * *

"Why wouldn't have the Imagineers—or the Cryptos, whoever—have collected evidence right away?" Willa asks.

She and Philby are approaching the bent Mickey statue in Toontown.

"Maybe they did," Philby says, his eyes narrowed. "Or maybe they tried to."

"Then why not tell us?"

"How do you react if you're about to do something and somebody tells you they've already done it? You do a half-baked job, is what you do. Joe's a smart guy. He tells us what he thinks we need to know and skips the rest."

"That's kind of weird, all things considered."

"He's a grown-up."

"Point taken." Willa gives a short bark of laughter. "And we're Peter Pan, I suppose."

"In his eyes? Yeah, probably. Kids forever. Same old, same old."

"I get so sick of that," Willa says.

Philby says, "Do you feel them out there? I mean, we know they're here, right? And vice versa. They didn't just show up in Toontown by coincidence."

"I don't appreciate your trying to scare me, Dell. I was the one with a knife at my throat, remember? Why couldn't someone else have taken on this assignment?"

"I'm not trying to scare you. And yes, I'm well aware this is not a casual stroll in Disneyland."

"Don't patronize me. It's not your style."

"Of course it is. It's exactly my style."

They reach the fountain and walk away from it at a measured pace, side by side, eyes on the ground. Fifteen feet away from the statue, Philby changes the pattern to the one he uses when he mows the lawn at home: big sweeps out and back. They cover the area between the fountain and the stretch of territory where the OTs stood during their showdown. It feels futile: Toontown has been swept, hosed down, and inspected along with every inch of the rest of Disneyland. Then—

"Got something," Willa says. They kneel, and Willa traces her finger in the air above a black S-shaped mark on the pale walkway.

"Yeah? So?" Philby says.

Willa points a foot or two ahead, indicating another, similar line.

Philby inches closer, squints. "I'm feeling dense. I don't get it."

"Who stood here?" Willa asks. She looks up, trying to catch anyone looking. Philby has infected her with fear. Only a few yards from where they now stand, she nearly lost her life. She wants to run—*now!*

"The OTs," he says. "Not Wayne. Not us."

"Correct. And who, if anyone, was barefoot?"

"Tia Dalma!"

"Correct."

"You think—"

"I *know* that Tia Dalma's feet looked dirty. Time practically stopped when I was standing there. Now I'm thinking it wasn't dirt, because the regular cleaning would have removed any mere dirt she left behind."

Philby traces the pattern and sniffs his finger. "Nothing."

"They'll get it off eventually. But not with water."

"Because it's oil," Philby says. "I see what you're saying."

"Took you long enough."

"Easy, prom queen."

"Hah. You wish."

"No, actually, I don't. I like you just the way you are."

"You pick the strangest times to say the things I always wish you'd say."

"I'm not good at this, am I?"

"You're good at everything. Don't kid yourself."

"Oil."

"More like tar, given how black it is and how it won't clean up. I remember when they tarred our school roof," Willa smiles, eyes crinkling. "Some kids got up there and dumped some of the roofing tar down onto the playground. There's still a stain." She pauses. "It's too *empty* here. I don't like it. We need to hurry it up." The surrounding attractions, gloomy and lifeless, seem to glower.

"Tar . . ." Philby taps a finger against his lower lip, staring into space. "So you think—what? She was on a roof?"

"Could be. Think about L.A. The La Brea Tar Pits, Philby."

"The grave of saber-toothed cats and—"

"Full of black tar."

"We need a sample," he says.

"It won't return with us."

"Good point."

The structures around them groan and creak. A breeze whistles through. Willa's skin turns to gooseflesh; she crosses her arms self-protectively.

"The Cryptos will have to collect it," she says.

"What's wrong?" he asks. "You're nervous. You're never nervous."

348

"A good man died here, Dell, you know? I . . . things were a little scary for me as well. Not my favorite place to be."

"Did I mention I can be insensitive?" Philby reaches out and takes her hand. "You're safe. I'll keep you safe."

She bites back a quivering smile. Her eyes sting. She nods—the best she can manage without coming unglued.

40

"THIS IS DEFINITELY messed up," Maybeck says. "Where are they?"

He and Finn have been scouting the Plaza from a bench. It's now several minutes past the scheduled rendezvous time, but no one has arrived.

"It'll be fine. Study it again. You're going to need to draw that once we've returned. It won't come with me."

Maybeck regards Finn's drawings, a sketch and a rubbing of the freshly carved marks on the table in Club 33. "Yeah, yeah. I can make a copy of this."

"It has to be perfect."

"Finn, I mean . . . come on."

"Yeah, I know. You're God's gift."

"True story."

"There!" Craning his neck, Finn points to Amanda and Charlene, arriving from the far side of the castle. The girls are out of breath; obviously, they're not all clear.

"What's wrong?" Maybeck asks.

"Nothing," Charlene says.

"We thought we were late, is all," Amanda adds.

"We were early—" Maybeck says.

"And we're still here," Finn says, completing Maybeck's thought.

"Philby and Willa? Are they in trouble?" Amanda hasn't taken her eyes off Finn; Maybeck can't stop looking at Charlene.

Finn shrugs. "Every ten minutes. That's what he said."

"Yeah, but if Philby never gets here," Maybeck says, "the clock never starts."

"Toontown," Charlene says, reminding everyone with only that one word of Philby's destination, the events of the recent past, and the threat that part of the park represents to the Keepers.

"So, no Storey Ming?" Finn asks.

"The ride's closed," Amanda says.

"We had to do a hologram thing to convince a Cast Member we were for real. Word was, the whole area stank of burning wires. Some kind of short, maybe. So we slipped through a wall, if you know what I mean, and—"

"It really did stink," Amanda says, interrupting. "We searched behind the final scene as you said we should. If Storey was there, she was hiding from us. And then we saw the burn on the scenery. A big black smudge, like a mark made by a laser—"

"More like by a blowtorch," Charlene says, cutting her off. "There was this panel that was scorched. Fried. But just in one spot."

"You think they got Storey?" Maybeck asks.

Finn is about to speak when his entire body starts tingling. He glances at his watch. It's exactly ten minutes past the rendezvous time.

* * *

Finn wakes up in his bed at the Studios and sits bolt upright. No matter how many times he crosses over, the return always freaks him out.

"Quick!" It's Philby, standing by Finn's bed. Finn jumps about a foot off the mattress.

"Tell me I didn't scare you," Philby says, sounding disappointed.

"What? You scared the—"

"*Shhh!*" Maybeck silences them both from the doorway.

"Get the door!" Willa says, instructing Finn, the last one through.

The theater they're in was once used for movie premieres. The Keepers clump together in the aisle, about halfway down.

"The Cryptos know we've returned," Philby says. "The server will show it. Sorry for leaving before you guys, but we had to get back fast."

"Because?" Finn says.

"Tar, or oil, on Tia Dalma's feet," Willa says. "She left tracks."

"We can't possibly know that," Finn says.

"There's a high probability, okay?" Philby says. "Who else has been barefoot in Toontown, other than us? And we didn't have beach tar on our feet." He explains that he and Willa wanted to take a sample, but like Finn's sketch, it wouldn't have returned with his DHI.

"So, the question is," Willa says, "do we tell the Cryptos or not? Philby and I didn't want to make a decision without you guys."

"Why wouldn't we tell them?" Jess asks.

The Keepers turn toward her, sighing almost in unison. The naïveté of the question is refreshing.

Finn answers gently. "Sometimes the Imagineers go in a different direction than we would."

Jess nods, still confused.

"How would we get down to Anaheim?" Maybeck asks. "That's what you're saying, right? That we do it ourselves?"

"Absolutely," Philby says, speaking for himself and

Willa. "Unless we could get someone to do it for us."

"Like Storey," Amanda says.

"Or that girl Brooke," Finn suggests. Heads turn toward him. "She helped me. It's a good possibility."

"I like her," says Willa, who stood guard with Brooke in the Court of Angels.

"I have her phone number," Philby says. "We texted."

Willa frowns; her face bunches.

"Regardless, we'll still need lab work to know what we've got," Philby continues. "The advantage of telling the Cryptos is that they could handle that for us."

"Could you do it?" Willa asks Philby.

"If I had access to a lab."

"Listen!" Charlene silences them all. "If it's tar, if it's Tia Dalma, then it's either the beach, the La Brea Tar Pits, or an oil rig."

"She was living on the beach on Castaway Cay," Willa says.

"If she was at the Tar Pits, that can't be good news. What's she doing?" Maybeck asks. "Raising a dire wolf from the dead?"

"Wait!" Jess leafs through her diary to the last page, her most recent drawing, and points to an object they'd tentatively identified as a grasshopper head. "It's not a grasshopper! It's one of those things on an oil well."

"The horse head," Philby says. "It's the business end of the beam in an oil rig. You had the right body part, but the wrong kind of animal."

"Wayne," Finn mumbles.

"Oh, Finn," Amanda says, throwing her arm around his shoulders. But Finn ducks away from her offer of comfort, squinting tightly into the distance. "Wayne said . . . he said, 'They must be stopped. Do not for a minute assume that earthquake in Mexico was a fluke. Be on guard to prevent it from happening again.'"

Silence shrouds the group. Maybeck looks at Finn as if he's worried Finn might be losing his mind. Jess studies her sketch. Like Maybeck, Amanda is worried about Finn. Philby and Willa look at each other; a special energy seems to cross the space between them.

Willa says, "Oil well. Earthquakes."

Philby says, "Fracking. 'Induced hydraulic fracturing.' September 2013. This small Ohio town."

"Youngstown," Willa says. "They had a hundred earthquakes, in a town where there'd never been one before."

To the others, it's as if they're speaking their own language. It's hard to piece together what they mean, the way they're finishing each other's sentences. They continue prattling on about other fracking incidents in Texas and elsewhere. Before anyone can interrupt, Philby turns to the other Keepers and says, "The earthquake in Mexico was no accident."

"They're planning another one here," Willa says.

Finn fights for breath. "Wayne warned me."

* * *

Philby being Philby, he's figured out the bus routes to get him and Willa from Burbank to Pepperdine University in Malibu. It's more difficult sneaking out of the Studios than traveling over the mountains and through Los Angeles to reach the school.

Philby and Willa stow away in the back of a small white panel van that makes routine courier runs between Walt Disney Pictures and the Disney-ABC television high-rise a few miles away. Getting in unseen is far easier than half the things the Keepers had to do on the Disney *Dream*; it's all a matter of timing. Maybeck distracts the driver, and Philby and Willa climb into the back as the van is backing up to leave.

On one of the many city buses they have to ride, they make eyes and play face games with a small boy in a stroller. Willa clutches Philby's upper arm and squeezes every time the boy smiles or coos. It's the first quiet time they've had since coming out west. For both, it passes much too quickly.

Entering the university campus, with its green lawns, red roofs, and white buildings overlooking the Pacific Ocean, briefly lessens their sense of purpose. Only miles from the Hollywood Hills, this paradise disguised as a university is so surreally beautiful, it seems out of place.

Philby has never met Brooke in person though Willa has described her as tall, thin, and pretty. Willa tells him this in the way girls talk about one another, as if these qualities are defects of some kind. Brooke greets them brightly and passes Philby the sample of oil from Toontown; she also has stained chips of the concrete pavement where they found the oil.

"That took a little doing," she says, grinning.

"I'll bet," Philby says, impressed. Beside him, Willa groans.

"There's a chemistry lab open in ten minutes," Brooke says, checking her Mickey Mouse watch.

Philby and Willa work in concert for the next ninety minutes. Brooke has lab experience as well; she sets up ahead of them, and cleans up after. Soon they have a wealth of data, but no way of knowing what it all means. Brooke summons a senior, Austin, who's been trying to get on her good side. He helps them feed the data into three different systems and hits Print.

"Bitumen deposits," Austin says. "Tar. I've compared the pure sample with the one containing the concrete, and discarded the inorganics we typically find there. Tar is basically oil degraded by bacteria, okay? So there are two things of importance to you in this sample: First, there's identifiable bacteria here, which is a real find. If you follow the Web sites, the only place it's been discovered recently was the excavation for the Black Gold Golf Club in Yorba Linda. Second, the contaminants mixed in with the bitumen include water, clay, and lauryl sulfate, a chemical used in—"

"Injection wells," Philby says.

Austin smirks, confirming what Philby has said. "The bitumens are hard to extract because of their viscosity. It's like heavy sludge. Lauryl sulfate thins the tar and allows high-pressure injection wells to pump it to the surface."

"So if you were guessing where this sample was from," Willa says, "would this golf course be at the top of your list?"

"Carbon Canyon, Chino Hills, Rowland Heights, Yorba Linda. Not the club itself. I don't know if there're any wells there."

"This may sound stupid," Philby says. That's a word he rarely utters, and in a tone he rarely uses. "But are there any fault lines that run between that area and Anaheim?"

"Are you kidding?" Austin says. "Definitely. Anaheim's located between two major fault lines." He pulls up a geological survey map on his computer screen and points out areas as he talks. "The Newport-Inglewood and the Whittier-Elsinore fault zones—the Whittier-Elsinore is located just northeast of Anaheim."

"You all right?" Brooke asks Willa, who has gone pale.

"What'd I say?" Austin asks. "What's going on?"

Philby looks like he's been frozen in place. Finally, his gaze shifts until he's staring straight at Brooke.

"No," Brooke says. Her eyes water, and she fights against crying by blinking rapidly.

"What?" Austin says. "Is anyone going to tell me what's going on?"

"You wouldn't believe us if we did," Philby says. He grabs his phone and texts Finn the news.

"We have no proof," Willa says. "We need proof."

"Do either of you have a car?" Philby asks.

"My roommate does," Brooke says.

"I'm driving," says Austin, intrigued.

* * *

Finn is no stranger to the power of playing for sympathy. He's used the technique effectively on his mother for years (his father is far less susceptible), and he's become not just capable, but competent, even skillful.

Now Finn dishes it out to Joe without having to play-act the grief he's experiencing over Wayne's death. Even talking about the event tightens his throat and fills his eyes with tears. He says he wants to "begin the process of closure," though he has no intention of facing that demon for some time to come.

As usual, Finn's instincts differ from Philby's. Finn works off intuition, while Philby maintains a procedural, forensic approach. From the moment Philby raised the idea of oil-tainted footprints, Finn's mind imagined the oil's origin being within Disneyland. The most obvious source of grease and oil is park maintenance; lubricants of various kinds keep the rides working. While hanging off the back of the train with Willa, Finn smelled lubricant and oil too, so another possibility is wherever park staff work on the trains and carriages.

With Philby off playing chemistry professor, Finn's impatience for answers about Wayne's death propels him to manipulate Joe into offering him permission to travel to Disneyland. Several times a day, Imagineers head to and from the park.

Finn asks to bum a ride, visit Toontown, and pay his respects. He promises to be punctual and meet up with whoever's driving at the specified time. Joe is openly skeptical.

Finn says, "I don't mean to be rude, but I'm going to do this with or without your help. I'd rather not break the rules if I don't have to."

This softens Joe, who nods and says, "Don't make a habit of it."

An hour later, Finn is on the freeway. Two hours later, the van parks backstage.

He's in.

* * *

True to his word, Austin's behind the wheel, driving Philby, Willa, and Brooke around north of Anaheim, looking for oil rigs.

"Nothing," Philby says after thirty minutes.

Brooke, riding shotgun, has been running searches on her smartphone since they left Pepperdine, muttering in disgust at the lack of available information. They're passing through a small hillside town called Sleepy Hollow when she lets out a squeal.

"Four miles directly east is an entire oil *field*! The fastest way there is to hang a U-turn!"

Austin swings the car around in the parking lot of Canyon Market, which advertises liquor, beer, and free deliveries. In the backseat, Willa wedges her hands nervously between her knees.

"What's wrong?" Philby asks. "You look like you're about to implode."

"Sleepy Hollow," she says softly, embarrassed. "Don't make me talk about this."

"About what?"

"What I'm talking about, Dell!"

"The teepees," he says.

"The teepees," she agrees.

"The Headless Horseman."

"If you'd been there, you wouldn't be grinning like that. Sleepy Hollow is where he comes from . . . I'm sorry. I know it's stupid."

"Not even close," Philby says, and then raises his voice. "Brooke, Austin, keep an eye out for anything unusual."

Brooke looks at the backseat. "Meaning?"

"Out of the ordinary."

"Overtakers?"

"Say, what?" Austin says. "What's that about an overeater?"

"Over*takers*," Brooke says.

But Philby signals her not to go there, worried Austin will think they're raving maniacs if they attempt to describe how they have reached this particular moment in time. Brooke doesn't know the half of it, and at this point, she already knows more than only the Imagineers, the Cryptos, and the Kingdom Keepers themselves.

"Think outlaw," she says to Austin, obeying Philby's wishes. "You know, like thieves. Highwaymen."

"In Southern California in broad daylight." Austin cannot contain his skepticism.

"I'm just saying."

"But what are you saying? That bandits are going to carjack us? This is a country club 'hood, like a hangout for old hippies."

"Just keep an eye out," Brooke says.

"Fine; I'll keep my six-gun handy, pardner."

"Wish I had one," Willa mutters, her hands still pinched between her knees, her body folded in on itself.

Philby presses his face to the window; Brooke cranes

forward to search the landscape. A shadow flitters across the grassland, and Philby twists to look up at the sky. He sees a jet on approach to landing—and catches the darting black triangle of a bird's wing.

"Nothing but a bunch of crows," Brooke says.

"Define 'bunch,'" Philby says, pressing his face against the glass as he tries to see upward. It's useless. Only pure blue California sky interrupted by a few soft cumulus clouds looks back at him.

"Yeah," Austin says. "I see 'em too."

"Eyes on the road!" Brooke says, bumping his shoulder with her hand.

"Shut up."

"How many?" Philby unbuckles, leans across Willa and, as she lowers the window, looks outside with her—to see a black bird dive-bombing. Philby can't get his head inside as fast as Willa; the bird's beak and talons scratch his forehead.

"Oh, Philby!" Willa exclaims. "You're bleeding!"

"Cripes," Brooke says, her face pressed to the windshield. "There are tons of them."

In fact, there are so many birds overhead, they block out the sun, making the car's interior dark.

"Those aren't crows," Philby says, mopping his forehead with his sleeve. "They're ravens."

"What's it matter what they are?" Austin asks.

"It matters," Brooke tells him. "Because Maleficent and the Evil Queen have pet ravens."

"Disney characters? Give me a break!" Austin says.

He might as well have signaled the birds. Within seconds, the unkindness of ravens envelops the car like a blanket dropped suddenly over the roof. Outside, it's a blur of feathers and beaks. Bird poop smears the windshield.

Willa is pressing the button to close her window—it will only ascend as fast as its electric motor allows. Before the window is all the way up, a head and beak stab through. Willa screams instinctively. Philby pulls her toward him, out of reach of the bug-eyed bird's menacing beak. He kicks with one foot at the bird while trying to reach the window control, but nothing happens.

"Ew!" Willa cries, stretching to reach for the window-control button while keeping her head in Philby's lap. She pushes the control up accidentally and the window squeezes the bird, forcing its black tongue from its beak. Willa quickly reverses the window, but the bird drops and falls to the highway, its neck broken. It is immediately replaced by a dozen more ravens, forcing their heads and beaks in and out of the closing window. As it shuts, the ravens begin to peck the glass. It sounds like machine gun fire.

Unable to see, Austin slams on the brakes. The kids lurch against their seatbelts and rebound off the seats. The drumming attack on every surface is deafening. Covering their ears, the kids shout at one another simultaneously so that no one can understand anything. It's chaos. Austin engages the windshield wipers and fires the wiper washer jets, diluting the mess on the windshield and startling the ravens.

Yet still the thunder grows. It sounds as though several tons of gravel are being dumped on the car. Willa resorts to singing a single note, trying to overcome the sound with her own. Austin leans on the horn, futilely trying to scare off the ravens.

Philby slips out of his shoulder belt and cranes forward between the front bucket seats, pointing off-road. "Bushes!"

Austin drops the car into low gear, bouncing off the asphalt, across the hardpack, and into a stand of tall bushes.

The screeching of branches against the sides of the car is nearly indistinguishable from the noise of the attacking ravens.

Finally, the car comes to a stop. Then it's just the deep cawing of birds, held at bay by the bushes that surround the vehicle. The abnormal dark returns as hundreds of ravens swirl overhead and cluster nearby.

But the kids can hear again. Austin curses. Brooke whispers to him, "I'm sorry I got you into this."

"What exactly are we into?" he says to her privately. "Look, I admit it, I wanted to impress you. I like you, Brooke. But who are these two? *What* are they?"

Outside, the birds fight desperately to reach the car. Their black feathers become streaked with red blood as they flap and claw through the thorny shrubs.

"They're not going to give up!" Brooke says. One poor bird strikes her window, leaving behind a red smear as it sinks out of sight.

"They're enchanted, under a spell," Philby says. "They're not going to quit."

"Okay! Time out!" says Austin. "*Now* I need an explanation."

"Later," Brooke says.

"Never," says Philby. "If we get out of this, you'll just have to forget it happened."

"As if! Is this like reality TV or something?"

The dark inside the car, the relentless efforts of the birds, and the terrible self-inflicted wounds they're incurring combine to break Willa. She covers her eyes and screams, "Stop it! Stop it!"

Philby shakes her, but it's no use. The windows are disgusting—a true horror show.

"I smell smoke!" Austin shouts.

The interior of the car falls silent. Willa drops her hands from her face; all the kids sniff at once.

"You're right," Brooke says. "Is the car—"

"It's wood smoke," Philby says. "Not oil."

"Not for long," Austin says. "And, oh, by the way, somebody owes me *an explanation!*" He looks intensely at Brooke, who purses her lips and squints uncomfortably.

"The catalytic converter," Professor Philby says. "There's your explanation!"

The fire rises from beneath the car, ignited by underbrush coming into contact with the extreme heat of the vehicle's emission control device. Austin is quick to back up and drive; as he does, they see that the tall bushes are black from the hundreds of ravens impaled on their thorns. The fire rises, feathers lifting with the smoke. Brooke turns away, averting her eyes as the conflagration consumes all but a handful of the birds.

Austin silently navigates the car back to the road as Philby watches coils of gray-black smoke billow from the pyre. Out of that smoke flies a single raven with a five-foot wingspan. It circles once, dives for the moving car, and comes within a few feet of Philby's window before rising again. Then it flies off to the southwest—the direction of Disneyland.

All but Austin watch it go.

"That's hers," Philby says.

Neither Willa nor Brooke has to ask who he means.

* * *

The steel structure housing Disneyland's trains looks as if it covers several acres. Inside, six rows of train cars and locomotives span its width, some polished and perfect, others disassembled for maintenance. It's longer than a football field, with a gray-painted floor as clean as a freshly scrubbed hallway. Lit by both electricity and skylights, the polished paint sparkles, the glass glimmers.

One of the Cast Members recognizes Finn, and fawns over him in that odd way all the Keepers have had to get used to. The guy introduces himself as Craig. He couldn't be nicer, telling Finn how his kids had been dying for the DHIs to finally arrive in Disneyland; they were part of the lottery offered to win the first DHI guiding experience when the system was still in beta. When the moment is right, Finn asks if he might have a look around. Craig is delighted.

Throughout the early going, Finn's looking for grease or oil. He's disappointed by the cleanliness of the place. Even the disassembled train cars look like museum pieces on display.

"Is there a place you grease them?" he asks Craig.

"Are you looking for something in particular?"

"Oil. Grease. Somewhere I might get my shoes dirty."

"The greasiest old girl here is Lilly," Craig says, and leads Finn to the back of the warehouse, where the multiple maintenance tracks merge into a single line heading out into the park. It's slightly darker here, and the famous open-sided passenger cars are densely crowded together, with barely enough room to walk between the lines. The only way to access the cars in the middle of the array is to climb up and down, passing through the cars in the outer rows. Finn and Craig have gone through several cars before Craig's phone acts like an intercom, summoning him to a meeting.

"Look, this'll only take a few minutes," he says apologetically. "Have a look around. Lilly Belle's at the back of the line, one track over."

"So not this track, the next?"

"Correct. We've rebuilt her, but she's been known to cry a little."

Finn looks at the man curiously.

"Her wheel journals."

Finn nods as if he understands.

Craig pats him on his back. He's surprised. "So . . . at the moment you're not . . . ?"

"No," Finn answers. "This is the real me."

"Pleasure."

"Same."

Craig climbs back down out of the car and is gone. Finn exits in the opposite direction, then grabs a rail to pull himself up and through the next passenger car. On the other side, he immediately spots Lilly Belle.

Unlike the open-sided passenger cars, Lilly Belle has the walls and windows of a real caboose. She has been impeccably restored, every detail spit-polished. Her tongue-in-groove paneling is painted a shiny burgundy with cherry trim and glossy black ironwork. Carved gold lettering proclaiming DISNEYLAND RAILROAD arcs across her side above the windows. She looks like a car from the Hogwarts Express.

Finn approaches cautiously. He sees no puddle of oil, no slick of grease. That alone should be enough to dissuade him from entering, but he's drawn to climb Lilly Belle's steps and face the impressive cherrywood door, which opens to reveal a miniature Victorian parlor with chairs and a couch all covered in red velvet and facing in toward the center. The drapes are pulled, dulling the luster of the interior's surfaces. Finn makes out an inlaid walnut Queen Anne end table sitting near him, below one of six large windows that run the length of the car on either side. The red carpet matches the furniture, with twisting gold ivy and heraldic crests woven into its design. Even in the gloom, Finn can see that the space is truly befitting of royalty.

"Well, well," a voice cackles from the dusk.

Finn jumps at the sound. Sitting on a settee at the far end of the car opposite him, unmoving, is Cruella de Vil. Her white fur coat, black dress, and black-and-white hair stand out in sharp contrast to the overwhelming red of the car's decor.

"Nice to see I've still got it," she chortles. "You hang around with these others for too long and you get discouraged." She bats her eyes, their lashes as long as the bristles on a barbecue brush, and waves her turquoise cigarette holder in Finn's direction. The pink cigarette is unlit, Finn notices; otherwise, he would have smelled the smoke.

Finn can't catch his breath. There was a time when he could somehow even push his mortal self briefly to all clear—a feat he has never understood—but he's out of practice.

"I think you should leave," Cruella says, "before something bad happens."

Finn spots a small stack of used paper plates and plastic sporks beneath her chair. She didn't just get here, that's for sure. The closed drapes make sense now, as does the car's musty smell.

"Why can't you children just play in the backyard or something?" Cruella moans. "You're such a bother."

As adrenaline floods his bloodstream, like jolts of electricity pulsing through him, Finn sees red—red that has nothing to do with the car's color scheme. Without thinking, he steps forward and grabs a porcelain vase of fake flowers, intending to hurl it at her—only to find the vase glued to the end table. He staggers back. But it's only a momentary setback. Blinded by rage and his instinctual desire to bring this woman to justice for Wayne's death, Finn races the length of the car. Before Cruella has time to react, he has her by the throat. She retches, clawing at his face; Finn can feel the exceedingly long fingernails through her scarlet satin gloves.

But Finn extends his arms, locks his elbows, and leans back. His vision hazed by bloodlust, he doesn't pause to contemplate his actions for a second. He squeezes tighter, and tighter still.

"Kid!"

Finn spins his head back to see a paralyzed Craig at the far end of the car. In his moment of distraction, Cruella slaps Finn across the face with so much force, he hears his neck crack. He loses his grip, staggers, falls.

"Who the . . . What the . . . ?" Craig shouts.

Cruella steals out the car's rear door, with Finn following close behind.

* * *

"Are you kidding me? It's called Oil Field Road?" Austin says from behind the wheel. Their car looks as if it has been tarred and feathered by the devil himself. The wipers have carved twin apertures through the goo, affording the only clear line of sight the four kids have.

Austin turns onto a paved road bordered by expanses of cocoa powder–like dirt, dotted with oil rigs that look like giant primitive birds endlessly dunking in rhythm.

"Yeah, I know," says Brooke. "Lame. But at least we found some."

"Where to?" Austin asks. "Back to campus would be a good answer."

Philby rolls his window up and down repeatedly, trying to scrape it clean. Then, abandoning the effort, he simply leaves the window down in order to see. Willa matches him.

"We'll know it by sight," Philby says. "Start high and get an overview. We'll work our way down to the various wells."

"There're so many!" Brooke says.

"And we have no idea if these are the right ones," Willa adds.

"Soil composition tells us they're strong candidates," Philby says, reminding her.

"And those ravens trying to stop us," Willa says, nodding. "We can't forget those."

"I will *never* forget them," Brooke says. "I've read about what you guys do. I've heard the stories. But let me tell you something: Being *right there*, a part of it? It was terrifying."

"Well, *I* have not read or heard what you guys do," Austin says, "so what *do* you do?" He's trying to look brave for Brooke, but wins only an apologetic look from her.

"We . . . fix things," Willa says. "At least we try."

"Like oil wells?" Austin asks skeptically.

Willa glances toward Philby, silently seeking his approval for what she is about to say. "Listen, if we're right about the oil well, about Tia Dalma, then there's no telling what to expect here. You guys understand that, right?"

Brooke nods. Austin's head swings side to side.

"What Willa means," Philby says, "is that if things go like they did back there, you need to let her and me handle it. Okay, Austin?" Philby leans forward to make eye contact with Austin in the rearview mirror. "We've dealt with these . . . *things* . . . before, and they can be super-dangerous."

"I kind of think you're pranking me," Austin tells Brooke. "But that bird thing—I mean, *how did you do that?* That was awesome!"

"If either of you got hurt, it would be bad for you, for us, for Disney," Willa says. "Okay?"

"Got it," Brooke says. When Austin fails to agree, she pokes him in the leg.

"So Disney's behind this? Like special effects or something?"

"You've got to promise," Philby says.

Austin's silence produces an awkward moment. He steers the car up a hill through two hairpin turns and arrives at a large sandlot with a couple of shuttered trailers.

"You're pranking me! A fraternity hazing? Is this because I wouldn't pledge?"

"No cars. There's no one here." Philby pops open the door and climbs out. He walks the perimeter of the lot, joined first by Willa, then Brooke and Austin.

"Amazing," Brooke says. She directs this to Austin, disappointment coloring her words.

There must be seventy or more oil rigs, all pumping. Narrow paved service roads twist around the contours of the hills, but mostly the fifteen acres they're looking at is sand and scrub vegetation—dwarf trees and chest-high shrubs.

"There!" Philby says, pointing to some equipment a little way below them on the hillside. "That's the one we want. Those extra machines could be for injection."

"There's a pickup truck," Willa says.

"Yeah. Stay low."

They all scramble down the rocky slope to the next level area of sand and dirt, hunching over and staying in the scrub, using it as cover. The footing is inconsistent and the going tricky. Philby motions for Brooke and Austin to stay put. He and Willa move forward, closer to the machinery.

"Too many of us," Philby whispers. "We don't need a parade."

"They're helping. Be nice," Willa replies.

They continue another twenty yards. Philby glances back to make sure Austin has not followed. "Wait," he says, stopping Willa in her tracks. Brooke is crouching where they left her. Austin is not.

Willa tugs on Philby's sleeve and points out a lumberjack of a man, previously hidden by an open panel on the side of the equipment. He's well over six feet tall, broad shouldered, with a full red beard. He taps one of the dials and makes notes on a clipboard.

Philby scans the scrub for signs of Austin and finds him squatting on the opposite side of the lot, straining to reach into one of the mountain mahogany bushes.

"Idiot," Philby hisses.

Willa spots Austin. "He's okay."

"No, he's not!" Philby's anger gets the better of him, and he raises his voice.

The worker leans back, swinging the open panel out of his way. He moves stiffly, as if in pain, his head and neck swiveling mechanically atop his massive shoulders. He peers through squinted eyes directly at Willa and Philby, who remain stone still. The worker looks at them—through them—without any indication of seeing them.

The sound of breaking twigs turns the man's attention in the direction of Austin, who has leaned so far forward, he's fallen into the bush.

"Help—you?" the worker calls.

Austin's mistake is that he runs. Or tries to. He struggles free of the bush that claims him, calling out, "Brooke! Hit it!"

"Hey!" the worker hollers, moving toward Austin. The boy scrambles up the short hill to the parking lot above with Brooke following, drawing the worker in their direction. "You!" the man shouts.

Willa looks back at Philby—but he's gone. Searching with her eyes, she finally catches sight of him behind the open panel, studying the dials. The worker spins around and sees Philby as well.

"Don't—touch—that." The man needs only three strides to reach Philby and take him by the arm. "What's—going on—here?" His words are disjointed and robotic.

Willa is getting to her feet, but Philby's eyes tell her not to. She cowers lower in the brush.

"School!" Philby says. "A school project on the environment!"

The man loosens his grip, but does not let go.

"So . . . what's with the other . . . guy taking . . . off like that?"

"We don't exactly have permission to be here," Philby says. "But you're a big guy . . . with a strong grip."

"Sorry—'bout that." The man loosens his hold—then squeezes tighter. "What kind—of environmental—camp? Anti- . . . fracking?" He looks at the panel and back to Philby. "What are—you and your—friends up to?"

A car engine starts in the upper lot, briefly distracting the worker. Philby breaks free and takes off.

"Go!" he shouts.

He reaches Willa and tugs her along. They're running down the slope through cypress, coastal sage shrub, and scrub oak, the worker close behind.

"You—come—back . . ." The worker stumbles, falls. Then he's back on his feet as if catapulted up, flaming mad.

Brooke's friend's car appears to their right, motor racing. Philby spins out in front of the car as Austin brakes to a screeching stop. Willa's in. Philby's car door is still open as Austin guns it and speeds off.

"Fracking!" Philby hollers, too loudly for the car's interior. Only then does he realize he's sitting on Brooke's lap. Willa has the backseat all to herself.

"And there's this," Austin says, reaching into his pocket. "I found it in the bushes."

He pulls out a stumpy voodoo doll made of twigs and twine.

* * *

Finn pursues Cruella down the narrow aisles formed by the train tracks. She's headed for the back of the building a short distance away.

Finn is not guided by thought or planning, but something more primitive. He snatches a wrench from a portable workbench sitting near a partially disassembled train car, reduced—or is it elevated?—to the level of a caveman with his club. He's a faster runner than she. The distance between them closes quickly.

Cruella's fur coat sweeps behind her. She hasn't surrendered her cigarette holder, which she holds like a runner's baton. Reaching an exit door, she spins and shoots Finn a look that should stop him cold. Instead, it eggs him on. He wants her head on a stake.

Her coat is snagged in the closing door. Finn yanks the door open and swings his wrench, only to cleave air. Cruella has abandoned her coat, but is still wrapped in the ermine-trimmed mink stole she has been wearing underneath as she scurries on, trotting like a trained pony in her high heels. Layers of fur—so Cruella.

Finn is a matter of steps away when the dogs appear.

They come as a single wave out of the landscaping by the fence. They are not Dalmatians, but mutts and street dogs, savage and hungry, with wild eyes and dangling pink tongues. There must be two or three dozen, their wet noses aimed at Finn, their legs propelling them at ferocious speed. Finn is not going to outrun the dogs. They'll tear him limb from limb.

Finn's one chance is a passing golf cart. Its driver yanks the wheel away from the oncoming pack, away from Finn, who hurls the wrench at Cruella de Vil, several feet ahead. The heavy tool rotates end over end, like a prehistoric bone weapon hurled at a fleeing deer.

Finn has no time to see if the wrench connects as he dives, catching a metal rod that supports the golf cart's roof. He tightens his fingers around it, is lifted higher and slammed onto the rear-facing seat.

The cart driver regains control as the lead dog leaps and lands atop Finn. The driver slams on the brakes. Finn and the dog smash into the seat back, but Finn holds on while the dog cannot. As the cart bumps, the hound is sent flying out the open back of the cart, cutting the legs out from under the advancing pack. Dogs go down like bowling pins. The cart races off.

Finn looks to where he last saw Cruella. She couldn't possibly run fast enough to be out of sight, yet she's not visible. Only as he lowers his eyes does he see a mass of black-and-white fur and realize it's the Overtaker he was chasing, collapsed in a heap. The white ermine trim of the stole is stained red. The bloodstained wrench lies alongside.

What's black and white and red all over?

The cart turns sharply left, then right, as it follows the train tracks toward the park. Finn, sweating and out of breath, sits alone on the rear-facing seat, his hand held over his brow, his eyes searching.

There's nothing to see but a pack of crazed dogs scattering in all directions, the leader limping painfully and slowly toward where Cruella fell.

41

SATURDAY AFTERNOON IS a solemn occasion. The Keepers board a van to go to Wayne's memorial, dressed in the formal clothes they've pieced together from the studio's wardrobe department.

The van's driver is a Cast Member not known to them, a woman who looks to be nearing retirement. Philby asks her to turn up the radio; the kids huddle together toward the van's middle seat, and conference in whispers.

Philby goes first, describing the search for the oil rig, which ended with the discovery of a voodoo doll. To punctuate his point, he pulls the doll from his suit coat pocket; it's passed around, eliciting varying degrees of shivers from those holding it.

Finn follows with his discovery that Cruella de Vil is living or plotting inside the luxury of Lilly Belle, and his hurling the wrench at her. "I know this may sound stupid," he says, "but I didn't mean to hurt her. I mean, I did—I wanted to hurt her. But when it was over, I felt awful. Like two wrongs, you know? If they turn us into them, then who's won?"

Amanda reaches over the seat back and places her hand tenderly on Finn's shoulder. Maybeck gives an exaggeratedly heavy sigh and Charlene punches him in the shoulder.

"There's something else," Finn says, winning their undivided attention. "If she's living in Lilly Belle, where are the rest of them? The Evil Queen? Tia Dalma? Chernabog? We didn't think about this: these OTs show up from Disney World and the cruise, but their characters are already here—all but Chernabog, and he's not easy to hide."

"Interesting," Philby says.

"It's a small park," Charlene says. "It's not like there are a million places to hide."

"Storey might be able to help us," says Maybeck—the guy who never wants help. "She found a place to stow away in the park. She must have tried others."

"We need to find her," Philby says. "She may know others things we don't."

"What about Wayne's warning about Mickey?" Jess asks Finn. "I know you're all desperate to track down the Overtakers, but honestly, from where I am—from where Amanda and I are—Wayne has always known what matters. The rest feels like a distraction."

The van's wheels whine on the freeway. The radio blares.

Finn looks at the others. "She's right."

"I don't want to sound cruel," Jess says, "but what if that's the point? The Overtakers know how we feel about Wayne, and from what you all say, there've been a couple times in the past when they could have killed him."

"He sacrificed himself," Finn says. "He let it happen."

"Okay. I'm sure that's right," Jess says. "But would he have wanted us to spend our time on revenge? A few minutes before, he was sharing secrets with you, Finn. Things he *needed* you to hear. But for the past couple days, you've been focused—"

"On your sketch," Maybeck says, cutting her off. "There was an oil rig in your sketch."

"There's Mickey Mouse, octopus tentacles, fire, a grass-hopper or something," she reminds him. "Wayne's message to Finn was about the original sketch of Oswald."

"Of *Mickey*," Finn corrects her. "He said the OTs destroyed Mickey: 'A single sketch kept in a file in his office. Never far out of reach.' Whatever that means."

"But if they destroyed Mickey, wouldn't the magic be gone?" Willa says.

"Maybe it is," Charlene says. "Maybe Wayne and the Imagineers have kept things going by sheer will. But with the OTs reorganized and Chernabog rebooted, Wayne knew it wasn't enough. Look, he could have told us this years ago, right? So why now? Because time's running out, and he felt too old to get things done. He brought us in, coached us, spent time training us." It's the athlete in her speaking. "Now he's passed the baton. He sacrificed himself to save us—absolutely. But what if he also did that to push us?"

"Dang," Maybeck says. "I wish I could say that that sounds ridiculous."

"But it makes sense," says Willa.

"Times ten," says Philby.

"This sketch," says Jess. "Do you suppose it's still around?"

"That couldn't have been what the OTs stole from the Archives, could it?" Amanda asks.

"We've seen that stuff," Finn says. "There's nothing like that in there. They're looking for the sheet with the invisible ink. We don't know if they found it, if they even figured it out."

"We keep going around in circles," a frustrated Maybeck says. "It's driving me nuts."

"Jess is right," Finn declares. "Going after the OTs makes no sense. Stopping them is way more important."

"But they're the same thing," Maybeck says. He sounds increasingly agitated. "If we go after them, we stop them."

"I think what Jess and Finn are saying," says Charlene, "is

that there's something bigger going on. It's like in cheerleading." Maybeck stifles a groan. "There's your individual routine, but there's also the team's routine. Wayne talking to Finn was about the team routine. Not our team, the Overtakers'. He decided we were ready to coach ourselves."

Willa says, "If that's a metaphor, I don't think it works. What exactly is our team routine?"

"Something bigger," Finn says. "Charlie's saying we've got to see the bigger picture. We're chasing oily footprints instead of trying to figure out what Wayne was saying about Mickey."

"But those footprints led us to this," Philby says, holding up the voodoo doll again. "And you found Cruella. It's not like we're wasting our time."

"It starts and ends in lightning," Jess says, recalling the revelation that came to her in the Indiana Jones attraction. "There's lightning in my sketch. And fire."

"We have to follow the leads we're given," Philby says. "To defeat an enemy, you have to establish his vulnerabilities. All we're doing is pursuing leads. We have to do that!"

"But following the footprints," Charlene says, "is following leads given to us by the Overtakers. Whose leads do we trust, theirs or Wayne's?"

The van slows. The Cast Member turns the radio down. Ahead, the Keepers glimpse the mortuary, a stucco building called Sunny Skies, which looks like a country club. There are cars everywhere, and dozens of people streaming inside.

A woman wearing a spectacularly colorful dress and a big red flower over her ear greets guests at the door.

"Look!" says Charlene. "It's Wanda."

* * *

As Finn approaches Wanda in the long line of arriving guests paying their last respects, a lump closes off his throat and his eyes brim with tears. As they hug there's an energy that passes between them. Wanda pours out stuff about how much Finn meant to her dad, how grateful she is that Finn came into his life even if late in his years. She talks about Finn being the "son Dad never had," which makes Finn feel guilty for causing a man's daughter to feel this way. He cries all the harder, thanks her, pulls away and moves on, comforted by Amanda and Jess.

"Can you wait a moment please?" Wanda asks Charlene once everyone is done with their condolences.

Charlene steps to one side.

Fifteen minutes later, with the last of the guests inside, Wanda pulls Charlene deeper into the building and corners her.

"I need to ask you to do something for me." Wanda's eyes mist over. She takes Charlene's hand and presses something into it. "My dad's watch. He wanted Finn to have it. Made me promise to give it to him. But honestly, Finn is just so much like my dad that when I . . . you know, just now . . . I couldn't bring myself to do it. I knew I would just fall apart. You know? Keep it. Give it to Finn for my dad. He wanted me to tell Finn 'It's all about time.' He made me promise I'd say it just like that."

Charlene nearly interrupts to tell her that Wayne *already* passed along that same message to Finn when they met in Club 33, but the timing, the mood are all wrong. She keeps it to herself. Instead, she nods a little too fast, overcome by emotion herself. "No problem," Charlene says.

Wanda thanks her profusely. They hug. Charlene is still overcome when she sits down at the end of a row next to Maybeck. She looks down the row at Finn. He catches her staring at him and she waves. This is no time to bother him; she wouldn't be able to get a word out without bawling. Besides, it wouldn't be fair to Finn.

He's listed in the program as one of the speakers.

* * *

"I didn't know I was going to be up here," Finn says from behind the lectern. He and Wanda exchange a look. "Wayne was always full of surprises and I guess his daughter is carrying on the tradition."

Those gathered chuckle. Finn is facing a sea of smiles, which makes him feel much more comfortable.

"Wayne was actually my boss. He hired me to model for Disney. I met a group of kids because of that and they've become my best friends on earth. The best friends, ever. Like any friends, you go through a lot of challenges, and we've had our share, for sure." The Keepers grin up at him. Amanda and Willa are weeping openly.

"It's too late now to thank him, but I think when you give someone else a friend, you give the most awesome gift ever. He gave me *six* friends. So I guess that makes it exponential or something. Philby's the math guy."

More laughter from the crowd.

"I have wonderful parents and grandparents, so I don't know where exactly a guy like Wayne fits in, but he was sort of all of those and more, and all at once. I guess what I'm saying is he taught me a lot of things. And I don't mean facts. Not like that. Not like school stuff. He taught me that fear makes us"—Finn addresses the Keepers now, who are all nodding at everything he says—"imperfect and vulnerable." When Finn feels he's about to lose it, he looks away from his friends' eyes.

379

"Wayne taught me there's real magic in the world and to trust that. To believe it. To live it. Easier said than done."

Again the crowd chuckles, but Finn didn't mean his remark as funny and the reaction takes him aback.

"Wayne taught me that leadership is about what you do, not what you say. That sometimes you feel super alone when you're doing the right thing and that's what makes it so hard. But you do it anyway.

"He lived all those things. That's the thing about him, what made him so different. He always kept his cool, always knew exactly the right thing to say. He knew stuff no one else will ever figure out or understand. Not ever. Particle physics. Stuff that only people like Einstein understood."

Finn feels frustrated as he's getting *Isn't he cute!* looks from most of the adults—all but Joe, Brad, other Cryptos, and Imagineers, all of whom are sitting together in one long row, all of whom seem to be hanging on Finn's every word, afraid he's going to spill state secrets.

"My guess is, there will be books written about Wayne and everything he's done. Someday there will be. Maybe movies. People will come to the Disney parks and see them in a whole new way. See them . . . for what they really are. Wayne was more than a dreamer. I know I could never have dreamed up everything he gave me and my friends, everything he gave the company—Disney, I mean—and the parks, and everything. There's only one Wayne Kresky." Finn feels tears running down his cheeks; he didn't know he was crying. "And I don't know about stuff like heaven and immortality. Maybe I'm too young; maybe I'm too naïve. But if real immortality—can you even say that? *real immortality?*—is about never dying because all the people around you, all the people who loved you, will never let you out of their hearts, and if they never let you out of their hearts then you're never gone in the first place, then Wayne's already immortal." Finn touches his chest and, to his surprise, the Keepers all stand and place their hands over their hearts as well. And then, almost incredibly, one by one, two by two, others in the crowd stand and do the same. Some are weeping; others, laughing. Some look up to the ceiling; some hang their heads.

An infant cries in the back of the room. It breaks whatever spell held the audience in thrall.

As Finn returns to his seat, Wanda stands and embraces him fiercely. There's a collective sigh, and then a teary-eyed Wanda faces the crowd and speaks. "Like Dad always said, I love this boy."

* * *

Finn is nearly mobbed after the service by well-wishers and people thanking him for his eulogy. Charlene has passed him Wayne's watch, but the gift feels wrong in a way he can't explain. More than one person tells him it was the best part of the service. He and the other Keepers keep close to Wanda and are with her when the main room finally empties out. Tea and cookies are being served down the hall, but no one's hungry.

Wanda praises Finn for being brave enough to share his emotions honestly. She thanks all the Keepers for making the end of her dad's life "mean something."

"It isn't over," Philby says. "Just like Finn said."

"I wanted to give this back to you," Finn says, proffering the watch.

Wanda instinctively yanks her hand away when she sees it, and the watch falls to the carpet.

Philby bends to scoop it up. "Huh!" he says. "Check this out. There's stuff on the back."

He shows it to Finn, and the others gather around.

"The drawings made with the invisible ink could easily have been these same images," Philby says. "Wayne's carving in Club 33 is like a piece of this stair thingy." Philby traces the lines engraved in the metal surface of the back of the watch with his fingernail. "It hasn't been cleaned in a long time."

"Dad hasn't worn that for as long as I can remember. It must be very old," says Wanda. Maybe a memory hits her, or maybe it's this day, but she suddenly looks as if she wants to speak, but can't. She reaches out for all of the Keepers, and they fall into a group hug that lasts through laughter and tears, but suffers from the gravity of the moment, the inescapable feeling of finality.

"He would have hated to miss this," Wanda says.

And led by Wayne's daughter, they all begin laughing, louder and more fully than any of them has laughed in days.

42

THE SECURITY PERSONNEL FINISH sweeping the room for listening devices and give the okay. Everyone around the table watches as Joe sees them out and locks the main door to the Disney Archives. Returning to sit at the head of the library table, he addresses the group, which includes the Keepers, the two Fairlies, Brad, and Becky Cline, who oversees the Archives. Becky holds a large box; a number of oversize portfolios sit beside her on the table.

Joe holds up an enlargement of the photo of Wayne's watch that Finn now wears. "We have stairs, an eyeball, and some kind of biblical-looking king. We know that when Wayne was given the watch, it didn't have this inscription on the back. He had it put there. He also wanted the watch passed to Finn. But there's more. Much more," Joe says. "Wayne mentioned the importance of time to Finn—"

"And *the* watch to Wanda," Charlene says interrupting.

"When he said that to me he held up his watch for me to see," Finn says. "This watch." Finn rattles it on his wrist.

"Yes." Joe doesn't take well to being interrupted. "There's the discovery of Tia Dalma's possible presence at an oil drilling site."

"Possible? It's a voodoo doll." Philby points; the doll lays on the table in front of Becky Cline. "Right, Becky?"

"I'm not an expert in the occult, in witchcraft. However, I'm not altogether unfamiliar with it, either. Certain spells and powers possessed by our villains fall under that category.

We have discovered similar items on a few occasions—even on Castaway Cay." Becky opens the archival gray cardboard file box. Inside are three different twig-and-twine dolls, all extremely similar. "To my uneducated eye, I would say this new doll fits well with these others. But that's as far as I'll go."

"And we have this," Maybeck says. He's sitting next to Jess. They've both had their heads down, sketching furiously. To look at them, one might think they're bored and doodling, but that's far from the truth. Jess holds up a photocopy: the page from the stolen file, with the watermarks and invisible ink. Maybeck holds up another photocopy, of the rubbing that Finn made in Club 33. "Check it out," Maybeck says.

They have each drawn over their photocopies. Jess has filled in the areas suggested by the water spills; Maybeck has deepened the shading in order to make the rubbed images stand out more boldly.

Silence falls over the table.

Jess presents three images: a set of steps, an eye, and a bearded man sitting. Maybeck's sheet shows what looks like a chair. Joe silently slides the photo of Wayne's watch alongside the other two sheets. They all depict the same images.

"Well," Brad says, "that takes care of that."

"Becky?" Joe says.

"There's one fact I can add to the mix," Becky says. "Despite Wanda Kresky's assertion, neither Wayne nor any other Imagineer was ever presented with a gold Mickey Mouse watch. Moreover, in Walt's time, the watches were made by a company in St. Louis. Wayne's is from New Jersey. It must have been something Walt ordered himself, a custom watch made expressly for Wayne. I find that interesting—from a historical point of view."

"It speaks to how special Wayne was to him," Brad says.

Finn turns to Becky, speaking over Brad. "Is there any chance the steps and the eye are used for black magic? Or whatever magic the OTs use—the Disney villains, I mean."

"I know all about the Overtakers, Finn. Wraiths and all," Becky says. "Give me a moment." She leaves the table and heads into the back room.

"The OTs have gone to a lot of trouble to get Chernabog back here," Philby says. "We should include that on our list. Do we have a list?"

"Yes," Joe says, making a note to himself. "We are keeping extensive records of all known events. Both for the sake of Becky and the Archives and—" He can't finish his sentence.

"In case none of us is around at the end of this," Willa says.

Joe smirks. "You said that. I didn't."

"All the OTs we've encountered," Charlene says. "The headless horseman, Madame Leota, the ghost of the Native American—I mean, is that normal?"

"Not normal," Brad says. Joe shoots him a condemnatory look, and Brad shrugs defensively. "What? Joe, we're giving Philby a key to the Crypt. We've agreed: no more secrets. They're over eighteen. They can handle it. They *have* to handle it."

Joe clears his throat, clearly uncomfortable.

"I'm getting keys to the Crypt?" Philby says, joy rushing across his face.

"We," Joe says, "and by that I mean some select Imagineers, as well as some chief executives, believe that recent events may—*may*—suggest an endgame on the part of the Overtakers. That this in turn necessitates an aggressive strategy for intervention and cessation on our part."

"You're saying it's now or never," Willa says.

Again, Joe smirks. "Perhaps. But that adds a kind of

melodrama we all feel it's important to stay away from."

"Killing Wayne out in the open triggers the endgame," Finn says. "Funny how no one thought like that when the OTs killed Dillard out in the open."

"I'm glad you mentioned that," Joe says. He makes a phone call. "We're in the library at the Archives," he says to whoever's on the other end. "Make it a yard west of my GPS fix . . . Yes. Now is good."

"What's going on?" Philby says. He knows this is something tech-oriented.

"Hey, Finn."

Dillard Cole stands a yard away from Joe.

Charlene screams loud enough to shatter glass. Finn stands up so fast, he sends his chair flying behind him. He takes two steps—and falls to the floor. Philby's there to grab his elbow and help him up. Joe rolls up out of his chair to block Finn's approach.

"It's okay! It's okay!" Joe holds Finn and Philby back. "He's a DHI."

All anyone hears is Finn's excited breathing and Charlene's sniffles.

"Impossible," Philby says. "You don't have the proper files. You wouldn't be able to—"

"His parents lobbied hard for this," Joe explains. "We resisted at first. Frankly, it struck us as morbid. But they pressed us, despite our concerns and caution. What convinced us to attempt this was their selflessness. They don't want him for themselves—would rather never see him. They wanted him for you, Finn. A reminder of your friendship, a gift."

"He's dead," Finn manages to choke out; he can hardly breathe.

"Think of him more as a walking encyclopedia, as portal to

386

the Internet. One that looks like your friend, has some of the memories of your friend, but will never replace your friend."

"Memories? How?" Finn looks around at the Keepers and the two Fairlies. "You were all a part of this?"

"They didn't know why we were asking, Finn," Joe says. "Nearly all the data was supplied by the family. Their memories. Home videos. His schoolwork."

"Joe told me they were just trying to get some background information, you know, to fill in the blanks," Willa says.

"Dillard is version 1.6," Joe says, "but you should see him in 2.0. Outstanding. It's too bad we've bunkered those servers and software, but for what it's worth, he's actually 1.6.3, thanks to the work Philby's done. In fact, you all will be upgraded to 1.6.3 before you next cross over. If you think of Apple's Siri, and move her about five generations forward, that's what Dillard's running on. It's an artificial intelligence software that gets phenomenally close to real-time reasoning and response."

"RTRR," Philby says, "is only theory."

"*Was* only theory," Joe says. "Disney has no obligation to share the technology while we're filing for patents, and that process takes several years. So, for now, we have RTRR and the rest of the world will have to wait."

"It's Nobel Prize stuff!" Philby says. Turning to the vision of Finn's lost friend, he tests it. "Dillard, who's in the room?"

"You, Philby. Amanda—hello, Amanda and Jess."

They answer in kind.

"Terry Maybeck. Wil—"

"Amazing!" Philby declares.

"Video face recognition," Joe says. "Like the TSA uses at airports. We're still building his database."

"But not his personality," Finn says. "You can't build that."

"No, of course not. Never. Not possible," Joe says. "But how do you like his voice?"

Finn shakes his head. "I can't do this."

"Please, Finn. He's here to help." Joe stands, walks around the table, and places his hands on Finn's shoulders; he leans down and speaks so that only Finn can hear him. "Think of him as a device. A gateway. Try him for a few days. His parents believe he can help with your grief—with your misplaced sense of guilt."

Finn shakes his head and looks away. "It's not misplaced."

"You see," Joe says, "you do need him."

The others at the table study Finn and Joe, saying nothing.

"You can do this, Finn," Joe says confidentially. He moves back to his chair and speaks at a normal volume. "The more you talk to him, the more you remind him of things you've done together, the more he'll retain and relate your stories to other events and instances, past, present, and future."

The door opens, and Becky reenters, her arms full. Dillard crosses the room to meet up with her. "Hello, Ms. Cline," Dillard says, "I'm Dillard Cole. It's a pleasure to meet you." She places down her materials and reaches out to shake his hand, but Dillard awkwardly avoids making contact. There's a breathless pause as everyone in the room waits for her to realize Dillard is a hologram.

Becky gives up on the handshake. "Nice to meet you, Dillard." She glances toward the door to make sure it's still locked. "Funny, we have a bell in the back that goes off if someone . . . and I didn't hear . . . Well, anyway."

Dillard turns robotically toward Finn, who can barely keep from squirming.

"What?" Becky asks, noticing that everyone is looking at

her. She wipes her mouth, her nose, as if afraid there's something unwanted on her face.

"Nothing," Joe says, also eyeing Finn. "We just wondered what you'd found."

Dillard takes an open seat next to Willa. Finn can't stop looking at him.

"Well, let's see." The portfolios are oversize. Becky dons a pair of clean white gloves and opens the first. "This is the original cell artwork for—"

"*Sleeping Beauty*," Willa says, seeing the first sheet. "Wow!"

The artwork is breathtaking—actual images that appeared in the film and are therefore familiar to everyone at the table. Becky works through the stack, keeping a sheet of special protective paper between each cell, moving through the first third of the film.

"Nothing," she says, returning the material to its box. "Let's look at this." She unties the ribbons on a portfolio and opens it. "These are alchemical emblems."

"Meaning?" Maybeck asks, squinting at the images. The symbols are circles, crosses, X's, tridents, and more.

"The occult," Becky says.

The Keepers come out of their seats and gather around her.

"The symbol for the letter L," Jess says, pointing but not touching. "That could be from this woman or king or whatever it is. Maybe that line is his beard."

"But the L is backward," Maybeck says. "I don't think so."

"We're close," Finn says.

Dillard remains in his chair, Jess's drawing on the table before him. "This figure is the Egyptian hieroglyph for 'throne,'" he says, his hologram finger pointing to the boxlike glyph the Keepers have been calling "stairs." The comment, directed at no one, silences the room.

"This is the eye of Horus, the all-seeing eye," Dillard continues. "It is a symbol of protection, health, and royal power, commonly associated with the pharaoh, another hieroglyph that therefore moves us toward an Egyptian translation." His finger slides lower and to the right. He's pointing at the human figure.

"Am I missing something here?" Becky asks Joe while looking directly at Dillard, who is sitting up as straight as a pharaoh himself.

"Show her," Joe instructs Finn.

Finn swipes his hand through Dillard's hologram. Becky startles, jerking so hard in her chair, she nearly tips over. "Good gracious!" she gasps.

Joe gives her a brief history of Dillard's hologram.

Finn stares at Joe and says, "The Dillard I know struggled to get C's."

Joe smiles. "I told you we'd upgraded him. He's not like you or me, Finn. Through the server he has access to Wikipedia, to dozens of extensive Disney databases and reference materials. He's a virtual Einstein. We're working on moving the technology to your DHIs."

"Wait a second." Maybeck sounds outraged, but also impressed. "Are you saying we're going to be smarter as DHIs than as our normal selves?"

"That wouldn't be hard," snaps Philby, winking at Maybeck.

"Ha-ha," Maybeck fires back.

"Right now," Joe says, "Dillard has access to more knowledge than any human ever will. What he lacks is intuition. That human trait is impossible to program. We believe we—UCLA, actually, one of our partners—are coming closer to an AI model that teaches itself unique responses, ones that approximate intuition. But right now, Dillard is a fiber-optically generated reference library—a historian, weatherman, bundle of facts."

"He's our new Philby!" Charlene cries, clapping her hands together.

One boy in the room does not like her comment. As if to prove his worth, Philby asks Dillard, "Egyptian?"

"Yeah."

"Throne. Pharaoh. King."

"Or god. Yeah."

"What about together? Do they mean anything in this particular order?"

Dillard studies the photograph of Wayne's watch back and closes his eyes, thinking.

"This can't be happening," Finn whispers.

Dillard is now looking at Philby. It's as if this is a private conversation—or competition—between them. "Osiris. That's his Greek name; there are about ten different versions in Ancient Egyptian. He is the lord of the dead and carries a crook and flail."

"Lord of the dead," Willa mutters.

"And of the underworld and the afterlife. In Egyptian mythology, he is generally represented with green skin, which is a sign of rebirth."

"*Green* skin?" Willa sounds like she might vomit. "As in—"

"Wait!" Finn can't keep from interrupting. "Rebirth? Renewal? Starting over!"

"Yes," Dillard says. "The lord of the underworld possesses the power to renew life."

Finn seems to grow a few inches taller as he addresses the

gathering. "Don't you see? It's a code. A clue passed from Walt to Wayne to—"

"You," Amanda says.

"Never mind me," Finn says. "It's a plan, and it goes as far back as . . ." Finn addresses Becky. "How old is the folder the wraiths helped steal?"

"The notes from *Fantasia* are dated 1938."

"And *Sleeping Beauty*?"

"That would be 1957 and 1958."

"And Disneyland opened in—"

" In 1955," says Willa.

"So," Finn says. "As early as 1938, when Walt first dreamed up Chernabog, all the way through the opening of the park and the making of *Sleeping Beauty*, when he chose to make *a character's skin green* just like Osiris's skin, Walt was already devising a code to save the Kingdom from—"

"His own imagination," Philby says. "He foresaw where all this might lead."

"Or something happened in those twenty years that made him realize it could all go impossibly bad," Finn says. "Impossibly wrong."

"So he made a backup plan," says Maybeck.

Joe is on his feet. "A plan he hid in invisible ink beneath a sheet about a production meeting that discussed Chernabog's powers."

"And he passed it on to a very young Wayne, so that Wayne would know the Kingdom had a chance," says Charlene.

"Wayne passed it to Finn," Philby says, drawing everyone's attention to Finn.

Maybeck breaks the silence. "You're the new Wayne, dude."

43

"WHAT NOW?"

Finn stands by his bed, looking at the boy in the doorway. A boy he has cried over, a boy that caused him to throw a wrench at Cruella, a boy that resulted in the death of a dragon.

A boy who isn't there. Not really.

"We don't have projection in our rooms," Finn says awkwardly.

"Of course you do." Dillard steps inside and closes the door.

"But we were told—

"Enough lies to keep you where they needed you."

"I beg your pardon?"

"Think about it, Finn," Dillard says. His voice is smooth and uncharacteristically confident. "Whose side do you think I'm on?"

"I don't even know who you are. I know *what* you are, because I've been one myself, but I honestly don't know if I like having you around."

"And yet. Here I am."

"Here you are."

"They blew it, Finn. In wanting me to know so much, they programmed me through their server, right? I can't act like the real me around them, because they'll reconsider what they've done."

Finn plops down onto the mattress. "I'm lost."

"Their server has all their files, e-mails, even texts. They seem to think communication is only one-way. But by its very definition, communication involves a minimum of two. I have no idea when it happened. It all happened so fast! But it was amazing."

Dillard sits on the bed near him. Finn can see them in his mind's eye, in his room back home, sitting just like this. Finn stands, his hands clenching into fists.

"I'm sorry!" he cries. "I can't do this."

"What's happening?" Dillard asks. "Do what?"

"Pretend like everything—Pretend like you're—"

A distant police siren hangs in the air like a mosquito's whine.

"Oh." Dillard stares at the wall, the floor, anywhere but at Finn.

"It's just that—"

"No! Don't. I recognize your regret. I'm not stupid."

"Stupid? You're like a supercomputer stuck inside my best friend, and I don't know what I'm supposed to do."

"Do nothing," Dillard says. "Do what you'd normally do."

"Normal? Are we really going to go there?"

"I feel like the unwanted Christmas gift, Finn. Like your parents give you last year's cool game and it's not even the right version for your new machine."

The analogy is so Dillard. He always loved gaming. Finn forces his mind back to his friend—this hologram of his friend—and his words.

"You read the Imagineers' files, e-mails, and texts? Seriously?"

"Finn, I don't have to read them. I know them. They don't call it random-access memory for nothing. It is totally random. And I have full access."

"For example?"

"Name a subject. I need prompting. Think of me like Siri on the iPhone."

"Amanda and Jess," Finn says.

"Internships in the company have been discussed in . . . sixteen e-mails among seven Cast Members. Five e-mails concern full scholarships at community college. The two Fairlies are currently designated as international visitors, which has something to do with concealing their identities and location from the government, which may be looking for them. Some of the e-mails refer to an encrypted system to which I have no access."

"Sheesh!" Finn drops into a chair and cradles his head in his hands.

"I'm here to help you, Finn. You and the others. I want to help."

"But that's a recorded phrase. Scripted, right? Do you know what it is to want something?"

"To feel or have a desire for. To have need of."

"Not the dictionary definition. Do you know what it is to want something?"

"I can only repeat myself. Based on what I observed earlier, that will not appeal to you. I see no positive outcome from trying this."

"You're Spock!" Finn shouts.

"Mister or Doctor?"

"What?"

"Dr. Benjamin McLane Spock, born May 2, 1903, died March 15, 1998, was an American pediatrician whose book—"

"Stop!"

Dillard is frozen in place.

"Dillard?" Finn tests. "Hey!" Dillard looks like DVR video in pause mode. "Play." Nothing. "Continue."

"Mr. Spock, a fictional character in the Star Trek franchise written by Gene—"

"Enough!"

"You asked me a question," Dillard says. "Questions require answers."

"Yeah." Finn slumps back, staring at the ceiling.

"Do you not feel well? You are assuming a position suggestive of—"

"Oh my gosh!" Finn laces his fingers behind his head and leans his forehead to his knees. "That's enough talking, please."

Seconds pass. Minutes. Finn sits up, thinking Dillard must have left, but the hologram remains where it was. Only the blinking eyes reveal that someone's home.

Finn makes a face at the hologram. There's no reaction.

"Lift your left arm." Dillard's arm rises to shoulder height. "Now that's interesting," Finn says. "Talk to me."

"What is interesting?" Dillard asks. "Can you be more explicit?"

"Stop talking." Finn studies the hologram. Bile stings his throat. He inhales sharply, recoils, holding his legs against his chest.

He bawls like a baby.

* * *

Finn awakens some time later. How long, he's not sure. Dillard remains in the exact same spot on his bed, looking at Finn with unflinching eyes.

"Did you enjoy your rest?"

"You don't sound like the real Dill." Dillard says nothing. "That used to be a joke with us: the real deal! The real Dill!" Still, nothing. Finn focuses on asking a question. "Do you laugh?"

The hologram laughs. Surprisingly, it's Dillard's laugh.

"Joe mentioned home videos," Finn says. "So I get where most of you comes from. Do I have to ask a question to get you to talk?"

"Conversation is the informal exchange of ideas through words. I am capable of several levels of conversation—casual, formal, technical—but I did not detect the desire for conversation in your inflections, Finn. Have I misinterpreted?"

"A person would say, 'misunderstood.'"

"I will replace that response. My parameters expand with each conversation cycle. Feel free to correct me. Thank you."

"I can't do this, Dillard. I can't train you."

"How do you wish to train me? Physically or verbally?"

"Never mind." Finn lets out a deep sigh.

"If you instruct me to—"

"Tell me," Finn says. "We would say, 'If you would tell me.'"

"If you instruct me to 'return,' my projection will cease. You can verbally program me to project as you would set a calendar event, and you can preprogram me for an action at the time of projection if you wish. For example: upon projection I will wake you, defend you, advise you. And so on." Dillard's hologram looks forward, away from Finn. "Should you fail to program me to project at a later time, you must contact the appropriate Cast Member and request projection."

Finn sits for a long time, studying Dillard in profile. A part of him wants to instruct the hologram to return and never appear again. Another part considers Dillard his own private genie. He doesn't know what to do, how to feel. He tells himself this is not Dillard, that nothing will ever be or replace Dillard in his heart. The hologram is a toy, a tool.

Wayne would tell him to use whatever resources were available.

Learn how to use this to your advantage. Wayne's voice apparently resides at the back of Finn's brain, whispering to him like Obi-Wan Kenobi in *Star Wars.* Finn doesn't know what immortality is, but once again he thinks this has something to do with it.

"Talk to me," Finn says. "What are the possible relationships between what we've observed of the Osiris images and the Disney villains . . . or Mickey Mouse?"

"I can tell you about: the Osiris myth; the comparison of the Disney character, Maleficent, to Osiris; Osiris in fantasy literature; Osiris shoes; Osiris, the near-infrared integral field spectrograph."

The hologram's clinical delivery of topics reminds Finn that this isn't his neighborhood friend. He actually appreciates that distinction. This is not Dillard, it's *the Dillard.*

"Osiris myth," Finn says, leaning forward and resting his elbows on his knees.

"In Plutarch's version, or ancient Greek, Typhon arranges a banquet and issues a challenge, tricking Osiris into climbing into a chest. In Egyptian mythology, the god Set is responsible for the ruse. Osiris is locked in the chest and dies. The chest is set afloat and arrives at the shore of Byblos, where a tree grows around it. The goddess Isis, Osiris's wife, eventually removes the chest from the tree. The tree becomes a center of worship. This explanation is unknown in Egyptian sources dating to the New Kingdom."

"The *what?*" Finn says. "Let's start at the word *kingdom.*"

"The most prosperous phase in Egyptian history is known as the New Kingdom. The five hundred years between 1600 and 1100 B.C. marked the peak of Egyptian power and influence."

"The New Kingdom," Finn repeats reverentially, reaching

for a pencil to make notes. "That is not a coincidence. It can't be."

"Is that a question?"

Finn laughs. "No, Dillard. Hang on."

The hologram grips the edge of the bed.

"Let go of the bed. The expression *hang on* means 'wait a moment.'"

"I've added that. Thank you. The command is 'Pause.'"

"Pause," Finn says. He writes down everything the Dillard has told him. "What about the Egyptian version?" He waits. There's a prolonged pause. "Resume! Please inform me about the Egyptian version of the Osiris myth. Make it abridged and include facts relevant to our current situation."

"One moment . . . editing. The story is much the same as the one I just relayed. In the Egyptian version, Isis discovers Osiris's corpse in the box embedded in a tree. The tree supports the roof of the palace of Byblos on the Phoenician coast. In several versions, Isis then casts a spell that allows her to conceive a child with her dead husband."

"Gross!"

The Dillard continues without comment.

"In this version, Set comes across the body and cuts it into fourteen pieces."

"This is more and more disgusting!"

"But Isis recovers the parts and bandages them back together. The gods are so impressed that they resurrect Osiris and appoint him god of the underworld, lord of rebirth and resurrection."

"Pause," Finn says, his mind whirring. He scribbles down what he's heard. "Resume. Are you aware of my conversation with Wayne at Club 33?"

"Yes."

399

"The topics?"

"Yes."

Finn debates how to ask the Dillard his next question. "Is there a relationship between my conversation with Wayne and the Osiris myth?" Finn feels like he's on a television game show. Everything hinges on asking the right questions.

"Wayne Kresky's reference to the destruction of the Mickey Mouse illustration could be taken as an analogy to the pieces of Osiris. Isis, the personification of whom is yet to be defined, would accept the assignment—"

"To gather the pieces!"

"—to collect and reassemble the various—"

"Pause!" Finn shouts. There's no visual reaction to Finn's raising his voice. "Resume. You need to blink more often! Pause."

The hologram blinks, but then the Dillard is caught with his lids closed; he looks like he's fallen asleep sitting up.

Finn writes quickly:

> Walt understood how to resurrect Mickey.
> Osiris code given to Wayne, given to me.
> Collect and reassemble the parts.
> Are the Imagineers the "gods" who can
> restore Mickey's power? Or the Keepers?
> Must find the parts!

"Resume. If the Mickey Mouse illustration was destroyed by the Disney villains, is there still a chance of finding the pieces?"

"Of the fourteen missing pieces in the Osiris myth, thirteen were collected. Some believe this gave this gave rise to the superstition that thirteen causes bad luck. The number represented incompletion, a state of being not whole. Since 1956, Cast Members employed by WED Enterprises have scoured Disneyland for the missing pieces of the Mickey artwork, which they believed were dispersed by an unknown entity."

"The Overtakers!"

"During the reconstruction that turned Canal Boats of the World into the Storybook Land Canal Boats, work halted for two full days while WED Enterprise employees cordoned off the work area. They were seen to be sifting earth."

"This is from?"

"*The Imagineers Almanac, 1950 to 1957.* Five volumes."

"Can you get me that almanac?"

"I have no way to print from my memory."

"Of course you don't. Sorry about that. How tricky!" Finn says. "They give me access to information I can't substantiate one way or the other."

"Is that a question?"

"No. Where are the pieces of Mickey that've been recovered?"

"In the vault in the Disney Gallery."

"Of course! If you want to hide something, hide it in the open."

The Dillard does not respond. Finn is getting used to him, is even coming to like him; he's not sure if the feeling is real, or part of the rush he gets from seeing all the clues come together.

"Would you like to hear an interesting fact?" the Dillard says.

"Sure."

"Disney Gallery is in the Opera House, one of the first buildings erected in Disneyland."

"If you weren't a hologram, I'd hug you!" Finn says.

"I'll take that as a compliment."

"Yeah. You should. So, do you know which Imagineers are aware of the Mickey pieces?"

The Dillard hesitates, and Finn can imagine some hard drive spinning in an underground room as the hologram searches his vast supplies of data. "No e-mails . . . no mention in annual reports . . . Ah! Here is something: a remodeling of the vault in 1998 follows by four months the recovery of the twelfth piece of Mickey."

Finn makes a note. At times, his mind starts to work so fast, it's like a locomotive about to jump the rails. He loses the ability to hold his thoughts together; they act like sparks shooting away from the white heat of a welder's torch. He wants to snag them in their flight, but trying to catch the flashes of thought will only burn him badly, so he watches them go.

"Why is there a vault? Is it for show or for real?"

"Prior to the Disney Gallery, that space housed a bank from 1955 to 1998."

"This is making a lot of sense!" Finn practically shouts.

Again, no reaction to his raised voice. This is one of the oddities Finn has to get used to: the Dillard lacks emotional responses to what he hears; but when speaking certain words, he has been programmed to make the appropriate facial expressions. The dichotomy confuses Finn, keeps bringing him up short. The Dillard is real—until he's not.

"More comparisons between Disneyland and Osiris?" Finn says.

"Egypt is one of the world's oldest agricultural civilizations. The Egyptians lived mainly on grain," the Dillard says. "Their staple food was bread, which is made from grain. When you 'bury' seeds, they sprout, confirming rebirth and life after

402

death. The Egyptians associated Osiris and death with burial and rebirth. There were celebrations and festivals when it came time to 'bury the seeds,' in celebration of the resurrection of Osiris."

"Festivals—parades, fireworks," Finn says.

"Yes. The similarities are unmistakable. Disney parks, including Disneyland, celebrate every day with parades and fireworks. Grains of many forms, especially wheat, are sold and eaten in the parks: breads, pastries, pretzels, desserts, ice cream cones, snacks, sandwiches, et cetera."

"The festival of Osiris."

"Daily," the Dillard says without emotion.

"But the Disney Osiris is missing."

"Incomplete would be a better word. Only twelve pieces of the original Mickey illustration have been recovered. The most powerful of the 'Disney gods' remains powerless."

"Allowing others to rise to power."

"History provides ample testament to the filling of power vacuums."

"You sound like a textbook."

"Apologies. My use of vernacular will modify with my exposure to common spoken terms."

"And again!" Finn says. The Dillard does not respond. "The Imagineers sent you to help me put this together," Finn mumbles, thinking aloud.

"I am projected, not delivered."

"Pause." Now Finn reaches for his mental sparks, corralling as many as possible. He's immune to any pain from their heat; this is too important. He must not lose any of it; he must retain the ability to explain all the things he's coming to understand to the other Keepers. On the pad, he scribbles random thoughts; he'll organize them later. They burst like the fireworks he just mentioned. "Wait!" Finn says to himself.

The Dillard's head swivels, but he doesn't speak. He looks like a dog eagerly awaiting a command.

"Resume," Finn says. He will instruct the Dillard later to "learn" from Finn's pauses, to evolve into a more conversational companion. For now, there's a more pressing question. "Search every available database and tell me: Did Walt Disney or Wayne Kresky leave any clues other than the hieroglyphs we discovered in the invisible ink, on the back of Wayne's wristwatch, and carved into the table at Club 33?"

The Dillard sits motionless for ninety seconds. Finn times the hologram's blinking, realizing they may signify how the search is progressing. At first, when the Dillard blinks, his lids stay down for a full second. Near the ninety-second mark, he blinks so quickly Finn, can barely spot the action.

"Walt Disney is believed to have created six private documents referenced in his last will and testament as 'The Manto Manuscripts.' As you may know, Manto, a daughter of the seer Tiresias, was a prophetess of extraordinary abilities."

The Dillard is doing his textbook thing again, but this time Finn doesn't complain. Between Philby and the Dillard, he is surrounded by know-it-alls. After all these years, he is kind of getting used to it.

"The Manto Manuscripts," the Dillard continues, "include the Stonecutter's Quill. There is no information available on the remaining five."

Finn wants to ask who has access to the Manto Manuscripts, where this information comes from, but there's a more pressing need.

"The Stonecutter's Quill required 3-D glasses for the recovery of much of its information," Finn says. "Is there anything like that with the Osiris hieroglyphs, beyond that invisible ink?"

"Information on the Manto Manuscripts is limited. That said, only basic concealment technologies were available at the time. It is logical to assume that use of such technologies would have been applied to the Manto documents."

"I think I understood that." Again, Finn finds it hard to keep his thoughts under control. He wills his pen to move faster on the page. The Dillard made his last comment on his own. He wasn't quoting an information source. The Imagineers have apparently given him such massive bandwidth that he can process data, calculate, and reason at lightning speeds. Finn tests his thesis. "How likely is it that a technology like 3-D glasses would be required to recover all the information in more than one of the Manto Manuscripts?"

The Dillard's eyelids lower and remain that way, seemingly confirming Finn's belief that this indicates processing. "There is a forty percent probability of this technology use recurring in another of the documents."

"Your movements are too mechanical," Finn says. "You need to be more natural, more fluid."

"So noted. Whose motions should I emulate?"

"Not any of the girls. Only boys."

"So noted."

"Maybeck has good moves, but I think you'd look stupid trying them. No offense."

"So noted. None taken."

"Philby's a little stiff."

"So noted."

"You were probably programmed based on family videos. Do you have access to those?"

"Yes."

"I wish you could project them."

Nothing.

"Use those," Finn says, clearing his throat. "Access and study them."

"So noted."

The Dillard can become tiresome. "Don't repeat phrases so much."

"Copy that."

Finn laughs aloud. It feels better than his earlier tears. Maybe the Dillard's parents knew what they were talking about.

* * *

Stage 3 in the Studios back lot is the size of several airplane hangars. Currently, a large section of flooring at its center has been removed, exposing a rectangular tank of black water bigger than a basketball court. A giant sheet of green-screen fabric hangs behind it.

All five Keepers, Amanda, and Jess wear green bodysuits covered with dozens of small metal disks. The Dillard stands beside Finn, looking the way he always looks.

Willa is not thrilled with the way the suit fits. It's like a second skin. The others look great. She thinks she looks more like a Shar-Pei.

"Don't worry about it," Jess says confidentially.

"Easy for you to say. I had no idea you were so fit. You always hide your body."

"It's no big deal to me. I mean, I guess I'm more cerebral, always trying to listen in on my own brain."

"You should have my body."

Jess nudges Willa's shoulder with her own and smiles gently. "I'm sure this won't take long."

406

Brad calls out, his voice echoing in the cavernous space. "We need to update your water abilities in order to ensure your safety as DHIs."

"The fact is," Joe chimes in, "we don't know what the OTs may throw at you. It's important that your DHIs be compatible and upgraded to the highest level of projection we can manage, short of version 2.0."

"It may be possible, through wire work, to give your 1.6.3 DHIs the ability to leap or jump great distances, run faster, and swim farther," Brad says, motioning toward the tank, "all while limiting some of the human-body aspects of 2.0 that could compromise the general population or the military, were the technology to fall into the wrong hands."

"Basically," Joe says, "we'd like to make you superhuman, but we have to stop short of super. Starting today, though, we'll be adding enhancements."

"Now that I look like a piece of asparagus," Finn says, winning laughter from the other Keepers, "I need to tell you what the Dillard told me."

"The Dillard?" Maybeck says.

"I'll explain later," Finn says.

Joe nods. Finn doesn't have his notes handy, but he easily explains what he and the Dillard reviewed. The others listen spellbound as Finn recounts the Osiris myth and the way it fits perfectly with the Mickey illustration and its one missing piece. Finn doesn't want to give away the Dillard's widespread access to the Imagineers' files, so he puts it out there as a theory—something cobbled together from his talk with Wayne in Club 33.

"All the pieces of Mickey might be out there in the park," Finn finishes breathlessly. His words resonate, and then fade in the vast soundstage.

Joe's obvious reluctance to share such secrets hangs awkwardly in the air.

"You're close," he says finally. "We believe the Overtakers did in fact steal the original artwork. And that they tore it up and distributed it so as to make reassembly nearly impossible."

"Why not just burn it?" Maybeck asks.

"Turns out, it can't be destroyed. Of course, not even Walt knew this at the time. But it couldn't be burned or shredded or eaten by acid—and yes, we put a tiny piece through all these tests. There are a dozen theories as to what it all means, but our best guess is that it was indeed torn or cut into thirteen pieces. This may have been possible because of the illustration's relation to storytelling—Mickey is mythic, after all! In the past several decades, we've recovered twelve. They're currently stored at a secure location."

Finn says nothing about his knowledge of the Disney Gallery's vault.

"But now you've been able to tie the engraving on Wayne's watch to the Osiris myth. That's new. We—generations of Imagineers—have known about the hidden Mickey, have tried to use our guests to help us in our search. We've planted hidden Mickeys all over the parks, hoping someone might see something out of the ordinary and report it. Four of the pieces were recovered this way, but that last one has eluded us."

"I don't get it," Philby says. "Why would Walt Disney not share the Osiris myth? That doesn't make sense."

"Timing," Joe says. "Maybe he didn't want the illustration made whole because it might have been stolen again. He may not have known how powerful that first illustration was. It could have caught him by surprise, even scared him. He was protective of his mouse, of his kingdom."

"So he gave it to Wayne in case it was ever needed," Charlene says.

"For a moment like this," Amanda says, nodding to herself.

"Maybe so. Our guys are trying to see if it means anything at this point, or if, over time, it's lost its meaning. We're only missing the one piece. It's hard to see how the reference to the Osiris myth could help much with that."

"But it must mean something!" Willa stands on her tiptoes as she speaks. "First the invisible ink. Then the watch!"

Finn clears his throat. "We should get on with the green-screen work."

The Keepers, Amanda, and Jess shoot him looks that border on disdain. Finn's expression remains intense, even grim. Amanda is the first to pick up on it.

"Finn's right," she says. "There's no time to waste. We need our DHIs to be as able and capable as possible."

"Let's get to it," Joe says.

Finn intentionally bumps into Philby, who's about to object, whispering, "We know something they don't."

Philby's lips clamp shut.

"Everything all right?" Joe asks.

"Couldn't be better," Philby says.

44

HAIR STILL DAMP FROM THEIR SWIM, the five Keepers, along with Jess and Amanda, cross over onto Disneyland's Plaza shortly after the fireworks' grand finale. The Dillard's projection awaits them. It's a balmy southern California night. Amid the commotion of departing guests, whose attention is focused on Main Street and the gates, the arrival of the DHIs goes unnoticed by all but a few children. And even with the Disney magic, their parents don't believe their claims that a kid wearing 3-D glasses materialized out of nowhere.

By previous agreement, the team divides into two groups of four. Philby leads Charlene, Maybeck, and Jess to inspect all the clocks in the park—Wayne has referenced time persistently, after all. Finn takes Amanda, Willa, and the Dillard on a mission to search for where clues might have been left.

The Keepers have agreed that the "king" in the Osiris hieroglyphs must be Walt himself—who else? Any location known to be both original to the park and specifically associated with Walt thus falls onto their list of places to visit. Somewhere in the park, the Keepers believe they will locate at least one other Osiris hieroglyph. Quite possibly, this will identify a missing piece of the torn Mickey illustration. Because of the Dillard's reference material about the Manto Manuscripts, they have the option of the 3-D glasses, which they hope might reveal the ancient symbol.

"I am now connected to park Wi-Fi," the Dillard announces.

"What's with that?" Willa asks Finn in a whisper.

Finn says, "Pause," and addresses the girls, who stare at the frozen Dillard. "Listen, even though Joe told us about the Dillard's abilities, they are mind-blowing."

"*The* Dillard?" Willa asks.

Finn hears concern in Willa's voice, and wonders if she's just worried about Philby or if there's something more. "Yeah, *the* Dillard. Philby is not going be too excited when he realizes the Dillard knows more than he does."

"I'm *sure* that's right," Willa says.

"Hey, you're all right with the Dillard, aren't you?"

"Of course." But she doesn't sound persuaded.

"Trust me, he's a big help." Finn makes sure Amanda's listening. "We've got to remember he's pure hologram, like our park DHIs. He can't touch anything, and nothing can touch him. He's a simple hologram . . . if that isn't contradictory. He can't help us physically, but his knowledge base is bottomless."

"You are so right about Philby not liking him."

"He'll adjust. The Dillard grows on you."

"Fine," Amanda says, trying to close the discussion. "So where to?"

"Resume," Finn tells the Dillard. Willa looks on dubiously. "What location inside Disneyland gives us the highest-percentage chance of finding a symbol hidden by Walt Disney?"

The Dillard's eyelids lower for five seconds. Then they blink open. "Top three locations in descending order of importance are: Walt Disney's private apartment at sixty-eight-point-eight percent; the Swiss Family Robinson Treehouse at twenty-seven-point-two percent; Pirates of the Caribbean at eighteen-point-seven percent."

Willa gives Finn a look that prompts him to say, "I know."

Then Finn asks, "Who votes we start at Walt's apartment?"

The Dillard raises his hologram hand at light speed. Amanda and Willa follow.

"It's unanimous," says the Dillard.

Yes, Finn thinks. Willa is jealous, just as he expects Philby will be.

* * *

Philby has assembled a list of clocks and timepieces in Disneyland. They head first to the Haunted Mansion. "The later it gets, the scarier," is how Philby defends this decision. "Going now is better than going in at two in the morning. Trust me!"

"Charlie and I disagree," Maybeck says. "We didn't like our last visit so much."

"It's only to look at the clock," Philby reminds him. "In and out. Besides, the park is in a soft close. It'll still be running. We're all right."

"I'll go with you," Jess volunteers. "Terry and Charlene can stand guard."

"I'm not saying I'm afraid," Maybeck says.

"No worries," Philby says. "One of you takes the front, one the exit. Jess and I go in through the back and cut through the 'chicken-door' passageway to the clock, since it's near the front."

"How can you look so calm?" Charlene asks Jess.

"We're DHIs," Jess says.

"But when we're scared, we're mortal."

"When I'm scared, I have my dreams. Nightmares, whatever you want to call them. So this is kind of an opportunity for me."

"In a sick kind of way," says Charlene.

"Definitely. Now you understand why I cringe when people call it a gift."

"I guess I do," Charlene says. "I hadn't really thought about it."

"Let's go," Philby says.

He and Jess sneak into the exit, through the unobtrusive door that offers a shortcut through the building for any riders who get too spooked, are too chicken to continue to the end. Moments later, the two are heading for the Doom Buggies. The attraction is surprisingly quiet, given that park hours have just ended. Typically, there would be Cast Members around at this hour, but not tonight. The ride must be "down" for maintenance or cleaning.

The few lights left on cast ghoulish shadows on cobwebs, portraits, and props. The v1.6.3 holograms glow slightly, forming a haze around Jess and Philby as the two slip past the buggies, feeling their way through the gloom.

"You picking up on anything?" Philby whispers.

"Not yet."

The sound of swirling wind comes from up ahead, swishing in waves like ocean water licking the shore.

"Wraiths!" Philby whispers, his voice cracking with tension. "Hurry!"

Jess follows him, but they've lost their all clear, so pushing past the Doom Buggies is slow work. It'll be just as slow trying to get back out, she thinks, and feels a cold rush of fear.

"There!" Philby spots the grandfather clock to the right. The rush of wind intensifies. He turns. "Jess?"

She's not behind him.

"Jess?" Torn between the clock and Jess, Philby calls, "I'll be right back!" and heads toward the clock.

Jess, sitting in a Doom Buggy with her eyes closed, is

overcome by a vision of broken earth spewing black smoke and orange fingers of fire. The images shift—she sees flags flapping and wraiths dive-bombing from overhead. Her arms extend to fight off imaginary ghouls. An instant later, her eyes pop open and she catches herself flailing in the dark. It takes a moment to reorient herself.

She spots Philby, wearing his 3-D glasses, standing in front of the grandfather clock. As she joins him, he speaks in his level, Professor Philby voice, the one with a tinge of a British accent. "It's quite clever, really." The clock is numbered for thirteen hours, not twelve. "I might have missed the hieroglyph altogether, but I was intrigued by the clock only having one hand, and happened to look where the hand joins the mechanism."

Jess dons her pair of glasses. On the metal stub that connects the clock's one hand to the mechanism behind the face is a tiny Osiris hieroglyph, no bigger than a collar button.

"Thirteen," Jess says, "as in the thirteen pieces of Osiris."

"Yeah. And a hieroglyph to make sure that number is noticed."

The wind grows louder and closer, pressing against them. Jess's hair lifts. Philby wrestles with the door of the clock, but it's locked.

"If the missing piece is in there, it's worth breaking it."

"No," Jess says.

"I know what to do." Philby pockets his glasses and kneels. Jess tucks hers away as well. "You watch for trouble!" he calls, trying to sound confident. Philby holds his breath and, confident of his all clear status, eases his hologram head into the base of the clock. His DHI's faint glow illuminates dust, cobwebs, and a set of tarnished keys. Nothing resembling a torn piece of paper. Next to the keys is a stick of caramel-brown wood, too small to be hiding the missing piece behind it. The chunk of wood seems out of place inside a grandfather clock.

Philby spins his head to look up and see if the bit of wood broke off of something. A black, hairy spider the size of a Ping-Pong ball creeps from a corner. Philby jerks back—*but can't move.* His fear of the spider has partially solidified him, sending a band of intense pain through his shoulders where they meet the wood of the clock.

"Hurry!" Jess calls. "Wraiths!"

He feels Jess pulling on him, but he's frozen, locked half in, half out by his fear. He curses v1.6.3 for its limitations; he's corrupted in part by his mind's relentlessness, his inability to turn off his thoughts. The more he thinks, the less chance of all clear. The idea is to let go, to find internal quiet, but quiet is not in his repertoire.

Jess's voice arrives, muted by the wood of the clock, the increasing roar of wind.

"Think of Willa," she says. "Your best times with Willa."

The mention of her name brings a rush of emotion. It's as if a dark cloth is laid over that part of Philby's brain that refuses to slow; a gateway to a part of him he rarely explores opens. His feelings. The resulting flood of joy and laughter momentarily blots out all thought, and Philby stops straining against the clock's hold on him. In that moment of relaxation, he sits back, falling out of the clock, caught by Jess.

The four wraiths are upon them, charcoal ghosts bearing down, arms outstretched and mouths agape. The stream of ghouls aims to suck the life out of them. Philby and Jess duck. The wraiths miss. The kids are up and running scared, weaving through the Doom Buggies, back toward the chicken door, the nearest exit.

Despite her forward motion, Jess sees her hair blow in

front of her and knows the wraiths have recovered and are closing in.

"Duck!" She pulls Philby to the floor of the waiting line. Once again, the wraiths miss.

They reach the chicken door and vanish through it. The wraiths smash into the wood, howling in agony and rage.

Once outside, Philby hisses at Jess and motions Charlene off the path. The kids scurry into the graveyard, hiding behind gravestones. The wraiths soar out of the exit line and hover briefly before darting out into the park, looking for the Keepers.

Jess starts to move. Philby whispers, "Stay!"

He's guessed correctly. Just a moment later, the four wraiths return, hover once more near the exit, and then bleed like smoke into the hallway. Jess, Philby, and Charlene hurry away from the mansion, gesturing to Maybeck, who sees them and follows.

"Fantasyland!" Philby says, and they're teamed up again.

Maybeck and Charlene demand an explanation of what happened, and Jess and Philby relay the story, panting with shock and nerves.

"They look so transparent," says Jess, "so ethereal. But when they hit the wall—"

"Yeah. I saw that, too." Philby isn't slowing down. "At least we know they aren't holograms."

"I think I might have liked it better if they were."

"And the clock?" Maybeck asks. "What about the clock?"

"The clue was *thirteen*," Jess says, glancing at Philby for confirmation. "The Osiris hieroglyph means it's important."

"It's a minor clue," Philby says. "A hint, more like. It's something to get someone thinking, but not enough to put it all together."

416

"It must go back forever," Charlene says. "Forever and ever. To Walt himself."

"He wasn't going to leave this to chance," Philby says. "Multiple clues ensured that the myth would be uncovered, that questions would be asked. I mean, what if something had happened to Wayne before we showed up?"

"The Imagineers know most of this. They've been looking for that thirteenth piece for a long time." Maybeck sounds discouraged.

"But it's been left to us," Philby says. "Specifically to Finn, not the Imagineers."

They slow, keeping to the shadows, trying to conceal themselves. Calmer now, Philby leads the way toward the Fantasyland clock tower.

"Do you think the Overtakers are trying to stop us because they know what you're—we're—doing?" Jess asks. "Or just because we're us and they know we're the enemy?"

"The OTs created the Hidden Mickey. Maybe they know the Imagineers have recovered all but the one piece of it. That might make them pretty desperate," Philby says, shrugging and putting a hand to his side; if he weren't a DHI, he'd have a stitch from all the running. "Obviously, they couldn't harness the power of the illustration or they wouldn't have shredded it in the first place. They fear the Kingdom regaining that kind of power. If they figure out that we stand in the way of that, I have no idea what they'll throw at us."

"Are you ever optimistic?" Charlene asks.

Philby is about to answer, but then stops and asks instead, "What happened to you back there, Jess? I turned around and you were gone."

"I had a . . . moment."

"And?" says Charlene.

"The ground was burning. There were flags, and . . . wraiths. The four wraiths we saw, I suppose. I've never had one of my dreams come true so fast. I know it means something, but I don't know what."

"Maybe it's not important," Charlene says sympathetically. Maybeck and Philby exchange a look.

"It is," Jess speaks with quiet resolve, peering around the corner of a building. "I've learned so much since the visions began. How often they happen, how often they take to come true—it's all part of it. It's all important. It connects, like one of those Christmas chains you make out of paper loops."

It's a funny image, so specific. Philby smirks. "You and Amanda have never told us much about your Christmases, your pasts."

Jess doesn't speak. Her hologram head hangs toward the ground, and Philby can sense contained pain, resistance, like something electrical heating up.

"None of my business," he says.

"No, it is. You all deserve to know. We've entered your lives uninvited. I suppose when you think of an enemy within, one or both of us gets the top spot on the list."

Philby hasn't forgotten about an enemy within, but he hasn't exactly dwelled on the idea either. The reminder is sharp, like a prick of a fingertip to draw blood. He would like to deny it, but he respects Jess too much to lie. "Suspicion is a poison." This is why he'd given up puzzling about the enemy within: the process became toxic. But now the problem has surfaced again.

"The story about a spy came from both Wayne and the Imagineers. It has to be true."

"None of us wants it to be. I'd rather not talk about it."

"Of course not. But I promise you, it's not Amanda or me.

I know—I'd say that same thing even if it was us. That's why we haven't said it already."

"Not knowing is the worst," Philby admits. "Not knowing—and living with suspicion."

The Fantasyland clock tower appears before them.

"What now?" Jess asks, her voice colored with caution.

"Now it gets interesting," Maybeck says.

* * *

"Interesting," Finn says. The hanging chain that blocks off the stairs to Walt's apartment is swinging loose to one side.

"This chain is usually left closed," the Dillard says. "Danger warning. Possible intruder."

"We don't want to crash a party," Willa says.

"But you're curious," Amanda tells Finn. As if it's news to him.

"Always," he says.

"I will stand guard," the Dillard says, his eyelids falling. "There is a light in the window that looks out onto the street. It once indicated when Mr. Disney was in residence in the park. It remains burning at all hours as a tribute to a great man. I can access the electrical circuit for that light over the local area network. I will terminate illumination from the light should I encounter anyone or anything untoward."

"Untoward?" Amanda teases.

"You can do that?" Willa says simultaneously. Finn raises a hand to stop her, but it's too late. The Dillard has launched into encyclopedia mode.

"I have access to eleven hundred and sixty-seven switch-able circuits. Another twenty-two hundred breakers, all public address—"

"Pause."

Finn tells the others to limit the number of open-ended questions they direct at the Dillard—"Or you're in for the full rundown," he adds. Then he gathers Amanda and Willa together with his eyes. "Okay, we're going up there." To the Dillard, he says, "Resume."

They hurry away as the Dillard continues to recite the litany of his capabilities to no one.

"Will he stop?" Amanda asks Finn.

There's a white feather caught by the breeze, floating before them. Willa waves it away.

"Who knows?" Finn says. "It's all new to me."

They don't know if the door to the apartment is locked; they don't bother using it. Inside, the group crowds the small entryway, then moves into the apartment's sitting area, which is to the right. They keep silent as they explore the tiny apartment. It takes only a minute or two to determine that they're alone.

"It's small," Willa says. "So much smaller than I expected."

"It's pretty," Amanda says.

"My grandmother had a quilt like that," Willa says, gesturing to a throw on one of the couches.

"Look at the huge Minnie!" Willa says. A huge stuffed Minnie Mouse sags against the table holding the lamp. "Couldn't you just hug it? Maybe all night long? I would love to have a stuffed animal like that! I wouldn't care who saw it!"

"It'll have to wait. First we search all the rooms without 3-D glasses, then again with," Finn instructs. "We're looking at photos, embroidery, anything with letters or images. Whatever we find may need to be decoded—open minds here."

He and the girls separate. As he searches, Finn keeps an eye on the lamp in the window. It's a small, simple light with a white glass shade. Nothing pretentious or unusual, but perfectly preserved—as is every other antique in the apartment: two twin beds against opposite walls; the table holding the lamp; books, figurines, and a half dozen photos placed carefully around the walls. Near the short hallway is a tall wooden case with a curved top and an inset glass window. Finn is drawn to its unusual design. It looks like an old-fashioned jukebox—like something from *Grease* or *Teen Beach Movie*—but made of wood.

He steps closer. Behind the glass window, he sees bronze-colored discs the size of power saw blades. He's normally able to figure stuff out on the fly; it rarely takes two looks for him to understand an object's purpose. But for the first time in a long while, Finn is stumped. The thing's function and the strange discs it contains baffle him.

Face to the glass, Finn squints into the strange-looking machine. The painted words have decayed over the years, but he's able to read:

The Music Box Co.
Rahway, N.J.

It *is* a jukebox, or a predecessor of one. The huge metal disks are like giant CDs. It has to be very old. Finn finds himself wishing the Dillard were here; discovering that feeling interests him.

"I've got something," Willa says. She looks like a librarian in the oversize 3-D glasses. "Lower corner."

Amanda moves toward her and pulls her glasses down in front of her eyes. "Yup! It's tiny, but it's there."

Finn joins them, donning his glasses. A dime-size Osiris hieroglyph glows green, illuminating the black-and-white photo of a group of men in jackets and ties and women in dresses, all of whom hold shovels.

"That's Walt," Willa says, leaning in and gesturing toward the photo. "His wife, Lillian, and I think that's Marty Sklar, the Imagineer. I don't know the others."

The date behind the superimposed Osiris hieroglyph is 1957.

"The Dillard will be able to identify everyone. I'll get him."

Finn heads for the door, but he's only taken three steps when a girl's voice sounds. "You can't go out there."

Shocked, Finn jumps back, loses all clear, and smacks into the wall. Willa emits a partial scream, which she quickly muffles with her hand.

"Don't freak out!" The girl's voice speaks again.

And then she materializes, blocking the hallway to the door. Her jet-black hair cascades over her face, revealing one blue eye. She's wiry, high school age, wearing a red spandex suit, black shorts, and tall leather boots.

"Violet!" Willa says.

"Who?" Amanda asks, studying the young woman.

"From *The Incredibles*," Willa says. "She looks so—"

"Real? Well . . . yeah! I'm right here, you know?" Violet says. "And you are?"

"Finn," he says.

"I know your name, genius," Violet says. "I'm asking if you're human or . . . whatever-you-call-it."

"Whatever-you-call-it," Finn says.

"Which would be holograms," Willa adds. "We're holograms."

"It was you who lowered the chain on the stairs," Amanda says.

"Gold star," says Violet. "Though not for myself. And you are?"

"Amanda. I'm kind of a friend."

"Real or whatever-you-call-it?"

"Not real. More whatever-you-call-it."

Willa says, "If you didn't lower the chain for yourself, then who?"

"There's a friend of ours out there," Finn says simultaneously. "I need to get past you, please."

"If you go out that door, Finn," Violet says, "you will be eaten by Shere Khan."

"The tiger? He's out there?" Willa says.

Violet nods. "Shere Khan and Si on this side, Scar and Am on the other."

Amanda's eyes widen.

Willa's eyes narrow, and she asks, "And you know this how?"

"Really?" Violet says. "I come in here. I leave you a clue—the chain—and you think, what, I'm here to pass the time? I know this because I live here, Willa. I'm here because we characters are under instructions to help the Children of Light however we can, and I happened to be chasing down my little brother when I saw the kitty-litter crew surround this place. I got the little annoyance back to our parents, made myself invisible, and slipped inside. FYI: you walked right past *all* of them."

"Then why didn't they attack?" Willa asks.

"How should I know? Maybe they're waiting to see what you find."

"Thank you," Amanda says, shooting Willa a look. "We appreciate everything you and the others are doing to help us."

"Very much," Finn adds.

"Have you found what you came for?" Violet asks.

"We think so," Willa answers.

"No, you haven't," Violet says immediately, shaking her head.

"It might be faster," Amanda says, "if you didn't talk in riddles. We kind of have enough of those on our plate at the moment."

"I'm just measuring your intelligence," Violet says. "We hear about how you guys are always outwitting the Dark Ones, but I'm honestly not picking up a lot of that right now."

"Look. You didn't come here to warn us, or to protect us," Finn says. "You're assigned to protect whomever it is you lowered the chain for. After all, you could have stepped over it, no problem."

"That's better," Violet says.

"The white feather—the one I nearly inhaled," Willa says. "Daisy or Donald Duck."

"Very good!" Violet bows slightly. "But wrong, I'm sorry to say. The feathers are from her hand mirror."

"What hand mirror? Who . . . *her*?" stammers Finn.

But Willa doesn't hesitate. Spinning to the street side window, she practically shouts, "Oh . . . my—"

"You can get up," Violet says.

The stuffed Minnie is not stuffed. As it sits up, all three Keepers jump back—even Willa, who's speechless.

"Minnie Mouse?" Amanda gasps. "*The* Minnie Mouse?"

The tiny figure stands about four feet tall and is "So-o-o-o-o cute!" as Willa says.

Minnie claps her gloved hands appreciatively.

"Can you speak?" Willa asks, performing a half curtsy, though she's not sure why. A silence falls across the room.

"She didn't when she helped Amanda and me in the Magic

Kingdom," Finn says. He asks Amanda if she remembers. Amanda nods violently, starstruck.

"Through me she can speak," Violet says. She pauses, listens, and then speaks, apparently translating the mouse's words. "Minnie wants to thank you and your friends for your attempts to save the Kingdom."

"We're not done yet," Finn says.

Violet says, "Minnie wants you to know this: 'That which you seek will give everyone much comfort and happiness.'"

"Has she told you what that is?" Amanda asks.

"No. Think of me more as a bodyguard—or a bouncer, but with better hair." Violet stops again and seems to listen to the silence. "She says the person you are seeking foresaw the coming of the Children of Light."

"You're making this up!" Willa complains. "She can't possibly know—"

"Let me tell you something. When it comes to this place, Ms. Minnie pretty much knows all."

"I think we should listen," Finn says.

Violet nods, pauses. An enormous tear spills from Minnie's right eye. It splashes to the floor and pools; it looks like someone spilled a glass of water. Then Minnie points to her ear, and Violet speaks again. "'He told me, *It's up here.*'" Violet motions to her temple, the same way Minnie is doing. "'He was humming a tune. He kept pointing and repeating, *It's all up here.*'"

Minnie wipes away another brimming tear that threatens to fall. Her large eyes are fixed on the Keepers. Finn can't tell if it's hope or sorrow he sees in her gaze.

Violet continues to translate. "'He told me they wouldn't stop me, that I had to do it before it was too late. If he tried, they would follow him. That would ruin it all.'"

Violet looks at Minnie doubtfully and shakes her head, but Minnie isn't finished.

"Excuse me," Finn says to Minnie. "Who wouldn't stop you?"

Minnie smiles at Finn. Violet speaks for her, saying, "'I remember you, too. We . . . Pluto and I . . . helped you to get to the island.'"

Finn inhales sharply. He says aloud, "I love this place!"

"'I do, as well,'" Minnie says, still speaking through Violet.

"Your friend told you they wouldn't stop you. Who did he—"

"'The bank.'"

"Of course," Willa says.

Amanda shifts her eyes from Finn to Willa; she's lost.

"You tore it up," Finn says, "not the Overtakers."

Minnie smiles away her tears. "'He told me you would understand.'"

"The bank would let you in," Finn says, "because you're you."

Another smile. It needs no translation from Violet.

"So, are you guys going to tell me what's going on?" Violet says.

"No," Finn says. "We can't."

Minnie steps forward and hugs Finn. Only Finn.

Violet says softly, "'You are the next.'"

"Was that you or her?" Willa asks.

"Her," Violet says.

"Oh . . . my . . . gosh," Willa says softly to herself.

Minnie releases Finn.

"'I did as he asked,'" Violet says for Minnie. "'Of course I did. Just in time, as it turns out. The ghosts arrived and took it from me. Took it right out of the bank with everyone crouched in terror behind them.'"

426

"But not you," Finn says. *Wraiths*, he's thinking.

Minnie looks as if she might cry again. She shakes her head.

Violet says, "'I knew I would like you.'" In a more caustic tone, she adds, "For the record, that's all her, too."

"Surprise, surprise," says Willa.

Finn is transfixed by Minnie. For him, there's no one else in the room. He taps his head. "The *power* is all up here. It's in our heads."

"'I wish I knew,'" Minnie says through Violet. "'He tapped his head like that. *It's all up here*, he said.'"

"And he was humming," Amanda reminds everyone.

"'A pretty tune.'" Violet hums a lovely melody. When she stops, a brittle silence hangs in the room. No one wants to break it.

"Can we get you guys out of here now?" Violet asks. "And FYI, this is me again, not Minnie."

"'We?'" Willa repeats.

"You don't think I'm going to attempt this alone, do you? Bagheera and the Tramp are hiding outside, waiting."

"We have a friend named the Dillard out there as well."

"So what are we waiting for?" Violet asks.

"A plan?" Finn asks.

"Ah, yes," Violet smiles and tosses her shock of dark hair. "That would help."

45

THE CLOCK TOWER in Fantasyland wears several faces. Philby and the others inspect each one, a painstaking process that eats up precious time. Jess is once again lagging behind, but now Charlene stays with her, making Maybeck and Philby the group's investigators.

The two boys move on to Innoventions. Inside the sign is hidden yet another clock, which Philby is certain will reward them. It does not. No visible clues, with or without 3-D glasses. At last, the girls catch up to the boys.

"We do Town Hall in Toontown last," Philby says, "because I think we're all terrified of Toontown. Agreed?" No one objects, not even Maybeck. "Excellent. But . . . that leaves Small World."

"Oh joy," says Maybeck. "Not like we've had any problems there before."

Philby says, "The dolls come out every fifteen minutes like cuckoos. If Wayne's telling Finn, 'It's about time,' we can't exclude it."

"As long as we don't have to go inside," Charlene says. Philby nods, and turns to Jess.

"You okay?" he asks.

"Fine, thank you."

An instant later, Philby jumps and shouts, "Rat!"

Maybeck bunches his fists in a fighting pose, but the two girls have little or no reaction.

"That's not a rat," Charlene says, "I mean, of course it's a rat, but it's Remy. And the one next to him is Django. As in: *Ratatouille*."

Remy nods.

The girls move to meet the rat. The two boys aren't nearly as eager. Charlene and Jess kneel, and then squeal and coo about how cute Remy is. Playing to the crowd, the rat shakes Charlene's index finger with both paws.

"Can we save the Adventure Club for another visit?" Maybeck says.

Remy points, his long whiskers twitching toward Small World. He shakes his head violently, then waves in a different direction.

"He wants us to follow him!" squeals Charlene.

From the shadows a hundred rats of all sizes appear. Adorable rats, not scary ones, with big black eyes, long whiskers, lips twitching in rat-size smiles that show their two front teeth.

"An escort," says Charlene, delighted.

"Why can't we go that way?" Maybeck asks Remy.

Remy's eyebrows arch mysteriously.

"Overtakers," says Philby.

The rat nods.

"Satisfied?" Charlene asks.

At Remy's signal, his cousins, friends, and teammates surround the Keepers like a wave of brown water. The rats herd the group at a quick pace, containing them within their undulating shadow and offering a protective force field.

The route moves away from Fantasyland and past the Mad Tea Party toward the Matterhorn, then swings left in the direction of Small World. Remy leads them in an arc through the trees, and they pop out on the far side of the Small World pavilion. Here the parade starts, but the park ends.

"We need to see the front," Philby says in a whisper.

Remy's button nose twitches.

"One or two of us could sneak along the topiary," Charlene suggests. She gives Maybeck a look that indicates she's volunteering. "We reach the front and do what we have to without attracting attention."

"That would be me and you," Maybeck says.

"Correct," Philby says.

Jess is lost behind her own eyelids again. Charlene speaks gently to her. "Jess, you and Philby are going to wait for us with Remy and his friends in the trees."

Eyes shut, Jess nods faintly. "An oval and a spiral. Chains." Her eyes pop open. She starts to draw in the dirt. "Did I say something?"

"Yes," Philby says. "I didn't like the last part."

"It's near here. It only happened as we got closer." Her sketch looks like a rifle sight: a large circle with a pin at its center.

"No offense, but we're wasting time," Maybeck says. He signals Charlene. "Ready?"

"I'll wear the 3-D glasses," she says, "even though they make me dizzy. You never know."

"I'll be your Seeing Eye dog." Maybeck has a way of being inappropriate without trying; Charlene smiles wryly at him. Then they crouch, cross the path, and steal into the shadows of the topiary trees, all carved and trimmed into geometric shapes. One is shaped like an upside-down teardrop, another like a cube.

As they pass beneath another, Charlene hisses for Maybeck to stop. She points to a stone in the ground.

"The eye," Charlene says. "From the photo! It's on that rock."

Maybeck inspects the stone closely. The simple ideogram of an eye carved on its surface—nearly identical to the hieroglyph—looks old and faded, but it's still unmistakable.

"You think it's under the rock?"

"One way to find out." Maybeck tries to move the carved stone, but it won't budge. He and Charlene start digging. After a second, Charlene stops.

"Come on!" Maybeck says encouragingly.

"We know better diggers," Charlene says, and whistles. Remy's nose pokes out from behind a tree. A minute later, two dozen rats are moving earth from all four sides of the stone like a machine. Dirt flies into symmetrical piles. In concert with their efforts, Maybeck shoves and wrestles the stone until it comes free.

Remy alone digs at the bottom of the exposed hole. His efforts are careful, so as not to tear a piece of paper should he encounter it.

"A little deeper," Maybeck says.

Django tugs on Charlene's pant leg.

"What is it, little friend?" she says.

Django clearly wants her to follow him, and she does. They dart across the path and look back at the topiary trees. Django turns. Charlene turns. He gestures with his head. Charlene has no idea what he's trying to tell her.

Sighing, Django fixes all four of his feet on the ground, lifts his right front paw, bent at the elbow, and then stretches and lifts his nose; his long tail goes as straight as a sipping straw. He's imitating a setter—a pointer dog.

Charlene looks, sees nothing but tiny amounts of dirt escaping the deep hole across the path. Then it occurs to her: lie down at the rat's level, and look up. The greenery of the tree they face, the one beneath which the rats have been digging, is carefully shaped into topiary like a giant doughnut, its leaves and branches curved into a wide circle with a large hole at the center.

"Oh, how pretty," she tells Django, annoyed that he has distracted her for this, but trying not to show it.

The rat shakes its tiny head back and forth.

"No?" Charlene studies the tree again. "It *is* pretty," she says.

If the rat shakes his head any harder, he will snap his neck.

Like a camera focusing, Charlene looks *through* the hole, allowing the tree to act as a round picture frame. In the middle of the frame she sees a twisting metal sculpture on the top of a spire that reminds her of the image Jess described.

"Terry!" Charlene calls.

Maybeck hurries across, wary of showing himself. Charlene points. He sucks in a sharp breath.

"We won't know until we check," Maybeck says, but she can see him nodding.

"We're supposed to *see*, to look from that spire," Charlene says.

"You're going to climb Small World," he says, doubtfully.

"I am."

* * *

The idea is for the Keepers and the Dillard to act as a decoy out back while Minnie uses the front stairs to access the street and Walt Disney's secret door into the Disneyland Fire Department. Once there, she can wait and then move effortlessly to safety.

Finn checks with Willa and Amanda. "You realize the need for all clear?" The girls nod. "In the face of a tiger attack."

432

They look troubled, and their nodding slows. "Si will probably go for our eyes," Finn says.

"Up our backs and over our heads," says Willa, "like in the wild. The tiger will go for our Achilles tendons or our necks."

"I can stop them," Amanda says.

"I hope so!" says Finn. "Without you this would be a suicide mission."

"But only once. I won't have the strength after that."

"The Jungle Cruise is behind us," Finn says.

"Yeah, and the tigers happen to call that home," says Willa. "We'll need a better plan."

"The Dillard can help. He should be able to access maps and lead us through the Jungle. Both the Treehouse and Pirates are almost directly behind us. Both were built or were being built when Walt was still around. Even before it opened, Pirates had become his favorite. Where better to hide something than where there's already buried treasure?"

"Don't worry about the tiger," Violet says, patting Minnie's shoulder and moving to join the group. "I can be really annoying."

"You'll want to stay close to us until Amanda does her thing," Finn warns. "Whatever."

Violet's hair obscures so much of her face that it's a wonder she can see. "If anything were to happen to you . . ." she says to Minnie, who places her hands on either side of her own round cheeks and shakes her head. Her expression says that Violet's being silly. "If anything happens, Minnie, Bagheera is just outside on the sidewalk. I'm not a big animal freak, but I'm thinking a panther pretty much scares the tar out of a tiger."

Minnie nods and pats Violet on the head.

"Be safe," Amanda says to Minnie, who blows her a kiss.

Violet opens the apartment's front door. The Keepers

watch Minnie go, each reeling from the intoxicating effect of having been in the presence of real Disney royalty.

Pulling themselves together, they gather at the back door as tightly as they can. Finn plays the role of captain, bringing up the rear. Willa opens the door and they proceed in order: Willa, Violet, Amanda, Finn. They slither across the metal fire escape walkway and over the flat roof, moving toward the stairs.

"Duck!" Amanda shouts.

Finn dives and reaches for her ankles, holding on for dear life.

Amanda pushes, throwing a force field directly at the charging tiger. Shere Khan lifts off his paws and is airborne, as if pulled up into a tornado. The tiger flips head over tail, a tumbling circus cat, and slams into the roof, sliding down, semiconscious.

Si, a Siamese cat, comes from the side, launching herself at Amanda. Finn, having lost his all clear, floats in midair, held only by his grip on Amanda's ankles. Out of the corner of his eye, he sees the darting cat and warns Amanda at the last second.

She strikes the cat as if hitting a tennis backhand, diverting Si around and past her. The cat lands on all fours.

Willa is already down the ladder. Finn lets go, gripping the metal banister, and Amanda follows. Then Finn rolls, throws his feet over, and finds the rungs with his toes.

Shere Khan is treading with both front paws, his head held low, haunches flexed, preparing to spring. The big cat's front claws tear loose shingles, rip free entire boards. His wild yellow-and-black eyes are the size of beach balls.

Finn stops. There's not time to get lower on the stairs; he's exposed from the waist up. He closes his eyes, exhales in

434

a steady stream, and searches the resulting blackness for a pin-prick of light. As he opens his eyes, Shere Khan sails through the air, snapping his white-toothed jaws shut on Finn's neck. Finn is eye to eye with the beast; he can see his own face reflected in the curve of the cat's corneas.

Failing to gain a purchase on the landing, Shere Khan begins to fall, no man-child caught between his jaws.

Finn punches the cat with an uppercut to the windpipe as, letting go, he swings one-handed off the ladder. Loosening his hold, he slides like a fireman down the handrail. His panic makes him whole again, and when Si drops like a hat onto his head and sinks his claws into Finn's eyebrows, Finn cries out. Shaking his head instinctively, Finn bonks the cat against the stairway handrail, once again flinging Si off. Just as he is about to crash onto the bottom stairs, Finn's own fall is cushioned by Amanda and Willa.

"Thanks for the warning light," Finn says to the Dillard.

"But I did not give you the signal," the Dillard replies.

"Never mind," Finn says. They'll work on sarcasm later. His mind flashes to the music box from Rahway, New Jersey; if only they'd had time to investigate further. But they didn't. Finn refocuses, saying, "We need to get through the Jungle Cruise to reach Tarzan's Treehouse. You'll lead, so run fast."

"I'll take second, to protect him," Violet says.

"Done."

They take off at a run. The Dillard actually has to slow down to allow them to catch up.

"Funny thing," Finn tells Amanda, the two running alongside one another. "Dillard—the Dillard I knew, I mean—was not exactly an athlete. Slow doesn't begin to describe him."

"I heard that!" the Dillard calls back. His image sparks and sputters, as do those of the others; the jungle interferes with DHI projections. Only Violet remains entirely herself.

"Just FYI," she calls back, "you guys are freaky."

"Wait till you meet the rest of them," Amanda says. "Us!" she corrects, and gives Finn a smile. "I still can't get used to that."

"You're doing fine," he tells her. "Just fine. It's us we need to worry about."

* * *

Ever impetuous, Charlene puts her climbing skills to use before consulting Philby or Jess. Maybeck sees it all go down, but is unable to stop her because of a slight distraction. Or not so slight: skeletons—in chains.

They're first spotted by Jess, who's hiding in the trees. Her reaction to an army of bones, some bound by rusty chains, some swinging the links at their sides like whips, is pure terror.

Where they may have come from no one knows. For Maybeck, they appear like something out of a zombie movie. There's no clatter of bone on bone, no creaking or cracking, only the singing of chains and the distinctive rattle and scrape of bony feet on the pavers. The sound is repetitive, like drumming with chopsticks on the edge of a table.

The skeletons aren't fast, but they aren't slow, either. Something about their motion is hypnotic, their approach mesmerizing; it stuns and freezes their prey. Maybeck wills his feet to move—*Run!*—but they disobey. The chains continue to spin, to blur and purr and chew their way through the warm night air like airplane propellers. Here we go, he thinks.

But now the rats emerge as fast as a quickly spreading plague, out around Maybeck, up the spindly legs of the

436

skeletons, ascending a pelvis, shinnying up a spinal column, and plunging their muzzles into eye sockets. Down go a few of the walking dead, colliding and tripping, crashing and splintering. When they fall, they come apart like toppled Lego sculptures.

At last free to think, Maybeck hoists the stone marker and holds it outstretched between his hands like a barbell. Its weight deflects the first spinning chain. The second wraps around the stone, which Maybeck releases, its weight pulling the approaching skeleton off to the side and allowing Maybeck to kick its legs out from under it. Again, the cacophonous percussion of two hundred bones scattering.

The rats, meanwhile, have put meat on the bones, covering the skeletons, bringing them down with their furry weight. As one falls, another is attacked. The marionette strings are cut, the dancing done. Maybeck dispatches three more before a remaining skeleton lifts one arm high, a signal to the few that remain standing to retreat and withdraw.

* * *

Charlene sees the approach of the skeletons and holds on tightly, transfixed by the aerial view of battle, believing in her heart of hearts that the skeletons are meant for her, that by her climbing, she has unleashed a darker spirit that intends to stop her.

Charged with new determination, she makes her way up the final few feet to the spire's pointed tip. A golden cone of coiled metal beckons. On a lightning rod ball mounted to the spiral is engraved the all-seeing eye from the hieroglyph.

"Yes!" Charlene cries.

She's impossibly high up, with no rope or net to catch her should she fall. Her fingertips hook a piece of tin fashioned like an Elizabethan collar below the golden spiral. There, inside the coil, standing like a sentry, is a small Mickey Mouse crafted of cast iron, rusted and pockmarked, welded to the metal beneath it. Its tiny mouse hand points decisively into the park, aiming at the carousel.

Charlene's heartbeat quickens. She has climbed to a great height, but it's not the altitude that excites her. She hugs the pointed peak of the spire and scans all of Disneyland, spread out below her like a glistening magical carpet: Sleeping Beauty Castle, the Matterhorn in all its magnificence, Main Street, the white spired roof of Space Mountain, the red rock of Big Thunder Mountain Railroad—all places she has been on an opposite coast, on another quest. In another life.

Swinging her head this way and that, over her shoulder and around the spire, Charlene absorbs as much of the view as possible. Whether it was put here by Wayne or Walt Disney himself, the miniature Mickey is no simple discovery. Combined with the piece of the Osiris hieroglyph discovered below, it has to mean something. It's a clue. Quite literally: a pointer, directing the Keepers toward the southwest, a vast section of the park. Too vast.

The pavement below is littered with the bones of fallen skeleton soldiers, and a swarm of rodents is moving like a stretching amoeba back toward Maybeck's solitary form. Charlene can't budge or remove the Mickey, no matter how hard she tries; the other Keepers will have to believe her. Working herself around to a position behind the miniature, she sights down his pointing arm. It is not pointing toward the horizon, the way a conquering general's arm might be. Instead, it is lowered a few degrees, pointing down toward a large boulder on Big Thunder Mountain Railroad. Charlene memorizes the location and begins to make her way down.

438

This can't be a coincidence, she tells herself, charged with excitement. But as she descends, a nagging question eats away at her. It was left there, sure. But for whom?

Charlene's whole body trembles; she's suddenly exhausted, and she holds on more tightly. The feeling grows inside her, as if the very earth is shaking. She fights off fear, knowing it will weaken her all the more. She is her own enemy, fighting a battle within to remain all clear. She wonders, as Finn has before her, if the betrayal the Keepers were warned of was internal, if the enemy within has nothing to do with a spy and everything to do with self-control, the ability to overcome and contain fear.

In a few seconds, her trembling ceases. The descent goes smoothly; she meets up with Maybeck and the others and, escorted by Remy, Django, and their fellow four-legged friends, the group makes for Big Thunder Mountain Railroad.

As they're walking, Philby says, "I'm so glad you could hold on."

"You're a climber, too," Charlene says. "It wasn't that hard."

"I meant during the tremor. The whole park shook. You didn't feel it?"

"I felt it!" Charlene looks over at the spires of Small World, wondering if the purpose of that tremor had been to cause her to fall—to her death.

46

THE DILLARD'S DATABASE identifies the locations of three rescue boats on the Jungle Cruise. He leads Finn and the girls to the nearest one and they nearly make it before Shere Khan catches up.

"It's no good!" Willa calls out. "Not going to make it."

"Yes, we will!" Violet hollers. "I'll catch you later!"

As the Dillard leads the group to the left, Violet shifts right and stands her ground.

Finn looks back in time to see her turn invisible just as the leaping tiger is about to land on her. Shere Khan flies into a patch of prickle bushes and lets out a roar of pain.

The Dillard is in the small skiff, sitting there like a schoolmarm. Finn unties the boat and pushes off as Amanda and Willa climb in.

As Shere Khan recovers, Violet tauns him. She takes off at a run, leading him in the opposite direction, and out of sight.

"The tree house?" Willa says. "Sure, we're looking for connections to the throne icon in the Osiris hieroglyph. Sure, an Egyptian throne *may* have been made of wood, and a tree is also made of wood. I heard the Dillard's percentage stuff, but this kingdom has so many princes and princesses, dozens of characters with thrones. Has the Dillard factored that in? This seems so . . . lame."

The Dillard hears a question and answers. "The percentage chance that a connection exists between—"

"Pause!" Finn addresses his group. "The Dillard initially

put Swiss Family Robinson second on his list. Now it's called Tarzan's Treehouse. It's a big tree that could have 'grown up around' a box or container that holds the hidden piece of the Mickey illustration. Look, it has to be an older attraction, right? This tree was here early on. Maybe the people in that photograph were breaking ground for—"

"No way!" Willa says. "That photo was dated 1957. Right, Amanda?"

Amanda looks pained but nods.

Finn bites his tongue, fighting down feelings of stupidity, and says, "Resume." He's feeling bad about pausing the Dillard. "What are the current odds of Overtaker presence in the Tarzan attraction?"

"Oh, really!" says Willa.

"Should I factor in the previous encounter?"

"Yes," Finn says. "And then compare the normal likelihood to the current likelihood, please."

"There is currently an eighty-eight-point-six percent chance of Disney villain presence in the Tarzan tree. During normal hours of operation, that is . . . zero-point-seven percent. The difference is more than one hundred times greater."

Finn addresses Willa. "If the threat's a hundred times greater than usual, there's a matching chance of our finding something of value here."

"Thrones, Finn. Thrones."

"Tarzan was king of the jungle," Finn says.

"Don't give me that. This didn't become the Tarzan attraction until long after Walt Disney was gone."

"Willa, you can search where you want. I won't stop you. Amanda, are you good, going with Willa?"

Again, Amanda looks pained to leave Finn, but again, she nods. "Sure."

"We'll split up. We're still in pairs."

"You're not. You're paired with a projection. The Dillard may be smart, but he can't help you in a battle. You're basically flying solo." Willa looks worried.

"Finn," Amanda pleads.

"You two check out the princesses. It's worth a look. Don't forget to use the glasses."

"Where do we meet?" Amanda sounds desperate.

"Pirates," Willa says. "Third on the Dillard's list."

"Is that a question?" asks the Dillard.

"I definitely need a break from this guy," Willa says.

"Pirates, then." Finn eyes the stairs at the base of the Tarzan tree, feeling the heart inside his partial hologram beat faster, as if trying to convince him that he's human.

The girls are off, Amanda looking back at Finn no fewer than four times.

"Okay, Dillard, we're looking for the hidden piece of Mickey. It's inside something, and it could be as a small as a thimble or as large as a trunk. Help me find it, please. Also, listen and look for any sign of active Disney villains and warn me the moment you detect them. Do you understand?"

The Dillard repeats Finn's instructions, putting them in formal language that sounds more appropriate to a military intelligence operation.

"If I come under attack, you will plot the most effective escape route and the best defense, and you'll stay by my side, advising me. Got it?"

Again, the Dillard repeats the instructions.

"You're good to have around, Dillard," Finn says.

"Is that a question?"

"Never mind."

As he starts up the stairs, Finn can't get Miley Cyrus's

"The Climb" out of his head. The song's a guilty pleasure, one he'd never confess to his friends. He's put the Dillard behind him—Finn wants to lead, and this reminds him of Wayne in ways he'd rather forget.

His grief has turned to anger. Wayne deserted him when Finn needed him most. He wonders if this was the betrayal Wayne himself warned of, if there's some irony he's supposed to take away from his mentor's death. It seems selfish of the old Imagineer to abandon the Keepers, his creations. Granted, his sacrifice had a purpose, yet Finn can't find it in his heart to forgive him. Not yet. Despite being surrounded by his best friends, he feels so alone. It's like the time the Overtakers brainwashed his mother, but somehow worse, because there's no hope. The hole inside him is deep and dark. Wayne had no right to push him to its edge.

The Dillard announces, "There are seven possible hiding places on the tree trunk. Most are intended as knotholes or woodpecker holes, and are small two-inch wide indentations recessed two to four inches deep. The largest is seventeen inches wide and is located near the top of the tree."

"Where did you find this out?"

"A posting on the Web site www-dot-w-d-w-radio-dot-com."

"Do you have access to any information about renovations done on the tree in the four months prior to Walt Disney's death?"

"Searching," the Dillard says.

The boys continue to climb. Finn's in no hurry, given the high likelihood of encountering OTs.

"There were limited modifications during the conversion to Tarzan's Treehouse."

They slowly work their way up the stairs.

"Would Walt Disney have been alive to see the tree?"

"Yes, it is one of the early attractions, along with the Tiki Room and this, the Jungle Cruise."

"All right then," Finn mutters. He spots a knot-hole in the tree and inspects it. Empty. "I don't see how it could be in one of these without being found a long time ago."

They pass Sabor, a painted lioness, poised to strike. Finn keeps an eye on the creature, whose menacing look cuts him deeply. He thinks back to a time when he wouldn't have given the image a second thought, a time when he was considerably younger and the Disney parks were a source of pure amusement and joy. How things have changed. He's not merely suspicious of inanimate objects like the Sabor, he anticipates trouble. He plans for it. Finn is realizing, perhaps too late, that he and the Dillard have entered what could be a perfect trap. There is only up and down, no alternate exists.

"Dillard, monitor the big cat."

"Are you referring to the sculpture we passed?"

"The same," Finn says.

"I request additional input."

"You aren't anything like Dillard."

"Is that a question?"

Finn sighs. "Monitor the cat for movement. Eyes. Breathing. Anything."

"It was crafted in 1999 of fiberglass. The sculptor was—"

"Looks can be deceiving," Finn says, interrupting him.

"I am familiar with that expression."

"Monitor . . . the . . . cat."

"I detect hostility in your voice."

"If anything moves anywhere around us, I want to know about it."

"The bougainvillea three yards from the base of the tree—"

444

"Anything threatening. Anything that might . . ." It's difficult to explain to a computer that vines can turn into snakes and sculptures into animals. Finn would have to reprogram the computer's logic, teach it to anticipate the illogical. He and the other Keepers live in a world where the rules have been rewritten, a world so outside the accepted parameters of human experience that it sounds unreasonable to other people, even crazy. And for a computer like the Dillard, it simply does not compute.

Finn senses the possibility the tree offers; it was built at a time when Walt would have had access; it's an iconic attraction; best of all, it fits well with the Osiris myth. He's on the lookout for a hidden door, a seam he might pry open to reveal a box, a jar. A piece of paper torn from a masterpiece.

The encounter with Minnie left his head spinning—her claim that she tore up the original illustration on instructions from Mickey, her reference to Mickey's pointing at his head. Each time the Keepers think they know something, they're challenged to rethink it. Facts reinvent themselves; stories are rewritten. The uncertainty that goes with being a Keeper pushes him to want to give up, to surrender to the external forces, but he hasn't given in yet, and he's not sure why.

They reach a landing where some of Tarzan's furnishings are on display. Finn studies each item carefully, knowing the best place to hide something is often in the open. How clever it would be to put the thirteenth piece inside a pepper shaker or coconut. But the transition between Swiss Family Robinson and Tarzan's Treehouse was decades after Walt's time in the parks. It is foolish of Finn to be wasting his time here.

Returning his attention to the tree—the all-important tree!—he sees the Dillard half-turned, transfixed.

"Dillard, what is it?"

"Technically, I do not have eyes in the back of my head. However, I am able to simultaneously monitor up to eight security cameras, or to put all the cameras into a rolling view."

"I don't need an owner's manual," Finn says.

"Humor," the Dillard says. "I detect motion in camera A-37. Camera A-37's view is below us, encompassing the lower stairs and the Sabor statue you instructed me to monitor. Eye motion was detected in the Sabor forty-six seconds ag—" He holds up a finger, interrupting himself. "Motion detected in front right paw. Motioned detected in front left paw."

Finn looks into the tree's green canopy. He pushes back the tendrils of terror wrapping around his legs, slowing him down, climbing and twisting higher through his hologram. He's flooded with the poison; his DHI sputters and spits photons like a Fourth of July sparkler. He's lost all clear when he can least afford to. It has happened more often since Wayne's death, forcing him to face that his grieving is not over; his emotions are winning the battle within him.

"Dillard, is there a way to slow the cat? To stop it?"

"Processing. A body of water. A tranquilizing gun. A net. A pit trap."

"Here. On this attraction!"

"Bow and arrow, twenty-six steps from your current location. A vine, six meters. A chest of drawers and vanity, two ladder-back chairs, and a table at the next landing."

"Got it," Finn says. "Keep up with me. When the cat charges, stand your ground. Hold it back if you can." The Dillard, being only projected light, cannot be injured. The Sabor doesn't know that.

"Understood."

"Can you find me if we separate?"

"Affirmative."

446

"Hold off the Sabor, and find me." Finn is feeling winded. His blue glow has lessened to a fine line, suggesting he is more his human self than a hologram. The activity of the climb and the panic caused by the big cat rattles him. He needs a few seconds to steady himself, a few seconds when he's not consumed by self-defensiveness and fear.

He checks behind him. The Dillard has stopped and turned, facing the Sabor as it slinks around the tree. The cat stops, tongue hanging wetly from its maw. Finn ascends, losing sight of the Dillard, whose presence has stopped the cat, buying Finn some needed time.

How much time, Finn has no way of knowing.

47

A KISS CHANGES EVERYTHING.

As the knowledge that she climbed the Small World spire in the middle of an earthquake sinks in, Charlene drops to her knees and kisses solid ground in front of Philby, Jess, Maybeck, and the rats.

A plane flies overhead on final approach, lights blinking on its wingtips. The lights are reflected on the ground in front of Charlene, off a faint, thin, shiny smear in the shape of an elongated *S*. Charlene presses her cheek to the pavement, sighting along the *S* in both directions.

"Are you okay?" Maybeck asks, his outline glowing a vibrant blue. He is tall and strong, entirely all clear. She feels safe with him close by.

"I'm not sure," she says.

"Charlie!" he drops to a knee. "Are you hurt?"

For all his rough-and-tumble persona, Maybeck has a thoughtful, caring side that Charlene loves. She attributes it to his Aunt Bess, one of the sweetest, most generous women Charlene has ever known.

"It's not me. I'm fine!"

"We shouldn't stay out in the open like this," Philby says.

"Wait!" Charlene makes sure Maybeck is paying attention as she points out the residual slime line on the pavement. "Snake."

Maybeck takes note. "But snakes aren't slimy. That's a myth. They look slimy, they can feel slimy, but they're dry."

448

"Not if they just came out of the wet grass," Charlene says, walking him along the line she has sighted.

"Maybe there was spilled ice cream in the grass," Philby says.

"Or suntan lotion or something," Jess adds.

"But the track dries out," Charlene says. "And it points that way." She gestures into the far distance, toward Casey Jr.

"So there's a snake in Disneyland," Philby says. "Big deal. It's California, Charlene."

"Terry," Charlene says, "put your head down on the path."

"Oh, come on."

"That's right, *come on*. Just do it."

Maybeck debates arguing with her. He kneels.

"All the way down."

"Why?"

"I'm waiting, Terry."

Maybeck flattens his cheek on the blacktop. "Satisfied?"

"Look directly up the snake line, like you're sighting along a sort of curving arrow. Good. Now look up, ever so slowly."

Maybeck's eyes move—and he freezes. He raises and lowers his head repeatedly. Charlene smiles.

"Now are you interested?" she asks.

"So this has nothing to do with the snake."

"We won't know until we get there," Charlene tells Maybeck.

"Where?" Philby asks, staring curiously at the ground.

Charlene is about to speak, but it's Jess who answers. "There!" she says. She stands slightly away from the others, as she often does. Jess, the ephemeral spirit, reluctant to speak, to join in, a bit of the wounded-bird look to her powerful eyes. Her pale skin is more like kitchen cling wrap, her formerly grandmother-white hair now red as that of a classic

Irish lass. Jess, the girl who remained Maleficent's prisoner for an unhealthy amount of time, the young woman captured and kept from all contact in a solitary space within Disney's Animal Kingdom. She doesn't ask for pity but seems deserving of it.

And the others follow her now without question. Jess and Charlene lead Maybeck and Philby on a short walk to the far side of Fantasyland, where Jess points up along a closed-off path with her thin hologram arm and delicate wrist.

"There's a building up there," Maybeck says. "You could see its roofline from back by Small World. It looks like a ski chalet or something. Who knows what it is actually? Wish we had the Dillard with us."

"Hey, I know!" Philby says defensively. "It's the Skyway Station. There used to be a tram here, like a gondola in the park."

"My dream. My sketch," Jess says. "I drew a ski lift. A gondola."

"Like that. Yes," Philby says.

"So what now?" Jess inquires. She has a knack for actually saying what everyone else is thinking.

Philby takes a long look at Jess, unable to dismiss her past history with both Maleficent and the Overtakers. Charlene saw something, sure, but it is Jess who has led them directly to this place. It's always been obvious why the OTs want Jess. Her ability to foresee the future is a powerful tool; her sketched dreams have repeatedly helped the Keepers steer clear of trouble or solve a puzzle. And she's close to Amanda, whose telekinetic power has saved the Keepers multiple times.

Philby has not forgotten about the repeated warning of an "enemy within." The Keepers don't discuss it much, but it hangs over them nonetheless. Jess could just as easily be a candidate as any of the rest of them. Philby adopts an extra-cautious stance as they approach. Is it impossible that Jess might betray the Keepers? Philby wonders. Maybe it's only as impossible as becoming a hologram in your sleep or dreaming parts of a future you've already been told will happen.

Philby studies Maybeck, who's clearly all in with the discovery of the Skyway Station. He looks ready to climb the hill and flush out the Overtakers. Charlene also looks hungry for battle. Gone is the L.A. actress; Charlie's back to being a misplaced cheerleader eager to justify time away from the gym. She wants—needs—to prove something about her ridiculously good looks, her physical abilities and her oft-overlooked brainpower. Rarely the young woman others believe she is, there are times like this when she rises to an occasion, when the brightness of her blue outline creates an aura of stark determination around her. She wants to get started.

"We wait," Philby says.

"Excuse me?" Maybeck reacts irritably, his chest swelling, eyebrows arching. Remy and Django also offer upraised noses, inquisitive expressions. The rest of their kind follow, surrounding the Keepers with expectant faces, and Philby finds himself the center of attention.

"What if the OTs are up there?" Philby says. "What if they're counting on us exploring? We'd be walking straight into a trap, like the zip line on the cruise." Philby keeps one eye on Jess, watching for her reaction. If she's against his plan, she doesn't show it. Why this makes him all the more suspicious of her, he doesn't understand.

* * *

The Dillard displays no fear because he has none. His hologram's "personality" is not programmed for fear, anxiety, remorse, or affection—human qualities difficult, if not impossible, to translate into computer code.

Instead, he makes eye contact with the Sabor and drops playfully into a prone position. The Sabor cants its head in curiosity, its animosity challenged. Its eyes brighten, its blood-lust gone. The Dillard rolls to the railing, like a cub playing. He covers his head with his hands and the distracted Sabor gently paws him, claws retracted.

A paw swipes through the Dillard, and the Sabor drops to its belly, engaged. It tries again; and again, nothing. The claws extend, the cat's expression now one of frustration. It goes after the Dillard repeatedly, one paw, the other, maddened by the lack of contact, increasingly aggressive and hostile.

The Dillard's internal counter has recorded eleven seconds since engaging with the big cat. The Dillard eyes the railing, rising to his knees. The Sabor's hackles rise as it lurches back on its haunches, obviously threatened. The Dillard's hologram passes through the railing and jumps. The cat leaps but misjudges the height and takes a bad fall.

Thirteen . . . fourteen . . . fifteen . . .

The Imagineers did not program pride, but the Dillard is a fast learner.

* * *

Higher up in the Tarzan tree, spying a sapling close to the railing that might bend under his weight and serve as a kind of express elevator—going down—Finn rushes to an extended landing that functions as a balcony. As he is about to take the leap, he looks back for the cat and sees instead a wink of golden light above one of the branches overhead, just out of reach.

With one leg poised to climb out over the railing, Finn

452

stops, his muscles willing but his brain refusing. He fights his own instincts, trying to ignore the golden wink, but he can't. Finn returns to the tree and jumps for the branch. Too high. Looking around, he sees what looks like a treasure chest wedged against the main trunk nearby. He drags it over to serve as a step stool. On tiptoe, he thrills at what he discovers: a hieroglyphic eye made of fine golden wire embedded in the tree bark. A great workman must have installed it; judging by the streaks of sap that leak like snail trails below the inlay. The symbol has weathered decades. Its placement is surely no accident.

Finn looks for any sort of hiding place for the missing piece of Mickey. The connection between the Osiris myth's missing thirteenth piece and the wood of the throne in the complete hieroglyph encourages him. He jumps and grabs a branch immediately above, pulling himself up just as the drumming of heavy cat paws rises like a chorus behind him.

Finn's hologram can't experience an adrenaline rush, but he feels the pulse of associated heat flooding his veins and again struggles to maintain all clear, cursing himself for not letting go of Wayne's tragic death. Not a good time to have an up-close-and-personal encounter with a Sabor bent on defending its realm.

Riding the tree limb like a saddle, Finn brings his legs up in time to avoid the fangs of the roaring Sabor. The beast snaps at air, falls, rights itself, and leaps again.

Finn looks down at the trunk he used as a stool, hoping beyond hope that the Sabor lacks common sense. But no. The cat springs up onto the chest as fluidly as rushing water.

Clinging on for dear life, Finn scoots away from the snapping jaws and comes face-to-face with a golden arrow. He concentrates and feels his limbs tingle—a good sign!—as he tries to work out the location to which it points. The tree limb he's standing on narrows quickly. He dares not venture much farther out. There's no sign of a trapdoor or hiding place. So why the arrow?

The answer comes in a burst of joy. Only Walt Disney or Wayne could have thought up such a clue! The synthetic leaves on the tree limb erupt in a sea of green, some large, some small—and some *missing*. The branch ends as if had been broken years before. From below, it would look like a gnarly, storm-bitten stump, two dead twigs extending like skeletal fingers. From above, the wounded bark looks exactly like three knuckles, a thumb, and an index finger pointing into the distance. Finn sights down the length of the branch, ignoring the Sabor's increasingly loud growls. He follows the line to the end of the extended index finger that points due north and he marks in his mind's eye the same directional line on the ground below.

Thrilled by his discovery, Finn spins around on the branch. The Sabor's wet nose is close enough for him to make out its leathery texture. The cat's mouth opens wide, spit flying as it roars.

"Hold on tight!"

It's Amanda's voice. Finn knows what's coming. Lacing his fingers around the tree limb, he wraps his legs tight as well and locks his ankles. The leaves invert, their silver undersides bent into the shape of a thousand funnels as the force of Amanda's telekinetic push hits both Finn and the Sabor, throwing the cat off the limb. Two claws remain stuck in the fabricated bark, separated from their owner.

As the Sabor lands below, it returns to its sculpted form, perhaps as a result of being removed from its domain. Amanda and Willa follow the Dillard, who's waiting below, up the stairs and reach Finn as he lowers himself to the main trunk and climbs down.

He sights the direction indicated by the broken tree limb one last time, and then turns as Amanda and Willa throw their arms around him. The three celebrate with a hug.

"Let's get out of here!" Finn cries, leading the way down the stairs.

The Dillard is prattling on about something to do with "seventeen seconds," but Finn barely hears, his mind overcome with his discovery. He takes deep breaths to restore his calm, and hopefully, his all clear.

"Jess needs us," Amanda says.

"Not now," Finn says, determined to pursue the golden arrow.

"Yes, now!" Amanda declares, with unusual firmness.

Her tone stops the three others.

"How could you possibly know that?" Finn asks.

"Why would you have to even ask me?" she counters.

Willa says, "Easy, you two! Seriously, Finn."

He describes his discovery of the partial hieroglyph and the golden arrow in a heated voice.

"Whatever it is," Willa says, "it's been there a long time. It isn't going anywhere."

Finn looks back to the Tarzan Treehouse, then into the girls' faces and the Dillard's holographic eyes. "Okay," he says. "I suppose you can tell us where to find her."

"Do I know, exactly? No. But she's somewhere in that direction." Amanda points. Finn's about to make a sarcastic comment when the ground shakes beneath their feet—a second tremor.

"We'd better hurry," he says.

48

THE REUNION OF THE KEEPERS takes place in a copse of trees with a view of Casey Jr. Remy, Django, and a dozen of their relatives find Finn and company, and, on orders from Philby, lead them back to Philby's group, which now includes hundreds more of Remy's kin.

As they meet up, all the Keepers begin to talk over one another while the Dillard looks on. The Dillard then demonstrates a particular aspect of his upgrade: the ability to record conversation and recite it like a script, so that when Finn asks Philby, "What'd you just say?" it isn't Philby but the Dillard who answers.

Then, prompted by Finn, the Dillard recites the other conversations, word for word.

"Incredible," Finn says.

"Unavoidable," Philby says, tugging Finn away. "It's amazing he can do that, yes. But think about it. He can record *everything we say.*" Finn stares at him, silent.

"Why would they program him like that? Why would the Imagineers add a ton of code to the Dillard's program, enabling him to record multiple conversations?"

"Oh, come on! Talk about paranoid!"

"I heard you ask a question, and I heard the Dillard answer. Honestly, I'm not sure we're supposed to know he has that ability."

"You can't be serious."

Philby's nodding. "He's spying on us, Finn. He's recording—

probably with video, too—everything we're doing. Transmitting in real time would be my guess. The Cryptos knew you'd keep him around. They played you. Played us!"

"You make it sound so . . . devious."

"It is!"

"We don't know that! And even if it's true, what if it's to protect us? Give them eyes and ears so they can bail us out or return us if we're in trouble."

Philby rolls his tongue in his mouth, chewing on the idea. Then he shakes his head, never breaking eye contact with Finn. "'The enemy within.'"

Finn sucks air. "No."

"Yes. All it takes is one bad Crypto with access to the Dillard and the OTs know everything we do—everything we even talk about doing. Wayne said we'd be sabotaged, didn't he?"

"This is crazy."

"Finn, sabotage is done to a *thing*: a machine, a building, a road. Not to people, not to a group. Why did Wayne use that particular word? And what makes it so impossible? The Dillard's your best friend."

"And I killed him."

"I didn't mean that! I mean he's the last person we'd suspect. Remember what Wayne said: 'Suspect everyone. Trust no one.'"

"Who can live that way? That's insane!"

"It's war, Finn."

"Do you trust any of us?" Finn counters angrily. "That's poison, Philby. You're poisoning us!"

"Am I?" Philby steps back, returns to the group, and raises his hand for silence. "Look at him. Find out what's going on."

The Dillard is crouched down outside a cluster of trees, looking away from the Skyway Station. He's posed like a scout, his head sweeping right to left, then back again. Finn looks around at the Keepers and Fairlies, all of whom are too busy talking to pay attention to what might be out there. It's hard for him to imagine that the Dillard's an Imagineer spy when the guy appears to be the only one who cares about their protection.

Finn approaches quietly from behind.

"There is someone coming, Finn."

It's disquieting that the Dillard names him without turning, without seeing who's approaching. Finn can imagine a GPS tracking system built into the hologram's database, allowing it to track and account for each of the Keepers' projections at any given instant. Again, Philby's accusations hang in his mind.

"Where?"

"Eleven minutes ago, security video recorded a breach fifteen yards east of the main gate. There have been no accompanying security alerts, leading me to determine that the breach has gone unnoticed by all but me. Allowing for an average human walking speed of 3.1 miles per hour, the individual could arrive at any moment."

"Can you see the security video?"

"I can."

"Description?"

"The individual is alone. Five feet seven inches tall. Approximately one hundred thirty pounds."

"So, a girl?" Finn says.

"Gender undetermined," the Dillard says.

"Current location?" Finn is learning to direct the Dillard by interrupting with questions.

"Approximately one hundred seventy-five feet southeast, hunkered down in shadow."

"'Approximately?' 'Hunkered?' Really?"

"Should I repeat?" the Dillard asks, missing Finn's sarcasm.

"No." Finn wishes he could pet the boy on his head like a puppy. Their relationship is developing the feel of a master and his dog. Finn hurries back and motions the others to gather round him. "A visitor!" he says in a hush. *"Stay here. Silence!"*

Finn turns and sneaks back up alongside the Dillard. "Dillard, how could this girl know where we are?" he whispers.

"Gender undetermined."

"Get over it! Answer the question?"

"The question is too broad. Can you limit the question?"

"What are the top three ways the individual could determine the location of our holograms?"

"Highest percentage: all projected holograms are currently geo-tagged and tracked."

Bingo, Finn thought. "The Imagineers can track us in real time?"

"Disney programmers possess our precise locations at all times."

"Do they track us?"

"Data not available."

"Next possibility?"

"Second-highest percentage: visual identification. On the Disney side, this includes the naked eye and security video."

"We could have been spotted."

"Correct."

"Explain what you mean by 'Disney side.'"

"Your adversaries may have spotted you."

Finn swallows away the suggestion. "Next."

"The individual's agents, irrespective of your adversaries, could have spotted you."

Irrespective? Finn thinks, but says nothing. The Cryptos need to work on the Dillard's vocabulary.

"Individual sighted," the Dillard says, duck-walking back into shadow.

Finn whispers, "You can see someone? Really?"

The Dillard points and Finn makes out a ripple in a shadow alongside a food kiosk. It looks like nothing more than a swirl of oil and water.

"Whoa," Finn murmurs, "you're good." He's still wondering how this person found out about him and the others. Most likely—though the Dillard didn't mention it—is that Charlene was spotted climbing the Small World spire. Her blue DHI outline would have been visible from a great distance. What's still a question is the person's intentions. Is he or she here to spy on them, warn them, or attack them?

"Gender: female. Race: Asian," the Dillard announces, unprovoked.

"I know who it is," Finn says. Spinning back toward the other Keepers gathered behind him in the trees, he hisses, "Storey's coming!" He signals Maybeck to sneak up behind her and keep his eyes open for anyone else in the area. Then he and the Dillard watch Maybeck surprise the girl, creeping up on her in shadow.

Ten minutes have passed by the time Storey is reunited with them. They talk quietly, standing in a tight circle under the trees, as Storey explains her mission.

"The characters—the good characters—are talking about the Children of Light being in Disneyland tonight. You've been seen multiple times, and the Overtakers know you're here, too."

"No kidding," Willa says. "We've met quite a few tonight."

"Remy's pack has spread the word that you may need help."

Remy crosses his little arms proudly at Finn's ankle and salutes. The hundreds of rats follow suit, rising and balancing on their hind legs.

"Now that's adorable," Storey says.

"And?" Philby asks. "Do we have any support?"

"Prince Phillip is organizing King Arthur's knights from the carousel. You need horses."

"Why?" Philby says.

"Aren't you planning an attack? Don't you know what's up there?" Storey asks, pointing toward the hill.

The Keepers shake their heads.

"There are those among us—good sorcerers, Fairy Godmothers, fairies—who feel the dark magic. Like old people who know a storm's coming."

The Keepers and Amanda look squarely at Jess.

"Yes," Finn says, speaking for all of them. "We know."

"Starting not long ago, about the time you all showed up, that dark power has grown stronger."

"Chernabog," Willa says. "Tia Dalma. Cruella. The Evil Queen."

"It causes headaches, makes characters feel unwell or puts them in bad moods. The moment I heard you were over here, I made the connection. *All* the characters who've fallen ill are from Fantasyland, It's a Small World, and the castle. You look at a map, they go out like spokes on a wheel from this hill, the—"

"Skyway Station," Philby says, interrupting.

"Abandoned for twenty years," says the Dillard, surprising everyone. They'd forgotten he was listening. "The Skyway once transported Disneyland guests from Fantasyland to Tomorrowland and back."

461

"Is that your friend Dillard?" Storey Ming asks, astonished to see him apparently alive.

"Don't ask," Finn answers. "Long story."

"It was closed in 1994," the Dillard continues, "when stress fractures were discovered in the tram towers inside the Matterhorn, through which the tram passed at that time."

"Hey," Storey says to the Dillard, who looks back, curiously.

"She's saying hello," Finn tells the hologram.

"Hello," the Dillard says, closing his eyes. Probably recording the expression in his voice recognition file, Finn thinks. When the Dillard's eyelids fail to reopen, Finn crouches down beside him while the others continue talking.

"The Overtakers are using the Skyway Station as a hideaway?" Amanda says.

"There *was* a building like this in my dream," Jess reminds them.

"Are you okay?" Finn whispers to the Dillard.

"So you're telling us there are OTs up there," Maybeck says to Storey. "Maybe the darkest of the dark. We've got a girl who can push telekinetically. Another girl who's a gymnast. Me, of course. And a couple of brainiacs. Then there's the OTs. They can cast spells, conjure, and transfigure themselves, and they're maybe hiding a jumpstarted monster that can crush us like bugs. Supposedly there's some Prince Charming—"

"Prince Phillip," Charlene corrects him.

"Respond," Finn commands the Dillard quietly. Nothing.

"Whatever," Maybeck continues. "He's coming over here with some pint-size knights in shining armor on knee-high plastic horses. The OTs have the high ground—another advantage—and may know we're coming." He pauses. "Did I miss something?"

Remy and all the rats nod.

"Excu-u-u-use me," Maybeck says. "Let's not forget our secret weapon: gourmet rodents."

He laughs at his own joke, failing to win laughs from the others. Judging by Remy's twisted snout, Maybeck has hurt his feelings.

The Dillard's eyes open and the hologram speaks confidentially to Finn. "I have identified only one Storey Ming in the White Pages. This is not she."

"It's okay, Dillard. She's probably under a pseudonym, kind of like the Fairlies. Reschedule query."

The Dillard blinks. His head shifts direction to take in the others.

Philby says, "That sounds about right, Maybeck. Better odds than we've faced in the past."

"We've never stirred the hornet's nest before, Philby. We've never faced all these guys at the same time, in the same place. Put on your professor's cap! What are we supposed to do, arrest them? *What's the plan, Stan?*"

Storey Ming produces a book of matches. "Did I mention that the Skyway Station was very old, and made entirely of wood?"

"No!" Willa's almost shouting. "We are not setting that station on fire!"

"It's isolated on that hill," Storey says, expertly flipping the books of matches between her fingers. She moves with extraordinary ease, as if she has eight fingers and a thumb, not four. "There's no wind, and Disneyland has its own fire department."

"The Disneyland Resort Fire Department's ladder company is located behind the Mad Hatter Store. It has an average park response time of under seven minutes," the Dillard says.

"We can't possibly be considering this," Charlene says. "It's arson. Arson's a crime."

"It's the Overtakers," Storey says. "Seven minutes? They'll barely get a suntan."

"No one asked you!" Willa shouts.

"Let's keep our voices down," Finn says. He eyes Philby, watching the gears grinding in his friend's head.

"We're all clear," Philby mutters.

"We should tell the Cryptos," Willa says firmly. "It's their park, their battle."

"Then why did Wayne bring us here?" Maybeck says. He's clearly leaning toward Storey Ming's way of thinking. "Not to guide the guests, that's for sure. He brought us here to solve—"

"Never mind!" Finn doesn't want Storey hearing about the Osiris myth or the Manto Manuscripts. It's a knee-jerk, instinctive reaction to stop Maybeck. His own action confuses Finn. Wayne worked with Finn for years, encouraging him to trust himself as a leader. Why this particular switch has been thrown Finn doesn't know, but following Wayne's mentoring, Finn trusts it. "We get the point."

"We don't even know who's up there," Charlene says. She's clearly agonizing.

"I can do reconnaissance," Maybeck says.

"Not alone, you can't," Charlene says, putting a hand on his arm.

And now Charlene's upset all the more, because she and Maybeck have taken opposite sides. She's pleading with her eyes, but Maybeck remains oblivious. Finn sees Charlene look away, hurt.

"Dillard," Finn says, "if the Evil Queen, Tia Dalma, Cruella de Vil, and Chernabog are up there, what are the odds of success?"

"Define success."

"Capture!" Charlene says.

Finn is thinking of Wayne and Toontown. "Capture or termination," he says.

"Without knowledge of the plan of attack—" the Dillard begins.

Finn cuts him off. "Skip the disclaimers. Cut to the chase."

"The chase?"

"The *percentages*, Dillard!"

"I do not have the necessary data on Ms. Storey Ming— still searching. Present company has an eight percent chance of termination, a sixteen-point-nine percent chance of abduction, and a nineteen percent chance of some combination of these two outcomes."

"We're toast," a disappointed Maybeck says.

"He doesn't like our chances," Finn informs the Dillard, who blinks, confused by the expression.

"Your percentages increase narrowly with the assistance of Prince Phillip and the carousel knights. However, you lack sufficient powers to counteract those of your opponents. They, your opponents, possess formidable dark magic and physical strength."

"And we've got squat," Maybeck says.

"You don't have to sound so crushed," Charlene snaps, stepping away from him and crossing her arms. Maybeck sneers at her. Finn closes his eyes. He can feel everything falling apart.

"We have this," Jess says, reaching into her front pocket.

The group looks at her.

Jess is holding Walt's pen.

49

"I REMIND YOU," Jess says, "I have no idea what I'm doing."

A swirling ground fog continues to rise around them and throughout the park. It grows thicker by the minute.

"Do whatever it was you did in Toontown," Philby says. "You saw something, right?"

"Not something I wanted to see."

"Still," Finn says. "It's worth a try. *Anything's* worth a try."

They're interrupted by the distinctive drumming of approaching horse hooves. The Keepers scatter and hide. A white horse appears from out of the fog.

"I know him," Amanda says, showing herself. The others come out from hiding with her.

Prince Phillip is little like his animated self. Certainly, he's square-jawed and intimidatingly handsome, but it's his commanding presence, broad shoulders, and deep, scratchy voice that beguile. His gray uniform and red cape might make other men look soft; not Prince Phillip. He lets his horse feed on the grass. Faintly visible beyond are another dozen horses—real horses, not carousel miniatures—mounted by fully armored knights.

"Chef Remy has informed me of your situation," Prince Phillip says. "I pledge my fidelity and that of my men to your cause. We, of the realm, are forever in debt to you, the Children of Light. Please know you may trust in us completely, that we shall serve you in whatever form of combat is required."

His bow, with a forearm across the waist, draws gasps

from Amanda and Willa. The girls exchange a look and giggle conspiratorially to one another.

"How may we be of service?" Prince Phillip asks.

Finn introduces the Keepers, presenting Philby as general of their war council, "Jessica" as an enchantress, Amanda as a conjurer capable of magical acts, and "Willow" as the kingdom's archivist. "We have alchemy on our side," he says, "as well as two others currently conducting reconnaissance on the enemy fortress."

"And the foe?" Phillip asks.

"No stranger to you, I'm afraid. The same foe this kingdom has battled for lo these fifty years." Finn enjoys trying to talk like someone from another era. Judging by Amanda's scrunched face, he has a ways to go.

"Witches, ghosts, goblins," says Phillip.

"The same. But with a new leader, a beast unlike any you may have faced."

"We have faced plenty, my friend, and conquered not a few."

"This monster is three times the size of any man. Part bull, another part god. He feeds on the souls of the good and sends forth ghosts to do his bidding. This beast has been brought under an enchantment, a renewal of his bond to darkness; we believe this has given new force to his powers. In his present form," Finn says, thinking of the stories of decapitation and murder, "he is unbridled, unprincipled, and quite possibly undefeatable."

"Then we shall change his form," says Prince Phillip matter-of-factly. "For no soul, no power, no force shall be allowed to storm our castle or threaten our kingdom. We here before you do solemnly swear to end this creature that lusts for power not rightfully his. We serve Oswald and all that come

467

after. There are legions more behind us, and legions again behind them. Know this, Children of Light: This day shall be remembered for all time. It is the day when the authority of good shall rise like the phoenix reborn and extinguish this enemy forever."

Phillip's horse somehow manages to choose this exact moment to break wind and do his business. The ensuing levity kills the Prince's momentum, but does nothing to diminish his message.

Maybeck and Charlene appear through the fog. They take in Prince Phillip. To his credit, Maybeck doesn't make a fool of himself.

Charlene speaks first. "We got up there. The Skyway Station."

"Charlie climbed to the roof," Maybeck explains, "which is a mess. Holes all over."

"I saw down inside. The Evil Queen. Tia Dalma. No sign of Cruella or Chernabog, but how far away can they be? There were workers in there, too. The card soldiers and the Small World dolls. Too many to name. They're working by candlelight; the station's boarded up on all sides. They've built some kind of . . . I don't know, some kind of set? Like for a school play. It's pretty big, and most of the OTs are gathered around, watching Tia Dalma. She's got maybe six of her little dolls and she's doing stuff to them. Moving their arms, legs. Whatever. The backdrop looks like hills, mustard-colored hills, and in front of it are these boxes and ladders and stuff."

"Tell 'em about the other wall," Maybeck urges.

"Yeah, across the room, on the opposite side, other OTs are building another backdrop. I couldn't see it that well. They've got this toy truck with the end part of a fishing rod glued to it. All very weird looking, like something out of the occult."

468

"I know," Maybeck says. "We're supposed to be looking for this Osiris thing, but whatever's going on up there can't wait. I didn't even see anything, but I could *feel* it, you know? Like when Maleficent's close. Like everything bad you can possibly imagine is about to come true."

Philby instructs Jess. "Do it. See if it works."

Jess uncaps the pen and begins to draw. She focuses on the Skyway Station and, as before, the ink takes on a life of its own. The others ooh and ah. Prince Phillip prattles on about magic, but no one pays much attention.

The hill and the Skyway Station are drawn perfectly. In pen on paper they look like a Christmas card. The moment the drawing completes, it animates. All the images, including the trees, shake. Horses climb the hill, eliciting comments from Prince Phillip. The Keepers appear as stick figures with their initials as their heads. The pen shows up in the drawing, adding flames on opposite corners of the station. The stick-figure Keepers enter the structure. Prince Phillips's knights surround it. The station starts breaking apart. The stick figures flee as it comes crashing down.

The drawing fades, gone from the paper on which it was drawn.

"What just happened?" Charlene asks.

"I think we won," Maybeck says.

A dark uncertainty encumbers the Keepers. The image of such complete destruction disturbs them all.

"How did we do that?" Finn inquires. "How *do* we do that?"

"Isn't it obvious? We attack!" declares Prince Phillip. "Mount your steeds!" he cries, looking around for horses that don't exist. "Our time has come."

* * *

Prince Phillip's detachment includes eight knights—two of them female, surprisingly—all on horseback of course. They are accompanied by eight squires looking suspiciously like the Cast Members who run the carousel. Each carries his own sword and shield and has another sword and shield slung over his back in case the rider to whom he is pledged should lose his or hers. These extra swords and shields are passed around to the Keepers, who practice their sword strokes and receive a few basic tips from the armored riders.

Phillip, Finn, and Philby kneel alongside Jess and her interactive drawing; it's Prince Phillip, not either of the boys, who now tests the power and speed of her sketching. "Have you heard the expression concerning the pen being mightier than the sword?" Phillip asks.

"Of course," answers Philby.

"Let's put it to work. Shall we?" He asks Jess to draw a small hole in the ground, not far from their current position. It takes all the men-at-arms to find it, but eventually they do. Jess has dug into the soft soil using nothing but a pen. She draws a rock—it appears as well. Finally, she scratches out the rock and, sure enough, the rock in the real world is gone.

"Please, fair lady, if you will," Prince Phillip says, "remove the tree to our right, just there." He points.

Jess scratches the tree out of her drawing. In the real world, it remains. Prince Phillip clanks over in his armor and fingers the branches. "Interesting," he says.

"I guess I can add and remove my own images, but not the things already there."

"A shame," says Prince Phillip. "T'would be fine to do away with that beggar's cottage and all within its walls. Alas, it is not to be." Despite his words, he sounds pleased.

What knight isn't ready for a good fight? Finn thinks.

"My men and I shall lead the charge up this trail, here." Prince Phillip points to the path leading up to the station. "We shall surround the cottage thusly, front and back, and capture any cretins fool enough to stand against us. Upon my summons, you and our squires will advance on two flanks, here and here. Sir Philby, to the northeast; Sir Finn, to the southwest."

"Once we are in position," Philby says with authority, "Jess will try to draw it again and see if there are any changes in the outcome."

Jess is already working calmly, but intensely, to draw a deep moat around the chalet. On its outside border, she sketches a line of long wooden stakes with sharpened tips. Overhead, she adds nets.

"You need to keep in mind, Prince Phillip," Finn says. "These are sorcerers, magicians, witches, who can conjure, throw spells, and transfigure. It's no ordinary army."

"And you must keep in mind, kind sir, that my regiment has been battling these spirits for nearly three score years. Our minds are as sharp as our blades, our hearts as devoted, our spirits as resolute as those of our founders. I assure you, we have faced such foes before and matched them s-sword . . . f-for . . . s-spell."

The ground beneath their feet shakes. The fog grows thicker. Phillip's last few words are spoken with a vibrating throat.

"We have some secret weapons of our own," Finn says. "So stay close."

"Then I bid you good fortune, gentlemen! The enemy awaits. May your swords be sharp and your eye true!"

Phillip bows to Jess, says, "My lady," and is gone before he can hear Philby's words.

"A simple 'good luck' would have been fine."

"I don't think there's anything simple about him," Finn says. He grabs the hilt of the sword stuck into the earth at his feet. Philby does the same.

"Are you thinking what I'm thinking?" Finn asks.

Philby nods, a forlorn, grieved look on his face. The words barely escape his mouth. "This is the one."

"For all time," Finn says, hoisting his sword. Then louder, "For all time!"

The Keepers pull into a tight bunch, swords raised and touching at their tips.

"For all time!" they echo.

A spark of lightning strikes their swords, or perhaps it's the other way around. Perhaps their swords throw a bolt to the heavens. The air buzzes and fills with the smell of ozone, and a faint crack of thunder is heard as if a million miles away.

50

THE TEAMS REMAIN THE SAME. Finn leads Willa, Amanda, and the Dillard to the base of the hill west of the station. The mass of Big Thunder reveals itself through the fog.

By now, Philby, Maybeck, Charlene, and Violet should be positioned on the Storybook Land side. The Dillard's inability to act in the physical world puts Finn's team at a slight disadvantage, but this is overcome by the power contained within Amanda.

"Should I alert the Cryptologists about our situation?" the Dillard asks. Finn wonders at the timing of the request, thinking back to Philby's concerns about the Dillard's possible spying.

"Are you in contact with them?" Finn asks bluntly.

"Define contact. I am, as you know, a hologram generated from a server under Cryptologist control. I am therefore constantly linked by upstream and downstream data. Your question implies a premise of autonomy that cannot possibly exist given my projected status. Do you wish to refine your parameters?"

"Later," Finn says. The Dillard can drive him crazy at times.

As the words leave his mouth, Finn is struck by a thought that literally stops his feet from moving. But it's jarred from his thought as screams arise from the top of the hill.

Jess is right on schedule.

* * *

Despite the egos involved, the inside of the Skyway is a model of efficiency. Two different stage sets have been erected against opposing walls. Tia Dalma manipulates a group of raffia dolls in front of the Oak Hills, California, backdrop, while the Evil Queen serves as foreman, directing a legion of Card Soldiers and dozens of Small World dolls, who are putting the finishing touches on a working model of Disneyland's Matterhorn Bobsleds. The Small World dolls work on ladders near the top of the backdrop, while the card soldiers are busy at the base.

All this is witnessed by an invisible Violet, who stands in a corner prying up a plank to make it easier for the rats to enter.

As the first wisps of fog seep through into the space, Violet next climbs up the timber-beamed wall and slips out through a hole in the roof. Reappearing, she descends the station's exterior and hurries through the thick fog, passing the steady breathing of unseen horses, and slides to a stop beside Philby.

"Between the Card Soldiers and Small World dolls, there must be more than fifty of them."

"Not the dolls," moans Charlene. "I *hate* those things!"

"Tell Finn," Philby directs Violet. "Get back here as quickly as you can. We need you!"

Violet hurries off.

"You're up!" Philby tells Remy, who's at his feet, waiting patiently.

Remy salutes Philby, then waves his tiny paw, urging his rat pack to follow him toward the station. Django and Remy split apart shortly thereafter, dividing their ranks, with Remy's battalion taking the southern side of the building.

Inside, the sudden appearance of mist wins the attention of the female OT leadership. But their minions do not break stride. The result is exactly what Finn and Philby intended: the villains' eyes track down to the floor.

Through the wispy fog appears the flow of rats, spreading from both corners like spilled ink across the floor. Screams shatter the working atmosphere into chaos.

* * *

"I know this is a strange time to get sentimental," Finn tells Amanda in a whisper, "but since we don't exactly know what's going on up there, I wanted to say how—"

"Shut it! Don't want to hear it!"

"What a good friend you are."

"Friend?"

"I'm glad I know you, Amanda."

"Better."

"When you're around, you know, I don't think about other stuff. I'm not wishing I was somewhere else, with someone else."

"No offense, but that doesn't exactly sound like you."

"Maybe I picked it up from a Nicholas Sparks movie."

"Do you watch those?"

"My mother does. So, I guess, yeah, sometimes."

"Wow, important information," Amanda says.

"I was just trying to say—"

"I got it, Finn. Thank you. That's very sweet of you. But don't go talking like we're going to die or something."

"It's the 'or something' I'm worried about. This goes wrong, who knows how we end up?"

"You're not helping any."

"Wow, important information," he says, and Amanda laughs in spite of herself.

"Better," she says.

"Good."

Finn smiles at her as shrieks peal from up the hill.

"The rats," Finn says. "It's started!"

* * *

Remy and Django know a thing or two about scaring people. As fog seeps through every crack and crevice to permeate the station, almost invisible in the rising mists, Remy and his friends lead their packs in swirling eddies around the feet of the Small World dolls and Card Soldiers, brushing their fur and whiskers against every ankle. The faster the rats sweep through the space, the more chaos ensues. As screeches begin to rise from her terrified minions, the Evil Queen stomps her feet again and again, injuring several of the valiant rats. Defenseless, the injured rodents scurry randomly about, creating still greater distraction. The more panic, the more perfectly they are fulfilling their mission.

* * *

Forty yards away, tucked between trees in the midst of coiling fog, Jess lowers her pen.

476

The scene that plays out before is much the same as the last: the approach of the Keepers and knights, the violent shaking, the collapse of the Skyway Station.

With no one around to see her fail, if she should, Jess tries adding lines, drawing flames on opposite corners of the structure as closely packed together as shark's teeth.

She looks up the hill. The fog stains orange—a *flickering* orange.

She draws a breath sharply.

"*FIIIRRRE!*" It's the voice of the Evil Queen, rolling down the hill like a scream of surrender.

* * *

As the doors to the station burst open, Prince Phillip unleashes his war cry.

The battle begins. Card Soldiers and Small World dolls pour from the station's front door and into the waiting moat, where the cards pile up quickly. Stepping atop their fallen comrades, the OTs' remaining troops advance toward the sharpened stakes, on which they are soon skewered like marshmallows prepared for roasting.

The Small World dolls move awkwardly, too, stiff-legged, rocking from side to side as if about to topple. But they stay erect, spilling into the trench, climbing up the other side, and slipping between the stakes, which they wrestle free from the earth, aiming the pointed poles at the oncoming knights like pikes.

Phillip's knights lower their swords, the blades glinting in the flickering firelight, aiming for the dolls as they pull their mounts sharply to avoid the sharp stakes. But the dolls grab hold of some of the horses' front legs and bring them down, throwing their riders. Card Soldiers turn sideways as

477

the knights attempt to strike them, all but disappearing; the knights slice only air.

* * *

Inside the Station is another matter. Tia Dalma does not move, refusing to acknowledge the hot smoke mixing with the cool fog. To her right, the Evil Queen stands like a sentry, protecting the voodoo queen as she works her dolls against the boxes, pulling matchstick levers, twisting button dials. Cruella is nowhere to be seen.

Charging through the smog are the Kingdom Keepers, brandishing their swords.

The Evil Queen extracts an ampoule of some blue concoction from a hidden pocket and raises her hand to throw it at the Keepers, but Remy and some of his intrepid friends claw up her dress and out onto her extended limbs; the weight of the creatures on her arms forces her hands lower, and her attempt to spray the Keepers with the charmed potion misses. Instead of the Keepers, the blue drops strike some of the rats, who instantly gray with old age, their faces shriveling, their teeth falling out. But there are more rats than she can hit, and they overtake her.

The Evil Queen hollers, struggling against the rats streaming up her legs and across her limbs. The remaining drops of poison fall on a few of the rats weighing her down. They too age and weaken. In desperation, the Queen takes to shaking the potion onto the undulating sea of rats as they swarm her. One by one they fall, lessening her load.

Finn sees what's coming. He drops his sword, worried that his strong hold on it may limit his all clear. As the metal clanks to the floor, drops of blue sail cleanly through his hologram, leaving him unaffected.

The stuff splashes the faces of some Small World dolls, who age horrifically, like plastic melting in flames, warping from frolicking child to wrinkled gnome. Their legs wither and break. Their fingers shrivel and bend.

The Dillard is unfazed. He studies the battle like an academic or a United Nations observer. His hologram head moves mechanically, taking a slow, all-encompassing panoramic view of the station's interior.

When he speaks, it's to Finn. There's no doubt about that, though he's looking in another direction entirely. "She is unimportant. The real threat is the one kneeling. You have approximately . . . twenty-six seconds to prevent catastrophe. Twenty-two seconds. Twenty."

"What catastrophe?" Finn has taken up his sword again. The Small World dolls are swinging tools at him and the other Keepers—blades, pieces of lumber with nails sticking out. Finn, Amanda, and Willa are in tight formation, backs pressed together, turning like a wheel as they battle the onslaught of dolls. Swords and wrenches clank and spark.

"We're outnumbered!" Willa calls.

"I need my hands free to push," Amanda cries. "But if I drop my sword—"

"Defend yourself! Do not lower your sword!" Finn shouts.

Through the haze, Finn sees Philby's team pinned against the far wall by wave after wave of Card Soldiers and dolls. Violet disappears and reappears, emanating small force fields that clear a narrow area around her.

"What catastrophe?" Finn repeats, shouting louder.

"It is too late," the Dillard answers. "Six . . . five . . . four . . ." The Dillard raises his voice. It's the first—and last—time Finn will hear him do so. *"Brace yourselves!"*

51

I<small>T BEGINS AS SEASICKNESS</small>, a loss of stability, dizziness. At first, the body wants to believe it's an internal malfunction, perhaps something amiss in the inner ear. It is the sound that brings the brain around to the possibility of an external influence: a booming growl, a cosmic resonance.

"Chernabog!" Finn shouts to those at his back.

The Dillard's voice returns to normal. "Probability, six-point-six percent."

"Who else can shake the earth?"

"I warned you," the Dillard says over the growing roar. "She is right there, Finn. Right where I said she was."

Philby and Charlene, also battling the dolls and cards, also back-to-back, fight their way to within shouting distance of Finn.

"That's Oil Field Road!" Philby briefly swings his sword toward the improvised backdrop, where Tia Dalma plays her dangerous games.

"Two-point-two. Two-point-six. Two-point-nine. Three-point-five . . ."

"What's with the decimals, Dillard?" Finn calls out.

Some of Prince Phillip's troops now spill in through the front door of the station, followed by a smoky line of wraiths. One of the wraiths lands on one of the squires, who instantly disappears, absorbed.

"Wraiths!" It's Willa's voice, not far from the man who has just vanished.

480

"Four-point-three. Four-point-eight . . ."

Finn's legs are not all that's moving. The station's ridgepole is swaying from side to side. The walls themselves are moving.

"Dillard!"

"I am using the Richter scale, Finn. I thought you would recogn—"

Clanging swords with the aggressive dolls, Finn turns to Amanda. "You . . . need to . . . push her! We're out of time—hurry! I'll cover you."

"Ready!"

"Go!" Finn shouts. He is battling three dolls at once. Amanda drops her sword, does a 180-degree pirouette, and shoves her hands at Tia Dalma.

The set explodes. Tia Dalma rolls into and across the painted boxes that model the Oil Field Road drilling station. The blowback sends Small World dolls toppling throughout the room.

The Keepers' DHI transparency serves them well; they remain standing. Everything else in the room has fallen.

And then the room itself falls.

"EARTHQUAKE!" Finn shouts.

52

W HEN FINN AWAKENS, he is atop a barren hill. The trees have fallen around him. It is still night, but fires burn brightly across the park, illuminating spirals of gray smoke against an oily sky. Finn sees that he is only partially projected.

Nothing around him appears to be level. He can't wrap his mind around it. The collapse of the station had nothing to do with their efforts; what Jess's drawing revealed represented the Overtakers' success, and specifically the results of Tia Dalma's voodoo magic.

Nearby, Maybeck's DHI sputters. Finn spots what must be Philby and Willa holding hands, their projections so faint he can see through them to the chunks of concrete and wood atop which they lie.

Finn rolls over and sees that the area just outside Disneyland is apparently unaffected. He's on an island of destruction, which includes the Disneyland and California Adventure parks, but nothing beyond the fences. "Bizarre," he says aloud.

Strangest of all, there's not a siren to be heard. No one else knows! Finn realizes, a shiver passing through his wounded DHI. Looking back, he rises to his knees—and jumps, startled.

"Don't do that!"

The Dillard towers over him, also sparking and sputtering.

"Where is everyone? Is everyone all right?"

"Define everyone."

"You—are—so—frustrating! The other Keepers—and Amanda, Jess, Violet."

"Of those you list as holograms, that is, with the exception of Violet, all are coming back online."

"Just because we're holograms . . . we aren't like you, Dillard. We can get hurt. Or worse. Are they okay?"

"I have no update on Violet." The Dillard closes his eyes, calculating, or whatever it is he does. Finn studies the landscape by the light of the flickering fires. Wooden structures like the Skyway Station and two buildings on Main Street have collapsed in ruins. Big Thunder Mountain Railway, Matterhorn Bobsled, and Storybook Land have all suffered.

"Searching . . ."

Four deep gouges run up Main Street like ugly scars; the roadway around the Plaza is cracked as well. Much of the damage is too far off and it's too dark for Finn to judge accurately.

The Dillard's eyes open. "No source data for the holograms is seriously impacted. The system rebooted only minutes ago. All holograms are coming back online presently."

"So they're all right."

"No lasting damage to source data." The Dillard does not seem to like repeating himself.

"Remy? Django?"

"Some of the rodents were lost in the battle. The leaders have survived."

"Where?"

"Unknown."

"The Overtakers? The villains?"

"Undetermined."

"What good are you?" Finn says it but doesn't mean it. Worse, the Dillard starts to list his processors and hardware. Finn stops him by withdrawing the question. "How bad is the damage?"

"The earthquake measured six-point-six on the Richter

scale. We are standing nine-point-five-four miles from its epicenter in La Habra, California. The resulting damage—"

"Wait! La Habra is where Philby found the voodoo doll."

"I believe it was a young adult named Austin, but point taken," says the Dillard.

"The rest of the city?"

"I don't understand the question."

"What's the *damage* to the rest of the city?"

"The damage is apparently contained to Disneyland and California Adventure."

"How is that possible? Never mind!" Finn says, realizing the Dillard will recite the probabilities of earthquakes, fault lines, and catastrophe rates.

Finn watches as some of the holograms reboot. His legs feel weak, hologram or not. His head is spinning. He thinks he might throw up.

"Hey!" Philby calls. Hand in hand, he and Willa head toward Finn and Dillard. Philby has only one leg and one arm. But as he nears, his DHI fills out. Though he's not entirely three-dimensional, his limbs are visible.

Maybeck rises from the ashes like a phoenix. But only when Amanda stands up from behind a huge piece of the fallen station does Finn take off at a run to greet her. Moments later, two-thirds of the Keepers are joined in a huddle, arms around one another's shoulders.

Amanda asks, "Where are—?"

"Everyone's coming online. We don't know about Violet."

"That fire just went out by itself!" Philby says.

"Not exactly by itself." A girl's voice.

"Jess!" Amanda declares.

At the bottom of the small hill, Jess has the battle plan laid out before her and Walt's pen in hand. "That was one of the ones I started." As planned, Jess controlled the fires and the fog in the Skyway Station, working to confuse the Overtakers.

"The knights?" Finn asks her.

"Retreated back to the carousel 'to fight another day,' as Prince Phillip put it."

"The OTs fled on foot," Charlene says as she and Violet come up the paved path. Charlene's partial hologram makes her look wounded. "They all survived, but Violet saw Remy and Django following them, so maybe there's hope we can track where they go next."

"There's a word," Amanda says. *"Hope."*

Finn thanks Violet for distracting Shere Khan at the Jungle Cruise. Instead of her usual sassy self, Violet nods solemnly. Clearly, the earthquake has affected her too.

Finn engages the Dillard. "Can you communicate with the Studios, Dillard?"

"Negative."

"But we're being projected."

"Yes."

"Explain."

"I cannot confirm."

"Best guess."

"Is that a—?"

"Yes! A question!"

"Installed within the last decade, fiber optics are considered to be buried lines and fall under federal guidance for earthquake sustainability. These data lines may have survived intact."

"Our projection is over fiber," Finn says. "Philby calls it 'light pipe.'"

"Correct."

"Can we communicate over fiber optics?"

"There are protocols, yes. A transmitter and receiver are required for encryption."

"So the Imagineers would have to have special hardware installed, and we'd need a special phone, something like that."

"Precisely."

"If I turn sideways, I'm two-dimensional."

"Yes, I have noticed." The Dillard spins as well; from the side, he's paper-thin. "'Best guess,' as you say, is that we are operating on a limited number of projectors, restricting three-dimensional projection. Technically, we are full holograms."

"Are we stuck here, Dillard?" Philby is beginning to grasp the scope of their situation. "Does that mean our human selves are stuck in SBS in our beds at the Studios?" The Dillard doesn't answer. Maybe the question or the terminology has confused him. Maybe he's short on bandwidth. "Are we on emergency power?" Philby asks the Dillard. "What's supplying the power to project us?"

"Technically, the Disneyland and California Adventure parks can operate on self-generated power during emergency conditions. The fuel for the generators is natural gas backed up by diesel. So long as the flow of natural gas continues, the park can generate enough power to remain in functional security mode at all times."

Looking out at the flames licking through the smudge of black smoke, Finn is almost certain not all natural gas is flowing uninterrupted. "If the park loses emergency power, then our projectors go down and we're in DHI shadow."

"Is that—?"

"No!" Finn says. "Not a question. A statement."

Philby says, "Our bodies won't wake up, our DHIs won't show up, and no one will know we're here. Technically, I suppose we won't be. If the Imagineers ship our real selves off to the hospital, the drugs will affect not only our bodies, but the behavior of our DHIs." Philby has had personal experience with medical intervention while in DHI state. "That's no fun."

"So, we're cut off from the Studios," Finn says. "We're on emergency power."

"No sirens," Philby says, echoing Finn's earlier observation. "That *has* to be the work of the OTs. They must have overridden the alarms or something."

"Under the rules of warfare," the Dillard begins, "such a strategy indicates that their efforts will continue through the night. The enemy has more planned."

"Great," Maybeck mutters, pulling Charlene into a hug.

"And it seems likely that no one will be coming to help," Philby says. "Even if they do, they may not enter such a risky environment."

Indeed, the cracks in the ground are still expanding, and the last standing trees are tilting toward the ground. The Keepers look among themselves from face to face, expecting the spark of optimism for which they're known. Nothing.

"The OTs have crippled and isolated the parks," Willa says. "Just like they've always wanted."

"We can't let this stand," Finn says flatly, determinedly, as the others look on in astonishment. "Can you imagine how it'll hurt people to see the park like this? We can't let that happen."

"Earth to Finn," Maybeck says. "Open your eyes. It happened."

"I'm up for finishing them off," Philby says proudly. He bends down to pick up a chunk of rock, but it takes him three tries. His DHI can't catch hold of it; as he lifts, the rock falls through his grip and back to the ground.

The others immediately try the same thing, with similar results.

"We aren't ourselves," Charlene says.

Jess climbs the hill to join them. She and Amanda share a long hologram hug. "Don't ask me to use the pen again," she says, "because I won't. I don't want to see anything more."

"Dillard?" Finn says, turning to face him. "Fact: we have six, maybe seven hours to conquer the Overtakers and restore the park. Is it possible?"

The Dillard's eyes flutter shut. "Rephrase, please."

Finn thinks.

Willa speaks. "First: How do we achieve maximum effectiveness against the Overtakers?"

The Dillard's eyelids flutter shut. Everyone hangs on his response. When it comes, his voice breaks several times, distorting digitally like a bad phone call.

"Two options. Number one: restore six park projectors. Override the northwest emergency shutdown valve of natural gas, restoring supply to Disneyland. Override the southeast emergency shutdown valve of natural gas, restoring supply to California Adventure." The Dillard needs no breath; he speaks in a continuous flow, a sound disconcerting to the ear. "Breach security and attempt to restore communication with the Walt Disney Studios and the Imagineers."

"Oh, is that all?" Maybeck quips.

"Number two: restore the thirteenth piece. Return Mickey Mouse to his rightful throne in the kingdom. Dispatch the Overtakers with Mickey Mouse as your leader and ally. Restore the kingdom."

"Dispatch the Overtakers," Maybeck says. "How?"

"It all comes down to time."

"Everything goes back to Wayne," Finn mutters. "Those are practically his exact words."

"I thought he meant his watch," Charlene says.

"The Osiris hieroglyph," says Willa.

Amanda puts her arm around Finn, leaning in close, but their holograms spark, forcing her to stand back.

"Fulfilling the Osiris myth's prophecy is crucial to your survival and that of the Disney kingdom," the Dillard says. "The power there will lead you."

"But lead us where?" Finn asks anxiously.

"That information is classified and inaccessible."

"Classified?" Philby says.

"Correct."

"The thirteenth piece." From Philby's voice, Finn knows he's become Professor Philby once more. "Restoring Mickey gives us the advantage."

"Correct." The Dillard suffers digital interference again, turning into colorful vertical bars of light like a video test pattern. He looks like the northern lights. Moments later, his flat hologram returns.

"What if none of this has happened?" Jess asks, stunning the others. "What if it's virtual reality or something? I mean, how can people not see these fires, the smoke?"

"A spell?" Charlene asks. "Can a spell make an entire population see what you want it to see?"

"I doubt that," Philby says. "But one might create an illusion of Disneyland from the outside, one that obscures the reality."

"People drive by," Charlene says, "but see—"

"What they want to see," Philby answers.

"They aren't going to wait two or three days to finish this," Finn says, staring out at the destruction surrounding them.

"It looks finished to me," Maybeck says, "but I'm game."

The Dillard says, "'You can design and create, and build

the most wonderful place in the world. But it takes people to make the dream a reality.' Quotation: Walt Disney."

"If people see this and stop coming, the dream is dead," says Finn. "The OTs win."

"Never. Not ever," says Charlene.

The Dillard recites again. "'When you believe in a thing, believe in it all the way.'"

"Walt was right. We have to believe this is going to work," Finn says. "No doubts. No limits. One thing at a time. We find and repair Mickey. Whatever follows, follows."

Amanda nods fiercely and moves to the common center. Maybeck, the tallest, raises his hand, and the Keepers pull together. Violet and the Dillard stand aside until Finn tells them to join.

"Dillard, lift your right hand!"

The group joins and cheers.

"Look! There!" Violet points to the Matterhorn.

Flickering orange flames rise from a rent in the path, sending dancing shadows up the mountain like dark matter. A lone figure stands silhouetted on an upward ledge of gray rock and ice. Even from a considerable distance, the curved horns on either side of his skull are apparent, as is the extended snout of a bull's nose.

The beast raises his furry arms toward the swirling fumes overhead and releases a moaning roar.

"Game on," says Maybeck.

53

LIKE RATS ON a sinking ship, the Overtakers come out of every crack and crevice in the crippled Disneyland, swarming the park in euphoric celebration.

In the shadows, Finn and Maybeck work to keep their swords from reflecting flashes of light. They have adopted stealth tactics in an attempt to secure some kind of stronghold or base of operations for the Keepers. With the park in ruins, its trees and lampposts scattered across the ground like pickup sticks, there's nowhere to hide. And hide they must. The Keepers are gravely outnumbered, their DHIs sparking and failing.

If they go dark, if they slip into SBS, then all hope is lost.

"You see those guys?" Maybeck says, and points.

"Yeah."

"They're putting the fires *out*. Why would they do that?"

Two teams of pirates move from one break in the asphalt to another, snuffing out the flames with blankets. Finn studies their actions, his mind whirling.

"You're saying, why not let the park burn?"

"Exactly!"

"No clue. Makes no sense."

The Dillard has come up with a list of possible hiding places nearby. None is more appealing to Finn than an abandoned tunnel across the Big Thunder Trail at the base of the mountain. Eyes fixed on their destination, Finn pushes Maybeck back as a pack of snorting hyenas charges by, led by Shenzi, Banzai, and Ed.

"Shades of the ship," Maybeck says, once they're gone.

"Don't remind me."

It takes a few minutes to find the tunnel, which is in the backstage area. When they reach it, the tunnel turns out to be more like a cave, since its far end is boarded up with lumber. The interior is cluttered with painting supplies. Maybeck and Finn leave the others outside as they inspect it.

"Our DHIs can pass through that wood at the end," Maybeck says, "Most OTs can't."

"Storey and Violet can't."

"We'll be vulnerable from the open end." Maybeck's voice echoes slightly.

"Yeah, but we've got to have a base, a place to meet up."

"Amanda could defend the opening."

Finn would rather have her by his side. He hesitates to agree. "Yeah. She could push any attackers, probably even push these boards away." He thinks it through. "Trouble is, pushing the OTs won't stop them. It'll just knock them back. And when Amanda does that, it depletes her. She needs time before she can do it again."

"What if we could contain Amanda's force, like in a pipe or something, so it's more concentrated, like a rocket launcher?"

Finn's immediate reaction is that Maybeck has been gaming too much—*rocket launchers?* But it's not that: rather, Maybeck's artist's eye is imagining Amanda's force somehow contained. "Whoa! There's an idea," Finn mutters. "Can you imagine *that* as a weapon?"

"You know we can find a big pipe backstage. They've got everything here. But what's the ammo we launch?"

"Pieces of concrete? We've got an endless supply."

"How 'bout the green goo? The magic brooms? If it's in Disney World, it's got to be here too."

"Killer," Finn says, enjoying his own pun. "The stage is on

Tom Sawyer Island here; it faces New Orleans Square. Take Charlie. Bring back as much of that stuff as you can."

"On it."

"Jess and the Dillard will stay here with Amanda. The Dillard's no physical help and Jess is better in a quiet place trying to dream up stuff."

"One question," Maybeck says. "If we're being projected, even poorly, then don't we assume the security video is probably working? So why hasn't Security called 911?"

"If you were the OTs, what's the first place you'd attack *before* causing the earthquake?"

"Okay. Got it." Maybeck pauses. "So they took out Security. But there's smoke and fire, so why hasn't someone called 911?"

"I don't know. Voodoo? A spell? Tia Dalma once made me believe I was killing her." Finn aches at the memory. "*We all saw her*, but not Dillard. Maybe if you're outside the park it looks perfectly normal."

"That's just plain strange."

"You and Charlie build the Mandy Blaster. It'll make this place defensible and safe. We're going to need that."

"Done."

With everyone now in the painting tunnel Finn realizes the Dillard's processing power is slow. He's spending a lot of time with his eyes closed.

"Is he all right?" Jess asks as Finn leads the remaining Keepers into the tunnel.

"I don't think he has a great signal, so he's slow processing," Finn says. "I've asked him to look at all the data we've collected before and after the earthquake and to offer a plan of attack." He pauses, and then adds, "As a side note, I'm worried about Remy and Django. I haven't seen them since the earthquake."

Overhearing them Philby speaks up. "If Dillard's processing, if he's still connected to the Internet—*which he must be* if he's doing all this data work—then why haven't the Imagineers called someone or done something?"

"Who knows who's connected to what?" Finn says.

The Dillard is crouching off by himself in a corner.

"What if they know exactly what's happened?" Willa says, joining in. "What if the Imagineers know exactly what's going on but know the only chance to beat these jerks is us? What if we're their only shot?"

"The *only* shot at what?" Finn says.

"If they're monitoring Dillard's search requests—and you can bet they are—they know we're looking for a strategy. They're not interfering. Not so far. So we have every right to assume our plan is better than anything they've come up with. Right? Or they'd program Dillard to talk to us."

"Brilliant!" Philby says. "Absolutely, brilliant! Listen, that also means we should be able to get messages to them through Dillard."

"We can use the Dillard like Instagram?" Finn says.

"A medium," Jess says. "Like in a séance."

"Creep me out, why don't you?" Willa says.

"Finn?" It's the Dillard. Finn walks over to him and crouches down.

"Here," he says.

The Dillard's eyes open slowly. "I require a park map and a writing implement."

Violet overhears and takes off at a run. Jess moves to join them and offers Walt's pen.

"I think that's only for you, Jess," Finn says. "Who knows what it'll do in someone else's hands?"

"I'll find something," she says, and nods to Amanda.

Together, the Fairlies begin to search the junk in the tunnel.

Dillard speaks in a secretive voice that Finn hasn't heard the hologram use before. "Initial search for Storey Ming has been fulfilled."

"We don't need that now, Dillard."

"Twenty-year-old Chinese-American female declared missing at sea the night of April 16. Believed washed overboard in calm seas."

Finn stares at his friend's partial hologram, watches as it dissolves and reappears. His mind feels numb, working over the Dillard's words. While he and his friends have aged considerably in the past several years, Storey's look is timeless. He knows some people—especially women—can seem to barely age, but Storey still looks like she did when they met her aboard the *Dream*. Coincidence? Tendrils of panic worm through him.

"Continue." His voice is rough.

"She was lost at sea. Believed deceased."

Finn feels an actual stab of pain in his chest. *Storey!*

"So she must have run away, or something." He says this, but doesn't believe it. Finn liked her immediately, remembers the other Keepers warning him about trusting her, and remembers how smug he felt when she turned out to be such a big help.

The others call to him. Finn is glad for it—he wants them to interrupt. Anything to mollify the sense of betrayal he's suffering. He directs the Dillard, "You will keep this information between us until further instruction."

"Information restricted," the Dillard answers clinically.

With two pens, a crayon, and a park map in front of him, the Dillard directs Finn to draw. Finn passes the chore to Maybeck.

"You okay?"

"You're the artist," Finn replies.

"You look . . . sick or something."

"I'm fine."

Maybeck calls for something with a straight edge. Willa finds a broken piece of wood trim.

Finn understands what's going on shortly after Maybeck extends the first line from a spire of Small World out over the peak of the carousel in Fantasyland and beyond—off the map.

"Why did we not think of this ourselves?" Philby asks.

"We were a little busy with the Skyway Station," Willa reminds him.

The group has reformed, huddling around the Dillard and Maybeck.

"The theory is based on two points of origin," the Dillard explains. "Both are elevated and difficult to access: the spire tower at It's a Small World and the branch in what is now Tarzan's Treehouse. Mr. Disney could ill afford to place such clues at ground level. He was aware the park would change multiple times over the years. But he could also be confident that two of his iconic attractions would never be torn down or replaced."

"Small World and Tarzan," Philby says, somewhat in awe.

"At the time, Swiss Family Robinson, but yes."

"From Tarzan—"

"Draw a line directly over that cupola," Finn says, interrupting the Dillard. As Maybeck draws, the two lines intersect at the entrance to the Mark Twain Riverboat ride.

"The boat is made of wood!" Philby declares. "And it was never going to be taken out of the park. That's where we find the missing piece! Brilliant, Dillard!"

"That's a lot of boat to search," Finn says.

"And we can't bunch up," Philby says. "We can't give the OTs that kind of target."

"I wish we knew where Remy was," Finn says, eyes searching the tunnel. "I'm worried about him."

"Rats tend to do better than humans in a natural disaster." Philby is clearly not worried. "They actually thrive. The plague, for instance."

"Shut up!" Charlene says.

Maybeck offers to "fly solo" on the mission to retrieve the magic brooms' green goo as part of their arsenal. He makes a point that these are exceptional circumstances and that they can't pair up for everything. Finn is about to argue, but he knows Maybeck is right. He accepts the change in plans.

"Go, now," he tells Maybeck. "We'll all meet back here in no more than an hour."

Maybeck nods, stares intensely at Charlene, who silently mouths, *Be careful*, and he takes off.

Finn instructs the Dillard: "Make two teams out of me, Philby, Storey, Violet, and Charlene. We need to search the vault in the Disney Gallery and the riverboat on the Rivers of America. Consider efficiency for both discovery and defense."

Philby leans closer as the Dillard closes his eyes. Typically, he and Finn decide the teams, usually based on which relationships are the most stable at that particular moment.

"Willa, leading Philby and Charlene," the Dillard says after a moment's hesitation. "Finn leading Violet and Storey."

"You rigged that," Philby says.

"Did not," Finn fires back. "Maybe the Imagineers, but not me."

The Dillard speaks up, uninvited. "The relative underdevelopment of your leadership ability, Dell Philby, may somewhat compromise your analytical skills if you are placed in a position of responsibility. At this moment, the need for access to your intellect supersedes any other mitigating factors."

"You're a real piece of work," Philby says.

The Dillard thanks him, which cracks everyone up. All but the Dillard, whose attempts at displaying emotion come too late to be relevant.

* * *

Willa leads her team with a barely contained sense of personal achievement. For six years, she and Charlene have been sidelined, left to watch Philby and Finn struggle for power. The two girls have borne the brunt of Maybeck's disparaging sarcasm, have fought to get their ideas heard and be recognized as better qualified than the boys for particular missions. Neither girl blames the boys. Finn, Philby, and Maybeck have never intentionally pushed them aside; it's more like they couldn't open their eyes or ears, couldn't *see* the girls.

It's funny, Willa thinks. She's never felt comfortable around other people. It wasn't until her DHI audition that she found a sense of belonging. Adults are adults; little kids are just that, little. But people her age confuse her. Some want to be fast on a field, others gorgeous, thin, witty, or funny. She never considered herself any of those things. Then came celebrity when she became one of the hologram guides in the parks, the ones you could swipe your hand through. Little did those guests making comments about how real she appeared know that she felt like her DHI: insubstantial.

But as a DHI, she wasn't alone. She was one of five, and those four others—fast, gorgeous, thin, witty—appreciate her for what she is: smart. You can't wear smart. You can't fashion it or show it off on a playing field, and if you show it off in the classroom, you're even more alone. So you learn to disguise it. But it grows in you, as it grew in her. She was so afraid others would see it. But at that moment of panic, the time in her life when she knew it would be impossible to keep it under wraps, the Keepers came along. Philby came along, a guy as smart as she. Four people accepted her, and that became something to build on.

Now, in the middle of a sea of devastation, sweeping in hologram form through displaced concrete and smoking holes in the pavement, Willa feels giddy with happiness. Whatever her path, it has led her to this moment: to be in charge and take the lead. If Chernabog wants to strike her down, then he'd better do it now, when she feels like nothing in the world could be as sweet as this.

Willa, Philby, and Charlene arrive at their destination, a nearly unscathed building on Main Street. Two royal-blue window awnings hang like fake eyelashes, revealing cracked panes. A burned but readable banner over the central doors reads: ANIMATION CLASSICS. Beneath it is a sign written in elegant script: *Disneyana*.

With a cry, Charlene stoops to help two birds on their backs, wings flapping frantically. She picks one up and tries to help it fly, but it's no use. The bird dies in her hands and she drops it, holding back tears. Philby and Willa are waiting.

Willa gestures for Philby, directing him to go all clear and pass through a wall far away from the main doors; Charlene will climb the facade, slip in, and come down from the second floor. Neither scowls nor questions her decision; Philby parks his sword against the outside wall and stands ready. She and Philby wait for Charlene to climb into place. Then, on a silent finger countdown from three, they glide through solid matter.

Willa sweeps through the main doors. A witch soldier from the Wizard of Oz stands sentry by the open vault, holding an iron halberd like a tall cane, a fuzzy hat secured to his head with a leather chin strap.

He stands his ground, leveling the halberd's deadly point at Willa, while its ax-like blade glistens, ready to cleave. The man's dark eyes twitch, taking in Philby, who's crouched behind a glass case on a walnut table. The room is made to look like a turn-of-the-century bank, all elaborate carvings and ornate molding. It is not a place meant for a fight.

Willa battles her own busy mind, aware that her overactive brain gets in the way of all clear. She need not contemplate how it is that her hands can grasp while her hologram remains fluidly transparent; that she can hit, yet not be hit herself.

The witch soldier glowers but does not speak. It makes him all the more menacing. His sole intention is to skewer Willa with the tip of the halberd and slice Philby's head off his shoulders.

The tingling in Willa's limbs confirms her worst fears: she can't trust that she's all clear. Philby's blue outline pulses from bright to dim, suggesting that he's faring the same way.

500

The soldier doesn't move away from the vault. The halberd sweeps side to side, aimed at Willa, then Philby. Even if they charge him simultaneously, one of them is sure to fall. Philby shakes his head. Willa eye-signals the interior wall, which produces a moment of confusion in him, but then she watches his blue outline strengthen. She's directing him away from the confrontation, allowing him to regain all clear.

Willa makes her first big mistake as a sliver of Charlene's face oozes through a wooden door to the soldier's left. It looks as if the door grows a pretty girl's eyes. Charlene disappears as quickly as she revealed herself, but Willa's distraction alerts the witch soldier, who glances in that direction.

As the soldier turns his head, Philby runs for the wall. The witch soldier spins and hurls the halberd like a javelin. He catches Philby in the shoulder, spinning him. Already halfway through the wall, Philby loses all clear and screams horrifically, his shoulder pierced, a solid wall running the length of him. It feels like he's been severed in half.

Willa experiences his agony as her own. He's more than a friend; he matters to her. She can't stop her feet from running to him; she pays no attention to the witch soldier's simultaneous advance. The soldier hooks her throat in the crook of his elbow and, lifting her, throws Willa against the outer wall. She slams and falls, breaking the glass of a display case.

Now she's mad. And he shouldn't have made her mad.

Pent up inside Willa are years of frustration at the world for not understanding her. This anger simmers like the belching lava of a near-dormant volcano. For eighteen years, she's managed to keep it under control, like a spring in a box. But this soldier has hurt her maybe-boyfriend, thrown her across a room, and challenged her leadership.

She's going to stop him. She will not fail.

54

FINN CROUCHES WITH Violet and Storey Ming in a clump of low bushes behind a pretzel stand. They're hiding across from the Mark Twain Riverboat landing; from here, they can see that the riverboat broke loose in the earthquake and drifted against the retaining wall next to the *Columbia*.

Finn put Storey on his team because of what the Dillard told him. He tries not to let her see the contempt he feels for her, and his confusion over her real intentions.

An enemy within.

In one short conversation with the Dillard, his trust has evaporated. Worse, it's been replaced by *dis*trust. He wants Storey close, where he can deal with her. His heart fights against him; he doesn't want to believe the dark things he has heard. She has helped him out so many times; why would one of Chernabog's Overtakers do such a thing?

Maybe the Dillard retrieved incorrect data. *Never trust anything from the Internet* is a maxim drummed into him since middle school. What is the Dillard but a talking search engine?

The distance between Finn and the boats seems enormous, an open expanse in which they will be easy to spot and attack. But the hilt of the sword has warmed in his hologram hand; it feels comfortable, part of him. Prince Phillip's brief training fills him with confidence.

"It looks empty," Finn whispers.

"I wouldn't count on it," Storey says.

It's different having these two at his side: non-Keepers,

but not Fairlies. The girls feel like trainees or interns. At the same time, he can't match Violet's powers, nor does he possess Storey's knowledge of the park and her otherworldly familiarity with Disney characters both good and evil.

"Thoughts? Suggestions?" he whispers.

"Be a nice place to lay a trap," Storey says.

"If I were them," Violet adds, "I'd put someone up top as a lookout."

"Interesting," Finn says, studying the riverboat more carefully.

"I'd go for the *Columbia*," Storey says, pointing to the masts of the tall ship. Following her gaze, Finn counts three platforms that would make good hiding places, one on each mast. A person lying down on any one of them would be able to see without being seen.

Two boats. Three people in his team.

"But they'd be looking in this direction, into the park, not out toward the water," Storey says.

"We attack from the water side!" Finn says. "Brilliant!"

"*I* approach the riverboat from the water," Storey says. "I'm a bit of a fish—I even held the record for swimming underwater . . . at my school. If I get behind those rocks over there, I can come around on that side of the riverboat and go up its far side."

"I'll take the tall ship while Storey takes the riverboat."

"Works for me," says Storey.

"I can't stay invisible forever," Violet says, "but I can get over there, no sweat. Once I'm on the tall ship, I can hide for a minute and recharge. When Storey's ready, I'll climb up the center mast and Storey will check the top of the wheelhouse on the riverboat. Once it's clear, we meet on the riverboat and search it."

Finn has understood for years now that good leadership

means allowing others to lead. He considers himself more a navigator than a captain, more a facilitator than a dictator. "Sounds good," he says.

Violet looks at him oddly. "Even Dash would disagree with some part of any plan I made."

"If I spot trouble, I'm asking questions later," Finn says spinning the sword. "Let's do this."

The girls take off. Finn doesn't see Violet again, but a shadow flows across the path in the far distance, over the wall, and into the water, as slippery as an octopus.

Finn has also learned that waiting is the hard part. Watching a plan unfold is far more difficult than being actively involved in it; patience is a warrior's most challenging skill to perfect. He does not waste the downtime, but spends it focusing on nothing. Like patience, this isn't easy. But nothingness is his avenue to all clear, his escape to transparency. And with the way he's been clouded by grief over Wayne's loss, he no longer trusts his self-assessment. This thought causes a ripple of worry, undoing his efforts of the past few seconds. Wayne, the man who introduced him to this unworldly world, now stands in the way of his owning it. Whoever said "Loss is gain" never tried to remain all clear.

Finn doesn't want to admit to himself that he should have been the one to remain behind in the tunnel, protected by Amanda, that he's not ready to return to his familiar role. He's stronger than that. He pushes himself to unveil the blackness, to allow a pinpoint of light. But as a Keeper, you do not push to become nothing. You accept it.

As Storey slithers over the far rail of the riverboat, Violet appears, hugging the tall ship's center mast. Their choreography could not be more perfect. Storey's movement down onto the deck looks so fluid that Finn recoils, looking away briefly. For some reason, it makes him sick to his stomach. But looking back, there she is, crouching as she crosses the deck. The girl he knows and likes.

On the riverboat, Violet ascends the mast with the confidence and skill of Spider-Man. She looks like a tree frog as she climbs, a red bug with a black thorax.

Storey does not reappear right away. She must be waiting to inspect the roof of the wheelhouse until Violet confirms her successful occupancy of the top of the central mast.

Six feet before she reaches her destination, Violet vanishes. A moment later, Finn sees a telescope swing back through the air, seemingly by itself, and drop again in a crushing blow. This is followed by Violet's reappearance, broken telescope in hand. There will be no more spying from the tall ship.

Facing in Finn's direction, Violet raises both arms in a questioning gesture. She is looking down at the Mark Twain Riverboat. Finn points, indicating Storey is there, but Violet shakes her head, *No.*

This is the problem with unfamiliar people, Finn thinks. You haven't worked with them, and you don't know what they'll do. His first guess is that Storey has gone rogue—she's entered the riverboat, intending to find the missing piece of Mickey and come out the hero. It makes sense, given Storey's uncanny independence.

But this is followed by a more chilling thought: what if Storey has no intention of sharing? What if she's in this for herself? How well does he know Storey and Violet? And yet, the two have been allowed to overhear all the Keepers' plans and theories. . . .

Finn is up and running before he makes any conscious decision. He moves in a zigzag, the sword gripped in both hands and held before him, ready to strike.

Strike what, he isn't sure.

55

CAUGHT HALFWAY through the wall, his hologram degraded, Philby moans, struggling to maintain consciousness. His right shoulder is stained red from the halberd spearing him.

The halberd lies atop the broken glass of a display case, just out of reach. A brief, long-distance exchange between Philby and Willa suggests that they understand each other and share a similar plan. If only Philby can seize the halberd in time. He catches another glimpse of Charlene, inside the vault and searching for the Mickey illustration.

Willa must keep the witch soldier distracted and buy Charlene time; she must also rescue Philby, though dislodging his DHI from the wall is something only he can do. The two tasks are part and parcel of the same problem: if she can win the witch soldier's full attention, Philby will have an unthreatened window in which to reach all clear and free himself.

She and Philby have come to the same conclusion: it all has to do with the halberd. A soldier and his weapon.

The soldier makes a move. In that instant, Willa, still holding Philby's attention, points to her eyes, her heart, and to Philby.

I . . . love . . . you.

With a pained cry, Philby lunges. His fingers hook the pole of the halberd and flick it. The strength required for such a move should make it impossible for the weapon to travel more than a few inches, but the seven-foot steel-topped lance flies across the room and into Willa's outstretched hands.

Philby now hangs at a precipitous angle, his body suspended above the jagged broken glass of the display case.

Willa cannot believe the weight of the soldier's weapon. It pulls her toward the floor. Only fierce determination allows her to regain her balance and swing it at the approaching soldier. He's too close; the blade impales his arm. He jumps back, his pinprick eyes a riot of disbelief.

"I didn't mean it!" Willa says apologetically. Recovering, she adds, "I meant it for your neck." She gets her legs under her and lunges. The soldier jumps back, folding in at the waist to avoid being spiked.

She has his attention now.

* * *

Charlene has the advantage of all clear. She moves silently, slipping through walls. The vault's interior is a boxlike space containing nothing but an easel with a poster on it, which block the door. The velvet-draped walls are lit by overhead track lights, giving it the look of an unused closet or prison cell.

Charlene can't figure out the implications of the empty room, the posting of a single guard, though admittedly a formidable one. Fearing an invisible foe is about to strike her down without warning, she keeps her back to the bland wall and moves as silently as possible. She sees nowhere to hide the pasted-together pieces of an illustration, no art on the walls, no shelves, no other doors. The emptiness of the room frightens her, and it worries her that there is nothing to be found here— that the presence of the single guard means that the Overtakers don't value the empty vault.

There is carpeting, but it's new. If clues once existed leading to the Mickey illustration, they are long gone.

What convinces Charlene to look more carefully is the room's size and shape. It's small, and wider than it is deep. Coming from upstairs, arriving in the former offices, she's seen the hallway that leads to the gallery proper, a hallway longer than the vault is deep.

As the sounds of struggle arise from the gallery, she taps the back wall with a knuckle. Faced with the decision to explore or rescue, her battle is not with the witch soldier but with her own desire to join the fight.

But the plan was diversion and execution. She would defeat their efforts if she joined Willa and Philby. The idea is not to bring down the witch soldier, but to discover and recover whatever he's protecting.

The sound behind her drumming knuckle changes as she reaches a point directly across from the vault's door. It's richer, deeper, more drumlike. The wall is hollow, suggesting a door-way boarded up years before.

Charlene exhales, blocks out the fight raging behind her, peers into the wall and sees lumber instead of concrete. She steps through and finds herself inside a dark, narrow space with three of its walls lined with safe-deposit boxes, many of them with their doors wide open, single keys protruding from one of the two keyholes in each door. The linoleum floor is strewn with debris and litter. Most of the boxes are small, but the three lowest rows have larger and wider ones. Safe-deposit boxes, Charlene recalls, can normally only be opened by the simultaneous use of a personal key, property of the box holder, and a master key, property of a bank. Even if she can locate a box containing the missing Mickey, she'll need two keys to open the box. But there must be a hundred or more keys scattered around, including both the ones on the floor and those left in the keyholes of opened boxes.

Several dozen of the safe-deposit boxes remain locked. The missing Mickey could be in any one of them.

Charlene releases herself to all clear, using a technique different from the one Finn has taught them. She doesn't focus on anything; she turns herself over to nothing, just as she does to move through walls. But this time it's a more difficult exercise. She enters the wall of safe-deposit boxes headfirst and studies the contents of several. But being blind to anything that might happen behind her with her head in a wall is terrifying, and she can't keep it up.

Feeling pressured to accomplish her task while Philby and Willa are dealing with the witch soldier, she finds it difficult to think. It bothers her how Finn and Philby are always doing the thinking for the group. It vexes her to not feel more in control of herself at the moment.

How can she identify the box containing the Mickey illustration? Why would Wayne or Walt leave no clue about which box to search and how to open it?

Believing there must be instructions lurking about, coded or disguised, Charlene reads and studies the scattered papers on the floor, tossing aside abandoned costume jewelry and discarded Disney memorabilia removed from the now-empty boxes.

Have the Overtakers beaten them to it? She won't go there—won't consider the possibility.

The instructions will be coded. She's certain of it. But there will exist some clue for the Keepers. As Charlene is thinking this, she spots a pair of black-framed eyeglasses amid the stuff spread around on the floor. She hurries to pull them on, but it's too dark to see clearly. Throwing papers to the side like a whirling wind, she comes across a small keychain flashlight, then another—and another. She nearly squeals with shock and surprise as she sees what's printed on each of them:

The trinkets are named for the Keepers, but there's an added word: INSIDER. Here she is, *inside* a bank vault that may hold the secret to saving the devastated park. How long have these flashlights been lying around in here? How is this possible?

Picking up one of the key chains, she squeezes the fob. The tiny light emits a soft, wide beam, turning the whole room vaguely purple. Charlene sees the vault's interior with a sudden new clarity, and realizes that the eyeglasses she has put on have 3-D lenses.

Wayne!

She carefully studies the vault's interior, knowing—no, *believing*—that clues only the Keepers could figure out are within her reach. Outside the doorless room, there's trouble. But this *insider* feels only hope. Her blue outline begins to shimmer.

* * *

When Philby slipped, reaching for the halberd, he inadvertently moved the stripe of pain caused by his mortal contact with the wall to his lungs and heart. It's as if an unfathomable weight has been placed on his chest. He can't breathe. His vision blurs as Willa, looking so small and fragile, stabs at the soldier. Philby is about to pass out; through the haze of pain, he realizes that to move as he did, he must have gone briefly all clear. Willa's signed message to him is the only possible reason. He thinks of her words. He fixes his mind on her. Seconds before drawing what would be his last breath, Philby turns his thoughts away from his own pain, away from the crushing wall, and directs his focus to the Willa and Charlene's safety, to Finn's success, somewhere out there in the park, to the continued protection of Amanda and Jess in the forgotten tunnel that's now KK Central Headquarters.

Philby tumbles out of the wall, through the broken glass case, and lands. He has no need to breathe, no room for pain. He is all clear at last.

Grabbing the witch soldier from behind, Philby spins him off balance. The soldier, nearly twice Philby's weight, crashes into the center display case, reaches overhead, and snags a chandelier for stability.

Willa lunges with the halberd.

"Do it!" Philby yells.

But Willa pulls back, unable to impale the man.

"I can't!"

"He's—not—human!" Philby snatches the halberd and thrusts its top spike into the soldier's chest. His eyes widen, fixing on Philby with a look of incomprehension.

"A child?" he says. The witch soldier turns gray and begins to crack. A pile of broken stone falls to the ground where he was standing.

"But . . . how . . . ?" Willa asks.

"They're bewitched! Brought alive by the ones with real power. We're killing illusions the real OTs want us to fear."

"You couldn't possibly have known that," Willa gasps.

"No," he admits. "Lucky guess."

"And if he'd been human?"

"I don't go there. I can't."

"But if he *had been*, you'd have killed him!"

"Where's Charlene?" he says. "Charlie!"

The girl's voice shouts an answer, but it sounds muted, like she's been gagged. Exchanging a startled look, Willa and Philby run into the vault.

"Empty," Philby gasps.

Charlene's voice is louder now, but Willa and Philby still cannot determine where it is coming from.

"Over here!" Willa tells Philby. "She's on the other side of this wall."

56

FINN DOESN'T NEED TO SIGNAL Violet. From her perch on top of the tall ship, she sees him running in a blur toward the riverboat. He jumps, grabs hold, and clambers onto the deck.

The wheelhouse is empty. Fear clutches Finn with its cold fingers as he follows the wet trail down the ship's steep ladder into the captain's quarters.

Empty likewise. But the captain's clock has been torn from the wall.

It's about time.

The wet path stops at a door bearing a brass plaque marked CREW ONLY. Finn twists the knob gently and eases the door open.

There's a small platform with yet another short set of stairs leading down into the riverboat's engine room, which turns out to be cluttered with pipes, valves, and gauges. Finn descends into the murkiness, letting the pipes pass through his DHI without a whisper.

"Storey?" He doesn't like that she's gone ahead without him and Violet, doesn't like that she created the plan and then didn't follow it. He feels like a runner at the back of the pack; he's waited too long to sprint and now Storey's in the lead, looking over her shoulder, sneering at him.

He sees her. Storey, pressed into a narrow area against the hull, in front of an old built-in chest held shut by a rusted padlock. She says nothing. She seems more shadow and shape than real girl.

"You didn't wait for us," Finn says. "That's not right."

"The water . . ." she says, her voice oddly low and guttural. "I thought . . . But I should have known. What does Dorothy say? 'There's no place like home'?"

From the little Finn can see, her neck and limbs are grossly swollen.

During their first meeting on the Disney *Dream*, Storey claimed she was sent by Wayne, something the Keepers' mentor never confirmed. Finn recalls being at the Castaway Cay stingray station with Storey, and how exceedingly comfortable she seemed around dangerous sea creatures. He sees now where this is headed—her swelling limbs, the way she slipped over the rail onto the riverboat. But he can't completely face it.

On the cruise, she led Philby and Willa to the *Dream*'s galley where they were attacked. She vanished for three years and reappeared in Ariel's Undersea Adventure, of all places! How did he allow himself to miss it? He's fraught with anger, embarrassed by how easily she won him over. He sees himself as small-minded and immature, so easily manipulated. He can't catch his breath, flush with a fool's fever.

"Why . . . ?" he gasps, taking a step back. "How?"

"Allergic reaction," she says. "I forgot it was freshwater."

"You lied." He pauses. "You've lied constantly."

It's no mere allergic reaction, it's a full-on loss of transfiguration. As she grows, Storey emerges partially out of shadow like a balloon being inflated. Purple, slimy skin, soft and unctuous. Finn faces her in her true form: Ursula.

"Ah . . . well . . . yes, there is that," the sea witch says. "As to why: it has remained locked away for a long time, this treasure. From the first I heard about the powers of the Children of Light, I knew the reason for your existence. I believed you would lead me to this chest inside wood. Of course I was right,

514

I am always right. Besides, you know what they say around here about believing. And I believed in you."

Distantly, he hears Violet, moving overhead on the deck. The sound is followed closely by a slurping, sucking sound that makes him sick to his stomach. He looks over his shoulder, squinting at the horrid thing emerging from the dark.

He shouts, "Down here! Quick!"

He hears Violet racing down the first set of stairs.

"In here!"

He doesn't dare look away from Ursula.

"You have got to be kidding me!" Violet says softly. "Where'd she come from?"

The sea witch answers. "That's a long and involved story, which is why I so appreciated the name of my former host in the first place. But enough, my dears; we haven't got the time for all that." She slides forward, a mass of tentacles and suction cups and a whole lot of ugly. "As to that," she says, "I'm afraid you've no time at all."

Her tentacles move like fast-striking snakes after Finn.

57

CHARLENE IS SMILING in spite of herself, in awe of Wayne's genius.

The 3-D glasses, used in conjunction with the trinket flashlight's eerie purplish beam, reveal an Osiris eye hieroglyph engraved on one of the dozens of flat brass keys protruding from the abandoned safe-deposit boxes.

Philby and Willa sweep through the wall, startling her. After hearing about the 3-D glasses and her search for a second key, Philby searches the unlocked safe-deposit boxes. Inside one he finds four more pairs of glasses.

"One for each of us," he says, "though don't ask me how that's possible."

Together, Charlene and Willa continue the search for a second key. Philby devotes himself to the lockboxes.

"Got it!" he announces.

Charlene hates him for finding it so fast. "How can you be—"

"Certain? Because there's a stair-step box glyph scratched onto the hinge. You wouldn't see it unless you were looking for it."

"Wayne," Charlene says.

"Or Walt, or an Imagineer. Yes. Whoever's behind this scavenger hunt."

Willa wears one of the pairs of glasses while carefully searching among the discarded keys on the carpet. She checks both sides of every key. *Nothing.* She double-checks with

Charlene, who turns from the keys on the floor to check those keys remaining in the safe-deposit box doors. *Nothing.*

"There could be more witch soldiers out there. We've got to hurry," Willa reminds them.

Philby squints behind the 3-D glasses. Think! "There's a number clue we're missing," he announces. It's right in front of us, so what is it?"

"1955," Willa says. "1971. Those are the most obvious."

"Try them!" Philby shouts.

He and Willa converge on box 1955. It's open and empty. So is 1971, the year Disney World opened.

"1901, Walt's birthday!" Willa says loudly. They hurry, and again the box stands open and empty.

Charlene suggests an address. "Is there one for the gallery? For the park?"

Philby actually jumps off the vault floor. His glasses bounce on his nose. "Thirteen thirteen!" He and Willa run to find it. It's locked. The glasses reveal a tiny image of a sitting Egyptian priest.

"Dang!" Charlene works a key from the door of an open box. "Tell me this isn't the master key!" She hands the key to Willa—not Philby—drawing her fingernail along the tag end of the key, which has been altered slightly, cut into a barely recognizable shape. Held up to the beam from one of the keychain flashlights, it resembles the profile of a bearded Egyptian pharaoh.

"To the contrary," the Professor says. "This is it!"

He places the two keys into the slots on box 1313. It opens. He steps aside and motions Charlene forward. It's the nicest thing Philby has ever done for her.

Charlene pulls the door open, removes the steel box from inside, and sets it on the carpet. There's a moment of hesitation. The three Keepers huddle close, as if gathering around the warmth of a small fire.

"Anybody want to do this?" Charlene asks.

"You go ahead," says Philby.

She opens the box's hinged lid, revealing an interdepartmental manila envelope with a string-and-button closure, aged to a leathery brown. There are only five signatures in the two dozen available spaces. Four are crossed out, starting with Walt Disney's. The bottom signature, not crossed out, is Wayne Kresky's.

"Whoa," says Philby.

"Seriously," says Willa.

For a moment, no one dares touch it. Then Charlene reaches in, careful not to fold or crease the envelope. As she moves to unwind the string from the cardboard button, the thin string decomposes in her DHI fingers, and the flap pops open. Charlene peels it back and reaches inside.

"Easy!" Philby warns.

"Rip the envelope," Willa says. "Tear the envelope away from what's in there—but don't hurt Walt's signature! We'll want to show the Imagineers."

"Help me."

Together, the three Keepers slowly work the envelope apart at its original seams. Inside is a milky-hued glassine envelope, which Professor Philby says reminds him of the waxy-looking papers of the sheets that protected his grandfather's stamp collection.

But there are no stamps inside. Even without opening the envelope, the contents show through. A dozen torn pieces of a pen-and-ink drawing, its bold black outlines clearly visible through the translucent inner envelope.

Philby coughs and sits back. The girls sit back as well. No

one wants to touch this treasure. After a minute or two, they cradle it together and return it to the steel box for protection.

"How are we going to get it out of here?" Charlene asks. "We need to make a hole in the wall, maybe where they sealed this room off from the vault."

"Stay where you are," Willa says, standing.

"What are you thinking?" Philby asks. He has several ideas about how to break through the wall, but he doesn't believe any one of them will work.

Willa grins. "A gift from the Overtakers. The halberd." She passes into the false wall, and disappears.

58

"FINN?"

Violet calls his name from somewhere back by the ship's ladder. Finn understands the tremor of rising panic in her voice; he can make sense of her shouting over the tumult of splintering wood as timbers yield around him under the pressure from Ursula's rapidly expanding body. He dances in the inrushing water, trying to avoid her tentacles.

The extreme tip of a slimy black-and-purple appendage wraps around Finn's all-too-human leg. The upper hull splinters, admitting enough light to see what his ears have already learned from the sea witch's hideous laugh.

Ursula continues to expand, bursting outward from what was once Storey's body.

An enemy within. No common spy or OT agent. The Keepers were thinking too small. Worst of all, his anger at being deceived by her, of having *kissed* her, roils inside him, giving him no chance to all clear.

What Finn faces is not small. He remembers seeing *The Little Mermaid* and thinking, That's one big ugly monster. Now, seeing the big ugly in person, terror overcomes him. He's trapped in the crowded confines of the engine room, with water all around and a long way up a pair of steep ladders to get out.

Ursula tugs with what turns out to be one of many tentacles. Can there only be six, as in the movie? It seems more like eighty. Finn goes down, falling hard, slamming into the hull. Another tentacle finds his waist and twists powerfully around him like an ever-tightening belt. Simultaneously, the tentacle holding his foot drags him closer to Ursula. Two more tentacles tear the chest from the hull. Cold water gushes in.

"Let him go!" shouts Violet.

A tentacle shoots for Violet, but stops abruptly; it's too short to reach her. Ursula oozes in Violet's direction, moving her tentacles within range, but Violet disappears, instantly invisible.

"Now, now," growls Ursula in a devilishly low voice. "Let's not play games."

She swings three tentacles in Violet's direction, one of which bends noticeably as it makes contact with the invisible girl. Ursula doesn't manage to grab her, but the resulting bang of metal pipes tells Finn that Violet can't be feeling great.

Water courses through the hull as Ursula's expanding size continues to splinter the wood. The sea witch wraps a coiled tentacle around the wooden chest, holding it tight.

"We are smaller in number, you see," she says to Finn. Her many tentacles continue, apparently without her notice, to pull down pipes, searching for Violet. It's as if her tentacles are part antennae and she's able to see by touch. "Not smaller in ambition or determination. You children were out to destroy them, which was fine with us. But you offered something else—intelligence. A quality frightfully lacking in most of us villains, I'm sorry to say. Ariel has it to spare. I've always hated that about her. Eric, too. Smart *and* good-looking."

She squeezes Finn playfully. He can't breathe. He chokes out the words, "Typhoon Lagoon?"

"Yes. My last attempt to stop you. Discretion is the better part of valor, as you humans say. Why fight when you can join?"

"The girl? The real Storey. Did you kill her?"

"That thing?" Ursula shifts to the side. An unconscious Storey Ming floats face up in the rising bilge water. "I borrowed her. It hardly matters. You will all die here. The hidden Mickey will give my small band the power it needs to defeat the rebels. Those . . . show-offs will be finished soon enough."

Rebels? Ursula is not with the Overtakers, Finn realizes. This insight provokes myriad questions he wants answered—*needs* answered. He recalls Maleficent once telling him, "I am but a humble servant to she who lives within. My powers are so small and insignificant." Had she meant Ursula? he wonders.

The last thing he sees before being sucked underwater is Violet reappearing behind Ursula. She has found a section of pipe and is holding it in a way that reminds him of Prince Eric ramming Ursula with the prow of the shipwreck he commanded.

From the moment his head goes under, Finn knows he's not going to free himself from Ursula's hold. He focuses on obtaining all clear—it's his only way out. But with air leaking from his nose and mouth, and his eyesight blurred by oily water, there's no dark vacuum, no pinprick of light.

He's beginning to faint. In his delirium, he remembers Storey's complaint about her allergy to fresh water. But the truth was, she—Ursula—is at home in water and failed to realize it would change her back to her real form.

The sea witch's grip on Finn briefly loosens; he imagines Violet has stabbed the purple octopus. But the respite comes unexpectedly; by the time Finn can react, Ursula has retightened her hold, which doesn't bode well for him or Violet.

Another remembered voice bubbles to the surface. Finn tells himself it's not Wayne's. Wayne is dead. Dead people don't speak to the living—except maybe in the Haunted

Mansion. For that matter, it doesn't sound like Wayne either, though it has a low, powerful, paternal timbre. Without thinking or planning, with a spontaneity that doesn't come naturally to Finn, he repeats what he hears.

The words unlock a memory from years before. Expelling the last vestiges of stale air in his lungs, Finn speaks in bubble talk: "Starfish wise, starfish cries"—the coded command King Triton gave him to summon help from the mer-people. In his oxygen-starved delirium, Finn expects Ariel's father to burst through the ship's hull, skewer Ursula with his trident, and drag her down to the depths.

Nothing happens. No climatic explosion, no loosening of Ursula's hold on Finn. With one more squeeze, the sea witch pops Finn's eyes open, practically right out of his hologram head—allowing Finn to see his sword below him, its hilt toward him in the oily water. Somehow Triton has managed to show Finn his sword—just out of reach.

Finn flutter-kicks like a swimmer, but he can't stretch far enough to grab hold. He fights Ursula, pulling on her suction cups, trying to tear them from her tentacles.

Above the rising water's surface, Violet disappears and reappears in Ursula's blind spot. Violet lunges with the pipe, stabbing Ursula in the back of the neck.

Below the water, a tentacle spasms.

Finn takes hold of his sword, curls forward, and slices off the end piece of a tentacle. Black ink clouds the water. He's free!

With visions of the Brave Little Tailor from Fantasmic! filling his head, Finn explodes out of the water. As Ursula strangles Violet with two tentacles simultaneously, he stabs the sea witch in the center of her chest and lets go of the sword, leaving it plunged two feet deep inside her.

Ursula reels, tips to one side, and demolishes what's left of the hull as she sinks from view, still clutching the wooden chest.

The riverboat floods, rolls, and begins to sink.

Finn swims for the unconscious Storey, grabbing the violently coughing Violet by the arm as he passes. A girl in each hand, he swims for the gaping hole in the hull, their only chance to escape this underwater coffin.

He's not strong enough.

What Finn takes to be a shift in the current turns out to be Storey Ming swimming both him and Violet toward the jagged hole. She pulls them at incredible speed. Before Finn can blink, they're out and headed up to the surface, where they break free and gasp for air.

"State breaststroke champion!" Storey says, giving him an enormous grin as the three tread water. "My senior year in high school." She wipes her eyes. "I'm Storey, by the way. Who are you?"

59

FINN SCRAMBLES UP to the dock as the riverboat founders in the dark water, recalling the times Storey helped the Keepers and fighting to make sense of Ursula's boasts. He gets to his feet, stumbling onto dry land, and collapses at the base of a huge rock. It sits like a small island, surrounded by blacktop.

Storey and Violet join him. Violet's hair is wet, but her superwoman suit looks dry. In contrast, Finn and Storey are soaked through. They exchange a volley of partial sentences, coughing and spitting as they try to get the words out. They're all breathing. Things could be worse.

It's readily apparent that there is more than just river water on Storey's face. Tears pour down her cheeks; she's shaking, as if freezing cold. She's going into shock, something only Finn understands. As a Disney character, Violet has no idea what it's actually like to be human, though she plays one on the big screen.

"Are you okay?" Finn asks.

Violet's kindness surprises Finn; she wraps her arm around the girl and holds her tight.

"Who are you people? Where am I?" Storey pleads.

"This is Disneyland." Finn is about to explain further when he's interrupted by Storey.

"What are you talking about?" she says, and nuzzles into Violet's shoulder like a child.

"What's the last thing you remember?" Finn asks more gently.

"My mom! Where is she? Where's my dad? My family? I

want my family!" She shudders and starts sobbing. "What was that thing down there?"

Finn wonders if people have been able to come and go from the park since the earthquake. The Keepers talked about a spell being cast. Was it a spell of appearance, or of exclusion?

"Am I dreaming or something?" Storey continues. "What's going on?"

Finn sees the way out. Together, he and Violet get Storey up and walking. "Dreams have a funny way of never telling you whether or not you're in one," he says. "But when you awake, you'll think that you were talking to Violet from *The Incredibles*. What are the odds of that, seriously? Isn't it more likely that you boarded the wrong ship by accident in Nassau? That maybe you banged your head or something and finally woke up in Disneyland a long time later? Your family is going to love seeing you again. And aren't you excited to see them? You've got to go back to sleep, so you can wake from this nightmare and start your life again."

"Ursula . . . Violet . . . I see what you mean. But who are you?"

"I'm kind of like your conscience," Finn says. "The part of you that understands how this all happened. You're going to wake up in a place called Club 33. It's nice in there, and there are phones, and you can call home. Everything's going to be all right again, Storey. I promise."

It's several minutes before they have her comfortably laid out on some pillows in Club 33. She falls asleep almost instantly.

"You're a sweet talker, Finnegan," Violet says. "I believed every word you said."

Finn mutters, "Ursula took the chest down with her. The missing Mickey."

"But we got out alive," Violet says. "And you saved Storey. That's got to earn us some points."

They're walking past the Golden Horseshoe when Finn notices a towering rock to their left. He's drawn toward the brass plaque at its base:

PETRIFIED TREE,
FROM THE PIKE PETRIFIED FOREST,
COLORADO

Finn skips to the bottom of the inscription:

PRESENTED TO DISNEYLAND
BY
MRS. WALT DISNEY
SEPTEMBER 1957

There's a long explanation that doesn't interest him. He can't look away from the credit at the bottom and the date: Mrs. Walt Disney, 1957.

"There's a photo in Walt's apartment," Finn says, rising to his feet. "Mrs. Disney, Walt, and some others with shovels. Like a—"

"Dedication," says Violet. "Breaking ground for the installation of something in the park. Something fifty-five to seventy million years old, weighing five tons."

"The arrows, the map—it wasn't marking the riverboat. It was this!" Finn says. "In the Osiris myth, the final piece of the god's body is found inside a *tree*."

"Locked away where no one can get to it." Violet studies the massive rock.

"Locked away so it isn't stumbled upon," Finn agrees. "It

527

has to be found. Searched for. You need to know what you're looking for." He paces back and forth, then blurts out what he's thinking about Ursula's reference to the Overtakers as "them."

"It's years ago. The Kingdom is threatened by a power struggle within the Disney villains. It fractures and threatens to overpower the park magic. Walt knows the power of the original Mickey illustration. Mickey, too. He knows the true source of the magic that made this place come alive and seem so real. Mickey tells Minnie to tear it up—basically, to kill him, put him into hibernation. She puts the pieces in the bank vault, but not *all* of them. Walt Disney or Wayne hides some. A story is invented for the sake of the Imagineers, saying that the Overtakers are responsible. It emphasizes the importance of protecting the original.

"And then . . . then Walt hides the final piece inside a gift he gives to his wife. She gives it to Disneyland, and a quest is built around it, a quest involving a myth certain to outsmart the OTs."

Violet nods excitedly. "The missing Mickey," she says. "Inside there."

Finn looks up and down the five-ton petrified tree.

"The insider," he utters under his breath.

60

"YOU DIDN'T THINK I was just along for my good looks, did you?" Violet asks Finn, who's giving her an uncertain look. "Stand back."

"Violet?" Finn inquires.

"Way behind me. Farther!"

Finn is ten yards behind Violet. "You don't have to do this! It's too risky!"

She's not listening. The slim girl's fists are tightened at her sides, her head cast downward in concentration. As Finn watches in horror, she starts to shake. He knows what's coming.

Finn is lifted off his feet and propelled backward, along with an uprooted sapling tree, a trash can, and a number of rocks. Umbrella tables at River Belle Terrace take to the air like kites. Finn crashes to the earth beside them; shaking his head, trying to clear his vision, he sees that the petrified tree has changed. It leans to one side, with dozens of cracks showing.

Violet looks back, her telltale swoosh of hair obscuring one eye, and sees that he's okay.

Violet emits her force field a second time; this time the result is more like a tornado. The petrified tree explodes into hundreds of flying chunks. Even the largest of the pieces takes to the air; as the force field diminishes, they come raining down on Violet like falling meteorites. The girl collapses to the ground in a limp heap.

Finn rushes to her aid. Violet's left leg is broken. Finn

wrestles a huge rock off her chest, but her breathing remains hoarse and shallow. Her face is the color of sand.

"Can't . . . breathe . . ." she gasps. She forces her bluish lips into an unconvincing smile. "How'd I do?"

Finn looks at the rubble of the destroyed tree. "You nailed it," he says, trying to smile at her.

"Really?" She coughs. Red stains her teeth. Finn can't look.

"Yeah. This place is a gravel pit," Finn says.

"What about the thirt—?" Violet can't complete the sentence. She breaks off into a horrendous wet cough that chills Finn to the bone.

Beside her, he spots a small box. No bigger than a jewelry case, it's made of cherrywood and has turquoise-blue panels on both ends.

"I think I see it," he says.

"Get it!"

But Finn won't leave her. "I'm about to give you mouth-to-mouth," he warns, "so you'd better pucker up. I've never kissed a superhero before."

"Oh no you're not!" She laughs, which is not a good idea.

"Stop talking and get ready!" he says.

"Shut . . . up!"

Finn's throat tightens. He doesn't really know Violet; he has spent only a few hours with her. But their connection runs deep. They share a common cause. She has supported the so-called Children of Light based on little more than faith, stories, and rumor. She's chasing a legend of which he's an integral part, which means it's a fiction: he can't be considered Disney legend. Not yet. Maybe not ever.

He'd have dived for the box a moment ago, but now it strikes him as petty, insignificant. What good is saving the Kingdom if it costs the lives of the wonderful characters who inhabit it? The good guys aren't supposed to die trying—like Dillard, Wayne, and now Violet. They're supposed to *win*.

But this, Finn realizes, is the Disney that's not Disney. The story behind the stories, the truth behind the legends. And he's a soldier, an ant in the colony, nothing more.

Finn bends lower, ready to put his mouth on Violet's to supply the air she's not getting. As their lips are about to touch, he hears the patter of footsteps, panics, and sits up. Is it Ursula?

No: it's Rapunzel.

"May I?" she asks Finn.

"But how—"

"You Children of Light seem to forget we're here to help. We try to help. We want to help."

Finn stands aside as Rapunzel kneels by the failing Violet. Partially unbraiding her divine locks, she lays her hair on Violet's chest, covering her waist and broken leg. Then Rapunzel starts to sing.

"Flower gleam and glow . . ."

It's her hair that gleams and glows. Radiating out from it is a wave of sparkling light, so intense that it blinds Finn, forcing him to look away.

When he looks back, Violet is herself again and Rapunzel is rebraiding her hair.

"You saved her," Finn croaks.

"My hair saved her," Rapunzel says. "You are Finnegan, are you not?"

He nods shyly.

Rapunzel stands—she's an enchanting beauty—steps close to Finn, and kisses him on the cheek. As her lips brush his skin, the world fades away. There are no fires burning in the park, no rising smoke staining the sky toxic gray, no distant cries of celebrating Overtakers. He's flooded with warmth, embarrassment, appreciation, and respect. Feeling his face flush, he realizes that more than fear can remove one's all clear.

"Thank you," he says, unsure whether his words are for the kiss or for saving Violet's life.

Rapunzel gives him a squinty-eyed smile, all white teeth and a blush in her cheeks.

With one look in that direction from Violet, Finn moves toward the box, frees it from the rubble, and opens it.

Inside is a single piece of torn paper: Mickey's eyes.

61

FIVE MINUTES BEFORE the Small World dolls attack the
Fairlies, the Dillard warns Maybeck, Jess, and Amanda of the
imminent assault.

"How can you possibly know that, Dillard?" Amanda asks.

"I am able to hear their feet."

"I'm serious," she says.

"So am I. Maybeck," he says, "you, Amanda, and Jess need
to move the Mandy Blaster and load it with the chemicals you
recovered from beneath the Fantasmic stage. It requires an
elevation of four degrees, meaning a fulcrum should be placed
nineteen inches from the front end."

"Are we taking orders from a . . . ? Wait, what exactly *are*
you, Dillard?" Maybeck asks.

"I am Finn's friend. A version 1.6.3 Disney Hologram
Interactive operating at—"

"Pause!" Amanda gestures for Maybeck to stand down.
"Leave it, Terry. Let's just do this thing."

"He's a calculator with legs!" Maybeck complains. "If the
Small World dolls are coming, we should be getting out of
here."

"And who told us they were coming?" Jess asks.

"That's beside the point!"

"Since when?" Amanda reengages the Dillard. "Dillard,
fight or flight? Justifications, please."

"This is the most effective concentration of Small World
dolls we have yet seen, second only to the mass grouping in the

Skyway Station. The natural restriction of space imposed by the backstage concourse suggests—"

"Okay! Okay!" Maybeck hollers. "Forget the pros and cons. Let's do this."

Once decided, the team is a model of efficiency. Maybeck and Jess set up a galvanized section of drainage pipe, loading it with rocks and two vats' worth of the brooms' green goo, which Maybeck found just as Finn had said he would. The Dillard stands alongside Amanda, who takes her place at the opposite end of the pipe, practicing dry runs with her telekinetic hand movements.

"I've never tried to funnel the push before, Dillard. What if I can't do it?"

"Failure to engage the Small World dolls will result in a battle during which you—or we, I suppose—will be outnumbered eight to one. We will likely succumb."

"But *how* do I do it? Do it best, I mean?"

"Processing," the Dillard says, closing his eyes. "Is the resulting force a product of eyesight or hand gestures?" Without being consulted, he adds, "Two minutes until initial contact."

"I don't know. I've never thought about it. But the pipe is only two feet in diameter. If I do this wrong, I'll send the whole pipe and everything in it out there in a gigantic mess."

"If it is a combination of hand and eye, a prone position will be most efficient."

"I should lie down?"

"Assume a position with a sight line through your hands as they make an outward motion."

"Are you accessing the paranormal hand guide or something?" Amanda asks, laughing, as she moves to lie down.

"I am unable to locate any paranormal reference material.

534

I am basing my theory on a description of setting a volleyball or making a chest pass in basketball, both activities my sources confirm should be familiar to a female of your age."

Amanda feels herself tingle uncomfortably. The Dillard's explanation is too clinical, too definite. She longs for encouragement, not a paint-by-numbers description of how to behave.

"I think I'll wing it," she says. "But I promise to keep the volleyball thing in mind."

"Is that a question?"

"Shut up, Dillard." She's immediately sorry for the outburst, but tells herself she doesn't need to apologize to a projection. When the Dillard fails to speak, she adds, "Time to initial contact?"

"Forty-three seconds," the Dillard answers dryly.

"Get behind me!" Amanda calls out to Maybeck and Jess.

"It's not ready! It's set too low."

"Thirty seconds."

"Get behind me, now!"

While Maybeck holds the pipe up, Jess adjusts the scrap of wood they're using as a fulcrum point.

"Twenty seconds. Fifteen . . ."

"Now! Please!" Amanda cries.

Maybeck and Jess abandon their efforts, run, and dive past Amanda as they see her winding up. Maybeck rolls back alongside Amanda, leaning in so he can whisper to her.

"Wait for it!" Maybeck says.

"Seven . . . six . . ." the Dillard counts.

The dolls emerge, heading down a backstage path. They rock from side to side as they walk, stiff and puppetlike. Their painted faces are cheerful and eerily immobile; they're happy little killers. Their jaws open and snap shut mechanically, hungry for whatever portion of the Keepers or Fairlies fails to maintain all clear.

"Five . . ."

"I hate those things," Maybeck breathes, his words barely above a whisper.

Two rows of dolls. Three. Four. There are thirty or more dolls in view, and more coming still, their legs marching in time.

"Three . . . two . . ."

Maybeck holds his hand over Amanda's back like the spotter on a shoulder-fired missile team.

"One . . ."

Maybeck taps Amanda on the back and ducks.

The drainage pipe makes a tremendous sound, an echoing *whoosh*, like a giant toilet flushing. Its contents spray out the far end, moving with such velocity that the fluid looks like a beam of green light. Chunks of goo-covered concrete hit the dolls like steel ball bearings fired at bowling pins, vaporizing everything in their path. The creepy-looking dolls explode and then disintegrate; one moment they're an army of advancing ghouls, the next, a cloud of plaster dust. Charred pieces of costume float in the air like giant snowflakes.

Maybeck stands up and jumps in celebration, banging his head on the top of the tunnel and winning laughter from all but the Dillard.

"We did it! We did it!" Amanda appears to almost levitate.

Jess smiles, claps. She's never seen Amanda so giddy and free.

62

USING THE OPEN-AIR STAGE on Tom Sawyer Island as the rendezvous for reuniting the Hidden Mickeys is an obvious choice, but a dangerous one. No place is more symbolic of Mickey's enormous powers than the Fantasmic! show, staged here. But the island's isolation poses serious potential problems.

As Philby, Finn, Maybeck, Charlene, Jess, and Willa prepare for what is starting to feel like a ceremony, the Dillard and Violet remain hidden on the mainland, with Violet ready to fire up the outboard motor of a service barge tucked into the bushes upstream. Amanda, still recovering from the energy she lost defeating the Small World dolls, is tucked inside a hole in the artificial stone facing the stage, which conceals a theatrical spotlight. She has two hundred degrees of view available from her perch, and can see beyond the multistory stage set should the OTs attack from the rear.

Only Maybeck retains his sword from the Skyway Station battle. The other Keepers have only their wits for weapons.

Philby lays out the glassine envelope on the concrete apron fronting the wooden stage. Finn cracks open the box from the petrified tree.

"We're good at this," Charlene says as Philby gently withdraws the torn pieces of Mickey.

"We should be wearing gloves," Willa says. "This is wrong."

"Maybe next time," Maybeck quips.

The Keepers, who have faced dozens of challenges and quests in their years together, are indeed good at puzzles. Ten hands dance together, reaching around one another, adjusting the torn pieces, gradually assembling the complete image. What Finn believed to be an eye turns out to be one of two buttons on the front of a pair of shorts. Another candidate for an eye turns out to be the character's nose—longer and more tubular than in current renditions of the Disney icon. He has a shock of wild, grassy hair; the ears that have become his hallmark look like an afterthought, trailing behind him and far more mouselike than in more familiar images. Both his legs and his right arm are drawn only in outline.

On and on they go. The pieces come together: nose; smile. Finally a mouse's eyes complete the picture.

"There!" Charlene says.

"That's it," says Willa. She pauses. "Now what?"

With the pieces realigned, the five Keepers raise their heads to watch the stage, expecting a miracle.

"I know!" Maybeck says. "Jess?"

"You think . . . ?" Charlene doesn't sound convinced.

"If you can redraw an entire park with Walt's pen," Maybeck says, "how tricky can a mouse be?"

Jess joins them. She has her pen out practically before anyone speaks. "I don't want to damage the original. It seems sacrilegious to even touch it. Shouldn't it be under glass or something?"

"It will be," Philby says, "as soon as we repair it. As soon as we make it whole."

The ground shakes. River water slaps loudly against the shore.

"You've got to be kidding me!" Maybeck snorts. "Again?"

"Most of the park is still standing," Finn says. "Maybe they're moving in for the kill."

A ripple of thunder announces itself far in the distance.

"Do *not* tell me it's going to rain," Charlene complains. "When are we going to catch a break?"

"I don't think you catch them," Philby says.

"You make them," Finn agrees. "We all do this together."

The Keepers place their hands atop Jess's, as in a sports team's pregame huddle. She gently touches the nib of the pen to one of the torn edges in the drawing. Nothing happens. She looks up apprehensively.

"Wayne had me squirt a drop of ink out of it from pretty high up," Finn says.

"*You* should do it!" says a nervous Jess.

"No! He gave the pen to you, Jess. It's meant for you."

"But if it doesn't work, *I wreck the original Mickey Mouse drawing for all time.* How am I supposed to do that?"

"Look. If doesn't work, none of this is going to be here anyway," Philby says, indicating the park. "Jess, don't think anyone's going to hold it against us at that point."

"It isn't just you doing it," Charlene says.

"We're all in," Maybeck adds.

The ground rumbles more violently.

"Look!" Willa points to a giant crane rolling down Main Street.

"We've got to do this now," Maybeck says.

Jess sits up taller.

"Form a windscreen!" Philby cries.

The Keepers wrap themselves together, arm in arm, creating a circle around the torn pieces of Mickey. Jess's fingernail finds the small ink lever on the pen and pulls it gently. A single drop of ink forms on the nib. It hangs, refusing to fall.

"A little more," Maybeck encourages.

"I can't . . ."

"*More*, Jess," says Finn.

The lever moves infinitesimally. Jess's throat catches as the blob of ink falls in what looks to all the Keepers like slow motion.

It splashes onto the sheet.

The Keepers hold their breath. Wind tousles their hair, but the Mickey illustration remains flat and unmoving.

"I knew it," Jess moans. The fallen ink splatters outward from the central blot, grossly altering the original sketch.

"Oh, crud," Maybeck says, seeing the results. "That's a bummer."

Willa sees a tiny flash of silvery white light spark from one of the torn edges. "Did anybody see that?"

"See what?" says Maybeck.

"There! I saw it!" Charlene is pointing to an opposite corner.

"Oh—my—word!" cries Jess as the illustration begins to glow. With each flash, one of the torn edges between two fragments mends. Then the transformation picks up speed as three fragments become one and attach to four others. By its very nature, the magical process is otherworldly, but to Philby's and

Willa's keen analytical eyes, there is more involved than the drawing's power to glue itself back together.

"Watch it closely!" Philby says. "It's working from the inside out . . ."

"In order to be perfectly smooth, no bumps," Willa adds.

The flashes of light form concentric glowing rings that spread like ripples from a stone tossed into a pond. As the rings roll toward the edges, the spilled splash of black ink vanishes, leaving the rips healed, the integrity of the work restored. As the last of the rings pulses to the edge and the glimmer fades from the surprised faces circled around it, a lustrous platinum smoke spews forth on the stage above them. Spotlights switch on—though there are no operators to run them. A dazzling spectacle that now includes a backdrop of pyrotechnics unseen in the Fantasmic! show plays out. There is majestic music; perhaps they all imagine the exact same melody and arrangement simultaneously.

From the midst of it steps, not Mickey, as the Keepers expect, but Mortimer Mouse, Mickey's first incarnation, the black-and-white character depicted in the illustration. He bows formally, an odd creature, who looks different from the one the Keepers know and love.

With a wave of his arm, the special effects disappear. There's only a small white cloud rising into the night sky as evidence that any of it took place.

"Look!" Willa says, gesturing off island.

But none of the other Keepers can pull their eyes away from Mortimer, who evolves with each footfall as he descends the stairs step by step. First, he becomes a black-and-white Mickey with a Steamboat Willie look, then a colorful Mickey with red shorts and gold shoes. Finally, the Mickey who approaches wears fire-engine-red shorts that ride high on his waist, yellow shoes, and oversize white gloves. He walks with a jovial, casual stride—not a care in the world.

"Hello, sir," says Finn.

Mickey takes a look over his shoulder, as if wondering who Finn is addressing. He gestures to himself as if to say, "You mean me?"

"She's there, Mr. Mickey," says Willa, ever the romantic. She points across the river. The opposite shore is crowded shoulder-to-shoulder with hundreds of Disney characters and well-wishers. Still more are arriving in droves from New Orleans Square, the Haunted Mansion, Big Thunder Trail, and all of Frontierland. It's as if they've lined up for a fireworks show, as if the earthquake never happened.

Behind them, the crane's looming steel finger moves slowly toward Big Thunder Mountain. Feverish dark work continues on and around the Matterhorn. Two worlds, diametrically opposed.

Front and center in the viewing area, directly across the water, stands Minnie Mouse, waving enthusiastically. As Mickey waves back and blows a kiss to his sweetheart, the enormous crowd issues a collective sigh. Applause starts quietly, and then builds to a fever pitch. Mickey waves both arms, bows, and then starts again.

Philby carefully returns the repaired illustration to its protective envelope and slides it up the back of his shirt to protect it from folding.

The cheering is thunderous, with high screams and whistling louder than at any parade.

"He puts the *king* in kingdom," Willa says, as the five Keepers trail behind the icon, raising their hands to join in the applause.

"Doesn't he see what's happened?" Charlene asks. "All the destruction, I mean. How can he not see it?"

"Because he sees only good," Finn answers. "He sees the characters, not the concrete. It's them he's missed the most. And one character in particular, I'm guessing."

Even from afar, it's clear that Minnie Mouse is crying tears of joy. Pluto and Goofy stand at either side, supporting her.

Abruptly, Mickey drops to his knees, and the crowd goes silent. He leans forward and kisses the shaking ground. The resulting roar sets the Keeper's hologram ears to ringing.

"He's b-a-a-a-ack!" shouts Philby over the tumult.

Mickey clearly hears Philby despite the noise, and gives a flicker of a look back at the teens—a mere glance, yet it bestows upon the Keepers a message of appreciation, determination, conviction.

Then Mickey kneels, the Children of Light standing behind him, the crowd going wild. The Keepers in the center, Philby, Willa, and Finn, lock arms on shoulders as Maybeck and Charlene wave to the crowd from the ends of their line.

Mickey places one hand on his heart. With the other, he points to the Matterhorn, where Chernabog clings to ice and snow, climbing his way to the top.

63

"WE WON'T GET ANOTHER chance like this," Philby says confidentially to Finn as they wave from behind Mickey.

"Agreed. I had no idea there were this many good characters in the park."

"I doubt they've ever assembled all in one place. Forget that we've probably made history. If we don't jump on this, everyone will go back to wherever they go to, and that'll be that."

The crowd continues cheering; they're waiting for Minnie to be ferried over to the island, to Mickey. The ferry is none other than the maintenance barge piloted by Violet, with the Dillard acting as crew.

Minnie's transport buys the Keepers critical minutes. They wave and move away from the legend.

"What now?" Charlene asks, voicing what's on all their minds.

"The OTs are not setting up for a party," Maybeck says. "They mean business."

"Mickey's the key," Finn says. "Wayne, and Walt before him, went to all this trouble to lead people like us to bring him back."

Maybeck says, "I think Wayne knew this battle was coming. From the minute the OTs rebooted Chernabog, he must have known. He got the pen to Jess, took himself out to save us, and left it up to the Keepers to figure it out and bring Mickey back."

"So Mickey can use the pen to fix things?" Willa asks. "There's no history of Mickey and any kind of pen."

"Look where he returned," Charlene says. "On the Fantasmic! stage. As in, *Fantasia*, which is one of the scariest movies I've ever seen, by the way. Mickey and all that fire? Ugh. Don't forget, Chernabog was in it too."

"How about this: *Fantasia* was Walt's version of a Jess sketch," Finn says. Even as he speaks, he's astonished at his own reasoning. "He has this nightmare about where his dream kingdom is headed and decides to make a movie of it. It makes sense! Otherwise, why make a movie like that in the first place? No talking. No soft little mouse bopping around. No princes or princesses. After *Snow White*, he was making money for the first time. Why do something as weird as Fantasia?"

"So that people like us would know what's coming," Charlene says under her breath.

"But who beats them down?" Maybeck says. "It *ain't* a bunch of holograms. It's Mr. Mouse himself."

"We're facilitators," Willa says. "Like in school, when the principal calls a school meeting and someone has to lead it. That's us. We make it happen."

"So are we done here?" Charlene asks. "Why doesn't it feel like that?"

"We're not done here," Philby says firmly.

"But how can you be so sure?"

"You want a nightmare, Charlie?" Philby sweeps his arm in a wide gesture that encompasses smoke and fires all around the park, the OTs' ongoing work on Big Thunder and the Matterhorn. "Mickey just stepped out of the past into this. Chances are he has *no idea* what's going on. Not only that, but he'll be thinking like a character from forty years ago. A lot has changed!" He punches Maybeck, his arm passing through the boy's DHI chest. "This place is nothing like it was in the 1960's, the last time he saw it. Willa's right, we *are* facilitators. We're like the rangers in Animal Kingdom and Mickey's the first guest through the gates."

"Without us," Maybeck says, nodding, "he's just a dude in red shorts, waving to a crowd, waiting for a script."

"So what now?" Amanda asks calmly.

The ferry arrives. Minnie crosses to join Mickey as the Dillard and Violet hurry toward the Keepers. Violet is wide-eyed. "I didn't see that coming," she says.

"Can you hear him the way you heard her?" Finn asks, recalling their first encounter with Violet and Minnie in Walt's apartment. The memory of the antique music box returns as well: the reason for the Osiris code's presence on it has not been explained. Everything Wayne does is for a reason, Finn thinks.

"I don't know. I suppose so. I'm a character, he's a character. Why not?"

"We need you to translate," Philby says. "Like for Minnie."

"I can do that."

"Jess, what's left on your drawing that we haven't seen?" Finn asks.

Jess is thrown off by the question. She concentrates for a moment. "We've seen the gondola and the drilling rig. The tea tray inscription was on the outside of the Skyway Station."

"I saw that!" Charlene says, supporting her.

"Wayne's Mickey watch," Jess says, working through the picture in her mind. "The eyes in the middle were probably the missing Mickey piece. The octopus was on it too."

"Storey Ming," Finn supplies, bringing up a story he's already told the others. "Ursula."

Violet shudders. "That was not pretty."

"I know!" Jess says. "The sorcerer's cap!" Her announcement wins everyone's keen attention. "There are flames," Jess continues, "but that's pretty obvious by now. And weird-looking flowers, and some arrows—but none of those images look like much of anything. The one actual thing left in the sketch is the Sorcerer Mickey cap."

"I don't mean to state the obvious," Maybeck says. "But who here remembers talking about *Fantasia* a couple minutes ago? As in Sorcerer Mickey?"

"That's stating the obvious," Charlene says, shaking her head.

Mickey glances in their direction.

"We've got to wrap this up. We've got to do something!" Willa says.

"Dillard!" Finn tries to take the boy's hologram by the shoulders, but of course he can't. He does, however, win the Dillard's full attention. "Joe, Brad, whoever, if you can hear me, listen up. Dillard, record everything you hear, starting now."

Finn addresses the other Keepers. "Everyone tell the Dillard anything and everything you've seen or done since we left the tunnel."

No one speaks.

"He can hear us all at once. There's no being polite here. Just talk!"

They start, Willa first. Then each Keeper chimes in until everyone, including Finn, is talking at the Dillard as fast as they can. The Mandy Blaster is mentioned, the Disney Gallery and the vault, the riverboat, Ursula. It comes at the Dillard in a tidal wave of raised voices, all calling to be heard. The Dillard stares straight ahead, showing no emotion.

The rush of tales trickles to a stop as Violet concludes, ". . . so we picked up Minnie and drove her across."

"Dillard?" Finn says.

The Dillard nods.

"Did you get all that?"

"Affirmative."

"Okay then. If you . . . If one works off all current data available, visual and audio, anything online or in Disney databases—anything you've heard or been told—then what is the most likely . . . the most likely . . ."

"Scenario," Philby supplies, knowing where Finn is headed.

". . . *scenario* for the Overtakers? If they want to end the park as we know it, what's their next step? And is it a next step or the final step?"

"We need to hurry," Willa says, noting Mickey's second glance in their direction.

The Dillard's eyes are closed; he looks as if he didn't hear the question in the first place. Then his lids snap open, and he makes eye contact with each of the Keepers, the two Fairlies, and Violet. It's as if he's assigning the dialogue he recorded to specific voices, sorting, evaluating.

Philby whispers into Finn's ear. "Oh, yeah!" Finn adds. "Prioritize by probability of efficiency, keeping in mind that the Overtakers have . . ." Finn consults the Wayne watch. "Five hours to accomplish their goal of ending the Kingdom."

"The Kingdom or the park?" the Dillard inquires. "Previously you said, 'to end the *park* as we know it.' Do you wish to edit that query?"

Finn checks with Philby, who shakes his head, whispering, *"The park and the Kingdom are the same thing to us, but not to him. Keep the question as is."*

"The original query stands," Finn says. "And we'd like to hear supporting evidence, if possible." He adds this because, while he's grown somewhat used to the Dillard's absolute statements, he's worried they may offend the Keepers and make them distrust his results.

"The following scenario has a probability of seventy-eight-point-seven percent."

"That's very high!" Philby comments.

The Dillard ignores him because it isn't a question. "Charlene observed two birds dying on the sidewalk in front of the gallery. She was unable to resuscitate one. Finn and Terry observed pirates attempting to extinguish fires in the pathway. They are correct in assuming the action of the pirates is counterintuitive to the stated aim of the Overtakers—that is, burning the park to the ground.

"Furthermore, the earthquake resulted in the buckling and destruction of much of the pavement and concrete in the park. I observed when Amanda pushed and destroyed the Small World dolls that the catalytic properties of what you have termed green 'goo' were not as reported. True, it functions as a corrosive, but the action was slower than previously reported and inconsistent. Much organic matter, including pieces of doll costume, remained behind."

"Where's this going?" Maybeck asks. Finn shushes him.

The Dillard continues. "Current observations in the park include an approaching storm and the advance of a tall crane down Main Street."

"Oh my gosh!" Philby blurts, straightening up.

"I believe," the Dillard says, "that Dell has arrived at a hypothetical given the current data. Do you wish to share, Dell, or shall I continue?"

Philby repeats himself, drawing the words out like taffy: "O-o-oh m-y-y-y g-o-o-osh."

"Continue," Finn instructs the Dillard. But Philby interrupts.

"The dying birds—they were canaries!"

"They were not!" Charlene objects. "One was a pigeon and—"

"Not literally, Charlie. Canaries in the coal mine! In the old days, canaries were used to detect gas leaks. If gas leaked into the mines, the canaries died first, alerting the miners to get out. Natural gas is C-O-T: colorless, odorless, tasteless. That stuff you smell when your stove freaks out is a perfume added by the gas company so you know it's leaking."

"I hate that smell!" Charlene says.

"Disgusting!" Maybeck adds.

Philby ignores them. "The earthquake was because of the fracking. Fracking is done to release natural gas. The birds died from the gas. The green goo lacked oxygen because of the gas. We're holograms! It isn't affecting us. These guys are all characters! Who knows what makes them tick? The pirates were *putting out the fires* because they don't want the gas burning off. They want it—"

"Collecting," Willa says. "Oh my gosh is right. Will it build up?"

The Dillard answers as though the question was directed at him. "So-called natural gas is ninety-five percent methane. It includes butane. Both have molecular weights heavier than air. When colder than the air it combines with, as when it emerges from the ground, natural gas will initially sink and therefore collect."

"I get it. They're putting out the fires," Maybeck says, eyes widening in horror, "so that gas doesn't burn off. The OTs want it to hang around until they can use it to torch the place."

"Lightning," Philby says. "The crane. The storm that's coming."

"Big Thunder Mountain!" Finn cries. "Thunder, as in

lightning. They're going to use the mountain as a lightning rod—"

"To set off the gas," Philby says, nodding. "That we can't smell and didn't know about until Charlene tried to save a bird."

"They're going to blow up the park," Jess says. "'It starts and ends in lightning.'" She quotes herself, the vision she had inside the park.

"And something tells me," Maybeck says, raising his head, "that only *that* dude can stop it."

They all look in time to catch a troubled Mickey and Minnie staring back at them.

64

Once they make it across to New Orleans Square, and among much celebration, Minnie leads the Disney characters on a short parade to Pirates of the Caribbean. Thanks to Violet's translation, Philby has instructed Minnie to find the underground treasure caves he's sure exist beneath the attraction, just as they do in Walt Disney World. Despite the aftershocks and the risk of explosion, the Keepers believe the good characters will be safer underground. The park will only explode if they, the Keepers, fail; they are not counting on that.

The Keepers and Mickey paddle canoes to the dock at the Hungry Bear restaurant and take shelter inside. Finn makes a second plea to the Imagineers, speaking directly to the Dillard. Several minutes later, all conversation stops when a man's voice, not the Dillard's, speaks from the hologram's mouth.

"Finn? Can you hear me?"

Only now does Finn realize how much he's come to accept the hologram as his neighbor and friend. When Joe's deep voice spills out of the Dillard, it's like something from *The Exorcist*, as if the Dillard has been inhabited by evil spirits. Steeling his nerves, Finn answers in the affirmative.

"We've managed to find a workaround to Dillard's isolation. We're aware of your situation down there," Joe's voice says. "We ask that you lead the group to the Central Plaza for an immediate return."

"That's not happening," Finn replies. "We're staying. The reason I reached out is this: we need Sorcerer Mickey's magic cap, the *real* one, as fast as you can get it." He looks up at the crane rolling into the place, at the flashing sky to the southwest. The storm grows closer by the minute. "You've got half an hour. An hour at most."

The Dillard's mouth opens, but only rough static comes out.

"Talk about jaw-dropping," Maybeck quips, winning nervous laughter from a few of the Keepers.

The Dillard says nothing.

"Tell me there's a real one, Joe," Finn says.

"Yes, it exists. But what you're asking . . . I'd have to wake half the company, including Mr. Iger, to get permission. By the time that happens, it'll be next week. I wish I were kidding, Finn. But even if I threw all that aside, it's maybe thirty minutes to the warehouse where the cap's stored, another hour or more to get it down there. Two hours minimum, and that's if I'm willing to be fired tomorrow."

"The park's going to be fired tonight," Maybeck says.

"Was that you, Finn?"

Finn stares at the Dillard, feels stupid for expecting his friend to know him better than that, struggling to rationalize Joe's voice emerging from Dillard's face.

"We think the plan is to torch the place," Finn says. He quickly explains that the earthquake was only part one of a two-part plan.

"I see," says the Dillard/Joe. He sounds as defeated as Finn feels.

"Mickey says, 'There is no future in the past, so let's make the future and live the present,'" Violet says to Finn pleadingly, seeming to hope that this will make more sense to him than it does to her.

"Did you hear that?" Finn asks.

"We were watching through Dillard as he came on stage. We saw Mickey and Minnie. Finn, there were more than a few tears here. And a lot of cheering. Congratulations to all of you."

Joe's words confirm Philby's suspicion that the Dillard is being used to monitor the Keepers, but Finn can't think about that right now.

"He says," Violet continues, "that 'the difficulty in life is not on how we struggle to survive the next day; it's on how we live today.'"

The Dillard's jaw flaps. Joe says, "Both those quotes are attributable to Mickey. I can't believe I'm saying this, but your Mickey is authentic. He's the real deal."

"Yeah, we kind of figured," Finn says. "We need his sorcerer's cap, Joe. The one from *Fantasia*. It's the final piece in all this. Without it . . . well, we'll have been through an awful lot for nothing."

"I wish I could help."

"We have to have it," Jess says softly. "I feel . . . I know now how important it is."

Finn nods, and tells Joe, "This is do-or-die on our end." The entire restaurant shakes from the force of yet another aftershock. "We don't have two hours," Finn says. He feels himself entering a more somber, reflective mood. "We've bunkered the good characters under Pirates. If anything happens, that's where to search first."

More static. Joe is apparently at a loss for words.

"We can't just sit back and watch this happen," Finn says. He looks into the eyes of his friends while speaking. He sees determination, commitment, and fear. Everyone's scared, including him.

Philby steps up to the Dillard and addresses Joe. "If the

Dillard is given the ability to control the projectors, couldn't he make us invisible and get us safely to the Plaza?"

"I suppose," Joe says.

"Because . . . if the Dillard can get us to the Plaza without being shredded, then you guys might be able to cross over the sorcerer's cap. Correct?"

"Green-screen it and cross it over to you," Joe says. The Dillard shows none of the excitement they hear in Joe's voice. "Into Central Plaza. Might actually work!" Joe sounds excited.

"We get the cap to Mickey and hope like heck it's got enough juice as a hologram to do whatever it is he needs to do to restore the park."

"If Mickey's going to repair things," Joe says, "it needs to be from the highest point available. Big Thunder's a hundred and four feet high. The Matterhorn's one-forty-seven. Otherwise, it'll be a partial job."

"I think we could have told you that," Maybeck mutters. He's unable to get a look at the Matterhorn, but all the Keepers and their allies have the same mental image of Chernabog climbing toward the mountaintop.

"Drop the firewalls," Philby says, talking over Maybeck. A demand, not a request.

"Done," says Joe/Dillard.

"Get us the cap," Finn says. "And throw in Mickey's conductor's baton, if you have it."

"We have it. Thirty to get them here. Maybe another fifteen to image. Forty-five to an hour."

"We haven't got that kind of time," Finn says. "But maybe we can stall them."

65

AND SUDDENLY IT'S UPON THEM: the advancing winds, driving angry storm clouds; the sight of Chernabog high atop the Matterhorn; dead birds littered at their feet; the smoke that continues to rise, apparently unseen by anyone not in the park.

Finn, Amanda, Philby, and Willa follow immediately behind Mickey, who's made it clear through Violet (currently at his side) that he won't be held back as the Keepers planned. Mickey's words are an odd mixture of levity and leadership; he's a lighthearted drill sergeant. The plan might as well have been sketched out on a sandwich bag.

What appears from a distance to be a slithering snake turns out to be Remy, Django, and their legion. There's a brief celebration as the Keepers drop to their knees and pet whiskers and chins. Remy salutes Mickey, bows, and rises on his haunches. His gesture expresses his message well: Here to serve.

"Half of you will go with Maybeck," Finn informs Remy. "The rest," he tells Django, "with us. But first, I need four of your best scouts."

Remy selects three extremely ratty-looking rats and one who's something of a show rat, a blue-ribbon beauty.

"Find Elsa the Snow Queen," Finn says. "Tell her Mickey and the Children of Light need her immediately. Two of you will look in California Adventure, in and around World of Color. Two others, in the cellars and tombs beneath Pirates. Do you understand?"

Maybe the cutest thing in the world is seeing four rats salute. It's a light moment in the gathering darkness.

"Off you go!" Finn turns to Remy. "So good to see you! We were worried."

Remy smiles coyly. In terms of attitude, he and Maybeck share more than a trait or two.

There comes a time when things become easy—like now, Finn thinks. He wonders if he seeks out conflict, given how comfortable he is with it. The crazier things get, the calmer he feels. Wayne has pushed him for years to accept a leadership role, and it took him far too long to realize acceptance isn't something you do, it's something you allow.

He pushes away worry because he has to: it's key to his survival, his all clear depends on it. Smiling, he reaches down, takes Amanda's hand, and holds it—in that special way that only holograms can hold hands—for a moment. Not long, but long enough. She smiles at him furtively.

"It's never felt like this," she says. She doesn't mean their friendship. He knows exactly what she means.

"It's him," he says, nodding toward Mickey. He walks like he's heading to a ballgame and can't wait to get there, kicking his feet out to either side. It's jaunty, silly. Violet is practically skipping to keep up.

"He's a game changer," Amanda agrees.

"I hope he'll let us do this our way."

"I wouldn't count on it."

"But we are. Counting on it, I mean," Finn says.

"Show him the watch."

"Why?"

"Trust me, when the time comes. Maybe it'll jog a few memories."

"You think he has memories?" Finn asks.

"That's not the question. The question is: Do you think he doesn't?"

"You've been hanging around Maybeck too much."

"Somebody talking about me?" Maybeck calls from immediately behind them.

Remy's team of several hundred rats has been in constant motion since the Keepers started walking. They scout ahead in groups of twenty or more, racing off like a long gray shadow. Minutes later, several return to report. They fan out in all directions, ahead and behind, right and left, tiny bodyguards keeping watch for any trouble.

It isn't long before Remy reports to Finn and Philby that Elsa's on her way. The girls spot her long before she reaches the group—as the Keepers continue past the Haunted Mansion— their girl-antennae warning of a formidable beauty's approach.

Formidable she is. From her French-braided white hair and glowing pink complexion to her form-fitting ice-blue dress, her posture and bearing confirm her royalty: Elsa the Snow Queen.

Mickey stops at the sight of her. The two seem to know each another; Elsa gracefully bows and curtsies for him, and they share a knowing exchange of expressions.

"What's going on?" Finn asks Violet.

"They're talking. He's telling her we need her. She says she's honored."

"Indeed," says Elsa, turning to face Finn and the group. Her voice is like a pleasant melody. "I am, of course, at your service."

Philby speaks first. "We know you can summon winter storms and ice. We've seen you do that! And wind. Lots of wind." He sounds foolish. Willa isn't the first to see that Elsa's beauty has charmed him, left him talking like a dolt.

"Perhaps it is wiser to tell me what it is you want, and permit me to be the judge of my own abilities."

Finn steps in. "We need to slow down the clouds, that storm." He points. "To hold off the lightning for as long as possible."

"Lightning happens in snowstorms, just as it does in rain," the Dillard says.

"Yes," Finn says, wincing. "We'd love to stop the lightning, we'd love to clear the sky and see the stars, but since that's probably not possible . . ." He pauses. Is it? "Then slowing it down will have to do."

"Cold fronts move faster than warm fronts," the Dillard says.

Elsa smiles and nods. "Strange but true. Mountains and warm water can slow a storm. We have mountains here!"

"This is not where we want the storm to slow," says Finn. "Just the opposite."

"Can you distract a storm?" asks Willa, eyeing Philby and brimming with jealousy. "Make it stop and ignore where it was going?"

"An interesting notion. You are Willow, are you not?"

"Close enough."

"We . . ." Elsa addresses all the Keepers, "are so grateful to you all for what you have done." She looks warmly at Mickey. Any warm-blooded creature would melt under that gaze. "Is this what you wish of me? To 'distract' these clouds, as you say?"

"We need extra time, ma'am . . . madame . . . Your Highness," Philby stutters.

"If I freeze the storm, it will only move more quickly. The lightning will become all the more violent. I'm afraid it will not do."

Mickey takes in Elsa. She looks at him.

Violet whispers, "He's asking her to use her magic as best she sees fit. Oh, how beautiful!"

"What?" Amanda asks.

Violet is practically glowing herself. "He said, 'What is done cannot be undone, but what is left to be done should not be left undone.'"

"Whoa," says Maybeck.

"You have given me an idea, Willow," Elsa says. "Distraction. Yes. As when two young women appreciate the same gentleman." Elsa steps closer to Philby. If Willa gets any closer, she's going to knock him over.

"There's no body of water between here and there," Elsa adds. "But what is wrong with a pair of unexpected snowstorms in Southern California?"

"A pair?" Finn asks.

"One here!" Elsa pushes her hand up and out, toward the sky. A blue streak of light shoots from her palm like rocket flames, erupting into the night sky, reminding Finn of Maleficent's fireballs. A flashing blue-white storm erupts to the south. A moment later, a second ice storm forms to the north. "Together, they comprise a triangle, something with which we're all familiar. Your warmer storm will want to move, but it will not know which way to go. Left or right? I've made sure your storm will be *distracted*, as Willow has said."

"An occluded front," the Dillard volunteers. "A cold front overtakes a warm one, forcing the warm air higher. The warmer mass will stall as it lifts. In this case, the warm front will prevail, but Elsa's right: the storm will be distracted and confused until it reforms."

"How much time?" Finn asks.

The Dillard calculates. "Twenty-six minutes."

"Is that enough time?" Elsa asks Philby.

"I . . . ah . . ."

Willa tries to shove Philby, but her hand passes through his shoulder.

"We'll make it work," Finn says.

Violet, speaking for Mickey, bids Elsa join them. They continue past Pirates, Finn separating them into two groups. Philby, Maybeck, Charlene, and Amanda, the mind and muscle team, while he and the others, including Mickey, take the lane toward the Tiki Room and the Plaza beyond.

The Dillard, no longer speaking with Joe's voice, is like a kid in a candy shop. "You will be interested in everything beyond the firewalls, Finn."

"You've been teasing me for the past few minutes, Dillard. I don't appreciate it."

"There is *so much* data."

"You can start by making us invisible."

"I am working on that. Have you considered that Elsa, Violet, and Mickey are not holograms?"

"Crud, I forgot," Finn snaps. "Sorry, Dillard. Feeling the pressure, I guess."

"You are grossly outnumbered, running out of time, and facing an enemy with supernatural powers that far outstrip your own. Given these conditions, emotional displays are not only expected, but predictable."

"Spare me the armchair psychology and focus on shutting down the projectors, Dillard."

"Understood. Engaged."

Passing through Adventureland and Indiana Jones does not come easily to Finn. The Temple of the Forbidden Eye brings to mind the temple in Mexico and Dillard's death, and the eye hieroglyph that is part of the Osiris myth. All that they have done and seen flows over Finn, threatening to overwhelm him.

Django appears and runs circles around Finn, stopping him. He points frantically, holding his paws in front of his eyes like a pair of binoculars.

"Spies!" Finn says, motioning his team to the near side of the path. "Dillard, shut them down, now! You all stay here and guard Mickey until Willa and I return."

The Dillard counts down. "Entering DHI shadow in three, two . . ."

Finn takes Willa's hand just before they, Jess, and the Dillard disappear.

Overtaking the Overtaker, a Sultan's Palace guard, is almost unfairly easy. Finn and Willa hold hands in order to keep track of each other. They follow Django and six other rats to the roof. The rats frighten the guard, who runs scared until he's pushed over the side by Finn and Willa. He falls into an umbrella, bangs his head, and is tied up and gagged by the remaining rats before he awakes. One down.

The Dillard keeps the projectors off. Those in DHI shadow form a daisy chain of hand-holding as Mickey, Violet, and Elsa lead the way into the Adventureland Bazaar.

Their dilemma is how to get Mickey across the Plaza to the Matterhorn when the place is swarming with Overtakers. Willa, selected for Finn's team because of her brains, just as Maybeck and Charlene were selected for Philby's team because of their athleticism, comes up with an imaginative solution.

Minutes after raiding the Bazaar, two girls appear, passing the Tiki Room and turning in front of the Jolly Holiday. Both wear turbans, jeweled veils to hide their faces, and flowing Arabian robes. One covers a superhero suit, the other a shimmering blue gown. Each of the girls is irreverently dragging an oversized stuffed character behind her. The girl under the white turban drags a mannequin dressed somewhat as an Aladdin lookalike, while the one wearing all black hauls a Mickey Mouse by its floppy wrist.

Blocking the view of the place the Partners statue should be is a pyre. It's being prepared to do away with all things Disney. Everything from toys to costumes is piled high.

Hades's henchmen, ghoulish spirits of the dead, patrol the Main Street end of the Plaza. They spot the girls.

"Hey! You there!" a henchman shouts.

The girls continue walking, as if they can't hear. Given the high level of activity around the Plaza, and the clatter and groan of the maneuvering crane, this is understandable.

"Add him to the lot!" the henchman shouts, indicating the pyre and laughing. "We can burn him for ya!"

"I'd rather toss him off the Matterhorn!" Violet shouts back, unable to pass up a golden opportunity. She could ditch the outfit and go invisible for the climb, but they might shoot at her even so. She elects to stay in costume. "Tell the others I intend to do exactly that! That way they won't shoot me when I climb it!" Under her breath she says, "Stay limp!" as Mickey squirms in irritation at the henchmen's disdain.

She and the second girl drag their booty toward the Little Red Wagon.

Just for a moment, the air around the girls seems to swirl in an oily, otherworldly way. The henchmen consult each other. "Did you see that?" one asks.

"What?" the other replies.

"Never mind. Me eyes ain't been the same since Mr. H melted me specs."

"I know what you mean," says the other. "He melted me gold fillings straight out of me teeth, he did. Me chompers

563

ain't never felt right since. But no complaining!"

"No complaining!" his partner agrees, echoing Hades's number-one rule and glancing over his left shoulder. Hades is never far behind, and he's *always* listening. They have found this out the hard way.

Like all the Keepers, Willa finds operating in DHI shadow thrilling. She has always felt so invisible throughout her high school years. Being truly invisible combines reality with fantasy in a way only old souls like her can fully appreciate. She feels right at home.

No one, including Willa, is sure how far Finn's team can make it, but slipping past the Plaza instills in them a renewed sense of urgency and confidence.

"We can do this," Finn says, turning them past the Little Red Wagon, up a short flight of stairs, across the umbrella-bedecked patio in front of the Plaza Inn, and beneath Tomorrowland's Astro Orbiter.

But Willa knows the truth: the worst is yet to come.

66

As Philby's team, comprising Maybeck, Charlene, and Amanda, nears Big Thunder Mountain Railroad, he wishes Amanda were Willa. He understands and agrees with the logic behind Finn's allocation of forces to the two teams: Philby's team faces the more physical task. Willa can help Finn think through solutions; Philby needs no such help. As the crane comes into detailed view, he puts the makeup of the teams aside. He understands what the Overtakers are trying to do.

Chained to the crane's hook, carried aloft as the crane extends, is the bronze Partners statue of Walt Disney and Mickey Mouse.

The Overtakers intend to attract a lightning strike to the most celebrated statue in the Kingdom, Philby realizes. Its bronze will melt as the park explodes in a swelling sea of gas.

Seeing this stops the Keepers. Philby checks his wristwatch: they have four minutes until the Dillard knocks out the projectors on this side of the park. Strategy is discussed. In the distant skies, the lightning storm renews its steady northeastward progress toward the park.

The teens hide behind a rock outcropping and boarded-up tunnel across from the railroad bridge and Big Thunder Trail. Philby is not one for pep talks; he leaves that to Finn. He's not given to sentimentality. His is a world of calculation and purpose, of numbers and common sense. He is practical, the professor. But at this particular moment, he can't help himself.

"It's strange to think that all of this, everything we've

done, would put us here. Agreed? The Quill, the battles, the cruise. But oddly enough, if we fail now, it's all been for nothing. Dillard. Wayne. Nothing. Granted, Mickey and Finn's team have to clean up the pieces, but we have to stop this or there won't be pieces to clean up." Another quick glance at his watch. *Two minutes* to shadow. "Sometimes we've worked well together, a lot of times we've disagreed." He looks to Maybeck, who smirks and claps him on the back.

"This is one of those times—*the* time—when we need to get it right the first time. We owe it to everyone, every character, every Imagineer, to stop the OTs. Corny, but for once it's true. If it means sacrifice, so be it. If it means doing stuff we've never done, so be it. We never talk of this again. We do what needs to be done. We end this. We end *them*."

There is the sound of a crane roaring nearby. Voices shout instructions. The approaching storm flashes and cracks. A mechanical whine interrupted by a ripple of the fire that continues to pour from rents in the earth.

One minute.

Looks are exchanged between them, things said that would never dare be spoken, kindnesses that cannot be voiced without tears and emotions that have no place on the battlefield. Each knows his or her strength, his or her value to the team and the mission.

As wry smiles steal across their lips and a telling agelessness gleams from their eyes, the Keepers and Amanda share a moment of communion, expressing a togetherness they have never felt this deeply before, not since they first stepped in front of a green screen so many years before.

The moment passes.

The remaining seconds run down.

They remain visible.

67

FINN, WILLA, JESS, and the Dillard, all in DHI shadow, are scattered across the Plaza, awaiting the crossover of Mickey's cap and baton. Willa is on the Adventureland side of the Plaza's circle, Finn is by the castle; Jess should be near Tomorrowland. Fearing that the cap will not go unnoticed for long, Finn's team is charged with its immediate recovery.

Finn looks right and left, eyes sweeping the pavement. He does his best to ignore the dozens of Overtakers coming and going inches from where he stands.

"Finn!" A familiar voice emerges from nothingness. The Dillard, invisible, is apparently standing mere inches away.

"I told you!" Finn hisses. *"Don't do that!"*

"Finn, it's Joe!"

But Finn could swear he heard the Dillard's voice. "Joe?"

A passing Stormtrooper stops and looks directly at the nonexistent Finn. "Who goes there? Declare yourself!"

Finn freezes. He wills Joe not to speak.

Joe speaks. "We are under cyber attack and must shut down the fiber op—"

The holograms of Finn, Jess, and Willa reappear instantly. The Dillard is nowhere to be seen.

Sorcerer Mickey's cap and conductor's baton lie on the asphalt halfway between Finn and Jess, who spot them simultaneously. Together, they run toward them. Jess snags the cap. Finn scoops up the baton.

"The OTs hacked the system!" Finn shouts at her.

"Yeah," she says, pivoting to run alongside him.

"You there!" shouts a menacing voice. It comes from one of a pair of patrolling wooden Christmas soldiers.

Finn tries shaking the baton at them. It's no use. "Give me that!" he calls to Jess, who passes him the cap. Willa appears on Finn's right, outrunning an angry Zira.

With one hand, Finn puts the cap on his head, clears his mind, turns, and aims the baton at the two advancing soldiers. "Away!" he shouts.

Both soldiers halt in lockstep, but only briefly; they're alarmed by Finn's actions, but no magic explodes from the baton. No curse is thrown. The soldiers grin malevolently and continue advancing.

Willa catches up, and she, Finn, and Jess leap across broken pavement in which the earthquake has ripped a five-yard-long hole. Jess skids to a stop by a leaning lamppost, its light flickering ominously. Finn tries to put on the brakes but slips and falls.

The Christmas soldiers advance, Zira nearly even with them.

Willa joins Jess in pushing against the lamppost, an act that makes absolutely no sense. The soldiers will just run around it!

"All clear!" Willa calls to Finn.

On the third try, the girls push the post down like a closing parking garage gate. It slams onto the broken pavement, creating an explosion that sounds like a bomb going off.

The girls' pure holograms, and Finn's near-all-clear state, allow them to survive the force of the blast and the flying debris.

The soldiers and Zira are not so lucky.

68

"SOMETHING'S OBVIOUSLY HAPPENED," Philby says, taking in his team. "The Dillard hasn't shut down the projectors, so we're not in DHI shadow. We're not invisible. We're completely outnumbered. We have to decide to risk an attack while we're visible or wait and hope the projectors can be shut down."

"Check out the crane!" Maybeck says. "And the storm! The lightning. We can't wait around!"

"Then we vote," Philby says. "Fair warning: if we're visible, if we lose all clear, then we may not be coming back from this. Any one of us could end up in SBS, maybe forever." There's a moment when he can practically hear everyone thinking. "No pressure. No judgment. I mean that! It's entirely up to each of us."

"I'm going," Maybeck says.

The others nod.

"Is everyone sure?" Philby asks. There are no dissenters. "Okay, we go as planned!"

There's no mention of all clear or how to protect the team from attack. They've been in similar situations before. Maintaining all clear is up to the individual. Ironically, the one who's usually best at that has led his own team to the Matterhorn.

Now Philby, Maybeck, Charlene, and Amanda face a swarm of the Sultan's henchmen, pirates, Stormtroopers, Thuggee warriors, and, overhead, wraiths circling like hungry vultures. The hive is Big Thunder, where the Overtaker minions are disassembling the roller coaster's steel rails and, using the bucket-brigade technique, passing them up the more easily scalable southeast face of the central peak. The crane has been positioned there as well. The rails are bound together with wire wrapping, like a giant grounding cable running from the mountain peak down to the existing track and beyond to the track laid around the Central Plaza. The network of steel creates a gigantic ignition switch that, when charged with lightning, will spark like a gas stove.

Maybeck and Charlene move up Big Thunder Trail in the direction of the crane. Philby and Amanda approach the Thunder Mountain railway bridge in an attempt to break the circuit should Maybeck and Charlene fail. The Keepers are taking nothing for granted.

"What's—the—plan?" calls Charlene, marveling at how difficult it is to keep up with Maybeck when she's slipped out of all clear. She works to calm herself and get it back. Everyone knows she's the fastest Keeper, yet Maybeck is moving at super speed.

"You're the climber," Maybeck replies. "So climb. I happen to love being behind the wheel, so that's where you'll find me."

Remy and company hear him. A gray, snaking line of coursing rat bodies divides before the two Keepers as Remy's troops fan out. Despite their short legs, the rats reach the crane well ahead of Maybeck. Unnoticed, they pass swiftly beneath the legs of several Thugs standing guard. Several dozen of the vermin begin chewing the rubber of the crane's right front tire.

Maybeck arrives at full speed and encounters a line of six turbaned Thugs in long red overcoats, each warrior brandishing a curved sword.

Lightning strikes the ground not a quarter mile away with an explosive sound, like TNT detonating. A cheer rises from the OT workers. A light rain begins to fall. Small drops that quickly approach the size of acorns.

Maybeck stops. The warriors have placed themselves directly between him and the crane. Six against one: Maybeck likes those odds. "You might want to put your swords down," Maybeck says, "so you don't get hurt." The Thugs laugh vociferously and raise their blades higher. "The thing is," he says, "when you miss *me*, you're likely going to injure one of your buddies. You can't say I didn't warn you." More laughter. "Allow me to demonstrate," Maybeck says. He walks—walks, not runs—between the two warriors in the center. One swings. The blade passes through Maybeck's hologram and decapitates the Thug next to him.

As the headless warrior slumps, Maybeck grabs the man's sword, spins, and puts the tip of his blade through the nearest man's chest. The second warrior falls. Wielding two swords, Maybeck backs toward the working crane as the remaining four Thugs slash and clang. They're expert swordsmen. The telltale tingling sweeps through Maybeck, and his blue outline dims. He's losing all clear. He removes the legs of one warrior below the knees. Severs the arm from the next: Two to go.

Pain shoots through him—one of the remaining Thugs has delivered a surface wound with a slicing stroke down his left arm, ten inches of screaming agony that Maybeck fights to overcome as he battles the remaining Thugs. He finds two swords too cumbersome; dropping one, he slips his wounded left arm behind his back, limiting its exposure. His wound won't allow all clear. He's just Maybeck, a recent high school graduate armed with a sword, fighting two trained warriors.

Wraiths sweep over the maimed and injured, pausing to draw out what life remains in the bodies. Only as Maybeck watches the two warriors grow gray from head to foot does he realize they are not being turned to smoke or stone: they're covered in rats.

* * *

Philby leads Amanda up a small hill to the Big Thunder mining cabin. They slip past two railroad men arguing over the explosive use of a locomotive's steam engine, and Philby kneels in front of a box of explosives.

"What are you doing?" Amanda whispers.

"Stealing some dynamite."

"You know, for someone so smart, you can be incredibly stupid."

Amanda has never spoken to Philby this way, and he's taken aback. "Excuse me?"

"We are trying to prevent an explosion, not cause one! You set off some dynamite, and the whole park may go up because of the gas."

"Duh!" he says, leaning away from the box.

"I thought that's why you brought me along?" She motions gently, both palms out. "To destroy the bridge without any sparks."

A devilish grin spreads across Philby's face. "Now I remember."

69

WITHIN THE BACKSTAGE area of the Matterhorn lies a network of catwalks and ladders that would make the Hunchback of Notre Dame queasy.

Elsa has frozen the two wooden Christmas soldiers pursuing Finn's team, turning them into red-black-and-white Popsicles. Once the whole team is inside and up the first ladder, she freezes it too, adding three thick inches of ice to prevent its use by their pursuers.

The group continues to climb. Violet stays close to Mickey, like a personal bodyguard, while Jess catches up to Finn.

"How do you know this is what Wayne meant for you to do?" Jess asks.

"I don't," he replies. "But your drawing helped."

"What if I got it wrong?"

"You know better than any of us that first we have to count on each other, second we need to go with our gut instincts."

"And if you're wrong? What if *we're* wrong?"

"We learn from it. Right?"

"Except that if we're wrong this time there's maybe not a next time."

"Feels kind of that way," Finn admits. "But we've never had Mickey before. He's not here to lead a parade, you know? He's connected to the Stonecutter's Quill. Something *good* happened that night. This . . . tonight . . . reminds me, reminds all of us of that. We know Mickey's the real deal. We know our best shot is to give him a chance to fix it. The Cryptos and Joe, they sense it too. You can't challenge yourself once you make a decision like this, Jess. It'll kill the magic."

"If there is any magic."

"Of course there's magic."

"But choosing this plan was your decision, Finn. More than anyone else's, it was yours. How do you deal with that if it goes wrong?"

"Maybe I won't have to—maybe it deals with me." He feels a shudder. He wishes she'd be quiet a minute.

"'It's about time,'" she says.

"I remember. I was there."

"I sketched the watch. It was in my dream."

"Again, I remember. There were thirteen hours on its face. That sealed the deal. The thirteenth piece."

"'It's about time,'" she repeats.

"Will you stop saying that? All you're doing is reminding me of Wayne."

"Good. Finn, Wayne wanted more than anything for you to have his watch. Not see a picture of it, but own it. Wear it."

"I'm not getting whatever it is you're trying to say, so why not just spit it out?"

"If I knew what I was trying to say, I would, but I don't, so I can't. Okay?"

"Okay." Finn checks behind him. It's a long, long climb. Mickey is slowing. Elsa has fallen back, too, though she's continuing to freeze the ladders.

"Number one, Main Street," Jess blurts out.

"I saw that on the back of the watch. So what?" Finn is beyond annoyed with her.

"You know what number one, Main Street, Rahway, New Jersey is?"

"A watch shop? Watch repair?"

"The nearest watch repair is on Irving Street."

"Spent a lot of time in Rahway, New Jersey, have you?" Despite his sarcasm, Finn does recognize the name of the town—and not from the back of the watch. But he can't place it.

"I consulted the Dillard. At that address there's a business called the Music Box Company."

Finn stops, three rungs up yet another ladder. He remembers now. "What?" RAHWAY, N.J. was written inside the music box in Walt's apartment. "Come again?"

"Why would the address on the back of Wayne's watch have nothing to do with watches?"

"Back up! No! Not literally," he says, as Jess, climbing right behind him, drops down two rungs so Finn will not tread on her fingers accidentally. "The Music Box Company. You're sure that's right?"

"Unless the Dillard is suddenly making mistakes."

Finn swoons, finding it hard to hold on to the ladder.

"Finn?"

"I'm all right." He continues climbing.

"What is it? What did I say?"

"What does a music box have to do with time?" he asks.

"I don't know! Music is timeless?"

Finn stops again, looks down at Jess. Then he turns and continues climbing, reaching what feels like the hundredth catwalk. A few feet in front of him, the surface is wet, slick. Finn forces his eyes up. Through an open hatch at the top of a ladder, he sees gray sky.

To one side stands a massive leg covered in brown fur. Above the leg, a curled horn comes into view.

What's up there needs no introduction.

Dispatching the last of the Thugs, Maybeck looks first to his wound, then up in time to see the Partners statue, hanging from the end of the crane's boom, swing into place atop Big Thunder. He's too late!

As he sprints to attack the crane operator, there's a loud *pop!* Lacking all clear because of his wound, Maybeck climbs the machine to the operator's booth. As he's reaching for the door handle, the entire crane shifts. He falls, but saves himself by snagging a handrail. His head thrown back, he sees the Partners statue swinging in space once again.

He looks down to see it was the rats chewing through one of the crane's tires that disrupted the OT's work. The statue swings away from its intended lightning-rod perch.

Nearby, Charlene scales the rock like a kid on a playground climbing gym. This is home to her, hanging precariously by a few fingers forty feet above certain death. The red spire shoots straight up; it's among the most dangerous free climbs she's attempted. Angling her body unnaturally, she wedges a heel and finds purchase: another finger grip. Flex. Push. Pull. Up she travels, slow as a caterpillar, determined as a Kingdom Keeper. Her destination is not the summit, but a small nose of rock facing the Big Thunder Trail.

But when the crane shifts, the Partners statue swings like a wrecking ball or a pendulum, first out and away from her, and then back, directly toward her.

Charlene loosens her grip, dropping fast. She squeezes

the cable hard to brake. Above, the bronze Mickey and Walt collide with her former resting place; fragments of rock rain down. Two more swings. Two more collisions. She dares to steal a look upward, blinking away the sifting debris and dust, to see the crane lifting the statue into position again.

She climbs recklessly fast, paying no mind to the sixty feet of open air now beneath her. The statue's smashing into the rock face has made the handholds easier, bigger. Reaching the damaged area, Charlene moves faster still to pull herself onto a protrusion of rock, a narrow shelf immediately above, tucking her feet in tight and squatting on the bridge of the sculpted figure's giant stone nose.

In front of her, the cable holding the statue has steadied. She stretches out to reach it, but it lingers just beyond her grasp: she's going to have to jump.

* * *

Maybeck can't believe his eyes: Charlene must have some kind of death wish. The Partners statue looks as if it's about to crush her. Cursing beneath his breath, he storms the crane operator's booth, swinging open the door.

It's Judge Doom at the controls. Amanda's push has broken his jaw, shifting it miserably to the left. He looks like a discarded action figure under a Christmas tree. His left leg isn't much better; twisted and ungainly, it looks more like the number three than a limb. But his hands work the seven hydraulic levers before him like those of a church organist playing Bach. Two television monitors, one in each corner of the booth's front window, show closed-circuit camera views from the boom's upper and lower sheaves. Doom pulls a lever, hoisting the statue higher. Another tug sends the jib forward and thrusts out the upper sheave's pulley.

If Charlene jumps now, he knows, it will be out into space.

Maybeck grabs the top sill like a pull-up bar and kicks Doom squarely in the jaw. Then he lunges for the middle lever and pulls back.

The statue drops. It's in free fall.

* * *

Charlene, airborne, collides with the hoist rope, a steel cable that was not there a fraction of a second before. She grabs hold and slides down like a firefighter, her hologram hands suffering severe rope burns due to her partial all clear. Her shoes slam into the hook, now a chain's length from the top of Walt Disney's metal hair.

The crane's hook contains an emergency release side lever, once brightly red-and-white striped, the paint now chipped. Charlene wraps her legs around the cable, prepared to invert herself.

As she does, the statue falls a second time.

* * *

Philby signals Amanda from the hut end of the Big Thunder Mountain Railroad Bridge. He's banging a rock against the rail in an effort to loosen the joint, something Amanda told him was not a problem. Philby wouldn't listen.

Amanda, at the far end of the expanse, near the miner's cabin entrance to the ride, spots the lantern headlamp of a railroad handcar in the darkness of the tunnel, immediately behind Philby, where he cannot see it.

Without all the noise, he might have heard it; without the near constant shifting of the ground from the thunderclaps overhead, he might have felt it. Two miners face each other on opposite sides of the handcar, taking turns pumping its teeter-totter–like mechanism up and down to drive it along. They aren't on a joy ride. As she watches the handcar speed up, Amanda knows with sickening certainty that their purpose is to reach Philby.

Instead of running away from the bridge as he should, Philby makes the mistake of running toward her *across* the bridge. If she pushes now, she'll probably kill Philby, who can't possibly be all clear.

The miners pump faster, closing on her friend.

In a moment of absolute clarity, Amanda knows Philby will not reach her before the handcar knocks him from the bridge.

"P—h—i—l—b—y!" she screams.

The handcar reaches him, shoving Philby off the bridge and sending him plummeting toward the bed of rocks below.

As Philby begins his fall he's overcome with fear. Without a speck of his body all clear, he falls like a stone. His one success is his ability to keep from screaming. Keepers don't scream.

He doesn't want to die. He has a lot to live for, starting with the friends he doesn't think he can live without. A family he loves. Willa. A computer that kicks butt. But while he's not as heartless as the Dillard, Philby's no romantic. It's going to hurt when he lands. He's going to suffer. It's not the death he would have chosen.

It feels like the tug of gravity is sucking him down like the Devil himself drawing breath from Hell. Spread out beneath Philby is the kingdom he has sworn to defend in flames, under the control of barbarians armed with black magic. He has devoted six years of his life to a singular aim, a goal with no personal gain—and that has made it the best ride ever. He and these friends have struggled to advance an ideal. He can live with that.

Or die with it, as the case may be.

* * *

Amanda sees Philby slipping away from her, claimed by gravity. Her heart sinks with him.

Her life so far has been full of opposites. Other people have families; she was claimed by an institution. Other people have hobbies; she has a power she can't escape. Other people have sisters; she has a fellow stranger who feels like her twin.

No thought, only pure instinct, motivates what Amanda does next. Pivoting on her heels, she reverses herself and *pushes*. She faces a four-story mountain of rock that isn't going to budge. The force of her thrust drives her straight back, as if a rocket had hit her in the stomach. She is propelled through space like a crash-test dummy thrown from a test car, except that she holds both hands palms down, facing out, ready for impact.

There!

Keepers don't scream.

She feels Philby's hand smack hers. He squeezes like there's no tomorrow, which, technically, there may not be. She carries him with her, his body outstretched, parallel to the ground, buckled forward as if she were working out on a rowing machine. Together, hand in hand, they sail backward and slam into a patch of sand between a small cluster of rocks. A puff of dust rises.

Philby coughs. Amanda wipes tears from her eyes before he notices. Her back to the mountain, she gives another huge shove with her palms. There's the sound of an explosion, but not sparks, no flames.

The bridge is spun like a turnstile, away from the moorings that hold it to the mountain.

The bridge collapses in an epic crash that challenges the shattering heavens for bragging rights. The miners and their car sail through the air to a dire fate awaiting them below.

The Overtakers' improvised grounding rod is broken.

* * *

Maybeck puts his fist where his feet were, punching his clenched hand into Doom's ruined jaw and separating its one remaining workable joint. The force of his punch leaves Doom's head swinging like a rattan porch chair in a warm summer breeze.

Simultaneously, Maybeck uses his remarkable agility to work the third of the seven levers with his foot, dipping the crane's jib into the rock face of Big Thunder Mountain. His ankle manages to trigger the winding drum's payout of hoist rope, lowering Charlene, whose remarkable bravery has freed the Partners statue, allowing it to free-fall to the ground below, where it squishes two Thuggee warriors flat like bugs.

Then Charlene and Maybeck jump at the same instant, whether by instinct or good judgment, neither knows.

A lightning strike hits the uplifted crane. A wild, rollicking jolt of several million volts of electricity races the length of the crane's boom and, finding no ground, builds to bursting on the crane's slewing platform. The crane melts like chocolate left in the sun and sags until nothing but a molten blob of metal remains.

Somewhere in the sludge is the Judge—doomed.

71

FINN HOLDS MICKEY BACK. The legend wants desperately to climb the ladder, though he is well aware of what waits above them, but Finn and the Keepers have other plans. Pushing Mickey's sorcerer's cap out of his own eyes, Finn climbs. Violet's hands are nearly on his heels, she is climbing so close behind him.

"The Queen! Tia Dalma! Where are they?" he shouts to Willa, far below. Were the witches caught and killed in the Skyway Station battle? It's the last anyone has seen of them. If Finn doesn't return, he wants Willa thinking ahead.

He doesn't anticipate the cloven hoof in his face. One moment he's climbing, the next, the ladder is knocked out from under him. The steel structure, bolted to concrete, crumples as if made of mere paper. Grabbing at the leg attached to the hoof, Finn finds himself on an express elevator to the penthouse, up and through the hatch. He lets go, the beast that carried him there none the wiser. Hitting the ground, he lands behind Chernabog, crouched on his hands and knees. Violet's not here. She must have fallen back to the catwalk, Finn realizes.

There's a thundering sound, but it isn't thunder. The beast stomps one hoof angrily. The steel hatch jumps off the deck, lifted by the vibration, and slams shut. The sound it makes draws Chernabog's attention; as he turns, he spots the parasite he carried aloft: Finn. The beast cocks his head at Finn and widens his black eyes, which are as big and as opaque as bowling balls. Hot, sour air blasts from his wet nose as he coughs and snorts.

Then, with a roar, Chernabog swipes at Finn as if he were a housefly. Finn ducks and feints to his right. The sunken deck at the top of the Matterhorn is instantly transformed into a boxing ring. Chernabog draws back a fist, the wing attached behind his shoulder trailing and echoing the windup, and swings. Finn dives between the beast's legs, rolls, and comes to standing mere inches away. If Chernabog steps back, Finn will be crushed or forced over the side to his death.

Finn steals a look down, past the edge of the sunken platform upon which they're standing, which has a surface rubberized against weather and is barely bigger than a backyard wading pool. The Matterhorn's icy white peak sits like a scoop of ice cream atop the cone of the mountain's jagged brown slopes. It's a long way down to concrete and asphalt.

In the second or two he has bought himself, Finn manages to go all clear. He attempts his spin technique, moving through Chernabog as the beast turns to search for him. Again, Finn comes out behind his opponent.

Not seeing Finn, Chernabog pivots back. Finn carefully times when to step through the beast. He succeeds undetected. Sensing the ruse this time, the beast turns yet again. He's quicker and cleverer than Finn anticipated. A flash of panic steals his all clear, and Finn bounces into, then off the beast's leg.

With another roar that seems to shake the heavens, Chernabog slams Finn with one mighty fist. But one wing tip snags on the lip of the sunken platform, reducing the force of the blow—it's not a square hit. Finn spins like a top and collapses, still conscious.

Chernabog raises his hoof and stomps. Finn crawls out of

the way at the last possible second. The beast rears back to kick Finn, but Finn hauls the escape hatch open. Chernabog's hoof cracks into the steel plate; the resulting collision sounds like a ten-car pileup. The enormous creature staggers back, growling in pain.

Seizing his advantage, Finn charges, his arms outstretched like lances, and slams into Chernabog. He might as well have hit a brick wall. Finn falls; Chernabog barely totters. But totter he does, and his sore hoof doesn't help. Finn lunges again, angrily this time, desperately. He is fighting not only for his self-preservation; he is fighting for Wayne's sake too.

Chernabog hits him cleanly this time, first with his hand, then with the tip of one wing, which catapults the boy off the platform, sending him sliding down the mountain's icy face. The surface is real ice, not fiberglass. It's real, and this beast means to kill him.

Finn claws his way up the snow, grabs a handful, and hurls a half-packed snowball at Chernabog. The beast tries to block it, but the ice ball explodes on contact, and the monster is blinded, at least for the moment.

Scurrying now, slipping and falling, but managing still to climb back up toward the platform, Finn throws more ice and snow into the beast's oversize eyes. Chernabog's reaction is to wrap his wings around himself and step forward.

Finn slips over the edge and back onto the sunken platform, scooping and throwing snowballs all the while, but the monster's wings open with a snap, revealing a red-eyed bull's head that is the closest thing to a devil's face Finn has ever seen. Chernabog takes two thunderous steps and knocks the hatch shut again, eliminating any chance for Finn's escape.

In the distance, an explosion rocks Big Thunder Mountain.

Like a crippled shooting star, the crane lifts and then falls, consumed in flames. Chernabog bellows his displeasure, making the Matterhorn shake with his cries.

Maleficent in her dragon form was vulnerable to Finn's attack. But she had outgrown a confined space, trapping herself and giving Finn the upper hand—literally: he tore her heart out with his hologram hand.

There will be no such simple end with Chernabog. The beast is free, he's angry, and the flesh-eating monster now towers over Finn. His massive black leathery shoulders cap bulging arm muscles and humanlike hands—but with long claws, bigger than lawn rakes. His blank, unforgiving eyes radiate a bull's brute ignorance and rage.

"I know you can hear me!" Finn shouts at Chernabog, who responds with an inquisitive look. Finn wants to cheer; he's won the beast's attention. "You cannot win! You kill us, and more will take our place. You destroy the park, another will be built."

Chernabog swings, but simply voicing his convictions has returned Finn to all clear. The surge of energy is brief, but potent. The beast staggers, thrown off balance by the force of his blow, which fails to connect, sweeping through Finn's torso.

"I'm not here," Finn says. "I'm magic. I'm everything you're not!"

Another swipe, another miss.

For the first time, Finn sees real puzzlement in the gaping black eyes. "There's no such thing as evil here!" he hollers. "No room for it in this place. In Disneyland, evil never wins. How can you beat the laws of nature?"

They are frozen, staring at one another, gazes locked. Finn wishes for Amanda's power to push. He wishes for Amanda.

Chernabog deserves to go over the side, or worse. The beast snorts, his eyes aflame.

"Take a look around," Finn says. "We're going to fix it. We're going to change it back to what it was—to what it's always been."

He can't decide if he's addressing a bull with a man's body or a man with a bull's head. He realizes that even if he manages to push the beast over the side, Chernabog will simply spread his wings and fly or glide to the ground. Finn eyes the closed hatch.

Another flash of lightning is followed almost instantaneously by a deafening crack of thunder. The storm is directly overhead.

"It starts and ends in lightning."

Jess said that. Had the Keepers misunderstood her? They had thought she meant that the park would be ended—destroyed—by lightning, and although that still appears to have been the Overtakers' aim, Finn wonders if there was a second meaning, one they missed.

Chernabog leans toward Finn, letting loose a moaning roar that sounds like a bull's grunting complaint and a man's pent-up frustration in one. And in that instant, Finn looks for something metal to attract the lightning. If this is his moment, if this is what Wayne meant to show him, that some things require the ultimate sacrifice, then he has no intention of going alone. If he's to die, his death has to mean something, it has to count. Again, Wayne's last words sound in his ears: *"It's about time."*

"For what?" Finn shouts, but he's afraid of the answer. He already knows.

Chernabog startles at Finn's outburst. The boy dives to one side, biting back a cry as a stream of green bile fills the

586

space where he stood a second before. The bile boils and bubbles on the rubber surface, melting away a section of the mountain. Finn forgot the beast could do things like that.

Finn rolls over and jumps to his feet. Chernabog shifts his weight, eyeing the hatch, apparently to be sure that it is still closed. He fakes Finn out, swiping at him with a casual gesture, as if merely fanning the air, catching the boy in the ribs and tossing him aside.

Landing hard, Finn looks down—and feels his stomach fall. He's once again over the edge of the recessed platform, hanging by his fingertips. In the flashing lightning, looking up at his wrists, he sees Wayne's watch, reflecting the storm in tiny bursts of light.

"It's about time."

It's about the watch, Finn realizes. He needs something metal to attract the lightning. If he's not fully all clear, the watch isn't either. If he's some part human flesh in this condition, then the watch must be some equal part its original self: metal. Gold-plated metal. Gold, one of the best conductors of electricity.

Did Wayne possess Jess's gift of prophecy? Did he foresee this moment?

Dozens of times in battle, Finn has reached for all clear by imagining a pinprick of light at the center of an endless black vacuum. He has pictured it like a train coming at him, the light growing until he is enveloped in it. He sees it now—that same intensity of white light. But the difference is that Chernabog has made his way into the basalt blackness.

Finn drags himself to the lip of the platform, crouches, and . . .

Jumps. He flies like a superhero.

Finn's boldness catches Chernabog by surprise. The beast

spreads his arms and his wings, trying to grab Finn, to crush him against his chest. But Finn arcs through the air with surprising speed and smashes into Chernabog's chest—and this time he makes the monster stagger.

As fast as he can, Finn climbs, ascending Chernabog's chest as if it were a climbing wall. He pulls himself up to Chernabog's shoulders, grabs onto one of his hideous curled horns, and stretches Wayne's watch toward the heavens.

Finn thinks of the old man. Here they are, teamed up together one last time, fighting this last good fight together. The pinprick of light in the sky expands and grows more intense, just as it has so many other times. But this time, the process goes faster than ever before. Finn's imaginary train has always moved slowly as it approaches through the darkness, washing out the fear and ushering the all clear in. Not this time: this time it comes as fast as lightning.

VIOLET AND ELSA recover the ladder only moments after it crashes to the catwalk. Although she has fallen from a great height, Violet's abilities protect her from harm. With Mickey standing aside, the two race to reattach the ladder, but the task proves to be physically impossible, because it has broken free from its supports. So instead, they work together to secure it well enough for Violet to climb back up to help Finn.

After several tries, Elsa's panic subsides, and she realizes that the tools she needs are in her hands. She instructs Jess and Willa to guide Mickey a few yards away for safety. With the three of them behind her and Violet in front holding the ladder in place, Elsa freezes the bottom of the ladder to the catwalk, leaving only a small gap at the top between the ladder and the Skyway Station's framework.

Violet is halfway up when an overhead explosion knocks her off the ladder a second time. Her horrified eyes fix on the ring of roiling blue electricity rolling down the mountain's exoskeleton. "Finn!" she screams. She leaps onto the ladder a second time and climbs with abandon, angrily knocking the hatch door up and open and pulling herself outside on top.

It's raining hard. Lightning flashes overhead; jagged bolts dance between the clouds. In the pulses of blue light, she sees the platform empty, abandoned. No Finn. No Chernabog.

Violet nearly hurls herself off the side, moving along the deck's perimeter to look down in search of them, terrified that she'll see Finn's bloodless fingertips clutching a handhold,

589

hanging on for dear life, but—nothing. Gritting her teeth, she dares to focus lower, on the concrete below, expecting the worst. But what she discovers is worse still.

Elsa, who has climbed quietly behind Violet, joins her on the platform. "Where . . . ?" Elsa begins, but she doesn't finish her thought. "Oh, no," she whispers.

Violet follows the Winter Queen's horrified gaze to the deck floor. One glance is enough. Stomach lurching, she averts her eyes.

The platform's thick blue vinyl-covered surface is charred black and boiled brittle, as if something was cooked there. No, not some*thing*. Some*one*, turned to dust, burned and vaporized by the same surge of energy that has blackened every streetlamp and bulb in the park. Violet sees residual fires flickering like candles in a dark room, sending shards of glancing light across what remains of Disneyland. She sees emptiness and finality, death. Her love for this place, its magic, its characters . . . that feeling struggles for air in a vacuum of evil intent.

"Finn sacrificed himself . . . for us," she whispers. She hears a peal of agony and sorrow carry like a clarion call over the park, and realizes belatedly that it comes from her own throat.

In the center of the still smoldering burn mark is Mickey's sorcerer's cap, somehow intact—the cap Finn was wearing when he climbed the mountain to meet his fate.

73

WHEN ELSA AND VIOLET return to the catwalk, they find Mickey standing alone.

"Where are the girls?" a shaken Violet asks. She passes Mickey his sorcerer's cap, which he pulls on. It stands regally atop his head, as though it has found its proper place at last.

Gone, Mickey says, speaking voicelessly to both of his fellow Disney characters.

"What? Where?" Violet cries.

Mickey blows a farewell kiss. Elsa moves as if to shake him, but Violet restrains her.

"Don't freeze him!" Violet begs.

"Where did they go?" Elsa shouts. Her words echo. "Jess! Willa!" Elsa looks down, awaiting an answer, but only darkness meets her. "Girls!" she calls again. No answer.

"If they took off that fast," Violet says, "there must be a reason. We have to stay positive."

"You cannot be serious! Finn . . . dust. Willa and Jess have run off! We have to stay positive? How?" Turning, Elsa trips over something—and bends to retrieve Mickey's conductor's baton, his magic wand.

Golly, Violet hears him say. *Is that mine?*

"It is," Violet answers, motioning to Elsa, who hands Mickey the baton and steps back.

Mickey swings it, as if testing its balance. Then, with his free hand, he pulls his cap on more tightly and directs the baton toward the ladder, which sparkles, shimmers—and the ice freezing it in place is gone. The ladder is restored, as they found it, in one piece, secured to the wall.

"You have been missed," Violet says demurely.

Mickey gives her his best, *Aw, shucks!* look.

Violet has overheard the Keepers discussing Mickey's importance, his role in what comes next. The endgame, Philby called it. She never figured she would be the one to see it through to its final moments. For a place once filled with such magic, such joy and fantasy, Disneyland feels nothing like that now. The Children of Light have been legend for years. Characters like her have hung their hopes on them. Finnegan alone took on a more than legendary, a truly mythical quality: the leader of the rebels, their heart and soul.

Without wanting to, Violet sees the charred outline on the deck in her mind's eye. For all her heroism, she has never considered self-sacrifice. She cannot imagine the strength it must have taken for Finn to allow himself to be struck by lightning.

Taking a deep breath, Violet turns to Mickey and speaks aloud. "He cleared the way for you. The Keepers—the Children of Light, the Children of *Life*—they believed in you, believed your powers alone could restore the park to its former perfection. They were guided by a man named Wayne, and by Walt Disney before him. Together, they made this happen. They sacrificed greatly for this chance. I guess what I'm saying is: they believed. And I believe too. It's time." She motions toward the ladder.

Elsa says gently, "We don't know how many of their leaders remain."

Mickey shakes his head sadly, but does not speak.

"They thought," Violet says hesitantly, "that if you . . . if the park could be made whole again, the trouble would pass. The Overtakers, the evil ones who have brought the park to its knees—they're wounded, if not destroyed. They've been set back years, if not forever. If—*when*—you heal the park and seal the earth back up, the evil will be sealed up too. The magic will be preserved."

Trouble has no place here, Mickey says silently. Elsa and Violet listen intently, hanging on his every word. *It never has; it never will.* He looks up the ladder to the open hatch. *You say the leader . . . ?*

Violet averts her eyes and shakes her head.

He flew away? Violet nods, on the verge of tears. *The leader, or the one called the Bat God?*

"Both, I think."

I defeated the Bat God once before, you know? Many years ago.

"Yes, I've seen it."

Seen it? You are too young! Far too young.

"I'll explain later. We must act now. The sun is nearly up. The park must be restored before any children see it like this."

Lead the way. Mickey nods, indicating the ladder.

Together, he begins to climb with Violet. Elsa stays behind, giving them room atop the mountain.

From the platform, Mickey and Violet survey the ruined park. Under a gray shelf of clouds, the sun burns in a pink line as it rises on the eastern horizon. Seagulls float not far off.

The park is empty! Mickey says.

"I think they—the villains we call the Overtakers—took off when Chernabog and Finn . . ." Violet works to keep the sorrow from her voice. "When they flew away."

You must not believe the pain, child. Like the magic in this park, it is only as real as you believe it to be. Hold on to the things you cherish. Leave behind all you do not.

She kisses him on the cheek. "Can you fix it?"

He giggles his Mickey giggle. It has been forever since she's heard that sound in films, and she has never heard it in person. It sounds lighter than she could have imagined.

Do you believe I can fix it?

"Yes, I do."

It's an awful mess.

"Yes, it is."

Together they take in the damage: the smoldering fires, the shattered concrete and fallen trees, the destruction at Big Thunder Mountain Railroad.

"It seems so unfair," Violet says. "The Children of Light should be here. This is their story. I have a feeling they would claim they are only visitors, that we are the ones who deserve to watch you. But that's another example of their selflessness."

Mickey puts his white-gloved hand on hers. Then he smiles. *How much do you believe?*

"Fully," Violet says. "Without a doubt."

Without a doubt.

Mickey likes that, she can tell.

Then believe this, child: the Children of Light are here with us. We witness with more than eyes and ears. The true test of one's faith is not belief, but commitment. From what you say, they have demonstrated that.

"More often than any of us," Violet says. "They lived it." And now at last she cries.

Below them, Elsa sheds tears of ice. They ring like tiny bells as they fall to the deck and burst apart.

Now, now, Mickey says, *there's no place for that here.*

He lifts his baton and begins to conduct a silent melody, as if leading an orchestra as big as the entire park itself, turning right and left, spinning in circles, childish, gleeful, ebullient. His cap flaps this way and that. Violet and Elsa can hear him laughing. The sound echoes in their hearts.

Sparkles appear like frost on the attractions and paths, and for a moment, Violet thinks Elsa is up to her Winter Queen tricks. But the sparkling frost is light, not ice. As it dances around the park, it restores the park as it was before the Skyway Station battle. Everything about it is new and untouched. The effect is slow to take hold. Magic, like a song, must take its own sweet time. Only the Skyway Station itself is left in ruins: the source of the wounds must be removed forever.

Violet has seen her brother run at speeds that blur her vision. She herself has appeared and disappeared in the blink of an eye. Yet, nothing has prepared her for this. All the magic of the princes and princesses, the bears and chipmunks, and even all the power of the Overtakers rolled up together would amount to little compared to the healing power Mickey unleashes.

Daylight breaks among the shooting sparks; radiant beams split the departing storms and spread warm golden light over a perfect Disneyland. In the distance, California Adventure glows. The attractions glisten. The paths shine, smooth and flawless once more.

From a distance, all around the park, the inhabitants of Disneyland reemerge from hiding to see a familiar silhouette standing high atop the Matterhorn, waving what looks like a baton.

One minute he's there.

The next, in a wink of light, he's gone.

The wink of light is the restoration of electric power to the park. Streetlamps flicker, but remain on. Neon buzzes back to life. Music floats from unseen speakers. A spotlight focused on the Matterhorn platform clicks on. Mickey steps into the cone of light; he was there all along.

Violet and Elsa are so enthralled by the changes to the park that they miss the growing cloud of colors at their feet and behind them. The shapes sputter and fight to appear.

When finally Violet turns, she screams as she sees Philby

and Willa, holding hands; Charlene and Maybeck likewise; and an inconsolable Amanda held tightly in Jess's arms. They are all there with them, just as Mickey said.

Finn lies at their feet on the deck, unconscious or dead.

Amanda pulls free of Jess and kneels beside Finn. "Help him," she says to Mickey.

Only Violet hears Mickey's reply. *I know him not. This kind is unfamiliar to me. I can heal magic, not flesh.*

"He's not breathing!" Amanda says. "Why bring him back if he's not breathing?"

Mickey can do no more than look down at her and smile his endless smile.

"It wasn't Mickey who brought us back," Philby says. "It was the power coming on. Finn . . . the lightning strike . . . Mickey restored the power. I was over at Big Thunder when that lightning struck. I have no idea how I got here. The rest of you?"

As Mickey smiles, the others shake their heads. All but Amanda, who is hysterical. "He's—not—breathing!" she wails.

Willa turns to Mickey, wringing her hands. "Megara, Rapunzel! Can you bring them here? Can you summon them?"

Mickey lifts and waves his baton.

"Look!" Charlene rushes to the edge of the platform. Out of the smoke from the fireworks Dumbo emerges, sweeping his ears with grace and ease. He's carrying Megara and Rapunzel on his back. The elephant hovers over the platform as the two women lower themselves and drop to Mickey's side.

Jess can't help herself. Through her tears, she waves at Dumbo, who winks and flies off.

Without instruction, Megara and Rapunzel tend to Finn. They work in sync, like two nurses with metaphysical powers.

Mickey, the Keepers, Violet, and Elsa form a semicircle around them. No one knows when exactly they all reach out and take one another's hands, but it doesn't matter. In the end they stand, unified.

The powers of the two women are transformative. The color returns to Finn's hologram. The burned and missing pieces of his DHI body are restored. It's as if Megara and Rapunzel are retouching a painting made of light.

Mickey giggles, turning each and every head. This time, everyone hears him. He covers his nose in embarrassment and blushes.

Next to Elsa, another orb of light pulses and flickers. The Dillard appears.

"Finn must be coming around!" Philby cries. "Look who's here!"

The Keepers and Fairlies clasp hands, celebrating the Dillard's reappearance. Charlene claps. The Dillard merely raises an eyebrow, emotionless as ever.

Finn sits up. Amanda gives a joyful cry and smothers him in a hug. The Keepers hug Megara; Mickey and Philby sneak in an embrace with Rapunzel.

"What has happened here?" the Dillard says.

Laughter rings from the top of the Matterhorn, the sound stolen away by the thunderous grand finale of fireworks overhead.

Finn lifts his arm beyond Amanda's embrace. The gold watch shimmers.

"Did it work? Did it work?" He manages to swing his head far enough to take in Mickey in his cap, bearing his baton. The peaceful expression on that familiar face seems to light up the sky along with the exploding fireworks.

Mickey and Finn lock eyes.

Finn sees someone behind those eyes he never expected to see again: Wayne—calling to Finn: *My job is done. It's your kingdom now.*

597

74

FINN WAKES, opens his eyes, and recoils at the sight of Philby, who is pressing his finger against his lips to indicate silence.

"What the—" Finn catches himself and returns the nod. Together, the two Keepers slip out of the actors' trailer serving as their dormitory and into a bathroom in the Frank G. Wells Building. Philby waves his hand under the faucet's automatic sensor, producing a hissing stream of water loud enough to cover their whispered conversation.

"Jess's latest drawing?" Philby says. "The one after it was all over."

The Keepers' past two weeks have been consumed with intensive debriefing sessions conducted by lawyers, archivists, and the Imagineers. Finn had nearly forgotten about Jess's unexpected nightmare, which led to her sketching a new image in her diary.

"The coffee cup?" Finn asks.

"No, the one after that. It shows you and Maybeck, crouched down near that mirror." Philby unfolds a copy of the sketch and passes it to Finn.

"Yeah? So what?"

"In it, you look like you're holding Walt's pen."

"Yeah, it does look like that. But that's not how it happened. Her vision is off. Besides, that was years ago. I was alone, Philby. Once inside One Man's Dream I tricked my way backstage in order to steal Walt's pen, and Maybeck wasn't with me. Other than that," he concludes sarcastically, "it's a perfect duplicate."

"Jess has never sketched the past. Always the future."

"Sometimes," Finn says, mulling this over, "she gets it wrong. Even she'll tell you that. But let's say she's right. We don't know it's Walt's pen in my hand."

"Of course it is." He pauses. "I need to show you, Finn. It's not something I can tell you."

"Okay. But why all the secrecy? Why just me?"

"Because I have my theories. Don't worry, we'll tell the others." There's an awkward pause. Finn wants to ask, "When?" but doesn't. Finally, Philby speaks, rubbing his neck uncomfortably, not meeting Finn's gaze.

"You're saying you haven't felt it?"

"I'm feeling things I don't ever want to feel again: regret, guilt, terror. Which do you mean? Take your pick."

"Hairs on the back of your neck, rising."

"That, too."

Finn has chalked up the sensation to the lingering effects of his near-death experience, his brush with permanent Sleeping Beauty Syndrome. Philby's confirmation that he has felt the same thing disturbs Finn.

"We know Maybeck melted Judge Doom. You fried Chernabog. But none of us saw what happened inside the Skyway Station after it all went down."

Finn looks away, twisting his lips. He doesn't want to revisit the feelings of disruption and panic. "I hear they're going to tear the rest of it down."

"I heard the same thing. No more Skyway Station. But that's not the point. The point is that both you and I feel things aren't exactly back to normal. And I'll bet the others feel it too. As long as that feeling's there, I trust no one, not even Joe."

"That's ridiculous!" Finn raises his voice. "We fixed the park! *Mickey* fixed it! We can't live our lives seeing ghosts around every corner. Or maybe you can, but I can't."

"It's not that simple."

"It is to me."

"No, Finn. I mean the 'fixed it' part. I'm not so sure we did. I think it's more relative." Philby pulls his hand from beneath the faucet. The water stops. "I have to show you this." He swipes his hand, gets it running again. "There are cameras everywhere. We know that."

"You're freaking me out, Philby. Can't we move on?"

"Not yet. I'm going to take you to the old Animation building hallway. Now, they could be watching us, so when we get there, I'm going to point out a picture, but I want you to focus on the *reflection* in the glass. Look at the photo across the hall reflected in the glass. Then we're going to wander around looking at several other photos. When we get back to the one in the reflection, take a good long look."

"At? Come on, Philby."

"You need to see it for yourself, Finn. That's the only way either of us is going to believe it."

* * *

The hallway in the old Animation building is long and empty. Finn follows Philby's instructions to the letter. Of all the Keepers, Philby is far and away the least dramatic. Finn might expect theatrics from Maybeck or Charlene, even Willa— though over the years she and Philby have grown so much alike that it's hard to tell them apart. Knowing this makes Philby's urgency all the more pressing.

In the reflection, Finn sees a poster-size frame containing a collage of several photos. The two boys begin to wander the hall independently, and Finn makes sure to take his time with the frame in question. Along the way, he studies several other images for a long time, hoping that when he stops in front of the crucial one, it won't seem suspicious—if Philby's even right about them being watched.

Then again, Philby's always right.

The collage commemorates the grand opening of One Man's Dream at Walt Disney World on October 1, 2001. There are a half-dozen color photos. Finn studies each carefully—and stops at the fifth one he examines.

In the photo, there is a mirror, of a kind often used for putting on makeup or shaving, and identical to the one in Jess's most recent sketch. The mirror is attached to a crisscross metal armature that can extend accordion-style.

Finn unfolds Jess's sketch. Her image shows only pieces of shelves. In the photo, they are revealed to be part of an animator's drawing desk, and the mirror is set up to allow the artist to study his own facial expressions as a guide to help in drawing his characters' faces. Her vision fits with what Finn sees framed on the wall, but he still can't make sense of it. He won't admit it out loud, but he *knows* that it is Walt's pen in his hand in Jess's drawing, and that it has no place being there.

After a while, he and Philby leave the hallway and step outside, where the security cameras may observe them but there are no microphones that might pick up their conversation.

"A drawing desk," Finn says. "One Man's Dream."

"Close. But not exactly."

"So? I'm the one who got the pen, remember? I was alone,

and I didn't find it on the drawing table. I found it on Walt's office desk."

"In a mug, like the one Jess sketched the first time. Yes. Did you happen to notice the shelves on the drawing table?"

"The books and stuff?"

"And in Jess's sketch."

Finn checks. *"Hmm."*

"Her drawing is not of One Man's Dream. Jess saw you and Maybeck next to a drawing desk, but not the one in the exhibit. It's *Walt's real drawing desk.*" Philby takes a deep breath, and then whispers, "'It's about time.'"

"Stop quoting that. You need sleep," Finn says.

"Wayne's watch," Philby reminds him. "The address—"

"Is actually the address of the Music Box Company. Like the thing in Walt's apartment. We've talked about this for the past two weeks. I'm sick of it! We're done, Philby. Done!"

Chirping crickets compete with the sound of traffic. A warm wind blows—judging by the smell, someone nearby is painting. Finn has lost two friends and nearly lost his mother, not to mention nearly losing his own life multiple times. With Wayne gone, with the park restored, he wants out. He has gained friendships worth keeping and working on. Experience, to be sure. But Mickey's designating him protector and defender of the Kingdom weighs heavily on his shoulders. He wants a break. He needs a break.

"We need to visit Walt's apartment," Philby says. "Scratch that. Wayne turned this all over to you, so *you* need to visit Walt's apartment. But you're bringing us along for the ride."

"Because?" There it is again, the reminder it's all on Finn now.

"I think Wayne left you a recording. If the music box can play recorded music, it can play a recorded voice, too. You know Wayne. Always up to more tricks."

"Okay. I'm good with that."

"Say, what?"

"If this will shut you up, I'll do it," Finn says.

"Just like that?"

Finn confesses. "The watch and the music box—that New Jersey address—it's been bugging me. I admit it!"

"If Wayne left you a message, it's not going to be a pep talk. It's going to be Wayne asking for you—for us—to do something. That's just who he is."

"I said, I'm in." Finn wants desperately to prove Philby wrong, to board a plane and return to Orlando, but there's no way he can turn down the chance to hear Wayne's voice again. Like having the Dillard along, it would assuage some of his grief. Despite himself, there's a flicker of excitement that burns somewhere within Finn. Wayne—another mission: could it possibly be true?

Professor Philby lays out the rules. "We can't tell the Cryptos what we're up to. Amanda and Jess are preparing for their internships. We don't need to bother them, either."

"Why so secretive?" Finn says. "Amanda and Jess are part of us now."

"I'm being cautious. So sue me."

"What's the big secret Wayne supposedly left us on this recording?" Finn asks.

"If I knew that," Philby says. "We wouldn't have to go there."

A bolt of excitement darts through Finn. And then he feels sick to his stomach. Each time Wayne has summoned them, the risk to the Keepers as well as to the Kingdom has increased exponentially. If Wayne left a prerecorded message, it could only say that he expected to die—or knew he would be killed.

75

THE KEEPERS TALK Joe and the Imagineers into allowing them into the park as DHIs during daytime hours, claiming that they want one last chance to act out their hosting roles, to show families around the park and see the joy the DHIs bring.

"We can't explain it," Finn says to Joe. He feels guilty about the lie. "After everything that's happened, it's just something we want to do."

"There's no repaying the debt we owe you," Joe says. "I don't need to tell you that. You have the keys to the Kingdom for life. And I'm hoping you'll all consider my offer of Imagineering School after college. You each have something unique to offer."

"Alone or together," Willa says, reiterating his earlier words.

"Yes," says Joe. "Speaking of which, what about Jess and Amanda?"

"They're busy. We'd like to do this by ourselves, if that's okay." Finn stumbles over his words, winning a curious look from Joe. "Sorry. We stayed up all night"—he glances at Philby—"so we'd be tired enough to fall asleep for the crossover."

"Sure," Joe says.

"We promise to return on time," Finn adds, holding up the precious fob that will allow them back.

"Off you go then! Get to sleep. We'll cross you over. Have a great time," Joe says.

"Oh," Philby says, "we will."

* * *

The Keepers cross over at 8:00 A.M., an hour before the gates open, and an hour before they are supposed to show up and guide guests through the park.

"Do you think he suspects?" Charlene asks, trying to brush a speck of lint from her hologram clothes, then realizing it's useless. No matter how many times she crosses over, she'll never quite adjust.

"The Amanda-and-Jess excuse was lame," Maybeck says.

"We're fine," says Charlene. "But it doesn't seem right. I mean, it's Jess's sketch!"

Philby says, "This is just the one time, Charlie." He receives curious looks from all.

"You suspect something," Charlene says defiantly.

"I do," Philby says.

"Do you know what Wayne's going to say? That is, if he says anything!" Charlene stares him down.

They can barely hear Philby's answer. "I think I do. Yes."

"And?" Charlene asks.

"You wouldn't believe me if I told you. Honestly? I don't believe it myself. But what I know—and I tried to tell Finn this—is that no one would believe me anyway. We have to hear Wayne's words from Wayne."

"Well," Charlene says, "you had me at: 'I don't believe it myself.' Since when? Let's do this thing."

They smile and laugh, caught up for a moment in the renewed warm feeling of their companionship. The years have gone by quickly. Not one of the Keepers has forgotten a single moment—the battles, both within and among themselves and against their enemies; the puzzles that so resisted being solved; the quiet moments and the loud. There's an awkward sense of pride they share but will not mention, a sense of accomplishment that also goes unspoken. Some of this is communicated with a glance or a grin, some not at all. Shared terror that is survived has a way of cementing companionship.

"Above all," Finn says, "we're a team."

For a moment it looks as if the others might tease him for this outburst. Surprisingly, it's Maybeck that comes to his rescue. "I'd never trade you guys for anything," Maybeck says, clearing his throat and staring at his shoes. "Wouldn't change any of it, even the worst stuff. I realize you two," he motions to Finn and Philby, "think something's going on with this music box, but I don't care. It isn't any of this"—he sweeps his hand through his hologram torso—"that's so cool anymore. It's this." He throws his holographic arm around Charlene and pulls her close.

"It is," Willa agrees, squeezing Philby's hand.

"You know, instead of another adventure, we could all apply to the same college!" Charlene says, winning more laughter from the group. "Yeah, well, it was a thought."

"We check out the music box, then we hang out in the park and actually have fun for a change. Right?" Willa says.

Finn reaches into his pocket and holds up the fob. "Right. And when we're done for the day, we take the one way back that's always worked. We . . . ?"

All the Kingdom Keepers respond at once, in brilliant unison: "Push the button!"

EPILOGUE

IN A WINDOWLESS ROOM at an undisclosed location—it looks a lot like the deep foundation dug to anchor the collapsed Skyway—a dark-skinned woman sits, cross-legged on the ground. Her matted dreadlocks and tattooed mascara suggest the costume of a Halloween trick-or-treater rather than that of the voodoo witch doctor she is.

The air smells foul, like lizard kidney and hundred-year-old eggs, the blood of a goat and wing of a bat. The stench emanates from the concoction bubbling softly in front of the woman, which simmers at a roiling boil, though there is no fire, no apparent source of heat of any kind.

The woman adds wings plucked from a living moth and the immemorial eye of newt, murmuring dark words under her breath.

This is no simple resurrection spell she is casting, but a charm for the ages, an experimental recipe she envisioned a long time ago but has never dared to try. The wing of bat was not from any ordinary creature. No. It was found near the base of the Matterhorn, after the disaster.

She dips a long finger in the brew, wincing at the heat, and withdraws, licking from the bowl of her inverted fingernail. Lacking sufficient volume of genuine spiderweb, she plucks out several of her own hairs—protein is protein—stirs them in, and smiles.

Perhaps there will be a bit of her in this one. . . .

From a leather pouch sealed with a piece of rawhide, she

withdraws three pale bones. She collected them on a day that feels like years ago, scrounging in a dank tunnel below a temple in the heart of the Mexican jungle: dragon bones—special bones that slide into the caldron and bubble on their way to the bottom.

The woman's eyes roll back in her head, entirely white, like two soft onions.

> *"Here within this devil's brew,*
> *Lost life restarted,*
> *One and one make two.*
>
> *Foundered but not sunken,*
> *As wild as the drunken*
> *Torment of the scorned.*
>
> *Bring these two*
> *Together,*
> *United in fright and fear.*
> *May its power know no limits.*
> *It lives now:*
> *Bring it here."*

ACKNOWLEDGMENTS

First, an effort to correct an oversight that I'd love to blame on the Overtakers, but in reality it was more likely my mistake. Please join me in congratulating the following for their help in naming *Kingdom Keepers VI: Dark Passage.*

Angie Annett
Natalie Zawadzki
Tim Russell

Now, for *Kingdom Keepers VII: The Insider:*
An ambitious undertaking, the writing of this novel included two publishers, four editors, a half dozen copy editors, and many readers. Along with one writer.

It's my pleasure to acknowledge the (often round-the-clock) hours of effort from the following:

Editors:
Wendy Lefkon (Disney-Hyperion)
Genevieve Gagne-Hawes (Writers House)
Brooke Muschott (Intern)
Christopher Caines (Copy Editor, Editor)

Coliloquy:
Lisa Rutherford
Jennifer Lou
Waynn Lue

Thanks for the access and the research provided by:
Disney Parks and the Walt Disney Company:
Kim Irvine, Disneyland
Becky Cline Director, Walt Disney Archives
Kevin Kern, Walt Disney Archives Collections Specialist
Richard Fleming, Entertainment Manager, Walt Disney World
Alex Wright, Creative Designer Lead, Walt Disney Imagineering
Jason Surrell, Show Writer, Walt Disney Imagineering
Joe Garlington, VP, Executive Producer, Walt Disney Imagineering
Betsy Singer, Merchandiser, Walt Disney Parks and Resorts
Misty Carroll, Events Specialist, Walt Disney Parks and Resorts
Karl Holz, President, Disney Cruise Line
Jodi Bennett, Relationship Marketing Director, Disney Cruise Line

And to the operational efforts of:
The Walt Disney Company and Disney Publishing
Chris Ostrander, Relationship Marketing Director, Walt Disney Parks and Resorts

MaryAnn Zissimos, Disney-Hyperion Publicity
Tim Retzlaff, Disney-Hyperion Marketing
Simon Tasker, VP, Sales Disney-Hyperion
Suzanne Murphy, VP, Publisher Disney-Hyperion
Jeanne Mosure, Senior VP, Publisher Disney Publishing Worldwide
Andrew Sugerman, Executive VP, Disney Publishing Worldwide

Design and Production:
Kelsey Gomez (Interior illustrations)
Joann Hill (Disney Design Director)
Arlene Goldberg (Designer)
Sara Liebling (Managing Editor)
Monica Mayper (Copy Editor)
Mark Amundsen (Copy Editor)
Marybeth Tregarthen (Production)
Allie Lazar (Intern)
David and Laurel Walters (Copy Editors)

Thanks for the daily help:

My office:
Nancy Zastrow
Jennifer Wood

And the professional support:
Writers House:
Amy Berkower
Dan Conaway
Bakara Wintner

Creative Artists Agency:
Matthew Snyder

Congratulations to the KK Winners:

Adventure_Willa	Allie Lazar
Amanda_Hologram	Aria Suzman
Bridge_Shadows	Miranda Thompson
Castaway_Fred	Reece Arabella Thorsland
Clouds_Willatree	Anam Shamsi
DHI_Sorcery	Doug Williams
Freedom_Kingdom	Olivia Madigan
Heightened_Crossover	Emily Mayfield
Holographic_Imagineering	Hannah Kirschner
Hyenas_Adventure	Madi Burke
Imagineering_Sorcery	Linnea Narducci
Jelly_Monorail	Anthony Doyle
Jez_Light	Karenna Blomberg
Keepers_Puzzle	Cassidy Artega
Kingdom_Willatree	Belle Ward

Levitate_Monorail	Randle Coker
Nightfall_Cruise	Taylor Dischinger
Pirate_Amanda	Kiara Mills
Popcorn_Seek	Jordyn Potts
Power_Accelerator	Christine Miller
Shadows_Crossover	Maxwell Mulbury
Twilight_StageB	Faith Bollengier
Visitors_Brave	Hayden Cagle
WillaTree_Circles	Hannah Dyer
Wish_Changerob	Beau Bellem

Congratulations to Fan Fiction contributors:

Winners	Honorable Mentions
Adventure_Willa	Adventure_Willa
Amanda_Firework	Amanda_Firework
Castle_Master	Brave_Imagination
Confidence_Elias	Cast_Radio
Dapper_Willa	Castle_Master
Dawn_Quill	Catastrophe_Master
Dream_Smiles	Chocolate_Flower
Fiction_Queen	Costume_Popcorn
Holographic_Creamery	Dark_Quill
Holographic_DHI	Dhi_Confidence
Holographic_Kingdom	Freckled_Monkey
Host_Sparkle	Freckled_Radiant
Imagineering_Castle	Greeks_Gloss
Jess_Swimming	Holographic_Creamery
Jez_Light	Holographic_DHI
Keepers_Puzzle	Imagineering_Castle
Light_Fairies	Jelly_Monorail
Music_Vision	Jez_Light
Mystery_Virtue	Keepers_Puzzle
Nobel_Reverse	Mission_Attraction
Owl_Runway	Music_Vision
Philby_Vision	Owl_Passage
Prescient_Rain	Pan_Reality
Shimmer_Lightness	Pirate_Clouds
Sleeping_Amanda	Popcorn_Coma
Stone_Philitup	Prescient_Rain
Stonecutter_Cannon	Reverse_Otherside
Twilight_Stageb	Reverse_Stonecutter
Willa_Changerob	Riddle_Rain
Willatree_Eclipse	Sea_Seek
Willatree_Quill	Shadows_Hyenas
Wind_Princess	Stonecutter_Cannon
Wish_Changerob	Tomorrow_Power
Wish_Dream	Wind_Princess
	Wish_Expedition
	Wish_Imagineering